1637

THE COAST OF CHAOS

THE RING OF FIRE SERIES

1632 by Eric Flint
1633 by Eric Flint & David Weber
1634: The Baltic War by Eric Flint & David Weber
1634: The Galileo Affair by Eric Flint & Andrew Dennis
1634: The Bavarian Crisis by Eric Flint & Virginia DeMarce
1634: The Ram Rebellion by Eric Flint & Virginia DeMarce et al.
1635: The Cannon Law by Eric Flint & Andrew Dennis
1635: The Dreeson Incident by Eric Flint & Virginia DeMarce
1635: The Eastern Front by Eric Flint
1635: The Papal Stakes by Eric Flint & Charles E. Gannon
1636: The Saxon Uprising by Eric Flint
1636: The Kremlin Games by Eric Flint, Gorg Huff & Paula Goodlett
1636: The Devil's Opera by Eric Flint & David Carrico
1636: Commander Cantrell in the West Indies by
Eric Flint & Charles E. Gannon
1636: The Viennese Waltz by Eric Flint, Gorg Huff & Paula Goodlett
1636: The Cardinal Virtues by Eric Flint & Walter Hunt
1635: A Parcel of Rogues by Eric Flint & Andrew Dennis
1636: The Ottoman Onslaught by Eric Flint
1636: Mission to the Mughals by Eric Flint & Griffin Barber
1636: The Vatican Sanction by Eric Flint & Charles E. Gannon
1637: The Volga Rules by Eric Flint, Gorg Huff & Paula Goodlett
1637: The Polish Maelstrom by Eric Flint
1636: The China Venture by Eric Flint & Iver P. Cooper
1636: The Atlantic Encounter by Eric Flint & Walter H. Hunt
1637: No Peace Beyond the Line by Eric Flint & Charles E. Gannon
1636: Calabar's War by Charles E. Gannon & Robert E. Waters
1637: The Peacock Throne by Eric Flint & Griffin Barber
1637: The Coast of Chaos edited by Eric Flint & Bjorn Hasseler

1635: The Tangled Web by Virginia DeMarce
1635: The Wars for the Rhine by Anette Pedersen
1636: Seas of Fortune by Iver P. Cooper
1636: The Chronicles of Dr. Gribbleflotz by
Kerryn Offord & Rick Boatright
1637: Dr. Gribbleflotz and the Soul of Stoner by
Kerryn Offord & Rick Boatright
1636: Flight of the Nightingale by David Carrico

Time Spike by Eric Flint & Marilyn Kosmatka
The Alexander Inheritance by Eric Flint, Gorg Huff & Paula Goodlett
The Macedonian Hazard by Eric Flint, Gorg Huff & Paula Goodlett

Grantville Gazette volumes I-V, ed. by Eric Flint
Grantville Gazette VI-VII, ed. by Eric Flint & Paula Goodlett
Grantville Gazette VIII, ed. by Eric Flint & Walt Boyes
Grantville Gazette IX, ed. by Eric Flint, Walt Boyes, & Joy Ward
Ring of Fire I-IV, ed. by Eric Flint

**To purchase any of these titles in e-book form,
please go to www.baen.com.**

1637

THE COAST OF CHAOS

ERIC FLINT
PAULA GOODLETT
GORG HUFF

Edited by ERIC FLINT *and*
BJORN HASSELER

A Baen Books Original

Baen Publishing Enterprises
P.O. Box 1403
Riverdale, NY 10471
www.baen.com

ISBN: 978-1-9821-2577-6

Cover art by Tom Kidd
Maps by Mike Knopp

First printing, December 2021

Distributed by Simon & Schuster
1230 Avenue of the Americas
New York, NY 10020

Library of Congress Control Number: 2021044391

Pages by Joy Freeman (www.pagesbyjoy.com)
Printed in the United States of America

10 9 8 7 6 5 4 3 2 1

To Rick Boatright

Contents

Maps   ix

Preface by Eric Flint   1

The Coast of Chaos   3
Eric Flint, Gorg Huff and Paula Goodlett

The Brothers   117
Walter H. Hunt

The People from the Sky   159
Eric S. Brown and Robert E. Waters

Remember Plymouth   185
Bjorn Hasseler

I Will Walk This Path Again   221
John Deakins

The First Conductor   243
Michael Lockwood

Confederation   271
Bjorn Hasseler

A Wide Latitude   323
Eric Flint

Afterword by Eric Flint   331

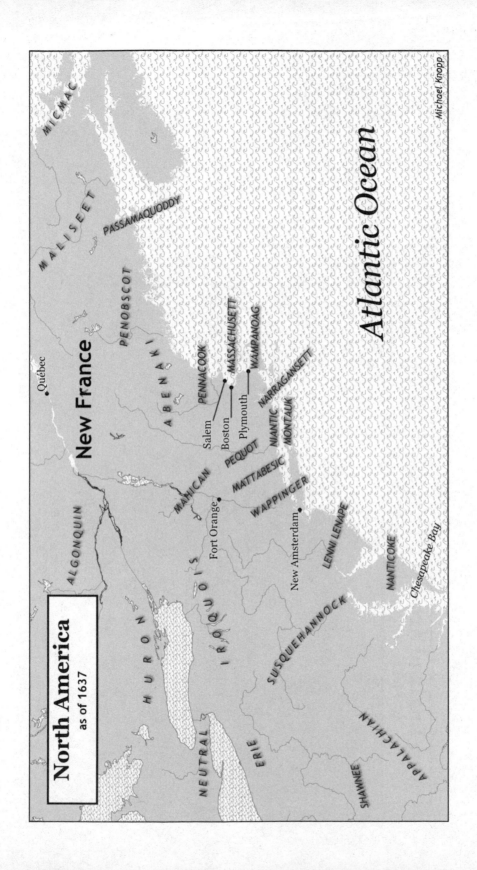

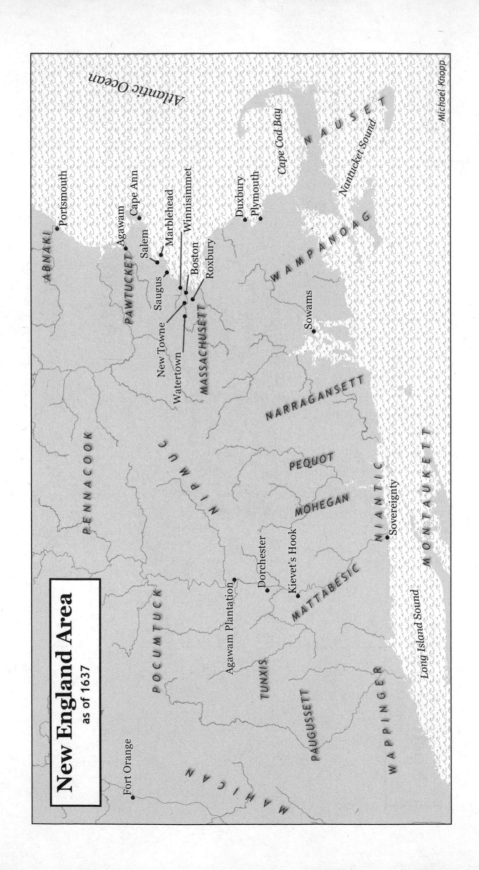

New England Area
as of 1637

Atlantic Ocean

Michael Knopp

ABNAKI
Portsmouth
PAWTUCKET
Agawam
Cape Ann
Salem
Marblehead
Winnisimmet
Boston
Roxbury
Saugus
New Towne
Watertown
MASSACHUSETT
Duxbury
Plymouth
Cape Cod Bay
NAUSET
Nantucket Sound
WAMPANOAG
Sowams
NARRAGANSETT
PENNACOOK
NIPMUC
PEQUOT
MOHEGAN
NIANTIC
Sovereignty
MONTAUKETT
POCUMTUCK
Dorchester
Kievet's Hook
MATTABESIC
Agawam Plantation
TUNXIS
PAUGUSSETT
Long Island Sound
WAPPINGER
Fort Orange
MAHICAN

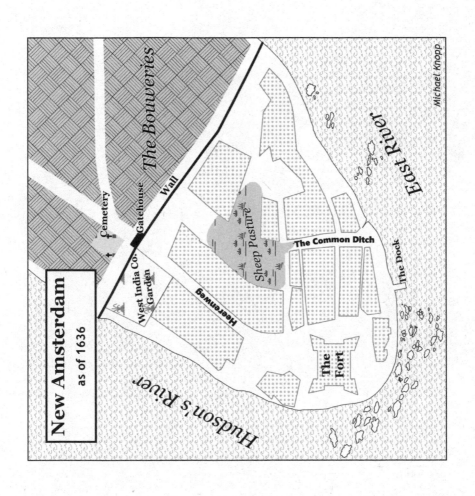

New Amsterdam

as of 1636

The Bouweries

The Common Ditch

Sheep Pasture

Heerenweg

Cemetery

Gatehouse

Wall

West India Co. Garden

The Fort

The Dock

Hudson's River

East River

Michael Knopp

1637
THE COAST
OF CHAOS

Preface

Eric Flint

1637: The Coast of Chaos is a hybrid volume, similar to *1634: The Ram Rebellion*. It's not a novel, since it consists of a number of stories written by several different authors. But unlike a traditional anthology, where the stories have no relationship beyond perhaps a broad theme (*Cats on Mars*, for instance), all of the stories in this book are connected to each other. Taken as a whole, the stories depict different aspects of the same dramatic center: the seizure of New England from the English colonists by France, and the ways in which the native and European populations react to that and deal with it—and deal with each other.

The volume begins with a short novel by myself and two of my frequent partners, Gorg Huff and Paula Goodlett. Our story stands a bit to the side of the others, since it is centered on the New Netherlands, the colony established by the Low Countries in what is modern day New York City, Albany, and the Hudson Valley and its environs. The reason we start there is because what happens in the New Netherlands—which includes their negotiations with the United States of Europe—sets many of the parameters for the rest of the volume.

The reason I chose to develop this portion of the Ring of Fire series in a somewhat unusual narrative framework is because I thought it would help capture one of the key themes in the way the series depicts the impact of the Ring of Fire on the New World, especially North America. Unlike the history of that

1

continent following its discovery by Europeans, in this alternate universe the developments are far more complex and chaotic. You don't have a few great European powers fighting each other until, by the mid-eighteenth century, Britain comes to dominate the continent. Nor do you have the huge wave of immigration from the British Isles that very quickly overwhelms the native populations.

Instead, there are many different (and much less powerful) centers of European influence, which includes Danes and Netherlanders and Swedes and different groups of the English as well as the French. And the indigenous populations are able to respond to the European encroachment on the continent in more effective ways.

It's something in the way of a literary experiment, but that characterization can be applied to the series as a whole. I think it works quite well and I hope you enjoy the volume.

The Coast of Chaos

Eric Flint, Gorg Huff and Paula Goodlett

Chapter 1

Brussels, capital of the Netherlands
May 24, 1636

Once everyone who'd be attending this meeting of the inner circle of the Habsburg court in the Netherlands had arrived, King Fernando invited them to sit with a gesture of his hand. Most of them had already planted themselves on their chairs before he'd even completed the gesture. The young monarch could be a stickler for formality on some occasions, but meetings with his closest advisers were held as casually as could be expected.

Understanding, of course, that "as could be expected" was measured by the care and caution of Europe's most powerful and long-lasting dynasty. The House of Habsburg had begun its rise six centuries earlier, founded by an obscure Swabian count named Radbot of Klettgau. He built his castle in a northerly portion of what would later become Switzerland and named it "Habsburg," which eventually became the name of the dynasty itself. The origins of the name are unclear. The most commonly held belief was that the count named it after a hawk—Habicht, in German—which he spotted resting on one of the walls.

The Habsburgs did not rise as a result of quick and dramatic conquests. This was not a family with the perspective and

3

temperament of Philip II of Macedon and his son Alexander the Great. Their preferred methods of advancement were, first and foremost, the making of advantageous marriages, combined with astute political alliances and obtaining positions for the family in the high ranks of the Catholic Church.

A bit over two centuries after Count Radbot's death, the Habsburgs took their first major step toward European royal preeminence when Count Rudolf IV was elected the King of the Romans on October 1, 1273. The man who held the title was generally considered the future head of the Holy Roman Empire, although that depended on the approval of the pope. But the initial period was a shaky one for the Habsburgs. They were not able to retain the position and spent the fourteenth and the first part of the fifteenth century engaged in more or less constant quarrels and maneuvers with other prominent dynasties on the continent.

Withal, they continued to progress, preferably with their tried and trusted methods of marital, political and ecclesiastical alliances. And if they were not especially adept in the use of military methods, they weren't all that bad at it, either. A coalition led by Rudolf defeated King Ottokar of Bohemia at the Battle of the Marchfeld on August 26, 1278. One of the outcomes of that battle was that the Habsburgs took possession of the duchies of Austria and Styria. In the centuries that followed, those duchies became the heart of Habsburg power and remained so until the final collapse of the dynasty in 1918, at the end of the First World War.

On March 19, 1452, Pope Nicholas V crowned Frederick III as the Holy Roman Emperor. The Habsburgs would retain that title in an unbroken line for the next three centuries, and reached the height of their power with the reign of Emperor Charles V in the first half of the sixteenth century. He was the single most powerful man in Europe since Charlemagne. After his death, the Habsburg dynasty split into two branches, the Austrian and the Spanish. Both of them remained among the major dynasties of Europe and usually cooperated with each other. The Austrian branch of the dynasty retained the title of Holy Roman Emperor.

Or rather . . . would have retained the title. But that was in another universe. In this one, created by the Ring of Fire and the arrival of the West Virginia town of Grantville in the year 1631, history had been changed.

Quite drastically. In the summer of 1634, Philip IV's younger brother Fernando—known then as the Cardinal-Infante—succeeded in reconquering most of the Netherlands for Spain, with only two small provinces and the great city of Amsterdam holding out against him, in the siege that made Gretchen Richter famous across Europe. (Or notorious, depending on how you looked at it.) Fernando then made a settlement with the Protestant Prince of Orange, Frederik Hendrik, which reunited the Low Countries. He gave himself the title of "King in the Netherlands" and shortly thereafter married his cousin Maria Anna, an archduchess of Austria.

At about the same time, Maria Anna's brother succeeded to the Austrian throne as King Ferdinand III. He made no attempt to get elected as the new Holy Roman Emperor, a title which remained vacant thereafter. Instead, he gave himself the new title of Emperor of Austria-Hungary. For all practical purposes, the House of Hapsburg had now divided into three branches.

Such, then, was the nature of the casual invitation to sit which the King in the Netherlands extended to his close associates. Relaxed—not quite languid but close—but still Habsburg.

Next to him sat the queen, Maria Anna. In the course of the two years since their marriage, Fernando had come to rely heavily on her shrewd advice—which was almost as detached and pragmatic as that of the old woman who sat on Ferdinando's left side.

She was his aunt, Isabella Clara Eugenia. The daughter of Philip II of Spain, she had ruled the Spanish Netherlands for two decades with her husband Archduke Albert of Austria and then another decade and a half following Albert's death. She had relinquished her formal power to her nephew upon his coronation, but she remained extremely influential.

Those were the two women in the room, of the seven people present. The four male advisers of King Fernando consisted of:

The famous artist Peter Paul Rubens. Now in his late fifties, he was as accomplished and prominent a diplomat for the Habsburgs as he was a painter.

The king's top military adviser, Miguel de Manrique. He had commanded the Spanish army that surrendered to the Americans at the Wartburg, and come close to being executed for it after his return to Spain. But Fernando, showing more acuity than his brother King Philip III's advisers, had taken him for his own service, figuring that Manrique's experience with the up-timers was what counted, not the results of it.

The newest addition to the court of the Netherlands' inner circle was the former Savoyard diplomat, Alessandro Scaglia. He was what you might call the theorist of the group, having advanced in his now-famous book *Political Methods and the Laws of Nations* the strategic approach he believed would best deal with the new political universe created by the Ring of Fire.

Finally, there was the last person sitting in the room, who was not part of the inner circle but whose presence was essential whenever major issues were being decided. That was Frederik Hendrik, the Prince of Orange. He was the leader of the Dutch Protestants who comprised roughly half of the Netherlands' population and accounted for considerably more than half of its industrial output and technical capabilities.

The gist of the settlement which he and Fernando had made two years earlier came down to three things:

First, religious freedom was established throughout the Netherlands. This was not "separation of church and state" as Americans understood the term, because the king was allowed to subsidize the Catholic Church from tax revenues. The Prince of Orange had the same right to subsidize the Reformed church from his revenues. But neither the king nor the prince nor any of their state agencies could prohibit or penalize the free and open practice of other faiths anywhere in the nation. That included Jews as well as Christians of all varieties.

Secondly, the seven United Provinces in the northern part of the Netherlands all enjoyed a great deal of autonomy. For the most part, they ran their own affairs with the exception of foreign policy. (In theory, the ten southern provinces shared the same status; but, in practice, they were far more subject to royal authority.)

Finally, the Prince of Orange occupied a special place in the government of the Low Countries, being recognized as its second most powerful official. The situation was not one of a dual monarchy, certainly; but it might fairly be called a monarchy and a half.

Frederik Hendrik spoke first, a none-too-subtle indication of his status. He was careful not to step on Fernando's toes. But he made it a point to plant his feet as closely as possible to the king's during these meetings.

"Am I right in presuming that we are here to discuss the situation in the New World?"

Fernando nodded. "Mostly, I want to discuss the New Netherlands. But the French claims on the territories sold to them by King Charles will inevitably figure also."

"Has there been any sign yet that the French intend to press their claims?" asked Manrique.

"Not that we are aware of," replied Maria Anna. "But the situation in France has been unstable since their defeat at Ahrensbök. It is by no means impossible that Gaston will accede to the throne, in which case..." She shrugged. "The man is unpredictable. We cannot assume that French passivity toward their New World claims will continue for much longer."

Rubens nodded. "So you wish to settle—"

"Please, Pieter!" exclaimed the king, smiling. "I think 'stabilize' is much the better term for it."

The artist smiled back. "Stabilize, then, your authority over the New Netherlands."

Isabella looked back and forth from one of them to the other. "Is that authority really in question? I realize we've kept a distance from the colonies in New Amsterdam and New Orange, but I hadn't gotten the sense that anyone there was tending toward revolt. By now, they should have had time to adjust to the new realities of power."

Fernando made a little gesture with his hand indicating the inherent fuzziness of political relations. "There's been no open talk of rebellion as such, no. But for all practical purposes, the West India Company has been operating completely independently for three years now. If we let that continue for much longer, it will become an ingrained habit with them, and—yes—that could lead to rebellion." He nodded toward his wife. "The queen and I both feel it would be wise at this point to reestablish our authority over them."

"Nothing heavy-handed," she said. "Still... we must be firm."

"What do you propose?" asked Rubens.

"To begin with, recall—and then dismiss—the current Director General, Wouter van Twiller. The man is reportedly incompetent as well as a swindler—"

"A drunk, too," chipped in Maria Anna.

"—and needs to be replaced. But I want to go further than simply replacing him. I want to discard the post of Director-General altogether and replace it with a governor—who will be accountable to the crown, not the West India Company."

The people sitting in the half circle facing the king, queen and Isabella exchanged glances with each other. Then, all looked to the Prince of Orange.

Who responded with a half smile. "Why do we Dutch have such a reputation for greed?"

"Because you're greedy?" suggested Manrique. But he made the jest with a half smile of his own. He and Frederik Hendrik were both soldiers and had a warm personal regard for each other, whatever issues over which they might differ.

The Prince of Orange shifted in his chair for a second or two. Then, shrugged. "In truth, I would not be in the least chagrined to see the high and mighty West India Company humbled a bit."

"It'll be more than a bit, Your Highness," said Scaglia.

"All the better," said Frederik Hendrik, his tone hardening. In that moment, all present were reminded that this man was the son of William the Silent and the half brother of Maurice of Nassau. All three of them had broken Spanish armies on the field of battle.

The high and mighty West India Company? Pfah.

The king nodded. "We're in agreement then?" He waited politely a few seconds to see if there were any demurrals.

When none came, he said: "What remains is to select our governor. I was thinking—"

He broke off, seeing the expression on Rubens' face. "Yes, Pieter? Do you have an opinion?"

"Yes, I do. A rather strong opinion, in fact. I think we would be wise to place Adam Olearius in the post."

Isabella frowned. "I've heard the name, but I'm not familiar with the fellow."

"I know him fairly well," said Frederik Hendrik. "He's certainly a capable man—a mathematician and geographer, in addition to his diplomatic work. And he's in his mid-thirties now, so he's mature enough for the post."

"Where's he from?" asked Isabella. The frown was still on her face. "And what's his religion? I don't insist he be Catholic, although

I'd prefer it. But if he's one of these disputatious Gomarists or Arminians, that's more likely to be a hindrance than a help."

"He's not Reformed at all," said Rubens. "He's of German origin, not Dutch. He was born somewhere around Magdeburg. I believe he's Lutheran"—the half smile came back—"a faith he wears in the reasonable manner you'd expect of a diplomat. But his principal qualification for the post of governor of the New Netherlands is his wife, Anne Jefferson. Olearius is the only diplomat we have who is married to an American."

The queen seemed to be stifling a laugh. "I've met her, as it happens. She's the one—the one—"

The smile on Rubens' face widened. "Yes, she's the one we used as our model for those famous postage stamps. What's more to the point, however—aside from her relationship to Olearius—is that she's a noted doctor."

"Registered nurse, technically, as Americans gauge these things." That came from Scaglia. "But that makes her someone I'd far rather seek treatment from than a down-time doctor who can expound his knowledge in both Greek and Latin with many a reference to the works of Aristotle."

The king had been following the discussion intently. Now he said: "Explain your reasoning, Pieter. I'm not opposed to the idea—I'm somewhat familiar with Olearius himself and I've met Jefferson. Impressive woman."

Rubens didn't respond immediately. His lips were slightly pursed and he seemed to avoid looking at anyone except Fernando. After a few seconds, he said: "That will require me to speak bluntly on a subject we have treated in a gingerly manner thus far."

The king opened both hands in a gesture of invitation. "Do so."

"I believe the prospects for the Netherlands are excellent, and are so in many respects. Since the reunification, we are too large and powerful a nation for anyone to go to war upon us without careful consideration. Not as powerful as the USE, certainly, nor France or Spain. But big enough and strong enough that we needn't fear any outbreak of major hostilities in the near future. And the longer that peaceful future continues, the stronger we become. Not in numbers, but in our technical capability and industrial might. We are second only to the USE—really, only to a couple of its provinces—in that regard, and in some areas their equal or even superior."

He paused again.

"There's a 'but' here," said the king.

"Yes, there is. But all of that depends on our maintaining good relations with the United States of Europe. First, because they are the one power in the world that could probably defeat us quickly in a war, if they brought all their might down."

"That's hardly likely, Pieter!" protested Manrique. "With them already at war with both the Ottomans and Poland?"

"I agree, it's not likely. But there's another reason we need the goodwill of the USE, and that's in case either France or Spain—or worse still, both in alliance—decide to wage war upon us. That wouldn't happen so long as Richelieu is in power, but..."

He nodded toward Maria Anna. "As Her Majesty said, Gaston may succeed in his royal ambitions, and the man is unpredictable. But if he—or Spain; or both—do launch a major attack on us, I believe we could count on the support of the USE. Tacit support, at least, if not an outright alliance. But I think tacit support would be enough."

He looked back at the king. "Provided..."

"There is no tension between us," Fernando finished for him. "Or not much, at least."

He planted his hands on his knees and leaned back in his chair. As he always did in these sessions of the inner circle, Fernando was using a chair that was no larger nor more ornate than anyone else's. Of course, they were all chairs you'd expect to find in a royal palace. Well made, if not precisely comfortable.

It was his turn to pause for a few seconds. Then he nodded his head. "I see the logic. The Americans are very influential in the USE and if they know that one of their own is directly involved in our reestablishment of authority in the New World, they are less likely to be suspicious that we have any intent against the USE. Which we really don't... except I'd prefer it if they didn't crowd our colonies too closely with any of their own."

"The Swedes have already established a colony not far from ours, Your Majesty," pointed out Manrique. "And they're planning to reinforce it, according to our agents."

"Yes, but that's a *Swedish* colony, not a USE colony," said Fernando. "As problems go, it's... What's that new expression the mathematicians are so fond of?"

"An order of magnitude smaller," supplied the Prince of Orange. Seeing the puzzled expression on the faces of several of the people present, he added: "It means something is ten times bigger or smaller."

Again, the half smile came back. "I learned that from Olearius, as it happens."

The frown came back to Isabella's face. "What you're saying is that we would be deliberately inviting what amounts to a USE spy to be at the very center of our project."

Rubens shook his head. "'Spy' is far too strong a term, Your Grace. If anyone were to even suggest that to her, Jefferson would be quite offended. After all the portraits I've done of her, I've gotten to know her quite well. She considers herself a doctor, not a politician." He spread his own hands. "Still, if she were to notice anything she found truly disturbing, she would certainly let one of her up-time friends know about it—and one of those friends is a man named Ed Piazza."

"Who, according to all estimates we've heard," said Maria Anna, "is probably going to be the new Prime Minister of the USE not long from now."

She leaned back in her own chair, although without any planting of hands on knees. That would have been most unladylike. (And if that attitude seemed at variance with her reputation as 'the Wheelbarrow Queen,' so be it. Customs are many things; logically consistent is not one of them.)

"I can see the reasoning myself, now. Since both Pieter and Frederik Hendrik are satisfied with the man's abilities, let us by all means make Adam Olearius our new governor."

"Yes," said her husband, which settled the matter. "Pieter, you'll handle the matter, I presume?"

It was a very Habsburg way of framing a command as a polite question. The dynasty's servitors had been mostly willing ones for centuries, and this was one of the reasons for it.

Chapter 2

Anne's physician's assistant, or apprentice doctor, stuck his head in the door to her office and hissed, "The queen is here!"

Anne was by now quite a well-established doctor in Amsterdam, with two other doctors in her practice, and was the preferred physician for the rich merchants of Amsterdam.

"Which queen?"

"The queen! Queen Maria Anna! Queen in the Low Countries."

"Well, show her in," Anne said, standing. She was an up-timer, but she was also Adam's wife, so this lady was her husband's boss's boss's wife. And even up-time that meant you stood to greet them.

A few minutes later, with the door closed and Anne and the queen seated with a tea service on her desk, Maria Anna admitted, "I'm actually here to ask you a favor."

"A favor?" Anne asked cautiously.

"I would like you to take on an assistant."

"An assistant?"

"The daughter of a friend of my brother. Lady Maria Amilia Alaveres. She is up-timer crazy and wants to be a doctor."

"Ah, which brother?"

"The emperor of Austria Hungary. Her father asked my brother, and he asked me and, well, she's in Brussels now."

"But you, or rather your husband, is getting ready to appoint

Adam to the governorship of the New Netherlands. She wouldn't be staying with me for more than a couple of months. You haven't changed your minds about that, have you?"

"Take her with you," Maria Anna said casually.

Anne Jefferson looked at the Queen in the Low Countries and knew she was being played. "Your Majesty, I am an up-timer and not used to the rules of court, so if I am being too blunt, please excuse me. Are you setting a spy on me or trying to get rid of Lady Maria Amilia Alaveres?"

"Oh, I'm used to up-timer bluntness," Maria Anna said with a bright smile. "I was well schooled in it during my time with Mary Simpson. And to answer your question, both. Amilia is quite bright and capable, but she is seventeen and almost as enamored of young men as she is of up-timers. And, well, she seems to go out of her way to scandalize the other ladies of the court.

"She will, of course, be sending me regular messages over the radio once you get it set up in New Amsterdam.

"And there is even a third reason. The wife of an assistant to an ambassador doesn't need female companions for propriety's sake, especially if she is an up-timer. But the wife of a royal governor does. Even if she is an up-timer."

New Amsterdam, North America
July 17, 1636

It was hot even in New Amsterdam. Not unusual for late July, but still a hot, sweaty day to be looking over lumber at the lumberyard next to the docks. Being next to the docks didn't make it cooler either, just muggy. Wolfert Dijkstra pulled a cloth from his belt and wiped the sweat from his forehead. As he did he looked over at the docks and saw that coming down the quay was a crowd just off a ship. No one could keep clothing clean and fresh on a long sea voyage, and with experience you could make a fair guess at how long a sea voyage it had been by how salt-stained the clothing was. This one was long, from Europe at a guess.

"Who's that?" he asked Joris, the cousin of the owner of the lumberyard.

"Refugees from their so-fucking-Catholic majesties and that traitor Frederik Hendrik," Joris said bitterly.

Wolfert didn't roll his eyes. Nor did he try to explain that the Prince of Orange hadn't had much choice, or that King Fernando was showing himself to be quite tolerant of the Protestants who chose to stay in the Netherlands, which was most of them. He didn't do any of that, because Joris was a Gomarist "refugee" himself. Which was why he was working for his cousin in America, not running his own carpentry shop back in Amsterdam. And because if Wolfert were to point any of that out, the prices here would go up, and the quality, both of service and the wood, would go down. Hans, who owned the lumberyard, was also a Gomarist, though not as fanatic about it as Joris.

Instead, he finished wiping his face, put the damp cloth back in his belt, and went back to examining planks of wood. There was a knot in this one and it would pop out within a year. He shifted it to the reject pile. These were split planks, not sawed planks. But they were cheaper and they would do for what he wanted. He would use the more expensive sawed planks for the interior molding, but these were to be coated in daub and white-washed. It was late afternoon and the day was starting to cool a little by the time he finished.

"You'll have that delivered to the site by tomorrow before noon?" he asked Joris, who nodded consent.

The walk home was a bit over a mile. He glanced at the sun. It was late. Nailah, his children's nanny, would have already fed the children. Sofie was four, and Daniel had just turned two and his favorite word was *no*. Wolfert's wife, also Sofie, died giving birth to a third child, which was why he'd bought Nailah's contract. He had to work and the children needed to be looked after.

Nailah had been brought in by the Dutch West India Company in 1633 and sold to Wolfert at auction. She was a half slave, a semi-official status that meant Wolfert allowed her to work for herself when she wasn't busy taking care of the children. She got to keep what she made, could buy real property, and even sue if the need should arise. She was a young woman with a small but growing Dutch vocabulary and quite pleased that she'd ended up here, not on a sugar plantation in the Caribbean. Those places were horrors from all reports. She took in laundry, and was working hard to put together enough to buy her freedom.

As he walked down the street, he thought about the problems caused by the immigration of so many Counter-Remonstrants, but didn't come up with any answers. He turned a corner and saw Mulder's Tavern and Boardinghouse. He could use a meal, and Brechtje Mulder made a good brew.

"Welcome, Wolfert," Brechtje called with a smile. "What brings you to this end of town?"

"Lumber. I have a wagon full of it to be delivered tomorrow. Spent the better part of a day selecting and sorting."

"Well, I guess if you're going to be designing and building buildings, you will have the occasional need for lumber." She gestured to a small table in a corner with two chairs. "Sit. I'll bring you some food."

She then called out, "Lijsbeth! Stew, bread, and some of the roast pork." Then, drew a mug of beer from the cask behind the bar and brought it over.

Brechtje set the beer on the table and sat in the other chair, turning it so she could keep an eye on the main room while they talked. Only Brechtje and Lijsbeth worked in the tavern and boardinghouse. Lijsbeth was indentured. "So how is the Bakker place coming?"

The Bakker place was the project Wolfert was working on now. It was to be a two-story house with a cobbler shop on the ground floor and a residence on the second. He was using several of the cheat sheets from Grantville, translated into Dutch in Amsterdam, and arriving here over a year ago. The house would have a flush toilet and water pumped into the kitchen and a Franklin stove. The Bakker family had two of the Higgins Number Three sewing machines, the ones used for sewing thick leather, and a fair budget for construction.

"Fairly well, except prices seem to be going up every day."

From across the room there suddenly came loud arguing, and Brechtje jumped up to go take care of the problem. Wolfert got up and followed her. He was a fair-sized man, and reasonably well-muscled, because he didn't just design houses. He built them, and ofttimes that meant climbing up on the roof to install the tiles himself.

He didn't interfere. It was Brechtje's tavern, after all. But he was there to back her if needed. The argument was over one of the five points of Calvinism. Wolfert wasn't exactly sure which one.

"Irresistible grace doesn't mean God will choose a Jew if He wants to. It means He won't want to. If He wants a Jew, the Jew will stop being a Jew, and—"

"Gentlemen, if you wish to continue this dispute, take it outside. People are trying to eat here," Brechtje told them.

"What matters food, if the soul be lost?"

"Whether the soul is lost is up to God, you Arminian!" shouted the other man.

Wolfert stepped up beside Brechtje.

"I'm not an Arminian, you fool. You don't understand the five points of Calvinism."

"Outside!" Brechtje repeated.

They went, and then Brechtje needed to go around the dining room, comforting her customers. The place was busy. It usually was. It was both a tavern and rooming house with several rooms on the second floor. It was well situated and kept Brechtje busy.

But arguments like that were getting more common. When she got back to the table, Wolfert asked, "Were they roomers or just diners?"

"Those two were diners. They eat here a couple of evenings a week, and usually agree that the rest of us are going to hell, and that they don't have to treat us fairly because they are chosen of God." Brechtje sighed. "Putting up with them is part of the job, but they can make it difficult."

"It seems to be an invasion of Counter-Remonstrants," Wolfert said.

"I wouldn't mind so much if they would just feel superior, but they seem to think that their special relationship to God means that honesty and decency need not be given to those not of the Select. They also have a tendency to short on the bill. You have to watch the Select."

After he finished eating and left, Wolfert again wished that he hadn't had to take out that loan to start his building business. He built good houses, but his profits were barely enough to live on and keep up the payments on what he owed to the moneylender. And he couldn't saddle Brechtje with his debt. He just couldn't.

Even assuming she'd have him. Brechtje was a good woman, kind, with a friendly word whenever he stopped in, but Wolfert wasn't sure how much of that was for him and how much was for the customer. She was also quite attractive and had turned down a proposal from Herr Gruber since her husband died.

Meanwhile, the invasion of the Counter-Remonstrants was not as good for business as it might be, because too many of them only wanted to deal with others of the Select. And all of them expected special treatment because they were the chosen of God.

So Wolfert lost business to church members who did shoddy work, overcharged, and got away with it because the reverend insisted that only members of the congregation should be employed. What the Counter-Remonstrants had managed to do was drive up the price of pretty much everything that he used in the construction of buildings, making it harder to make a living.

They caused other problems as well. New Amsterdam was a polyglot community with a generally easygoing attitude. The Counter-Remonstrants were less tolerant of Catholics and Jews, not to mention the natives, many of whom were out-and-out pagans. That was bad enough, but they were increasingly insistent that the government, which was the West India Company, become less tolerant as well. They wanted to turn New Amsterdam into a New World version of the tightly knit and cohesive towns they'd come from in the Dutch seven provinces.

Which was making it harder to clear his debt and get to a position where he might ask Brechtje to marry him.

He got home about then. Nailah greeted him and told him the children had eaten and been put to bed.

Nailah was dressed to go out, and as soon as he was in the house she was out of it, on her way to meet her beau. He was a nice lad; another Counter-Remonstrant, but, unlike so many of them, was not belligerent about his religious views. Eduart Jansen worked as a day laborer for Wolfert.

"Go ahead, but don't you let Eduart take advantage of you."

Nailah said something in the African tongue she spoke, and from her tone Wolfert probably didn't want to know the translation. Nailah was a Christian now, but she wore her Christianity somewhat lightly and often harkened back to the beliefs of her tribe in Africa.

Brechtje watched Wolfert go and didn't shake her head. She liked Wolfert, and for practical reasons she needed to get married. Just she and Lijsbeth weren't enough to run this place, and with the amount of new construction and new devices since the Ring of Fire, you couldn't hire good workers for love nor money. That meant that you had to buy contracts of indenture, or slaves, or half slaves.

There were immigrants pouring into New Amsterdam, but mostly they weren't poor and desperate for work. Mostly they were people from the Dutch provinces who were moving because their side had lost and they were not reconciled to the new situation. But no one had driven them out, which meant they'd had the time and opportunity to bring their goods and their money.

Brechtje was aware of all that in the back of her mind, and she'd even read some of the new books on economics that were showing up all over the place. These days it seemed that every ship brought as many books as people and that was a lot of books. And even more pamphlets and the cheat sheets that were so popular these days.

But mostly she was thinking that the inn was just too big, she needed help, and didn't know how to get it. She'd refused Herr Gruber, and not just because he was a grubby little fat man with dirty hands that wandered where they shouldn't, but because she knew that the only reason he was offering marriage was to get his hands on the inn. And if she married him it would stop being her inn. Wouldn't even be *their* inn. Instead, it would be *his* inn, and he would probably sell it.

She also knew Wolfert's situation, and even respected him for not wanting to saddle her with his debts. But in spite of those debts, she wished he would stop trying to protect her and ask. She figured the two of them together could retire the debt soon enough.

Chapter 3

Nancy, capital of the Duchy of Lorraine
August 4, 1636

After she handed her jacket to the servant, who took it away to be hung somewhere, Anne Jefferson took a few seconds to examine the chamber she was in. Had she still been in Grantville, she would have thought it to be a modest-sized living room. Here, given that her hosts' quarters were situated inside the palace of the dukes of Lorraine...

"I swear, Missy, you and Ron somehow manage to turn frugality into ostentation."

Missy Stone, who was in the process of pouring coffee into two cups at a sideboard, looked up with a frown on her face. "What's that supposed to mean?"

"You're richer than anyone in Lorraine except maybe—*maybe*—the duchess herself, and you chose"—she waved her hand about, indicating the surroundings—"this barely-more-than-a-cubbyhole apartment to live in? I bet it was a servant's quarters."

Missy handed her one of the cups, into which she'd already spooned a bit of sugar. Despite the age spread—Anne was now in her mid-thirties, twelve years older than Missy—the two of them were half sisters so they knew each other quite well. Certainly well enough to know each other's taste in coffee, given the expense of the beverage.

Before responding to Missy's question, Anne took a long sip. Coffee was not to be treated casually.

"Lord, that tastes good. At least you're not stinting on the variety."

19

"It's Turkish. Ron can't tell the difference between good coffee and garage swill, but I can. And what's with the wisecrack about the apartment?"

Anne sat down in one of the armchairs, carefully, making sure she didn't spill any coffee. "It wasn't a wisecrack about the *apartment*. It was a wisecrack about you."

Missy sat down on the divan across from her, balancing her own cup with care as she did so. The expression on her face was a bit defensive. "Look, it suits us fine. And, yes, it was a servant's quarters—but she was one of the duchess's dressmakers, so this apartment is just down the hall and around the corner from the Grand Old Lady's suite. Which means—"

She waggled a finger in that direction. "We're close to the one and only up-time-designed flush toilet in the whole damn palace. And we got visiting rights—I made sure of that before I agreed to this arrangement."

She took a sip from her own cup, holding it in both hands, followed by a little shrug. "We only need one bedroom, since we sleep together." A little grin flashed on her face. "And, boy, does that seem to scandalize people more than anything else we do."

Anne chuckled. It was taken for granted in the here and now that lower class couples slept together—more often than not, sharing their bed with their children—but seventeenth-century upper-crusters were expected to maintain separate quarters. That made sense, of course, given that most noble and almost all royal marriages were practical matters involving wealth and politics. Often enough, a husband and wife slept together only infrequently, and then solely for the purpose of continuing the family lines. But although Ron and Missy Stone were wealthier than most aristocrats, theirs had been a marriage guided by American customs. They were undemonstrative about it, but it was a genuine love affair.

"Other than that, we've got a decent-sized kitchen for the cook, as good a bath arrangement as you can get until we bring in up-time-trained plumbers, and we don't need much in the way of closet space since neither Ron nor I is a clothes horse." Her expression was now firmly righteous. "Besides, we're both busy as hell. We're not here most of the time."

"At least get some portraits up on the walls." Anne got a sly look on her face. "How about your grandmothers? They'd be suitably somber even for down-timers."

Missy sniffed. "Fat chance of that ever happening. I'd hang gargoyles on the walls before I'd put up any pictures of Vera and Eleanor, as nasty as they were when Ron and I got married. And as it happens, we *have* commissioned a couple of portraits. Artemisia Gentileschi's doing one of my dad and Ron's father is having one done by a painter named Francesco Albani."

"Let me guess. You found Albani in one of the encyclopedias."

"Well, he's in them—I looked him up. But it was Tom who recommended him once we told him we wanted his portrait done."

Missy finished her cup and set it down. "Okay, now you need to satisfy my curiosity. First, why'd you agree to go haring off to North America when you've got a booming medical practice in the Netherlands? Second, why'd you come all the way down here to have Ron provide you with pharmaceuticals—including a pharmacist? Can't His Royal Muckety-Muck the King of—sorry, 'in'—the Low Countries provide you what you need?"

"In answer to your first question, there are two reasons. One of them is as simple as it gets. I owed it to Adam. My husband has been completely supportive of me even though that meant he had to take a pretty big hit on his own career. Professional top-shelf diplomats are expected to, you know, *relocate* from time to time—and do it for extended periods, not just the short trips that Adam's been able to do so long as I was fixed in Amsterdam. And now he was offered the governorship of the Netherlands' major colony in the New World. You think I'd be dumb enough to say 'no'?"

She shrugged. "And I was of two minds on the question anyway. Yes, my medical practice in Holland is going very well. But I can't think of a greater challenge to a doctor or nurse in the year 1636 than doing what I can to alleviate—no way to stop it, but something can be done—the worst medical catastrophe to hit the human race since the Black Death of the Middle Ages."

Missy made a face. "You're talking about the epidemics that devastated the populations of the Americas after Europeans arrived, bringing diseases with them that New World people had never been exposed to. Anne, I did some studying on the issue after Ron told me what you were planning. Most of those deaths have already happened—happened quite a while back now. The worst epidemics—"

"—would have come in the first century or two after Columbus landed. Yes, I know. By now, the indigenous populations who survived will have built up some immunity. But the operative word is *some*, Missy. They're still at greater risk than people of European stock."

"True." Missy extended her hand. "More coffee?"

"Please."

As Missy went to the side table, Anne continued: "Which sort of sidles into my answer to your other question. The reason I want my own direct connection to you and Ron is because you're Americans. We just don't look at this issue—nor slavery—the way down-timers do."

Missy paused as she was about to pour the coffee and looked over at her, her brow creased a little. "You don't trust them to follow through on their promises?"

"It's not a matter of 'trust,'" said Anne. "I don't think any of them are lying to me about their intentions. I'm quite sure my husband isn't. It's just…"

She looked out of the window for a moment. There was nothing to see beyond the glass other than a drizzly day. Not quite bleak but close.

"Things will come up, other demands will arise, and when you get right down to it they don't feel any sense of responsibility for the situation."

"Neither do I—nor do you, being blunt about it. Neither one of us—nor our parents or grandparents or even our *great-*grandparents—bears any responsibility for that history. The Civil War and slavery ended a hundred and thirty-five years before the Ring of Fire. The massacre at Wounded Knee happened in… 1890, if I remember right."

Anne shook her head. "It's not a matter of individual responsibility. It was still our *nation* which committed those things. The United States of *America*, not Europe. The citizens of a free and democratic nation have responsibilities as well as rights and privileges—and the way I look at it, one of those responsibilities is to do what you can to prevent mistakes, screwups, and for sure downright crimes from being done again."

Missy finished pouring the coffee and brought it over to her. "If you put it that way, I agree with you. And I know Ron does, from things he's said to me."

No matter how weighty the subject matter, coffee was coffee

and naturally came first. After draining a good third of the cup, Anne sighed contentedly and set it down. "But there's more to it than just a sense of responsibility. Down-timers are...well, down-timers. You know as well as I do that in some ways they just don't see the world the way we do. They're...I don't know..."

Missy was in her seat by then, and chuckled again. But the sound had no humor in it this time. "Callous? Even cruel? Cold-hearted? Wouldn't cross the street to give some water to a man dying of thirst? Like that, you mean?"

Anne winced. "That's putting it more harshly than I would. But...well, yeah."

"It's putting it more harshly than I would myself," said Missy, "if I were being fair and judicious about it—which I'm damn well not, plenty of times. The seventeenth century and its inhabitants can really piss me off now and then. Like maybe every twenty minutes."

She leaned back in her chair, sighing a little. "But if I'm more charitably inclined—which I am as a rule—I'd just say they were tough-minded. And then I find myself wondering just how tenderhearted and goody-two-shoes I'd be if half my brothers and sisters had died before they became teenagers, and I knew that any time I bore a child I was taking a significant risk of dying myself. And that if my father or brother or husband was a seaman that there wasn't better than a fifty percent chance he'd survive to retire—and then he'd probably have suffered a major and possibly crippling injury."

"Or that being a farmer is more dangerous than being a soldier," Anne chimed in. "Or that if you live in any city big enough to be called one it'll have to be protected by a star fortress."

"Yeah, that too." Missy smiled ruefully. "To think that you and I came from a time when the only reason people lived in gated residences was because they were rich snobs, not because they were worried about a siege."

"Or keeping out desperate refugees during an epidemic or a famine. Oh, twentieth century! We barely knew ye!"

They shared a laugh, then, which lightened the atmosphere. Right on the heels of it, there were the sounds of people entering the apartment. A few seconds later, Ron Stone came into the chamber, followed by a young man whom Anne had never met.

"I'm glad to see you're both in such good cheer," said Ron.

"If only you knew," said Missy. But she muttered it too softly for the men to hear.

Ron gestured at the fellow with him. "Anne, meet Bastien Dauvet. He'll be going with you to New Amsterdam, although it'll take a couple of weeks for me and him to assemble everything we can send with him. But he'll get to your ship with the equipment and supplies before you set sail."

He smiled. "I know he looks like he just turned nineteen—that's because he did, last month—but he's really good with pharmaceuticals and has a pretty decent grasp of medicine in general."

Anne did her best not to look dubious. At a guess, she would have thought Dauvet had just turned seventeen. He really did look like a teenager.

Still, she was inclined to trust Ron's judgment. The middle of the three Stone boys had turned out, against the odds and certainly most expectations, to be almost frighteningly competent—and he was only twenty-one himself.

Besides, she reminded herself, beggars can't be choosers. Finding a good up-time-trained pharmacist willing to relocate on short notice across the Atlantic was almost impossible, given the need for them at home and the salaries they could demand.

Which brought up, though . . .

"Why are you willing to come?" she asked. "You don't have to answer that if you don't want to, but I'm curious."

She'd asked the question in Amideutsch, not the idiomatic American English she'd been using with Anne and Ron. But Dauvet answered in the same English. His accent was pronounced—Walloon or Lorrain, she thought; maybe Alsatian—but his grasp of the idiom was excellent. Clearly, he'd been spending a lot of time with Americans.

"What can I say? It sounds like an adventure—which my home town of Namur certainly isn't."

Walloon, then. "Adventures have a way of getting out of control," she said. "I'll try my best to keep this one within reasonable bounds, but . . . you never know. When I come from, they didn't call it the 'Wild, Wild West' for nothing."

Of course, no one had referred to New York City that way in the late twentieth century that she'd actually come from, but they were now in a very different "when." New Amsterdam—what would become New York in that other universe—had only been founded twelve years earlier. It was still very much a frontier town.

Dauvet just grinned. Clearly, the youngster was not given to fretfulness.

She turned back to Ron Stone. "How much help will you be able to give me?"

"Hard to say, at the moment. We're just getting up and running here in Lorraine, and the situation's not all that much better in Hesse-Kassel. And, obviously, we've got some major medical problems to deal with right here. But I'll send you whatever I can, Anne—that's a promise. We're Americans, not down-timers. They've got a multitude of challenges and problems to deal with in the New World. So do we—but we've also got a debt to pay, on top of that. And since we can't pay it back, we're obligated to pay it forward."

Anne was gratified but a bit surprised that his thoughts ran so closely parallel to her own. Some of that must have shown in her expression, judging from his next words.

Ron shook his head. "One Trail of Tears was enough."

Chapter 4

The North Atlantic, aboard the Stormwing
September 1, 1636

Adam Olearius watched as Barend de Haan crawled under the steam engine. It was made in Amsterdam from parts made in Magdeburg and Essen as well as in Amsterdam. And it was finicky. Most of the trip they would be traveling by sail, but this engine and the tons of coal in the hold meant that they wouldn't be becalmed. They didn't have enough coal to make the whole trip under steam, but they had enough to travel several hundred miles at an average speed of three miles per hour.

In spite of which, they would be taking the southern loop to the Canary Islands, then the trade winds to the Caribbean, the engine to get to the Gulf Stream, and the Gulf Stream to New Amsterdam. Most of the trip by sail, at an average speed of around ten knots, and only a bit at the slower but more constant speed provided by the engine. And some by a combination of sail and steam.

Adam was watching and chatting with Barend because steam power was, he knew from that other history, eventually going to replace sail for transport, if for no other reason because steam power—adequate steam power, which this wasn't—allowed a ship to travel in a straight line from point to point, rather than being a slave to the winds.

"Got it," Barend said then. "Ow, that's hot. Turn it on, would you, Governor?"

Adam pulled the long handle and the steam engine began

to turn. Then slowed, as Barend was climbing out from under the engine.

"That's all right, Governor, you can close it again. We need to build steam for a bit. I just wanted to make sure that the gasket didn't leak, and the engine would turn. You can close the valve again."

Adam pushed the long handle back to the upright position. "If you're done, let's go above deck and join Anne and Bastien."

"No, I have to wait till the steam is up, then inform the skipper, and handle the engine till we're out of the harbor." He pointed first at a gauge, then to the Bakelite phone, and finally back to the long handle that Adam had pushed and pulled at his direction.

Barend was the chief engineer of the *Stormwing* and already Adam wished that he could steal the young man to put him on his staff. But Captain Lange would have threatened his life if he tried.

Anne, Lady Maria Amilia Alaveres and Bastien Dauvet were in the medic's quarters inventorying supplies to make sure that they had everything. They did. This was the third inventory and the first two had caught few errors.

"Hello, Your Royal Governorship," Anne said as Adam came to the door. "How is the greasy old steam engine? Does it need a tonic?"

"No. Apparently Barend's latex band-aid worked," Adam said. "If you two can tear yourselves away from the papers and the counting of vials and beakers, I suggest we adjourn to the deck and get our last look at Amsterdam for some time to come."

On deck, they stood together at the railing as the lines were cast off and the ship backed out of the quays and turned under steam power, then the sails were raised and they got underway.

They stood there, holding hands and watching Amsterdam slowly recede for almost half an hour.

September 7, 1636

The storm came out of the southeast. It was a hurricane making its way across the Atlantic and would fetch up somewhere in Mexico as a Category 3 storm a couple of weeks later. At the moment, it was a Cat 1 and they were just on the edge of it, but that was enough so that most of the sails were reefed, and the steam engine was in use to try and get them out of its path. A job made more difficult by the fact that they didn't know what its path was. There was no Doppler weather radar in the seventeenth century, at least not yet. And in this day and age, you didn't chase storms. Storms chased you.

Or at least it seemed that way to Adam Olearius and Anne Jefferson, neither of whom were particularly good sailors, at least not in what Anne described as a ship the size of a bathtub toy. In fact, the *Stormwing* was two hundred feet long and forty-two feet wide at the beam.

But the waves they were facing were thirty feet deep, and the rain was traveling horizontally, with a fine disregard for gravity. So was anyone or anything on the ship that wasn't tied down.

Adam threw up into the commode again. The commode wasn't what Anne would think of as a commode. It was a modified chamber pot in a closet with a catchall under it. The catchall was replaced and emptied daily by a crewman. Except at times like these, when the crewman in question was on deck, tied down with lines and trying to keep the various items of ship's equipment functioning and not flying away.

"Move!" Anne croaked with passion. Adam moved just in time, as Anne took her turn bowing to the porcelain god.

The floor moved. A moment before the commode was uphill, now it was downhill, and Adam grabbed Anne's hips to keep her from doing a header into the full pot.

Three hours later, they weren't out of the storm, but they were out of the worst of it. No longer likely to erupt, partly because they were both quite empty by now, but also because the ship was rolling fairly gently, not trying to imitate the vomit comet from up-time.

Anne looked over at her husband. "Once we get to New Amsterdam we're staying there. I am never doing this again."

"I fear we're going to face storms even more severe once we get there, love," Adam said, sounding concerned. "And I'm not sure I'm what's needed to batten the hatches down."

"Why not?" Anne asked, though she thought she knew the answer. They'd talked about this before.

"I'm a diplomat, not a governor. I provide those who govern with the information they need. I take the proposals of one lord to the next, and take his response back. I carry messages. I don't make the sort of final decisions that lead to war or peace, pardons or executions."

"Bull! I've seen you operate. You're a lot more than some glorified messenger boy. You know your stuff, and you're ready for this. But you're not going to believe me or anyone. Not until we get there and you start handing down directives and passing laws. Just don't let the power go to your head." Anne didn't mention that within a week of their arrival in New Amsterdam, they were going to be in contact with Brussels. Because while the new tubes were still in short supply, they had three of the things, and four aqualators. They were going to be able to signal bounce, Maunder Minimum or not. So, in spite of what he was afraid of, he wasn't going to be completely on his own.

Anne wasn't sure that she liked that, because Adam could be a royal governor completely on his own. He had the knowledge and ability, and he had the will. It was just that he was used to subordinating that will to the will of another.

She hoped that Fernando would send back messages saying, "You're the man on the spot. Do what you think best."

Chapter 5

New Amsterdam
September 10, 1636

"Have you considered Boston or Plymouth?" the fat toad asked.

Dominie Karl Brouwer finally stood in the presence of Wouter van Twiller, director-general of New Amsterdam. It had not been worth the wait.

"I know it's English—well, French now—but you might find the company more to your liking. Here, we have a lot of trades-men. Even a few Jews."

After waiting a week because they were unwilling to bribe Egbert Wessels, the Director-General's clerk, they were finally able to present their petition for a new township on the isle of Manhattan, with a house of worship and land for shops and farms.

"You're sure?" the Director-General went on. "Very well. But as to your petition, no, I am afraid not. There would be fees, you see, and the West India Company already owns that land. So, I have to protect their interests. And if I were to put their interests aside, well, there would be fees. And you would have to, ah, persuade me to take up your cause. And you were apparently unable to come up with the wherewithal to persuade my clerk to bring you in to see me early."

The meeting went downhill from there. In cold, hard truth, Karl Brouwer hadn't expected it to go much better. He didn't expect to have the Director-General give them land owned by the Dutch West India Company.

What he had been hoping for was a counteroffer. A place near

30

New Amsterdam where they would be able to set up a township and establish their own laws.

Karl Brouwer had read a lot about the United States of America, and especially about their breaking away from the rule of England. He thought that if a bunch of English could do it, certainly his Gomarists could do it. But not yet. First they needed a base to build from. And they needed to work fast, before their most Catholic majesties, Fernando and Maria, started paying attention to the Americas again.

There were a lot of Counter-Remonstrants in New Amsterdam by now, pushed here by the capitulation of the Prince of Orange to the Spanish Cardinal-Infante—who now styled himself the "King in the Netherlands."

After another fifteen minutes—and at least twenty requests for bribes, each a little less veiled than the last—they were escorted out.

"Very well," Karl Brouwer said to his cousin and the rest of the party. "We do it from here."

"I don't know why you even tried," Conradus said. "We have money and every ship brings more hands to our cause. And the United Provinces, even combined with the Spanish territories, aren't England at the end of the eighteenth century. England today isn't England at the end of the eighteenth century."

"And we aren't thirteen colonies stretching across most of the east coast of North America," Karl said. "Don't get ahead of yourself, cousin. This isn't going to be easy."

Egbert Wessels was shaking his head as he entered the room. "With respect, sir, it might almost be worth it just to be rid of them."

"Quite. But I couldn't allow it. It's the principle of the thing," Director-General van Twiller said.

"Principle, sir? What principle is that?"

"That no one does anything in the New Netherlands without paying me my fee."

Egbert Wessels grinned. "It's so nice to be working for a well-principled man, sir."

"What do you have there?" The Director-General gestured at the several sheets of paper in Egbert's hands.

"Complaints about Bogardus, sir."

"Maybe we should give Bogardus his own town. Somewhere far up the Hudson."

"He wouldn't take it, sir," Egbert Wessels said.

Dominie Everardus Bogardus was increasingly a thorn in the side of the Director-General. Bogardus didn't approve of slavery. Having read some of the up-timer histories that had arrived by ship over the last three plus years, he had come to the conclusion that slavery had always been an offense against God. More accurately, he had his beliefs confirmed by the future history, and intended that slavery should be ended before the blood debt for it would lead to a war in this timeline, like unto the American Civil War in that other history.

"What is it this time? More dire predictions about a war to end slavery in a hundred years?"

"It's not the sermon this time. It's the congregation. Bogardus had Africans, including half slaves and full slaves, in the pews right next to slave owners."

"Not that there are a lot of slave owners who attend his services."

"No, sir. And the ones who do aren't the ones who are complaining. It was several of the other slave owners. They don't like the notion that slaves, or even free blacks, should be accepted into a white congregation, whether it's theirs or not."

Wolfert Dijkstra placed the ruler on the sheet and drew the line. It was another change in the design after the customers had walked through the half-finished building last Friday. Now they wanted a dumbwaiter between the shop on the bottom floor and a storeroom on the second floor.

It was actually a good idea. Wolfert just wished they'd realized the need before the second floor had been put in in that part of the house.

Eduart Jansen came up to him. "Ah, Mister Dijkstra. Did you hear about the sermon?"

Wolfert had indeed heard about the sermon. Or more accurately about Dominie Bogardus' congregation. "Yes, I heard. What about it?"

"Do you think slavery is an offense against God?"

Wolfert considered. "I honestly don't know. The New Testament doesn't mention slaves. Jesus threw the moneylenders out of the temple, but he didn't go around smiting slave owners. It seems to me that there are an awful lot of things that offend the Lord, and which ones are the worst depends on who's telling the tale. None of us can avoid offending Him to some degree. All we can do is the best we can manage, and hope that He'll forgive us for the rest.

"As to slavery in particular, I think it's probably wrong but I'm not at all sure it's a wrong that can be avoided. There are all sorts of servitude, managed in all sorts of ways. But what you're really asking about is Nailah and my owning her. Isn't it?"

Eduart looked at the ground as though he was ashamed to have asked the question. And Wolfert didn't know why he should be. It wasn't as if Eduart owned a slave, even a half slave. If anyone ought to be looking down in shame it would be Wolfert himself, who was starting to think he should be. Just starting to, though, and a long way from actually feeling shame.

"The way I look at it is, I'm getting her service in exchange for the money I paid when I bought her."

Eduart looked away and Wolfert waited, but finally Eduart nodded and went back to work.

Nailah put the soup and bread on the table and called the children from their game. She, too, knew about the sermon and the congregation, and had her own opinion. But she also had washing to do, meals to cook, wood to gather, and all the other jobs that were necessary for maintaining a household in the seventeenth century. And that was what she was spending her time on when she wasn't thinking about Eduart and his shy smile and big shoulders.

If asked—which she hadn't been—she would have pointed out that she never agreed to her purchase, nor did she receive the money that Master Wolfert paid for her. But she was very grateful that she was here, and not down in the Caribbean being worked to death on a sugar plantation.

Chapter 6

Brussels, capital of the Netherlands
September 11, 1636

They passed by the Palace of Coudenberg as they came in for a landing. Situated on a small hill, the palace provided an excellent view of the city of Brussels, and was an impressive structure in its own right. For Rebecca's tastes, the extensive gardens adjoining the palace left something to be desired, since the designers had substituted quantity for quality. Still, it was quite a suitable residence and court for a dynasty that was one of the most prominent and powerful in Europe as well as the most recent.

The rest of the Netherlands' capital city...

"Place is a dump," pronounced Rebecca Abrabanel's pilot, Lt. Laura Goss. "I admit, I'm prejudiced by the so-called 'airport.'"

She was approaching the one and only runway that graced Brussels' airport—and it wasn't much of one. The authorities in Brussels had decided that since most of the air traffic in and out of the city would be flown by the Royal Dutch Airlines' Jupiters, which were planes with air cushion landing gear, they'd make themselves a shallow lake instead. A lake that was fine for the Monsters, as the planes were called because of their size, but didn't work at all well for other sorts of aircraft.

For planes such as the one that Laura and Rebecca were flying in, the "airport" didn't really deserve the name. It was more in the way of an airstrip with two small open-sided sheds that made do as hangars and a control tower whose second story "tower" resembled an ironclad's pilot turret more than it did anything that would be very useful in helping an aircraft to land.

It *did* have a radio, at least. "You are clear to land," announced the air traffic controller.

"No kidding," muttered Laura. "The only thing we're sharing the sky with is a flock of geese about half a mile away."

"Be nice," said Rebecca, fighting down a smile.

"I *am* being nice, Boss. I didn't say it over the radio." She picked up the mike and spoke into it: "Coming in now."

There was a stark contrast between the airport of the Netherlands' capital city and that of Amsterdam, which was the nation's largest city and a much more commercially active one. By now, Amsterdam was the second-largest industrial city in Europe, being surpassed in that regard only by Magdeburg and being equaled—perhaps—by Hamburg. Its airport was actually busier than Magdeburg's, due to the priority the Netherlands' monarchy had placed on developing aviation.

You couldn't dismiss Brussels as a sleepy provincial town, though. It was not only the political center of gravity of the Netherlands, but it was also becoming a manufacturing city in its own right, albeit not on the scale of Amsterdam. In particular, the wool and textile industry was booming, having benefited from the introduction of steam power.

Rebecca was pretty sure that her pilot's less-than-enthusiastic attitude toward Brussels had more to do with the capital's culture than its commerce. Lieutenant Goss was what Americans referred to as a "party girl," and the freewheeling spirit of Amsterdam suited her a lot more than the stuffy atmosphere that prevailed in Brussels.

Her way of putting it was: "Amsterdam's got more saloons than you can count. Brussels? More nuns than you can count."

But Rebecca made no criticism of her pilot's habits. Whatever Laura Goss might do when she was off duty, she was always ready and on time—and sober—when Rebecca needed her services.

When the plane taxied to a halt in front of the control tower, Rebecca saw that a small delegation was there to greet her. Heading it were Pieter Paul Rubens and Alessandro Scaglia.

She was pleased to see them. Partly, that was because sending two of his handful of closest advisers was King Fernando's way of making clear the importance he placed on her visit. Mostly, though, it was simply because she was looking forward to their company. She and Rubens had been on friendly terms—even close ones, in some respects—for several years now. And while she'd only met Scaglia briefly on two occasions, neither of which had allowed much time for conversation, the two of them shared an odd sort of companionship. Each of them was the author of one of the continent's most currently famous political treatises, Scaglia's *Political Methods and the Laws of Nations* and her own *The Road Forward: A Call to Action*. Perhaps more to the point, the two books had been written in large part in contention with each other.

Someone else might have been hostile to her ideological opponent, but Rebecca's temperament was that of an intellectual. She found the debate stimulating, and given that Scaglia had maintained a polite tone in his public pronouncements, she'd seen no reason not to do the same. They weren't what you could call "colleagues" without stretching the concept into a pretzel, but they weren't exactly enemies, either.

"Frenemies," the Americans call it. Thankfully, the grotesque term hadn't made its way into the Amideutsch lexicon.

Yet. Rebecca was fairly certain it was just a matter of time, though. The new part-German, part-American idiom that was becoming central Europe's lingua franca was a veritable sponge when it came to vocabulary.

They rode into the city on a steam-powered vehicle whose type Rebecca had never seen before and so far as she knew did not exist in the USE. The best description of it she could think of was a cross between a small autobus with a total capacity for eight passengers along with a driver and engineer in a front compartment, and a low-slung tractor with very wide wheels. The reason for the second aspect of the vehicle was obvious: most of the streets of Brussels were still unpaved and while the main thoroughfares were cobblestoned, that would have made for a rough ride had the wheels not been so broad and coated with what she thought was some form of latex.

"It's mostly for showing off our industrial progress," Rubens admitted to her. "There are only three of them, all of which are reserved for official use." He winced as the engineer enthusiastically blew the steam whistle for perhaps the twentieth time since the trip began. "Personally, I'd just as soon ride in a litter, but the king adores the things."

A litter slung between horses probably would have been faster as well as more comfortable, but she found the trip more interesting this way. And there was this much to be said for the device—it had no difficulty making its way up the hill atop which the palace was situated. Of course, horses wouldn't have had any trouble doing so, either.

The royal audience was held in one of the smaller chambers in the palace. Calling it an "audience" was more of a formality than anything else, since the seating arrangement was as casual as such things ever got in a court whose customs were still largely Spanish. The king and queen sat in chairs that were larger and more ornate that any of the others, but still fell quite short of what anyone would call "thrones." To either side of them—the elderly archduchess to Maria Anna's left and the Prince of Orange to Fernando's right—sat Isabella and Frederik Hendrik, in chairs that were just a tad smaller and less decorated than those of the royal couple.

Those four chairs were positioned in a shallow arc. The "audience" faced them in chairs that were only slightly smaller and arranged in a straight line. Miguel de Manrique sat on the far left, facing the Prince of Orange; Alessandro Scaglia on the far right, across from the archduchess. Rebecca and Rubens had the two seats in the middle facing the king and queen.

After the initial pleasantries, King Fernando leaned forward and said: "I trust you have had time to consider the letter we sent you and Prime Minister Piazza."

She would hardly have come to the Netherlands for this meeting if she hadn't, of course. She and Ed Piazza and a number of other people had spent quite a bit of time discussing the matter before arriving at their decisions. One of those people, although her communication with him had been quite informal in nature—what up-timers (somewhat crudely, in her opinion) called "pillow talk"—had been with her husband Mike Stearns.

As a mere general in command of one of the USE's army divisions, Stearns really had no business participating in such high matters of state. But that thought had never once crossed either her mind or her husband's—nor, had they known of it, would it have occurred to the prime minister or, for that matter, Emperor Gustav II Adolf. Mike Stearns was the man often called "the Prince of Germany." When it came to the realities of power as opposed to its public protocol, the seventeenth century was nothing if not practical.

But she simply responded with: "Yes, Your Majesty, we have considered your missive at length."

She didn't refer to it as "your proposal," since technically no proposal had been contained in the letter although its intent had been obvious. In essence: *What assurances can you give us that you won't try to thwart our ambitions in the mid-Atlantic region of North America? And what would you want for such assurances?*

"We are generally amenable to what seems to be your principal concerns," she continued. "It has been one of the cornerstones of the foreign policy of the United States of Europe since my husband took office as our first prime minister to have as good relations as possible with the Netherlands"—some awkwardness needed to be glided over here—"once the political situation in the Low Countries stabilized."

The slight quirks in the lips of both King Fernando and the Prince of Orange indicated that she'd successfully navigated that possible shoal. So, onward:

"That policy has the full support of Prime Minister Piazza as well."

There was no need to make reference to the intervening regime of Wilhelm Wettin, since it was essentially irrelevant. For all practical purposes, Prime Minister Wettin had had no policy regarding the Netherlands because he'd been completely preoccupied throughout his term with the internal affairs of the USE.

"We believe an outright alliance between the USE and the Netherlands would be counterproductive," she said, "given the complex"—that sounded much better than *thorny*—"relationship Your Majesty has with his brother the King of Spain."

"We agree," said Fernando, nodding his head firmly. "Please go on."

"But short of that, we intend to maintain the friendliest possible stance toward the Low Countries, both diplomatically and commercially." She was finally coming to the point of this meeting, so all the people listening to her leaned forward a bit, intent on her next words.

"Accordingly, with regard to the New World, we would like to assure Your Majesty that the USE has no desire to impede the progress of your colonies in the continent of North America."

She put just enough emphasis on *the continent* of North America to make clear that the issue of the Caribbean and its many islands might need to be handled separately, depending on...

This and that, and this and that. There were a host of factors involved when it came to the Caribbean. She and Piazza had agreed that it would be premature to try to resolve any of those issues until the overall situation became less uncertain.

"Specifically, we offer the following. The United States of Europe will neither establish a colony nor sponsor any privately financed one on the continent of North America north of the thirty-fifth parallel and east of the Appalachian Mountains. We reserve the right to found colonies anywhere south of that parallel of latitude and west of the mountains."

She stopped there, to allow her audience to absorb the statement. Some of them—Manrique, of course, as well as the king and the prince of Orange—obviously knew the geography involved well enough to immediately grasp what she was proposing. Others were just as obviously unclear on the matter.

The archduchess was frowning. Not in disagreement, simply from lack of knowledge.

"Where..."

Fernando looked to Scaglia. "Could you fetch us a map, Alessandro?"

"As it happens, I brought one with me." The Savoyard reached down into a long valise he'd had resting next to his chair and drew forth a rolled-up map.

"Give me a hand, Miguel," he said to Manrique. Between the two of them, they unrolled the map and stood up, displaying it to the other members of the royal party.

"The thirty-fifth parallel is...here," said Scaglia, looking down and pointing to a line with his finger.

Isabella squinted at the map. Her eyesight was no longer very good, but the old lady was either too stubborn or too vain to make use of eyeglasses.

"It begins on the coast at Pamlico Sound and runs westward until it reaches the Mississippi River about...here." His finger came to rest on a spot some distance south of the confluence of the Mississippi and Ohio rivers. "If I recall correctly, the American city of Memphis—in the universe they came from—is located there."

Rebecca wasn't surprised by Scaglia's detailed knowledge of the geography of her husband's former nation. He was the sort of man for whom careful preparation was second nature. "Just a bit south of there," she said. "The thirty-fifth parallel marked the boundary between the USA's state of Tennessee and the states of Georgia, Alabama and Mississippi. Most of what they called North Carolina was north of the line; almost all of South Carolina was south of it—as well as Florida, of course."

"This will place you in conflict with Spain," Maria Anna pointed out.

Rebecca made a little shrugging gesture. "That ship has already sailed. There is no way any longer for us to avoid conflict with Spain in the New World."

Which, of course, was one of the principal factors making an overt alliance between the USE and the Netherlands impossible, at least for the moment. There was already a great deal of tension between King Fernando and his older brother, Philip IV of Spain. So far, though, both of them had steered clear of open hostilities—and the king in the Low Countries was determined to maintain that state of affairs if at all possible.

It could be argued—plenty of courtiers at the Alcázar in Madrid had and continued to do so—that Philip's younger brother had betrayed him after reconquering most of the Netherlands. Instead of turning over control to the king of Spain, Fernando—then known as the Cardinal-Infante—had declared himself the "King in the Netherlands" as part of his settlement with Frederik Hendrik.

The Spanish king's more astute advisers, however—including his chief minister, the count-duke of Olivares—had viewed the situation differently. The Cardinal-Infante had been stymied when Amsterdam successfully withstood him and there had been no prospect for a quick end to the ensuing siege. The great victory of the USE over the League of Ostend's forces at the battle of Arhensbök soon afterward would have made it impossible for Spanish troops to remain in the Low Countries. Torstensson's triumphant army would have marched into Holland and reached Amsterdam within two weeks—three, at the outside—and Admiral

Simpson's ironclads would have reached the Zuider Zee even sooner, which would have completely broken the siege.

There had been no chance that Frederik Hendrik would have agreed to a settlement that restored direct Spanish control over the Netherlands. By making the deal he had with the Prince of Orange, the Cardinal-Infante had at least kept the Low Countries within the orbit of the Habsburg dynasty.

And even if one allowed that Philip's younger brother had stabbed him in the back, at least he had—so far—refrained from twisting the knife in the wound.

"I notice that your proposal would allow you at some point in the future, should you so choose, to establish control over that area of the continent that Americans refer to as 'the Deep South'—and which was the region where chattel slavery sank its deepest and most intractable roots."

Rebecca looked at Scaglia. "Yes. If need be—we hope it won't come to that—the USE will suppress slavery by the crudest and most far-reaching application of brute force. Which brings me to a discussion of the price we will ask for, in exchange for our assurances that we will not hamper your ambitions."

"You want us to ban slavery and the slave trade," said King Fernando. There was no trace of surprise in his tone of voice. Quite obviously, he and his close associates had discussed this matter at length also and had come to the correct conclusion.

"Yes," she said again. "We want slavery and the slave trade banned—completely banned; we will accept no half measures— everywhere the authority of the king in the Low Countries holds sway."

"Ah!" That exclamation came from Rubens. "That's an interesting way of putting it. 'Holds sway' is a term that applies to actual as opposed to theoretical power."

She now looked at him. "Prime Minister Piazza is not impractical and neither am I. And neither—although his limits are likely to be more stringent—is the Prince of Germany."

Her use of her husband's informal title was deliberate. Formalities be damned. Ever since his arrival in the Ring of Fire, Mike Stearns had been an elemental force in European politics. No one in their right mind—certainly no capable ruler—was likely to forget that.

Again, she made a little shrugging gesture. "We realize that

Your Majesty's control over much—perhaps most—of the Netherlands' territory in the New World is . . ." She smiled, rather sweetly. "A complex matter, shall we say?"

That elicited a little laugh in the room, joined in by everyone except Miguel de Manrique.

"The problem is the West India Company," he said. "It is a troublesome reality that the West India Company—as well as the East India Company—possess far more influence and leverage than they ought, in their respective spheres of influence. They will not fail to see that the game board is changing."

"That probably won't matter at first," said Rubens, "so long as the regions affected are on the continent. Slavery as practiced in New Amsterdam and New Orange is of little concern to the West India Company. In the islands of the Caribbean, however, the situation is quite different."

"We are aware of that," said Rebecca. "Still, the tail can only wag the dog for so long."

"When it's a very big tail and a small dog, it can wag for some time," said Frederik Hendrik. "The awkward strategic reality is that most of our naval strength in the New World is in the hands of the West India Company, not Admiral Tromp. And what makes the situation still more awkward is that not all of the company's men in the New World are . . . How to put it? As imbued with loyal sentiments—forget outright patriotism—as they should be."

"What do you recommend?" asked Fernando.

"I suggest that in the case of the Company's continental managers that our public explanation for their removal concentrate on their scandals and corruption."

"Evidence for which can be easily furnished," said Scaglia. "We don't even have to fabricate any of it."

The Prince of Orange flashed a quick grin. "The reason I make this suggestion is that it will not send a full alert to the masters of the far more valuable—and therefore, influential—properties in the Caribbean and the Pacific. They will not see an individual introduced as a 'governor' of the crown as a move toward a permanent reshuffling of power, just a local expedient—and in a locality to which most of them are indifferent because they have no personal interests at stake there. Hopefully, that will give us the time needed to make the rest of them—redundant."

"Redundant?" Rubens echoed.

Frederik nodded. "As we speak, relations with both the native and enslaved peoples of the Caribbean are in the early stages of great change."

"Yes," Fernando agreed. "We have seen the reports."

"Then you no doubt also have been apprised of how ferociously the representatives and factors of the Company are resisting them. To add the perception of yet another threat to their self-supposed mastery of those territories and peoples could have unfortunate results."

"Are you suggesting they might revolt?"

"I am suggesting, Your Majesty, that they might seek to discuss the matter with the Spanish viceroys and governors in the region."

"So ... collaboration, not open revolt."

"Such affairs invariably exist on a spectrum," said Frederik Hendrik. "I merely suggest that we attempt to keep the hues dim until such time as we may clear the palette of them entirely."

He looked at Rebecca. "Would that be acceptable to you? We can ban slavery quickly in the colonies on the continent, but we need to be more cautious elsewhere. I believe the American expression is 'make haste slowly.'"

Rebecca frowned. She wasn't intrinsically opposed to such a maneuver but...

"The Americans have an apt saying," she said. "'The devil is in the details.' Making haste slowly can all too easily become no haste at all."

The king leaned forward. "And how will you gauge that, if I might ask?"

"There are two aspects to that question, Your Majesty. The USE now has quite a few assets in the New World." She didn't specify *the wife of your new governor* since that was obvious, and she saw no reason to tell them that contact had been reestablished with the Chehab expedition. There was certainly no reason to inform them of the Louisiana project. "So I am confident—as is Prime Minister Piazza—that we will be able to monitor your progress when it comes to the eradication of slavery and the slave trade."

She paused and drew in a deep, slow breath.

"And the second aspect is...?" That came from Queen Maria Anna.

"The second aspect has to do with the person or persons who

do the gauging. I may gauge things one way, and so might the prime minister. Another man..."

She paused again. "I spoke with my husband shortly before I left, on this very subject. What he told me was that negotiations were my affair, and he did not presume to second-guess me. But he also asked me to convey to anyone who expressed an interest that in the world he came from his nation sacrificed the lives of more than six hundred thousand soldiers to put an end to slavery. In the battle of Gettysburg alone, the casualties were around fifty thousand—that is to say, more men than are even present in most battles of this era. He added that if his nation was prepared to kill that many of its own countrymen, people should consider how many foreigners they might be prepared to kill if it becomes necessary to do so in another world."

She looked from one to the next, to the next. "Finally, he said this to me: 'I am not involved in negotiating the issue of slavery and the slave trade any longer, nor do I intend to be again. I have a different profession now. I am simply biding my time.'"

The evening which followed was pleasant, in the way such formal diplomatic events often are when they are well managed. Toward the end of it, Rubens wound up in private conversation with his monarch.

"I did his portrait once," he said. "Stearns, I mean."

Fernando looked surprised. "I've never seen it."

"No one has, Your Majesty, except his wife. I did show it to Rebecca. Since then, I've had it stored away in one of my closets."

"Why—?"

The artist shook his head. "I painted it during the siege of Amsterdam. Showing it publicly to anyone except her seemed inexpedient."

"Even to *me*?"

Rubens' lips quirked. "Perhaps especially to you, Your Majesty."

"Well, I want to see it now."

"Yes, I think now would be a good time. I will bring it to the palace tomorrow morning."

The portrait was superb. No surprise, that—Rubens was recognized as a great artist in two separate universes. But King Fernando was struck by how unusual a portrait it was, for this particular artist. It was as if the man who was both one of his closest advisers as well as a genuine friend had become imbued with the spirit of a painter from an earlier era.

Hieronymus Bosch, perhaps.

The portrait showed Stearns reclining at his ease in a chair that was a bit too small—but just a bit—to be called a throne. His arms lay on the armrests with both hands open. Children, most of them infants, came spilling out of his left palm, growing in size as they neared the floor. From his right palm spilled out a stream of monsters of various kinds: demons, imps, gargoyles, manticores, dragons. A large gorgon had reached the floor first and was surging her way forward.

What was most striking, though, was the portrait of the face. The king recognized him easily, having spent a number of hours in Stearns' presence. But the expression was nothing he'd ever seen before. In person, he'd found the USE former prime minister to be a lively and even friendly fellow. Here...

Nothing. There was no emotion at all on the man's face. Just a sort of watchful readiness that could be transformed into any emotion. Kindness, fury, joy, rage—anything at all.

"What did you title it?" he asked Rubens.

"*The Choice.*"

The king nodded. "A good title, I think. It's still not suitable for public display, of course, but I'll buy it from you. I think it would be wise for me to have it hung in my private quarters."

Right about the same time Fernando made that decision, Rebecca met Laura Goss at the airport.

"So how'd it go, Boss?" asked the captain, giving Rebecca a helping hand into the cockpit. "If that's not a state secret, of course."

"Well enough. I can't discuss the details, I'm afraid. But... well enough."

Laura grinned. "I hope you put the fear of God in 'em. These damn royals need it, you ask me."

"God? No."

Chapter 7

New Amsterdam Harbor
October 12, 1636

The *Stormwing* steamed into New Amsterdam harbor. The winds were unfavorable, and they had plenty of coal to bring up steam for the short haul. So it was a largish ship with its sails furled that pulled up to the docks.

"Grab that line!" a sailor shouted to a dock worker. "And tie it off. There's a good fellow."

The dock worker made a rude gesture, but grabbed the tossed mooring line and tied it off. More lines were tossed and soon the *Stormwing* was secured and the boarding ramp was pushed out. Adam Olearius went down the ramp first, and was followed by six men at arms in the brand new royal uniform of the Low Countries army. They wore blue trousers and gray tailcoats, with leather belts and a cross-draw holster for the pistol. The helmets were gray with the royal crest painted on the front, and bore a definite resemblance to American military helmets from the latter half of the twentieth century.

Once down, Adam, flanked by his guards, headed up the dock for the shore. The port facilities in this day and age were mostly located on the East River, not the Hudson.

Wolfert was again at the lumberyard. And he was again distracted, this time by a ship coming into dock with its sails furled, then by the flag of the king in the Low Countries, which was flying from the top of the mainmast.

46

If it was just another ship full of Gomarists, Wolfert would have stayed at his task, but this was looking like it might be important. He headed for the docks.

Adam stopped at the end of the dock and looked around, remembering the map and comparing it to the ground in front of him. They didn't match very well. He thought of pulling the actual map out of his pocket, but that wouldn't help. His memory was fine. It was the world that had changed almost completely out of recognition.

He looked around again. There was the beginning of a crowd. He saw a large man, reasonably well dressed, but healthy and looking right back at him, not with hostility or fear, but curiosity.

He gestured and the man came over.

"Afternoon," Adam said. "I'm Adam Olearius. Would you mind directing me to the Director-General's residence? My map is apparently a bit dated."

The man nodded. "There's been a lot of construction in the last couple of years," he agreed. "And the Director-General no longer makes his residence in the Fort. I'm Wolfert Dijkstra, by the way. I'll take you there." He pointed to the northwest, and then started walking. Adam followed, and the guards moved up to flank them.

"What's going on?" Wolfert asked.

"I'm the new royal governor of New Amsterdam and His Majesty isn't overly impressed with the former Director-General's loyalty or honesty."

"Ha!" Wolfert laughed aloud. "The rats in the cellars of New Amsterdam aren't impressed with Director-General van Twiller's honesty."

"Hence our unannounced arrival and my hurry to get there before van Twiller has time to respond."

"Are these all the men-at-arms you brought?" Wolfert asked, sounding concerned.

"No, but again there is the matter of speed. We want to be in van Twiller's residence before he has an opportunity to respond."

"This way." Wolfert pointed again, and they turned the corner moving at a brisk walk. From this vantage point, Adam could see the fort that dominated the southern tip of Manhattan Island.

It was more or less a standard star fortress with thick, sloping packed-earth walls to absorb cannon fire, except it had only four sides with a bastion on each corner.

They were going to be passing by the fort on its eastern side, heading north toward the broad avenue—using the term loosely; it was a dirt road, nothing fancier—that Adam could see angling to the northeast. That matched the map, at least. It was the Heerenweg—the "Gentlemen's Way"—which in another universe would become Broadway.

Passing by the fort confirmed what Adam had already suspected while still in Europe. However well built it might be as a fortress, it was not suitable for the sort of Government House that was needed now. If for no other reason, because Government House would also serve as his own residence, and there were some issues over which his up-time wife had firm American opinions.

Plumbing, first and foremost. They had brought with them the materials to provide a newly built edifice with the sort of facilities that Anne would insist upon—and which, being honest, Adam much preferred himself. Even with the skilled and experienced craftsmen they'd brought with them, trying to retrofit a star fortress with such facilities didn't bear thinking about.

As they entered the Heerenweg, Adam asked his guide: "What do you do, Mister Dijkstra?"

"I'm an architect and builder."

"And why did you happen to be there when we arrived?"

"Lumberyard," Wolfert said, keeping most of his breath for the brisk walk.

A few minutes later they got to the Director-General's residence, which was located on the eastern side of the Heerenweg. It was disappointing. First, because of shoddy construction. Second, because they were on the side of the Heerenweg that wasn't too far removed from the commons known (for good reason) as the Sheep Pasture. Adam couldn't see it, but he could certainly smell it.

He made a mental note to himself. *Drainage and sewage. Top priority.*

"Did you build that?" he asked, using his chin as a pointer.

"No!"

Adam looked at the man. He sounded offended. "If you wouldn't mind waiting here for a few minutes, Mister Dijkstra,

I would like to speak to you some more after I have finished my business with van Twiller."

"I'll wait."

Adam knocked and then without waiting opened the door to the Director-General's residence. There were two gentlemen in the foyer of the building. They took one look at the soldiers who accompanied Adam, and decided they had business elsewhere. Adam proceeded to the most ornate door from the foyer, passed through it and found himself in a smaller room with a man at a desk. His guards followed.

"Who...who are you?" the man squeaked.

"Who are you?"

"Egbert Wessels. I'm the Director-General's secretary," he said, apparently gaining confidence by the recitation of his name and title. "And you aren't allowed in here carrying guns."

"I have a dispensation," Adam said. "Where is Director-General van Twiller?"

Wessels' eyes flicked to the door to the side and back to Adam, and that was all Adam needed. He headed for the door.

"You can't go—" Egbert Wessels' voice cut off abruptly as one of Adam's men stepped forward. He didn't point his rifle at the man, but hefted it enough to make clear he easily could.

Adam strode through the door.

A short, fat man was standing, and the chair he'd been in a moment before was pushed back. "Do you know who I am?" he almost shouted.

"You are Wouter van Twiller, the nephew of Kiliaen van Rensselaer, and you *were*, until quite recently, the Director-General of the New Netherlands. However, the New Netherlands no longer have a Director-General. Instead, they now have a royal governor. That would be me—and you are now unemployed."

"My uncle won't stand for—"

Adam held up a hand. "A compromise of sorts has been reached. You're not going to be arrested for taking bribes. In exchange, your uncle is not objecting to the crown taking direct control of the New Netherlands. You have two choices—and only two. You can take the ship I came on back to the Netherlands, or you can stay here as a private individual. A factor for your uncle, perhaps, but with no legal authority beyond that."

It took a bit more discussion and the presenting of documents, all with the presence of Adam's guards making clear that his orders weren't simply legal, as the new government in Brussels saw things, but could be enforced.

Finally, it was done and the former Director-General was gone, muttering vague threats as he went.

Adam then had a chance to look about the place, and it was a dump. A fancy dump, but a dump nonetheless. The walls were painted, but not well made, and there wasn't enough room for what he needed. Nor was this place nearly as defensible as Adam wanted.

He sent for the builder who'd showed him how to get here.

Wolfert watched the invasion of the Director-General's residence with a mixture of pleasure and concern. Wolfert was Protestant, and he'd emigrated from the Netherlands when it was still fighting a war against rule by a Spanish king who was trying to force everyone to be Catholic. Now the Netherlands did have a Catholic monarch, but one who was apparently willing, at least so far, to let people decide for themselves what religion they were to follow.

Van Twiller was a fat toad, who insisted on a bribe to sign his name. But how could Wolfert be sure that this new royal governor was going to be any better?

Adam Olearius was Lutheran, not Catholic, so apparently the new king in the Low Countries really meant it about freedom of faith. Wolfert was tempted to leave, just to make sure he stayed out of trouble. But the new governor had asked him to wait, and starting off his relationship with the new authority in the city by running off after he'd been asked to wait seemed a bad idea.

Eventually, one of the soldiers came and got him.

In the office that until a few minutes before had been van Twiller's, Wolfert and Adam discussed what the new royal governor and his entourage, including soldiers, were going to need. They were still discussing it when more soldiers arrived, escorting the governor's wife, an actual up-timer named Anne Jefferson.

She seemed quite casual and friendly. "It's not just us and a few soldiers. We also brought experts. Not nearly as many as we would have preferred, but a few. I'm going to need a clinic and that means beds, hot water, and distilled spirits. So we need a bigger place."

"I can build it for you, but it will take time."

"The question is: what do we do in the meantime?"

"You could stay at Mulder's Tavern. Brechtje owns it now, and it's not just a tavern, but also a boarding house. It's pretty full at the moment. A bunch of Gomarists who left the Netherlands to..." Wolfert trailed off.

"To get away from the King in the Netherlands," Adam finished for him. "And his corrupt Catholic government, who are going to grab all the good Protestants by their coattails and drag them down to hell."

"Yes, Governor, that's the way they see it."

"We can look for additional accommodations. If necessary we can quarter some of the men on the local residents," Adam said, watching his wife.

"The Bill of Rights..." she started.

"Which Bill of Rights is that, dear? The one that won't be written for another hundred and fifty years, or the one that is the law of the State of Thuringia-Franconia? Not the USE even, just the SoTF. Which has no Third Amendment. So if we need to quarter troops on civilians, we will. We will do it with as much respect as we can manage but we will find quarters for our people. And it won't be in tents, not with winter coming on."

Anne Jefferson didn't look happy, but she didn't say anything further.

Wolfert didn't know what they were talking about. Housing troops on the populace was standard practice when a fort was unavailable or inadequate. Everyone did it. Some more gently, some more harshly. Apparently Adam Olearius was a gentle sort, and that was good. "I suggest that we go talk with Brechtje and see what she has available. We can get a good meal at the same time."

Brechtje listened to the raging argument between Dominie Brouwer and his cousin, Diederik Hendrix. The Dominie was arguing for wait-and-see and Diederik was dithering between direct and immediate attack, and running away to Indian country. They weren't speaking loudly, but were speaking quite intently, and Brechtje had excellent hearing.

Then Aloysius, the stable boy, came running in. "Bunch of soldiers coming with Mister Dijkstra. Pa told me to tell you."

The stable wasn't owned by Brechtje, but she had an arrangement with the stable owner, who was Aloysius' father. She fed and housed the people, and he did the same with the livestock.

There was silence in the tavern portion of the boarding house. Brechtje went to see, and opened the door just before a Dutch soldier in one of their new blue-and-gray uniforms could do so.

Aloysius' report had been accurate, but not complete. Along with Wolfert and the soldiers came a woman wearing pants, and someone who, by his dress, was probably the new royal governor that Karl and Diederik were arguing about. For just the briefest moment, she was sure that Wolfert had informed the new governor who the leader of the Counter-Remonstrants in New Amsterdam was, and the soldiers were here to arrest everyone and burn her place down in the bargain. But it was a fleeting moment, caused by the infectious paranoia of Karl and Diederik who saw a cloudy day as a plot by the king in the Low Countries, along with his brother, the most Catholic Majesty of Spain.

And there weren't that many soldiers. Just six, plus the governor, his lady, another man, and Wolfert.

"Hello, Brechtje," Wolfert called as a tall blond soldier with three little roofs sewn onto the arm of his uniform coat stepped around her into the taproom and examined the crowd. The soldier wasn't threatening.

Well, no. He was threatening, but he didn't threaten by word or deed. It was his presence and the long gun strapped to his back. And, perhaps strangest of all, the fact that the uniform he wore was as clean as though it was brand new. The trousers that went all the way down to the black half boots were pressed.

It made Wolfert, who was a neat and tidy man, look positively slovenly, and everyone not in the governor's party look a bit down on their heels. And Brechtje, even as she was intimidated by the man, wanted rather desperately to know how they did it. Especially how they did it after a month at sea with not enough water to spare any for washing.

But the soldier had washed. He was clean as a new babe, save where the mud of New Amsterdam streets had soiled his shiny black boots.

"This is Royal Governor Adam Olearius and his wife Anne

Jefferson." Then he added almost as an afterthought, "And this is Paulus van der Heide, who will be handling the bill."

That was enough to snap Brechtje out of her nervous hesitance. "What bill?"

"We're hoping you will have room to put us up while Wolfert here rebuilds the former Director-General's residence," the royal governor said with a friendly smile.

"Wolfert tells us your tavern has the best meals in New Amsterdam," Anne Jefferson said. "We would like a meal for ten. Whatever you have on hand."

There was a discreet cough from the blond soldier. And Anne Jefferson rolled her eyes. "A meal for four, and after that, a meal for three, and then three more." She leaned over to Brechtje and added, "Personally, I think Sergeant van der Molen has read too many novels about the Secret Service."

That comment made no sense at all to Brechtje. "This way, Governor." She led them to a table and saw them seated, then grabbed Wolfert by his arm—she wanted to grab him by an ear, but discretion won over peevishness—and dragged him away for a few private words.

"What's this all about?"

Wolfert explained while she set Lijsbeth to work on providing the best meal the kitchen could manage for their four guests.

"I don't have room. Royal governor or not, I don't want to throw out any of our present guests." Brechtje wasn't happy with Wolfert's presumption.

"I understand, and I am sure Adam will too. They just got here and are still working things out. They may end up quartering some of the soldiers with residents. But if you have the governor and his wife here—" He paused and finished poorly. "—that will be good."

And it would be, assuming that the royal governor paid his bills on time—which was not something that Brechtje was willing to take on faith. But whether Wolfert's help was in fact a help or a hindrance, it was done now and she had to find room.

Brechtje's tavern and boarding house was a large two-story building with a large root cellar. It had a room for her and one for Lijsbeth, plus three more downstairs rooms that were used for storage, not counting the kitchen and the taproom where her guests and others could have a beer and a meal. Upstairs, there were ten large rooms that could accommodate two to four people each in comfort, and up to eight if they were willing to be a bit crowded.

However, seven of those rooms were occupied. If she cleared out the storerooms on the ground floor, that was room for some more. But that part of the tavern was supposed to be family quarters—would be family quarters if the pox hadn't taken Robert and little Hans—and Brechtje didn't like the idea of soldiers, even nicely dressed soldiers, one door away from her or Lijsbeth. She had no objection to soldiers being quartered with civilians; she just didn't want them quartered with her and Lijsbeth.

Then Sergeant Peter van der Molen explained why he wanted the meals staggered. This squad of the company that the royal governor brought with him were the elite of the elite. They were assigned to the personal protection of the governor and his wife. And, yes, they had been reading about the practices of royal guards and presidential guards of the future and they had learned a lot. So someone was always on duty when the governor was eating or whatever, and when some guards ate, others watched.

That was why the staggered meals. After he explained it, it did make sense. "But why are you telling me?" Brechtje asked.

"Because if the governor stays here, you need to know what we're doing and why. So you can schedul—"

He turned as Karl Brouwer and Diederik Hendrix came up. "Is it true that papist lackey is going to be staying here? You must not allow it!!"

Up until that moment, Brechtje had been undecided about Adam Olearius and his party staying in her boarding house. Yes, assuming they paid, it was good money. But Brechtje's only interest in politics was to avoid getting stepped on by them.

"This is my place, Dominie Brouwer. And you don't tell me who can stay in my boarding house, or whom I may serve in my tavern!"

"Well, I can tell you this much. I will not be staying in your boarding house if you allow this, nor will any of my people!" He turned and stalked off.

Brechtje turned back to the sergeant. "Well, another room or two seems to have opened up. Dominie Brouwer and his wife and son have one room, and his cousin, Diederik Hendrix and his family another. And more may be moving out since he is one of the leaders of the recently arrived Counter-Remonstrants."

"Tell me how that's been working?"

"What do you mean?"

"Well, for instance, how long has Brouwer been here?"

"He moved in off the ship that brought him and his group. They arrived about two months ago and have been arranging other quarters."

"Two months to arrange quarters?" asked the sergeant

"New Amsterdam has been growing fast since the Cardinal-Infante invested Old Amsterdam. They have been coming from all over the United Provinces and some from the Caribbean. Anyway, every time Dominie Brouwer would get a place ready to move into, there would be another shipload and he would put them up in the house he just had built, and stay here longer."

"He's using only Counter-Remonstrate builders," Wolfert added. "Though not all of the Counter-Remonstrates are quite so fussy. There is a great deal of new construction in New Amsterdam. But I think the real reason Brouwer's been staying here has more to do with politics than preference. The boarding house is centrally located and the taproom is a good place to have a meal and talk."

"But not so good if you're talking sedition and the soldiers of the crown are one table over," Sergeant van der Molen added with a smile.

"That might be why he decided to move out," Brechtje agreed, "but why be so loud about it?"

"A mistake or a statement?" Sergeant van der Molen asked, but not as though he thought they would have an answer.

Over the course of the next three days, five of the seven rooms that Brechtje had rented were abandoned as the Dominie Brouwer's actions were taken as a call to arms.

Not all of Brechtje's rooms were rented by Counter-Remonstrants. She had a sea captain who rented one of her rooms so that he would have a quiet place on land when he was in port, and a fur trader who was also only in town part time.

By the end of the week, the new royal governor's party was moved in—or, at least, the diplomatic and medical people were, along with the small unit of soldiers who guarded them. Most of the technical and other people who'd come across the ocean had been provided with lodgings elsewhere; about a dozen had been provided quarters in the fort.

There were two reasons to get it done as quickly as possible. One, if Wolfert was to begin construction on the new governor's compound before the winter set in, he needed to do it sooner rather than later. Fresno scrapers were a good tool, but they didn't work well on frozen ground. Two, they couldn't stay on the ship because as soon as they got it unloaded and stocked with wood for the trip home, it was on its way back to the Netherlands, and no one knew where it would be sent next. It wasn't particularly well armed, but it did have steam power to augment its sails, so it was, over the course of a long voyage, much faster than a straight sailing ship. That made it valuable and expensive to use.

Quite a bit of its cargo was shifted into a hastily rented warehouse just off the harbor. While the new royal governor had only brought twenty soldiers with him, New Amsterdam had already had a garrison of two dozen or so. The men of the garrison were not up to the standards of the troops brought over from the Netherlands, but they were quite willing to accept his authority and that of Captain de Kuiper. Olearius had another fifty people who were technical specialists of one sort or another. There were also several large chests of silver coinage, and even larger chests of paper banknotes from the Wisselbank, which now had branches in Amsterdam, Antwerp, Brussels, and at least three other cities in the Low Countries. As soon as Adam's financial staff could set it up, the Wisselbank would have one in New Amsterdam as well.

The rest of the technical staff were medical, engineering, chemical, metallurgy, and surveying, plus everything that Adam, Frederik Hendrik, King Fernando and Queen Maria Anna, not to mention Fernando's aunt, could think of.

The goods were mostly the "tools to build the tools" sort of equipment, and it was going to take a while for any of it to get into production. Their job was to use what they had brought and the local labor force to build enough of a solid infrastructure base to allow New Amsterdam to grow rapidly. And while they were doing that they were going to be a labor sink, pulling workers out of other jobs.

Chapter 8

Work site, new governor's residence
New Amsterdam
October 18, 1636

Wolfert Dijkstra watched as Guss Teuling placed the charge and attached the fuse. The fuses were quite good, and though electrical ignition would be better, copper wire was still far too expensive to waste. But good quality black powder was available and up-timer knowledge allowed something close to a shaped charge.

After setting the fuse, and then repeating the process, Wolfert and Guss retreated to the place where the measured fuses connected. Then, after Wolfert retreated behind the berm they had thrown up, Guss lit the master fuse and joined him. They sat there, looking at Guss' pocket watch until the fuses burned down. Then there was a series of explosions rather than one single blast, and the director-general's former residence collapsed into a pile of rubble, and the Fresno scrapers moved in.

Wolfert regretted using the explosives, but not very much. This wasn't Europe, after all, but America. The whole continent was full of trees. Still, it felt wasteful. But they didn't have the time to tear the building down by hand, not if they were going to start on the basement before the hard freeze set in. Besides, it wasn't going to waste. It was going to be charcoaled to use as fuel for steam engines and forges.

Brechtje's boarding house, temporary Government House

Adam Olearius heard the explosions, because the future site of Government House wasn't too far from Brechtje's boarding house. But he paid it little attention, because he was looking at a large sheet of paper with considerable misgivings. Not because he disapproved, but because he knew this proclamation was going to be unpopular. It wouldn't affect just the slaves in New Amsterdam. There were slaves all through the New Netherlands, growing crops, and managing livestock for the patroons.

This was a royal proclamation. And right there at the top was the title in Dutch. "Emancipation Proclamation."

It went on to describe how the slaves and half slaves were to be freed. First, they would be sold to the crown at a set price that was fairly close to the recorded prices for slaves over the last few years. Then they would be manumitted by the king in the Low Countries. At that point, they were free to work for whomever was willing to pay them. The proclamation didn't include indentured servants, because the indentured servants presumably entered into their indenture voluntarily in exchange for money or passage to the New World.

It gave the present slave owners until December 1 to sell their slaves to the government. Thereafter, all persons held as slaves or half slaves were to be freed from bondage, in the name of Jesus and by the Act of the King.

That didn't give the slave owners a lot of time to complain. That was deliberate on Adam's part. Because of the rapid growth of the colony—some of it stimulated by the projects that Adam himself would be starting—labor costs were going to go through the roof. In fact, that had already started. The price of a slave was a third again what it had been the previous year, and it would go up even more if allowed. Which, of course, was the reason for the last clause in the proclamation:

The sale of slaves to anyone but the government is henceforth prohibited. The export of slaves and half slaves from the New Netherlands is also prohibited.

There were over five thousand copies of this proclamation in the supplies. Almost enough, they had thought when they left, to give a copy to every person in New Amsterdam. They were all copies. The original, on vellum, signed by the king and Frederik Hendrik, and stamped with the Royal Seal of the Low Countries, along with a proclamation that officially made slavery illegal in the Netherlands itself, was in Brussels, on display in the palace in a fancy wooden case with a plate glass top. Or at least, it ought to be by now. They would know once they got the transatlantic radio up and running.

There were two big radios in their gear, one for the directional transatlantic communication between New Amsterdam and Amsterdam, and hence into the radio communications network that tied the Low Countries together and connected them to the USE.

And the broadcast radio, which, along with cheat sheets for building crystal sets, would allow proclamations like the one in Adam's hand to be sent out over the airwaves to all the subjects of King Fernando in the New Netherlands. Neither of those radios was ready yet, much less the thousands of crystal sets needed to hear the broadcasts.

Adam put away his distractions and added the sheet to the pile on his desk. "Very well," he said to his secretary, Jaco van Vliet. "See to the distribution, and batten down the hatches."

Then he went on to the next thing. The judicial system in the New Netherlands was a disaster waiting to happen. Established in 1625 and superseded on Adam's arrival, it was based on a contract between the Dutch West India Company and the colonists who were here at the time. The local board of directors was both the legislature and the court, and handled appeals by locals from local magistrates. For now, all Adam could do was confirm, on an interim basis, the current magistrates, making them responsible to the crown instead of the company. He did make the appointments provisional, at least until he got to know the magistrates.

At the moment, with the population growing so fast and the former Director-General having made his appointment on the basis of who paid the biggest bribe, Adam was unwilling to make permanent appointments.

He had department heads that he'd brought with him, Attorney General, Chief of Sanitation, Customs and Levies, all the important departments, but they had no staff yet, and Adam's biggest problem was he didn't know who to trust.

Two doors down, Anne was sitting with Brechtje, trying to figure out where to set up her clinic. Brechtje was pretty insistent that she not set it up in the boarding house. "I lost my husband

and child to the pox. I'll not lose anyone else." Brechtje took a breath and added, "I'll help you find a place, but not here."

"All right," Anne agreed. She already knew that Wolfert had lost his wife and last child in childbirth. "We need a solid building, and something that can be cleaned and kept clean. Cleanliness may or may not be next to godliness, but dirty is certainly next to dead in this day and age."

Then they got into particulars.

October 19, 1636

Adam's secretary knocked on the door to the room he was using as an office. It was next door to the tavern room. When he looked up, Jaco said, "Dominie Everardus Bogardus is here to see you."

"Show him in," Adam agreed, curiously. As of their arrival, there were several reverends in the New Netherlands, but Bogardus was one of the first to come here.

The man shown in was middling tall, and starting to put on a bit of weight. Adam, from the rumors, knew he was not one to back down when faced with obstinate officials.

Bogardus bowed, but not like he had any practice doing so, then straightened and said, "I thank the Good Lord for showing His Majesty, the king in the Low Countries, that slavery is against the will of God."

Adam figured that the one who showed King Fernando that was Rebecca Abrabanel, but he wasn't going to argue. "Have a seat, Dominie," he said, waving to one of the chairs in front of his new up-time-designed desk. "I am pleased and a bit surprised to hear that you approve. Many of the patroons seem less than thrilled by His Majesty's decree."

"Thieves"—Bogardus waved a hand dismissing all the complainers—"who cry they are being robbed when the lives they stole are returned to their rightful owners."

"I tend to agree," Adam said. "There aren't a great many black people in Europe, but I have met Doctor Nichols, and the notion of him being denied the opportunity to become a doctor seems much worse than theft."

"What I don't understand, Governor, is why His Majesty is choosing to pay the thieves, ransoming the victims of this abomination and filling the coffers of its perpetrators."

"I agree again, and so does His Majesty, but we live in the world of 'realpolitik.'" Adam used the Amideutsch word and waited to see if Bogardus would understand or need an explanation.

Bogardus nodded and said, "I have read both Rebecca Abrabanel's *A Call to Arms* and Scalia's book. I incline toward her view of the situation."

Adam, who himself preferred Scalia's approach to Rebecca's, nevertheless nodded. Anne, after all, leaned to Rebecca's approach. "It's a question of what even a king can do. Especially a king whose army is three thousand miles of ocean away. In effect, His Majesty had to choose between freeing the slaves and punishing the slave owners. He didn't have enough force at hand to do both. Sometimes throwing money at a problem is a necessary part of the solution."

Again Bogardus nodded. "I understand. What can you tell me about His Majesty's position on religion? I know he is Catholic, but is he going to attempt to impose his popery on us here?"

"No. His Majesty isn't imposing Catholicism, even on those parts of the Low Countries that are Protestant. Instead, religious toleration is the law in all of the Low Countries and all of her colonies. You will not be forced to attend Catholic services or Lutheran services, but neither may you force a Catholic or a Lutheran to attend yours. His Majesty does support the Catholic Church, as Frederik Hendrik supports the Dutch Reformed Church. Jews may practice their faith in safety in the Low Countries in both those parts that were Catholic and Protestant before the treaty that ended the siege of Amsterdam and reunited the Low Countries was signed."

Bogardus didn't seem all that pleased with this revelation, but he did nod again. "While popery hasn't until now been legal here, it has been tolerated in the occasional visitor."

"I'm afraid that from now on, it's going to be more than toleration of the occasional visitor, Dominie Bogardus. Several of our party are Catholic, and we have a Catholic priest with us."

"Why would you do such a foolish thing?"

"Both the king and queen are Catholic. And while they are now willing to accept religious toleration in the hope of peace, they aren't willing to let their Catholic subjects be treated with less toleration than anyone else."

They talked for almost an hour, and found themselves in

agreement about a lot, disagreement about some, and parted on cordial terms, with Adam promising to attend at least the next Sunday's services.

Dominie Bogardus' church
October 23, 1636

Adam and Anne sat in the front pew of Dominie Bogardus' church, and Anne was pleased to see that a fair portion of the congregation was black. Bogardus had approached Adam the day after the Emancipation Proclamation was spread, thanked him and the king for their piety in freeing the slaves, and immediately invited them to attend Sunday services.

Adam reported that Everardus Bogardus was a logical and effective thinker, if a bit more certain of his righteousness than Adam would prefer.

The sermon began, and it was on the Good Samaritan and religious toleration, with King Fernando in the role of the Good Samaritan, the person lost to the true faith, but still a servant of God. He wasn't giving an inch on the notion that there might be something true or of value in the Catholic Church, but at the same time he wasn't pushing for their expulsion. Rather, he was exhorting his fellow Calvinists to act as good examples, to show them the proper path by example, rather than by coercion. And insisting that the religious wars that had ripped across Europe didn't belong in this new land. "Let America, in this history as well as that other, be the beacon of freedom and religious toleration for all the world."

It was a good and rousing sermon and effectively endorsed the new government, even if the king was a papist.

After they left the church, Anne said to her husband: "One thing I've really been surprised by since we arrived in New Amsterdam is how many black people live here. They must be at least one quarter of the population. From the little I remember from my high school history classes, enslaved Africans didn't start arriving in North America in any numbers until later in the century."

"That's an effect of the Ring of Fire, I think. Hundreds have arrived just in the last couple of years because of the expansion of New Amsterdam. That's been largely driven by the emigration of disgruntled Counter-Remonstrants from the reunited Low Countries."

"Are there *that* many of them here now? A lot of the people I've met don't seem to be especially concerned about the new political...what do I call it? Dispensation, I guess."

Adam shrugged. "Many of them aren't, perhaps even a majority. The expansion of the city driven by the Counter-Remonstrants also attracts other people—many of whom aren't even Dutch. Prosperity recognizes neither creed nor color, you might say."

Anne was frowning. "What's your sense of how well the abolition of slavery will go?"

"Too early to tell for sure, but I'm optimistic. One advantage we have is that the only major issue is economic. I've read quite a bit on the history of the America you came from, and the sort of savage and brutal racial animosity that existed there just isn't present here."

"No, I've noticed that. Look at Eduart and Nailah, for instance." She was still frowning, though. "But that's a *not yet* situation. If slavery continues much longer, you'll see that vicious racism come to life. It's the only way slave owners can keep justifying themselves."

"Quite true." He smiled at his wife. "But I think that will be another effect of the Ring of Fire—a much shorter lifespan for slavery."

"It's not called the Ring of *Fire* for nothing," said Anne darkly.

Anne's future hospital
October 24, 1636

Anne looked at the building. It was wood, rough planking filled in with daub and whitewashed. It had a wood-shingle roof, a fireplace, and a wooden floor. It would take some work.

She turned to look at Wolfert. He had a team at the former Director-General's residence, but what they were doing right now was mostly digging a big hole, so Wolfert's presence wasn't needed there.

"What do you think it needs?" Anne asked him.

"It depends on you. Are you still insistent on having your clothes and bedding washed here?"

"Yes, at least for now," Anne said. "I know you want Nailah to get the contract, but sterilization is important in this. And that means really hot water and or a sterilizing agent like strong lye soap, and neither of those things goes well with washing by hand."

Wolfert's former half slave, Nailah, was now a free woman, and employed by Wolfert as the nanny for his two children. Wolfert had taken the cash that he received for her contract and handed it to her as an advance on wages. She had handed it back to the clerk as a deposit in her Wisselbank account. She and her fiancé were saving for their own place.

She was also the washerwoman for the neighborhood, and wanted to become the washerwoman for the hospital.

"The washing machines you want her to use are expensive."

Anne was okay with that, except that she didn't want anyone doing hand-in-tub washing of the linens for the hospital. She wanted them machine-washed and rinsed in sterile water. And in New Amsterdam in 1636, that meant boiled water. Wolfert was right. Boiling that much water was expensive in fuel. There were other methods that would be used in other places, but for the hospital where you were going to have a lot of sick people crowded together, boiling was what Anne wanted. And she wanted it done right here in the hospital, where the cleaning staff would be less tempted to skimp on fuel and where the sheets, gowns, and so on would be less likely to get dirty on the trip from cleaning room to bed.

"I know, Wolfert, but a hospital needs sterilization more than just about any place else. And that includes linens."

"In that case, we will need a cistern to hold water for the piping..."

They talked about the design and function of the hospital, the installations of screens on the windows so that they wouldn't have to deal with flies in the summer, and all the rest.

He pronounced that she could start using the place in another week, but only part of it at first. He would still have crews working on the rest of it for a while.

Brechtje's boarding house, temporary Government House
October 26, 1636

Eduart Jansen walked over to the table where the soldiers sat, still not at all certain about this. When he mentioned the possibility to

Nailah, she'd been ambivalent. The governor's guards were hiring and while Wolfert Dijkstra was a decent boss, the truth was that day labor on a construction site didn't pay all that well. And it paid even worse in winter when half the time they couldn't work because it was snowing or sleeting, or the ground was frozen.

But a soldier got regular pay every month. Put that together with what Nailah was already getting as the nanny for Mister Dijkstra's kids, and they could get married now.

Nailah liked the idea of getting married now but wasn't thrilled with the idea that he might get shot.

Sergeant van der Molen was seated at a long table with a dozen other soldiers. The soldiers ate in shifts so as not to over-burden the cook. And in spite of that, Mistress Brechtje Mulder had hired another cook and a maid. He looked up as Eduart approached. "What do you need?"

"I was . . . well . . . I was thinking about joining the Governor's Guards."

The sergeant looked him up and down, sniffed and said, "Maybe. The Governor's Guards is an elite unit, lad. We don't take just anyone. Every man of us is literate and most of us have a second skill."

It was true, Eduart knew that. And he was literate. Well, he could read well enough, though his writing wasn't all that great. "I can read. I read the cheat sheets to the other workmen on the site sometimes."

"That's good. Are you free for some testing?"

That was the reason he was here. The rain meant that he couldn't work today.

"I can take your tests," Eduart affirmed.

The rest of the day he spent being tested. His reading, his writing, obeying instructions, loading and firing the Dutch rifles. Which he got to do standing in the rain and lying in the mud north of town.

It wasn't a fun day. The sergeants and Captain de Kuiper made their position clear. They were testing a lot of things, but the most important of them all was "could he take it." "It" being a combination of things: fear, cold, mud, physical and mental abuse, and obeying orders that made no sense without complaint.

They also wanted to know why he was interested in joining, and what his particular religion was. On finding out that he was a Gomarist, the sergeant shouted in his face that he was a Roman Catholic, and that Eduart should stay home and live as long as he could, because as a heretic he was going to hell.

Captain de Kuiper then informed him that he was a Lutheran, and both of them were going to hell, the sergeant for being a Catholic and Eduart for being a Calvinist. Which particular brand of Calvinist mattering not at all, since they were all going to hell. All of this being shouted in his face while he stood at attention unable to speak.

They asked him if he could take orders from a Catholic, a Lutheran, a Jew, or even an out-and-out heathen if they were put in command over him.

He could. Nailah was a Christian now, but she still respected her tribal gods from before she was taken as a slave. And Eduart couldn't believe in, much less follow, a God who would lock Nailah out of heaven.

Almost surprisingly, Eduart passed the tests.

That evening at dinner, Eduart's application to join the Governor's Guards came up. By now it was customary for Adam, Anne, and a varying group of others to have dinner and discuss the happenings of the day.

Today it was Captain Johan de Kuiper, Sergeant Peter van der Molen and Lady Maria Amilia Alaveres.

"Is he handsome?" Amilia asked.

Anne rolled her eyes, and Amilia giggled. Amilia possessed an open, honest, and unapologetic interest in the opposite sex. It was so far an academic interest, because she was fully aware of the economic, and even political, value of her virginity.

"I'm afraid he's taken," Sergeant van der Molen said. "In fact, his expressed reason for wanting to join our little band is that the regular pay will mean he and his girl Nailah can get married."

"That doesn't sound Dutch?" Anne asked.

"It's African. Some sort of a tribal name."

"You mean she's black?"

"She's Wolfert Dijkstra's nanny. I saw her when he brought her in a day or so after you announced the Emancipation Proclamation. She's darker than Sharon Nichols."

"And Eduart Jansen?"

"A blond lad, with blue eyes."

Anne wasn't surprised. The dehumanization of Africans had not always been true, nor had it happened all at once or at the same rate everywhere. It was a product of hundreds of years of slavery and occurred most strongly where the slaves were treated most harshly. It was, in cold hard fact, a conscious and intentional *lie*, meant to answer the question, "How can you treat people this way?" by the claim that they weren't people to begin with.

Here in New Amsterdam, where slavery was just getting started and slaves weren't treated much worse than indentured servants, it was barely there at all. There was quite a bit of racial intermarriage, in fact.

"I'm less concerned with why he's interested in joining," Adam said, "than I am in why you're considering taking him."

"Because there are a lot more Gomarists than we thought were going to be here. After His Majesty invested Amsterdam . . . well, few believed he was going to be as gentle on the Protestants as he promised." He looked over at his sergeant and added, "After all, who can trust the word of a Catholic when they can just buy an indulgence for all their lying?"

Lady Maria Amilia Alaveres stuck her tongue out at him.

"I don't let it bother me, Your Ladyship," said Sergeant van der Molen. "After all, he's only a Lutheran," He looked at Adam. "No offense, Governor."

"If you two will put aside your ongoing attempt to restart the religious wars that Europe has inflicted on itself these last hundred and more years, I want to know more about the military situation here," Adam said.

"Yes, sir. Well, with all the concern over how the Cardinal-Infante was going to treat the Protestants, plus the fact that a lot of the local Calvinists were less than thrilled to have a Catholic king, there were suddenly a lot more Dutchmen willing to take the risk of colonization. They wanted a nice, big ocean between them and the Cardinal-Infante and King Philip of Spain.

"Also, by then the story of America rebelling against England in that other history was common, if rather distorted, knowledge. So there was the notion that with an ocean between them and the Catholics, they could start a new republic conceived in Calvinism and dedicated to the proposition that all the nasty Catholics and Lutherans were too far away to do anything about it.

"A surprising number of the newly arrived Calvinists, mostly the Gomarists, came here with the intent that when they were strong enough, they would repeat the Dutch rebellion, but this time—with a whole ocean between them and Madrid—they would win. So not only are there more people here than we thought, but they are of—" He paused, looking for just the right phrase. "—a more boisterous nature."

His phrasing didn't help. They all knew that both the Dutch Revolution and the American Revolution had won in Anne's timeline. And they were out here with no more than fifty soldiers and about the same number of officials and technicians, looking at a colony that was at least four times the size they'd been expecting, and twice as likely to rebel as they'd thought.

"But isn't this lad a Gomarist himself?" Amilia asked.

The captain nodded.

"Can we trust him?" Adam asked.

"I think so, sir," Captain de Kuiper said. "He seems truly in love with his girl, and he's admitted that while nominally a Christian, she's about half pagan in her actual beliefs. I don't think he's all that likely to be spying for the revolutionaries.

"And he's a bright enough lad, but straightforward in his thinking. Not subtle, if you know what I mean."

"Good enough," Adam said. "The fact that he's a Calvinist and, especially, a Gomarist, will help as long as he's loyal. But keep an eye on him, because if things are as bad as you're suggesting, the revolutionaries are going to approach him before long."

"And we should attend the wedding," Amilia said.

By now Anne was moderately politically astute, but Amilia had grown up in that world and she breathed it with every breath.

Bogardus' church
October 29, 1636

Saturday was still cloudy with intermittent rain, so Wolfert wasn't losing a construction day by letting his crews off for the wedding.

The church was packed, and the groom was in his brand-new uniform. The bride was in her best clothes, which were none too good, but Nailah was unwilling to spend money that might be needed later on a fancy dress that would only be used once. And there was no father of the bride to foot the bill for the wedding.

Wolfert did pay Bogardus' fee and rental on the church building, and he gave the bride away.

It was a lovely ceremony, attended by soldiers and slaves,
as well as the new royal governor and his lady. There were full
slaves, half slaves and those already manumitted; soldiers, sailors,
crafters, and a marked absence of patroons for a wedding that
brought out the governor.

It was one more shot across the bow of the patroons, who
wanted even at this very early date to categorize Africans as "not
people," so they wouldn't have to treat them as people.

But for all that, for Eduart and Nailah it was a day to look
into one another's eyes and swear undying love each for the
other. As they said their vows and accepted Dominie Everardus
Bogardus' blessings upon their union, the politics faded away to
nothing and only the glow of their love shone in the dim and
cloudy day.

Chapter 9

Eduart was still very much a trainee in the Governor's Guard, but he was here anyway because the information for this came, in part, from Nailah. After the Emancipation Proclamation, news of it spread like wildfire throughout the New Netherlands, breeding anger among the patroons of the Dutch West India Company and hope among the slaves and half slaves. At this point in history, half slaves were not so much less common as less official. There were quite a few Africans who were, under the law, just slaves, but were, in fact, closer to half slaves.

Or had been, until the Emancipation Proclamation.

Now, a lot of slave owners were feeling cheated and were taking it out on their slaves.

In this case, a group of field hands from an estate on Long Island was being smuggled through New Amsterdam to a ship that would take them to the Caribbean for resale. At a hopefully better price than the government here in New Amsterdam was paying.

Eduart looked around the corner, and saw the wagon. What he didn't see was the field hands. And that was wrong. Nailah had a friend who worked in the kitchen of van den Heuvel, and she knew about the transfer, knew the day and time. And there in the wagon was van den Heuvel and his foreman, but the back of the wagon was empty except for a pile of stuff under a tarp.

Then the tarp moved. Not much, but enough, and Eduart knew

what was going on. It even made sense. The slaves knew that it was illegal to sell them except to the government, or transport them out of the New Netherlands. So all they would need to do was raise an alarm and the patroon would be caught. To prevent that and still have live slaves, they had to be gagged and tied.

The wagon rolled on past Eduart in the alley and turned to the dock. Then a squad of ten of the Governor's Guard came out in front of it. Sergeant van der Molen shouted, "Ready arms!"

Ten "Infantes" came up. All pointing at van den Heuvel and his foreman.

"What is this?" demanded Patroon van den Heuvel.

"This," said Captain de Kuiper as he stepped out from the same alley Eduart was standing in, "is a royal inspection of the contents of that wagon." The captain waved the warrant signed by the royal governor and bearing his seal, as more guardsmen, including Eduart, stepped out behind the wagon and presented their "Infantes."

Eduart loved that nickname for the Dutch Cardinals. Officially, they were the Low Countries Rifle, but everyone knew they were a copy of the French Cardinals. Before he became the king in the Low Countries Fernando had been known as the Cardinal-Infante, so members of the Royal Guards, and now the Governor's Guards, called the rifles "Infantes" as a sort of joke.

It was really weird what went through your head as you were standing with a rifle against your shoulder, waiting to find out if you were going to have to kill someone in the hours before dawn.

As it turned out, they weren't called on to kill Patroon van den Heuvel. Instead, Eduart was put to work freeing the slaves from the ropes and gags. One of them wasn't breathing. He was a large man and well muscled, but he wasn't breathing.

Eduart didn't know what to do. He called the sergeant. "Sergeant van der Molen, he's not breathing."

The captain ordered, "Go!" almost before the words were out of Eduart's mouth. And one of the troops, the company medic, ran around to the back of the wagon. He pulled a large and very sharp knife from a scabbard at his belt as he ran, and cut loose the rest of the slave's bonds. He checked the eyes and put his hand against the artery in the man's neck, then shouted, "No pulse! But he's still warm. Hot, actually."

The medic pointed at Eduart. "You help me with him."

Together they laid the man in the bottom of the wagon and the medic checked his airway. Then Eduart got a lesson in CPR.

Luckily, they caught him in time. In less than a minute of CPR, the magic had him breathing again. The slave, who was named Oringo, and was a captive from Africa, had just had a cold. The cold gave him a stuffy nose, and the gag had mostly blocked his airway. He'd gotten by until the arrest, then the excitement and increased heart rate was just too much, and he couldn't get enough air. Gagging him had almost killed him, and would have killed him if it had taken a bit more time for his lack of breathing to be noticed.

Shaking his head, the medic said, "People don't realize how fragile the human body is, given the wrong circumstances."

Lady Maria Amilia Alaveres looked at the tall black man as he was brought in. Oringo was laid out on the cot in the newly active hospital, and Amilia had the duty. She got the particulars from the medic, and set about seeing to Oringo. She had him rolled onto his side, so that with luck at least one of the nasal passages would drain, opening up an airway without him having to breathe through his mouth. She washed his head and chest with cool water to try and bring the temperature down a bit. He was a handsome man, even sick like this. Well muscled, with a strong face.

Over the next few days his fever spiked twice, but then it broke and he started to mend, and Amilia got to meet the man. He was a warrior of his tribe, captured in a raid, and brought here almost two years ago. And he spoke Dutch poorly. Well, Amilia's Dutch had a decidedly Austrian accent. But he had a nice smile, and seemed to take the world as it came.

Brechtje's boarding house, temporary Government House
November 2, 1636

The dining room was full, but not with diners. This was the first Royal Court, and the room was full of spectators. That was good, Adam Olearius thought, as he took his seat behind the table that had been put on a six-inch platform just for this.

Patroon Gijsbert van den Heuvel was defending himself and his defense was jurisdictional. He was a new patroon who bought his patroonship all of a month after King Fernando had besieged Amsterdam. A man who could see the writing on the wall, but wasn't all that good at predicting outcomes. He bought his patroonship on the assumption that Spain would win, but that the Low Countries would fight on from here.

It wasn't, Adam admitted, a bad guess, given what was known at the time.

Van den Heuvel sold his lands and businesses in the Low Countries to buy a patroonship, and the slaves to man it, and retreated to the New World in the confident hope that, just like in that other history, the New World would throw off the old.

Then Adam showed up and spoiled everything. Granted, the crown was offering to pay for the slaves, but not enough. And the important point was he had paid good money for his patroonship, and *he* had the right to make the laws within his patroonship, not the royal governor. It was in his contract. It was in the Charter of Freedoms and Exemptions, right there in black and white. Van den Heuvel went on for some time about the Charter of Freedoms and Exemptions, and Adam let him talk until he ran down.

Then it was Adam's turn. "Your contract was with the Dutch West India Company. The Dutch West India Company, in turn, had an agreement with the States General of those parts of the Low Countries that were then in rebellion against the Spanish crown. That's the Charter of Freedoms and Exemptions that you've been harping on.

"But that rebellion failed, and while the Treaty of Amsterdam did grant the States General recognition and certain privileges, its laws were subject to change by the victors. As they always are.

"In this case, the law making slavery illegal in all the lands under Dutch control was endorsed by not just His Majesty, but by Frederik Hendrik, as well. If you want part of your money back, the people you should sue are the representatives of the Dutch West India Company.

"None of that is news. It was all explained the very day I arrived. The government of the New Netherlands is no longer in the hands of the Dutch West India Company, and it wasn't when you took ten of your slaves, bound them and gagged them, and carted them off like so many bags of grain to a ship bound for the Caribbean with the intent to break His Majesty's laws. In so doing, you very nearly killed one of His Majesty's subjects.

"Understand, if Mister Oringo had died, I would hang you for willful murder, so you can thank Corporal Smit for your life. However, in light of your willful disregard not just of His Majesty's laws, but the lives of his subjects, this court is not inclined to compassion. Your property—*all* of your property in the New Netherlands—is returned to the crown. Mister Oringo and all of your other slaves are hereby freed.

"And as for you, you almost murderer and flouter of the king's law, you will receive twenty lashes. And once they are delivered, you will be branded as an outlaw. Take ship back to the Low Countries, or move to one of the newly French or English colonies, but you can't stay in the New Netherlands."

Gijsbert van den Heuvel stood there and felt his righteous rage fade into horror. This couldn't be happening. Whipping and branding? These were punishments reserved for slaves and peasants, not men of substance and property!

He'd known he was going to lose the case from the moment those troops stepped out of the alley. He'd even expected to lose the slaves without any recompense.

But all his property in the New Netherlands?

That was *all* his property.

Such a massive seizure was well past too much. Too much even if the slave had died.

It wasn't like Africans were really people anyway. Gijsbert didn't hold with the half slave nonsense. A slave was a slave, and that was all. A piece of livestock, no more. The death of a slave, while a financial loss, wasn't murder. Especially not the accidental death of a slave.

He was outraged when the royal governor seized all his property, but whipping and branding? It *couldn't* be. He still hadn't accepted that the royal governor meant it, when the guards came to take him away.

Anne Jefferson watched the trial, and wasn't all that much less shocked and outraged than Gijsbert van den Heuvel. *Whipping and branding?* What was this, the Middle Ages?

No, she realized. It was called "the early modern period." Whose distinction from the Middle Ages—or the Dark Ages, for that matter—often seemed miniscule to her.

But from Adam, she'd expected more of the modern and less of the early. You didn't torture people, not to get a confession, and not as a punishment.

Back in their room she asked him, "What's wrong with you, Adam? Have you been taken over by Ivan the Terrible or Torquemada?"

"No. By practicality and a need to make it clear that there *is* an iron fist in the velvet glove." He sighed. "And Oringo almost died. In a way, I really would have preferred to have the man executed."

"Why didn't you, then?"

"First because without Oringo's death, I didn't have grounds to." He looked her in the eye and his normally warm eyes were cold. "But also because I wanted him humiliated in a way that a simple hanging wouldn't accomplish. I need them to fear me. To know that they will suffer if they step too far out of line."

Anne wasn't sure what to say to that. It was cold comfort to realize that, given another century and a half of social evolution, Europe would replace the medieval headsman's axe with the guillotine.

Chapter 10

Residence of Hansje de Lang
November 3, 1636

The discussions were loud and acrimonious, but that wasn't what bothered Karl Brouwer. Nor was it the fact that a fair part of his congregation was on the royal governor's side in this. Karl didn't approve of slavery himself. No, what bothered him was the strident undertone of fear.

The notion that this could turn into a real fight, that the king in the Low Countries might actually send troops to bring the New Netherlands to heel as he did in the old Netherlands... That was new. Even after Olearius arrived with his honor guard and his high-handed ways.

For the Governor's soldiers were an honor guard, at least by the standards of the Old World. Fifty men wasn't much of a force to be reckoned with, even here. Back in Europe, a single tercio was three thousand men.

Granted, the whole city of New Amsterdam didn't have many more people than that, but that was just New Amsterdam. The rest of Manhattan Island had another eight hundred or so, Long Island had over five hundred, Staten Island almost a thousand, and there were more on the coast and, increasingly, upriver. There were at least ten thousand Dutch people in the New Netherlands, most of them young men. With time, they could raise a force of five hundred, perhaps more. And cousin Diederik was a soldier who had fought against the Spanish tercios before that fool Frederik Hendrik lost the war.

But it was going to take time, and the God-cursed governor wasn't giving them that time.

Mistress Sara de Lang came up to him. "Dominie, the Director-General, well, the former Director-General is here. He wants to talk to you."

"What does he want?"

"I don't know, but he asked to speak to you in private."

The de Lang house was a fair-sized house. Hansje was a tailor who'd managed to bring a sewing machine with him. "An actual Higgins," as he was prone to tell anyone who would listen. He'd also brought his wife, three surviving children, a journeyman, and two apprentices. In the European style, the ground floor was the business, and the second floor was the residence for the family and staff. The ground floor was where the discussion was getting strident.

"Sara, could I trouble you for the use of your sitting room?" Brouwer asked.

The sitting room was a small room at the front of the second floor. It had glazed windows, though not in the new large-paned style, but plenty good enough to let in the sunlight, since it was a southern-facing room.

"Of course, Dominie." Then she muttered, "I'll just have to clean it after he leaves."

Dominie Brouwer chose not to hear the mutter. He agreed with her assessment of the former Director-General.

Former Director-General Wouter van Twiller was looking a bit shabby these days. His friends were, for the most part, friends of convenience. With the loss of his power to grant favors, he'd also lost most of the "friends."

When Sara showed him into the sitting room, Dominie Karl Brouwer was already seated. He waved to a wooden bench. "Have a seat, Mister van Twiller. What brings you to me?"

"Whatever agreements my uncle was forced to make under the Cardinal-Infante's guns, I am still the Director-General of the New Netherlands. Any agreements were made under coercion and are not valid."

Karl Brouwer blinked. That sounded almost plausible. No...not almost. It sounded like a reasonable legal argument. Certainly as legal as that ridiculous Declaration of Independence the English colonists had issued in that other timeline. Not a fig leaf based on the so-called rights of the governed, but an argument of prior claim. "That is an interesting point, sir." Karl declined, for now, to use the title van Twiller claimed. "But can you back it?"

"Not by myself, perhaps, but in cooperation with others? Olearius brought only a very small force. And the strength of formation fighting requires enough men to have a formation. You need a mass of men for massed fire. Fifty isn't enough."

"In a fort, you don't need a tercio. No pikes needed to hold off cavalry, if you have thick earthen walls backed by brick and mortar."

"But they don't. At least, not yet, and not soon. They have torn down my house and dug a basement, laid up some earth. But, for now, for some months, they will be staying in Robert Mulder's boarding house. It's a solid enough building for wood and daub, but hardly a fort."

"Fifty men with those fancy guns of theirs make it a fort. We would lose men taking it, a lot of men. And even if we did take it, what about Admiral Tromp?"

"What about him? He's in the Caribbean, last I heard."

"He is also opposed to slavery, and has apparently made his pact with the Catholic devil who sits on the throne in Brussels. Were he to take it into his head, he could blockade the port of New Amsterdam and leave us all to the tender mercies of the local savages."

"The local savages aren't all that savage. In general, we Dutch have treated more fairly with them than either the English or the Spanish. And we are less prone to offer or receive atrocities from the natives. What concerns me more is that a blockade would cut off our trade with Europe and ruin our businesses," van Twiller said.

"However, we can get through that. It won't be easy, at least at first, but in one way, at least, Fernando did us a service when he sent Olearius." He grimaced. "Not Olearius or his soldiers, but the technicians and the tools. Even his wife. He has provided us the tools to make an industrial base of Manhattan Island. Not easily, but possible. Which means we will need to take the boarding house and the warehouse intact."

"And the clinic?" asked Brouwer.

"I would rather take it intact as well, but the important thing is that we capture Anne Jefferson alive. Both for her medical knowledge, and as a bargaining chip with Olearius, if he survives. And with Fernando and Tromp, if he doesn't. As for the clinic, you can use it as an example, if you need to."

"I may. Did you see Saturday's paper, about her immunization program?"

"Yes?" van Twiller asked cautiously.

"She wants to immunize the pagan savages who haven't accepted Christ at all, and without requiring any acknowledgment of the sacrifice Christ made for all of our souls."

"Ah, the part about herd immunity makes quite a bit of sense."

"It would, if you failed to include the fact that every inoculation given to a pagan savage is one not given to a Counter-Remonstrant Dutchman. It is God's herd that needs to be immunized, not the pagans." Dominie Karl Brouwer paused, took a breath, and changed the subject. "None of it matters, though, as long as Olearius and his fifty troops are sitting in that boarding house."

Brechtje's boarding house, temporary Government House
November 7, 1636

The rider from Fort Orange was mud-stained, but not injured. He reported a conflict between the new Gomarist religious community three miles from Fort Orange and the local Indians, apparently started when the Gomarists tried to convert several tribesmen who were bringing furs to the trading post. The rider, a Gomarist himself, insisted that the Indians were at fault. The commander of the fort wasn't so sure. At least, not that Adam could tell from his letter. But in either case, the situation clearly needed a show of force.

After the man was released to his meal, Adam, Anne, and Captain de Kuiper went to Adam and Anne's room for a private chat.

As the door closed, Anne asked, "Can Johan deal with this, or do you have to go?"

"From the level of confusion the courier reported, I think we are going to need a political solution backed by a visible military presence."

"I was afraid of that," Anne agreed, waving for Captain de

Kuiper to take a seat on a chair next to a small table stacked with papers. "How are you going to get there?" she asked, taking a seat on the bed. Adam remained standing.

"It's been a mild autumn thus far, so I see no reason not to use a small ship. And a couple of boats," said Captain de Kuiper. "We may need them to manage the bend at West Point."

"That seems the best plan," agreed Adam. "I'd like to use one of the steam engines, but there isn't enough time to install one in any of the ships we have."

The radios they had weren't the uptime radios, nor were they the crystal sets or the Ferguson alternators. They were tube sets using the first radio tubes out of the factories in Amsterdam. Those tubes weren't great by the standards of the up-timers. They had short working lives and a high failure rate. But they did work. And they allowed for FM radios and powerful AM transmitters. Powerful enough to bounce off the stratosphere and reach across the Atlantic.

Even so, to get any real range they needed fairly good-sized antennas. But the mast of a sailing ship was plenty tall enough to use to get a signal the one hundred and fifty miles to Fort Orange. Especially since it would be talking to the really tall antenna they were building just outside of town.

"All right, Captain, find us the ship and boats. I figure to take half the company."

"I don't need half the company," Anne said. "Leave me a squad. Ten men, eleven with the sergeant, should be plenty for all I am going to need to do."

It took a bit more arguing because Adam was worried about her, but she convinced him that if anyone was going to need troops, it was him. So, in the end, he took most of the garrison. Other than the unit assigned to guard Anne, he only left behind a handful to keep an eye on the fort. A corporal and five soldiers would be enough to keep thieves away.

New Amsterdam docks
November 9, 1636

Corporal Ivo Hoebee checked off a box on his sheet after reading the markings on the crate. According to his inventory, the small wooden crate was mostly filled with packing to keep the ten Mark 4 amplifying tubes safe. They were spares for the radio set that would be set up on the small ship. Once they got to their destination, they would take it off the ship and set it up in Fort Orange so that they would have regular instant communications between Fort Orange and New Amsterdam.

Ivo looked at the next box. D rations, canned pork—what the up-timers called SPAM, two hundred cans, each with enough SPAM to feed a squad. He checked off his box. Next came beans. Then freeze-dried cabbage. Freeze-dried and sealed in waxed boxes in a factory in Amsterdam. Another check mark.

The next box was filled with pre-made cartridges, lead bullets on one end of a waxed paper cartridge. You could shove the cartridge into the chamber. Closing the chamber would cut off the back end of the cartridge and all the rifleman would have to do is put the cap on the nipple, cock, aim, and fire. Another checked box.

And so it went. By the time the whole loading was finished, it was past noon.

The sun was over the yardarm before they set sail.

On the Hudson River, headed toward Fort Orange November 12, 1636

Specialist Jacob de Haan set the switch and watched the tubes light up. Most of the tubes lit up. One of them, a Mark 4, didn't. Jacob cursed under his breath, then sighed. This didn't happen all the time, not even half the time. It just *seemed* like it happened all the time.

"Sergeant, we have a dead tube again."

"All right. Go down in the hold and get one of the spares."

Fifteen minutes later, Jacob carefully opened the box that was supposed—according to the list—to have ten Mark 4s. It actually had fifteen Mark 3s. Jacob made several comments on the ancestry of the inbred idiots who had mislabeled the box. Then, carrying the box, went back to the radio to report to the sergeant.

"Well, fix it!" the sergeant ordered.

Jacob bit his lip to keep from commenting on the sergeant's ancestry. "It's not a blunderbuss. I can't bang on the bullets to make them fit. The impedance is wrong. The only thing we can do is go back to New Amsterdam and hope that all the boxes of tubes weren't the wrong sort."

The sergeant didn't look particularly pleased at that. Well, Jacob wasn't happy either.

"We haven't gone all that far, Governor." They were in the S curve that was just downriver of West Point. "We could leave the boats here, turn around and go back. If we're going to have to make another trip, anyway, we might as well."

"I would, except for the danger that we might have a massacre up near Fort Orange if we don't get there in time."

Chapter 11

New Amsterdam
November 15, 1636

The true American Revolution was going to start here in the New Netherlands, and this time it would bring forth a Calvinist America, not the secular abomination that was born in that other history. That was why the Good Lord had brought about the Ring of Fire, to give humanity a second chance to follow his divine will.

But Karl Brouwer was deeply afraid that the revolution they'd been planning for was going to be a bloody business. And he wasn't looking forward to that. Not at all. But God's will was clear enough to him.

He called to his cousin, who had just come in from outside. "Diederik, is there any news yet?"

"Yes, Dominie Brouwer." Diederik gave a nod that was almost a bow as he came over. "I just got word from one of my friends. They tried to use that radio of theirs to call the ship the governor is on, but they aren't getting any answer."

"Do you have any idea why?"

"No, nor do the papists. It could be all sorts of things. It might mean that the governor has run into trouble. But, more likely, it's a question of the radio itself failing."

"Do you think they can fix it?"

His cousin shrugged.

Karl bit his lip, considering. If the radio wasn't working, then they didn't need to wait for the governor to get all the way to

Fort Orange before they moved. It could mean that they had twice as long to carry out their plans as they thought they would. It was a gift from God, the radio failing as it had. "Gather the men, Diederik. We won't wait. We'll move today."

Diederik Hendrix nodded and went to start giving the orders that would gather the faithful to the banner of a free Christian state. The Free Christian State of America.

Twenty minutes later, two men approached the household of Wolfert Dijkstra. "This is stupid," said one.

"No. Eduart's a good Gomarist. He just took that job so that he would have the money to marry his"—the second man wagged his hips suggestively—"African girl."

The first man shook his head, unconvinced.

Wolfert Dijkstra was a builder and an architect. His house was large and well built. It had his office and a small warehouse on the ground floor, and the residence on the second floor. The sun was just coming up, but Nailah was up, with the Franklin stove on the ground floor heating and the oats soaking, when the quiet knock came. Eduart was in their room, putting on his uniform. He usually had breakfast with the family before heading to the boarding house to go on duty. Mister Dijkstra and the children were just getting up.

Nailah went and checked the side door near the kitchen. There were two men and she recognized them. They were members of Eduart's congregation, and she didn't much care for them. But she opened the door because they were Eduart's fellow congregants, and went to fetch Eduart.

Eduart came down the stairs buttoning his uniform coat. "What brings you here?"

They looked at Nailah. Then one took Eduart's arm and pulled him outdoors. And all of a sudden, Nailah was afraid. Things were coming together in her mind. Rumors among the slaves and former slaves about the alliance between the Counter-Remonstrants and the slave owners who were upset over the Emancipation Proclamation. And this barely dawn approach to Eduart, and them not wanting her to hear what they were saying. She went to get Mister Dijkstra. He was a smart man who knew the governor.

❖   ❖   ❖

Wolfert Dijkstra listened to Nailah's concerns without much concern of his own, but he went out onto the second-floor landing to see a reluctant Eduart being escorted to the room that he shared with Nailah by two young men, one of whom had a pistol not just in his belt, but angled in a way that made it easy to get at in a hurry. And his hand reaching for it in response to the opening door.

Wolfert wasn't a man of action, although he'd done some brawling in his youth. But he was closer to forty than to thirty now, and he had two young children and a business to look after. Still, this situation didn't lend itself to long pondering, and Wolfert was agile enough. He stepped forward and managed to get a grip on the hand the fellow had around the pistol.

Then he was out of ideas. He had no notion of what to do from here.

The man tried to jerk the gun away, and when that didn't work, he punched Wolfert hard in the belly. Wolfert uffed, unready for the blow, but still held onto the fellow's gun hand.

Apparently that was enough for Eduart, who shrugged off the arm of the man holding him and punched the man struggling with Wolfert in the kidney. The man uffed, side stepped, his foot finding air as he was next to the staircase, and almost took Wolfert with him as he fell down the stairs. He did take the gun, which went off, sending a lead ball into the roof, and gun smoke into Wolfert's eyes, effectively blinding Wolfert for the rest of the fight.

All three of the young men were in good shape, but Eduart had a bit more training, and his training was much more scientific and professional. Besides, one of the men was at the bottom of the stairs, making close acquaintance with a pot of boiling oats.

The other one faced Eduart alone, with his back to a staircase, and the example of his friend to encourage him to look over his shoulder to see his footing.

That gave Eduart the moment of distraction that his instructors had talked about. He struck two blows, the first a regulation jab at the solar plexus. The second, though, his unarmed combat instructor would make him do fifty push-ups, if he saw it. For that second blow was a haymaker that belonged on a farm. But it landed. And as useless as a haymaker is if the other fellow sees it coming, it delivers a lot of force if it gets through. Another fellow went down the stairs to land on the first, even as Wolfert was blinking gun smoke from his eyes and asking Eduart, "What was all that about?"

"They said they needed my rifle, that it was my duty to God to give it to them, to join them in smiting the papists. I tried to tell them the governor is a Lutheran, but they said he worked for a papist and might as well be one himself, since he brought a bunch of them with him. I didn't know what to do." Then, in almost a wail, "They were my friends."

"Maybe," Wolfert said, "they were, but if they were, they aren't any more. Eduart, run to the warehouse and get me some rope to tie them with. Whatever their reasons, we're taking them to Brechtje's boarding house."

They found the reasons surprisingly easy to discover. The young men, both in considerable pain and one suffering fairly severe burns on his face from the boiling oats, were only too happy to tell Wolfert, Brechtje and Eduart what their punishment was going to be when those chosen by God took New Amsterdam away from the papists and founded a Calvinist republic in the New World.

They took them to the new hospital that Anne Jefferson was still setting up. After all, both of them were injured, and Anne's was the best medical facility in the New World.

One and a half blocks from the boarding house, the New Amsterdam Hospital was a refitted warehouse, with a steam-powered electrical generator. It needed the boiler both to produce distilled water and for the electricity to run several pieces of equipment, including lights, which allowed surgery even at night. And a refrigerator for keeping things like insulin from going bad.

The wagon carrying Wolfert, the kids, Nailah, Eduart, and the two injured men arrived at the hospital. Brechtje had remained behind at her establishment.

It was Amilia's shift as duty nurse, and she was looking forward to getting off in another hour. Also, while she knew the basics from books and had some experience—New Amsterdam having rather more than its share of accidents needing medical attention—severe burns over three quarters of a man's face and another man who was apparently still half-blinded by a near miss from a black-powder pistol, were beyond her skills so far. She sent a runner to fetch Anne.

If Amilia's medical skills were still pretty limited, her political and military judgment was top-notch. She had the story out of Wolfert and Eduart in a short while.

She didn't wait for Anne to arrive. She immediately ordered everything that could be moved packed up for transport to the boarding house. "There is no way that ten soldiers can protect this place *and* the boarding house."

She looked over at Oringo, who was mostly recovered and now a recruit in the Governor's Guard, and the only one whom Eduart actually outranked. He, like her, had the duty last night. "Oringo, I need you to go to Dominie Bogardus and get him to gather his congregation and bring them and any weapons they have to the boarding house. With most of the troops on the way to Fort Orange..."

She stopped. "Blast it. The radio on the boat is out, at least that's what everyone thinks happened. Never mind. Oringo, go get Bogardus and his people. Eduart, I need you to go wake Sergeant van der Molen, and tell him we need to warn the governor the old-fashioned way."

"What about the fort?"

She shook her head. "Forget the fort. They will have sent enough men to keep the few soldiers left there from coming out. Even if we could use it, we couldn't get everyone there in time."

By the time Anne got to the hospital, the packing and transport of patients was underway. She treated the burn victim and washed Wolfert's eyes with saline solution and wrapped them so that they would rest. It would leave him blind for a few days, but was the best thing for long-term recovery of his sight.

As it happened, Bogardus had several rivermen in his congregation, so a boat was sent after the ship that the governor was on.

Less than an hour later a mob equipped with muskets and torches arrived at the hospital to take Anne Jefferson into custody, only to find an almost empty building. Cheated of their prey, they put the torches to use, and the building and anything of value that it might have still held went up in flames.

Dominie Brouwer wasn't happy.

Brechtje's boarding house, temporary Government House

Two hours later, the mob had invested the boarding house. Most of them were milling around on the Heerenweg, but dozens had come into the smaller street on which the house's front entrance was located.

"Okay, Eduart, how many are there?" Sergeant van der Molen asked.

"A lot!"

"I was looking for something a bit more precise." He looked to Oringo. "Recruit?"

Oringo, who Eduart knew was a former soldier for his tribe, looked out with a practiced eye. He'd already studied the crowd in the Heerenweg.

"Two, maybe three hundred all told, mostly young men. Half of them here, the rest mostly in the Heerenweg. But there are a fair number of women with them. I'd say about half have guns, but most of their guns are muzzle-loading smoothbore muskets." He laughed. "Some of them are matchlocks."

"Then let's pray for rain," the sergeant said, looking at a cloudy sky.

The ground-floor doors and windows were closed, shuttered, and barred. The second floor, though, had gunners at every window. It wasn't just the squad that the governor had left and the recruits Eduart and Oringo. Dominie Everardus Bogardus was here too, and he'd brought his congregation, many of whom had arms of their own. Mostly those arms were smoothbore muzzle-loading guns, but since they were inside, out of any potential rain, they were in a much better situation than the attackers. There were men, white, black, and red, and a few women with their household arms. The attackers had the numbers, but the defenders had the position.

Eduart looked out the window again. There was a group of young men at the fore, and Eduart recognized Diederik Hendrix leading them. He pointed and someone on the ground must have noticed.

Suddenly, the sergeant shouted, "Down!"

Eduart went down, and so did Oringo and the rest of the soldiers. Most of the civilians too, but not till the shooting started. Several shots rang out. One man was killed and two were wounded. The sergeant said two sacrilegious words, then shouted, "Get to your windows! Ready weapons. Target that mass of young men. Fire!"

Eduart fired. He was shooting into the mass, not aiming at any one person. But that apparently wasn't the case with the others.

Diederik Hendrix was hit three times in that first fusillade. Two of the wounds were mortal, one of them all but instantaneous. He went down, never to rise again till God rose up the dead.

"Reload!"

Eduart pulled his rifle in, opened the lock, inserted another round, closed the lock, cocked the hammer, pulled a cap from his pouch, and fumbled it on, while he tried not to throw up.

"Aim!"

Eduart aimed, noting peripherally that most of the civilians were still pouring powder into the barrels of their guns.

"Fire!"

Eduart closed his eyes and jerked the trigger.

"Reload!"

It seemed like forever, that cycle of aim, fire, reload, with a peppering of fire from the civilians, who by now weren't even trying to keep up with the soldiers. It went on and on and, at the same time, it passed in an eyeblink until, finally, fire wasn't followed by reload, but by "Odd numbers, clean your weapons. Even numbers, have your rounds ready, but don't reload yet."

Eduart was an even number. He checked his rounds. He had fired seven rounds at a rate of fire that was supposed to be three rounds a minute, although he was a bit slower. The battle had lasted less than three minutes, and the crowd was already running, leaving its dead and wounded behind. Clearly, they hadn't been prepared to encounter firearms like the Infantes. If they'd heard rumors of the rifles' accuracy and rate of fire, they hadn't believed them.

There didn't seem to be too many dead—yet, anyway—but there were quite a few wounded men out there. Blood was everywhere, as well as...

Eduart lost his battle with his stomach. He stuck his head out the window and vomited into the street.

Suddenly, he was jerked back inside. "Throw up in the corner, you fool! You want to get your bloody head blown off?" the sergeant shouted.

Dominie Everardus Bogardus came in, saw that people were mostly whole, and went on to the next room.

Elsewhere in the boarding house, Brechtje was busy taking care of, and berating, a blind and helpless Wolfert. Brechtje, it seemed, wasn't overly impressed by Wolfert's heroics. "You could have gotten yourself killed, you great fool!" Then she hugged him fiercely.

Wolfert wasn't sure what was going on, but he liked his prospects. He again considered his house and Brechtje's boarding house, and this time he had to consider the fact that he might well not have a house by the end of this. That mob that was getting itself shot up out there might well decide to burn his house down if they figured out the part he'd played in this morning's events.

Or, if the battle went badly, the boarding house might burn.

He decided not to worry about that last, because in that case, they would all be dead.

Anne Jefferson was mostly ignoring the battle. She had patients to tend. Aside from the newly wounded, there were two surgical patients, a mastectomy that may well have been too late, especially since she had no chemotherapy to follow the surgery, and a compound fracture that would have left the patient crippled. Both those patients were made worse by being moved before they were ready, so Anne was too busy seeing to sick people to pay more than passing attention to the shooting.

She spent her time wishing for disposable latex gloves. What she had instead were two—count them, two—pairs of dishwashing rubber gloves, which were cleaned between surgeries. At times like these, Anne wished for a lot of things from the disposable world of the twentieth century that she'd left behind. Then she went back to work saving lives.

Dominie Karl Brouwer, in a building across the street and down the block, silently cursed the papists. He cursed his fallen cousin, the up-timers, and himself. Cursed anyone and everyone, except God.

Even in the silence of his soul, he couldn't curse God. God, who by the act of the Ring of Fire, had spat in the face of all Calvinists and the doctrine of predestination by stepping in and changing the destinies of countless men and women, perhaps of everyone on earth by now. There were men from that other history, men of faith, who hadn't even been born in this history. How could they fulfill their destiny?

It was as if God had looked at John Calvin's doctrine and said, "Want to bet? I'll change it all!"

But he couldn't think any of that, for to accept that was to accept that Calvin and, especially, Gomarus were wrong. That God found the faith by which he'd lived his life offensive. And that, he could never accept.

Instead, he continued to curse the papists, and the up-timers, and the Remonstrants, and anyone who wasn't a committed Counter-Remonstrant, and plotted their downfall. In his anger, he turned the mob loose on the governor's partially built radio tower.

The papist governor's residence was also burned. What would burn, that is. When it was finished, the residence would be as much of a fort as a residence, with doubled brick walls with packed earth between them. For now, they were barely started. The basement was dug and there was a wooden framework that the bricklayers and plumbers were using for their work, and the whole thing was covered by tarps. But under Dominie Karl Brouwer's orders, the framework and the tarps were burned and anything easily smashed was smashed.

Hudson River, near West Point
November 16, 1636

It was late in the afternoon when they heard the gunshot. A sailor was sent up into the rigging and saw a boat approaching under oars. It was still a couple of miles back, but with the radio out Adam was wondering if he should turn back or go on. He had the ships turned about and went back to meet the boat.

Having gotten the report, he made sail for New Amsterdam.

Hudson River, approaching New Amsterdam
November 18, 1636

The sun was coming up and they were just now getting back to New Amsterdam. Unwilling to wait a day, Adam decided to abandon the careful scouting he'd planned.

"We go straight in, Captain."

Captain de Kuiper started giving orders. Five minutes later, before the ship was even tied up, soldiers in the blue and gray of the Netherlands were leaping over the side onto the dock and forming up.

Captain de Kuiper jumped over the side as the gangplank was being run out and shouted, "Company, forward march!" and they started marching. Then, "Company, at the double, march!" and they started running. It wasn't a sprint, but a steady, ground-eating formation trot. A trot that let them keep formation even as they ran.

Adam ran up and reached the front of the column, a little out of breath. He was surprised that Captain de Kuiper was ignoring the fort altogether. Instead, he was leading the troops alongside the Common Ditch, toward the Sheep Pasture.

De Kuiper paused the march and introduced Adam to a short man in his late forties or early fifties. "Mijnheer Visser. He knows the city well."

"Most of them are holed up in the Church of the Redeemer, Governor," Visser explained. "The ones with any fight still in them, anyway. There are maybe two dozen more who've seized the fort and taken the soldiers there prisoner. You have to know that it's not everyone who went crazy after you left. A lot of us are on your side. And a lot more are just keeping their heads down, not wanting to get shot."

"I understand. What we need to know is their dispositions."

He told them what he could. The Counter-Remonstrant church where the traitors were located was a large building made of half-brick walls, that is, walls that were brick up to a height of about three feet, with wood and daub above that. The Redeemer had a bell tower, but didn't yet have a bell because it was a new-built church and the bell foundry had run out of copper until they got in a new shipment. But the bell tower meant they might well have a lookout. The Gomarists had the sympathy of a fair amount of the city's residents. But a lot of the citizenry weren't in favor of the revolution, either because they were fine with King Fernando or, more often, because they didn't think the revolutionaries could win and didn't want to fight.

So what the Gomarists actually controlled was the Church of the Redeemer and a few houses right around it, the fort, and the area right around the boarding house.

Adam looked at his captain.

"Governor, I've seen more battles lost by fancy tactics than any other way. They probably know we're here by now, but they haven't had time to figure out what to do about it yet. So, most likely, they'll be forted up in that church, trying to figure out their best tactics. From what this fellow said, I think the boarding house is safe enough for the moment.

"We can deal with the men in the fort later. Few if any of their leaders will be down there. What we should do now is head to the Church of the Redeemer just as fast as we can get there, surround the place with our whole force, and call on them to surrender."

He pointed to the north, indicating a spot just past the Sheep Pasture that was still out of sight. "This is the fastest way to the church."

Adam considered. What he wanted to do was fly to Anne's rescue like a hero out of legend. But he was a reasonable man who listened to his experts, and here was his expert in matters military. "Captain, you have command."

"Yes, sir! Groot, take three men for a governor's guard. You'll bring up the rear."

Groot collected his men.

Captain de Kuiper shouted, "Company, forward march!" After three steps, "Company, at the double, march!"

And they were running again, with Adam in the rear.

It was less than two minutes later that the company reached the square in front of the church, and Captain de Kuiper had spent the run talking to his sergeants. All he shouted was "Execute!"

As they hit the square, four squads of men split off to surround the church.

From inside the church came three shots, fired apparently in panic and not hitting anyone.

Before long the squads were in place, one behind the gazebo in the square, one in the house to the left of the church and one in the house to the right. The last short squad went around back, and took the stable behind the church, shooting a stable hand who went for his gun.

Then the captain, who was stationed at the gazebo, shouted, "In the name of the royal governor and the king in the Low Countries, I call on you to surrender!"

There was a fusillade of shots from the church, and Captain de Kuiper shouted, "Ready!

"Aim!

"Fire!"

There was a fusillade of shots and at least two screams that Adam could hear.

"Go!" the captain shouted, and was up and running even as he shouted. Now the men weren't running as a clustered group. Each man was separated by several feet from the next, giving plenty of room for shots to miss. They'd been trained as skirmishers as well as line soldiers.

There were shots, but not many. Most had been expended in that first rush to fire after the call to surrender. It took considerable time to reload a muzzleloader, and Captain de Kuiper wasn't going to give them that time.

Still, one man went down as they sprinted for the wall of the church.

Adam ordered his protection detail to go get the man, but Corporal Groot said, "Wait a moment, Governor. We'll get Joep, but not until the captain makes the breach."

Now, against the walls of the church, the squads readied their grenades. These were the new grenades made in Amsterdam. They didn't have old-fashioned fuses which needed to be lit. They had a nipple for a cap, the same sort that was used on the rifle. Bang the cap against something hard and you had about five seconds before the grenade went off.

Whack!

One.

Two.

Toss through a window. Three.

Four.

Five. *Bang!*

The wall blocked most of the force and all of the shrapnel.

On this day, that was enough. No more of the Governor's Guards were injured.

As soon as the grenades went off Sergeant Claes Boogard stepped out from the wall, lifted his right leg, and kicked the door. Sergeant Boogard was six feet three inches tall and weighed close to three hundred pounds, all of it muscle. The double doors to the church burst inward, and the men charged in.

Now one of Adam's bodyguards went to fetch the downed man.

❖   ❖   ❖

Inside the church, it wasn't packed with people, but it was far from empty. Almost a third of the belligerents were women and some were children. Most of the members of the Church Council, which included Dominie Karl Brouwer and doubled as the leadership of the rebellion, were there also. Adam shook his head in disgust. *Heroes that burn down hospitals.*

"All right, Captain. Make sure they are disarmed, not a penknife among the lot of them, and that includes the women. And hold them here. It's as good a place as any, for the moment."

Of course, they couldn't leave just yet. They had to organize things here, take the bodies out of the church. There were seven of them, and thirteen wounded. Thankfully, all but one of the dead were men, but several of the wounded were women and two were children.

Searching the congregation for weapons also took time. Time that Adam didn't want to take, but knew he needed to.

Outside Brechtje's boarding house

The people outside the boarding house heard the shots and the muffled bangs of the grenades, and some of the mob knew what they were. They could all hear the direction that the sounds came from. New Amsterdam was still a small town, in spite of its growth, and this was still a walking-distance world. The boarding house was less than half a mile from the Church of the Redeemer. And shortly after they heard the shooting, they heard from a friend who worked at the lumberyard next to the port that the royal governor had arrived with his "whole" army. The rebels still had quite a few more men than the governor did, but by now they knew full well how much the Infantes added to the firepower of the Governor's Guard.

People started deciding that they had other places to be.

Derik van der Kleig called a friend over. "Peter, go to the church, see what's happening."

Peter ran off.

Minutes later Peter was back. "They were bringing out the dead, a bunch of them. I saw Hans. He had half his face blown off. And the fucking blue coats were looking barely scuffed. I'm getting out of here."

"Wait, what about Dominie Brouwer and the others?"

"I didn't wait to see, but if they aren't dead, they're surely going to hang. I'm leaving." Peter stopped and took a breath. "Look, Derik, we are in rebellion against the crown. We're traitors. At least, that's how the royal governor is going to see it. I'm not just leaving here, I'm getting out of New Amsterdam. Maybe Fort Orange, maybe the Indians. I may even go to Boston or Virginia. There has to be some place where His Most Catholic Majesty, king in the Low Countries, doesn't rule." Peter picked up his musket and left.

Derik would have followed, but he had a wife, two children, and a cobbler's shop, all here in New Amsterdam, and his wife wasn't going to leave her house, whatever he did.

Fifteen minutes later, when the Governor's Guard actually arrived, Derik and the last of the mob had slipped away. Derik went back to his cobbler shop and hoped that no one noticed that he'd been involved in the rebellion. Or if they had, that they keep it to themselves. Or if they didn't, that the authorities would choose to look the other way.

At the head of a column of thirty men—one squad was back at the church keeping an eye on the women, children, and the wounded—Adam Olearius marched to the rescue of his lady.

At the front of the boarding house, Anne stepped out and came to meet him. "It took you long enough. What happened to the radio?" Then, not giving him a chance to answer, she grabbed him and kissed him.

"A tube went out, and it turned out we had the wrong box of spares," Adam said when she let him come up for air. Then he kissed her again.

Chapter 12

The lot Anne's hospital stood on November 20, 1636

The hospital was all ash and ruin. Well, mostly. All that was left were a few boards, quite a few bricks, and—best of all—the boiler and steam engine had been burned, but not destroyed. With some cleaning, they would work. The autoclave might or might not be repairable. All in all, aside from the building itself, they'd lost a couple of thousand guilders worth of equipment.

The owner of the building wasn't happy, and Anne didn't blame him. He was demanding that Anne make good the loss. "Those fanatics never would have touched my building if I hadn't rented it to you. And you know that. I know it's not your fault, but it's not my fault, and the government is responsible for this."

"I will talk to my husband, Mister Rynsburger, Perhaps something can be worked out."

As it happened, Mister Rynsburger wasn't a Gomarist. He was a Counter-Remonstrant, but rather like Wolfert, mostly because he didn't much care about the topic. Especially since the Ring of Fire, which he figured was God telling all the priests and dominies and reverends for the last thousand years or so that He could do whatever He wanted, save whoever He wanted, and would do so as He chose without consulting them.

He was also a member of Dominie Bogardus' church, and while he wasn't with them in the boarding house, his brother-in-law was.

"Right now," Anne said, "my husband is at the site of the

Governor's Residence, seeing what damage was done. Once we get the radio up, we should be able to contact Brussels and the Wisselbank, and get some more credit, and perhaps another shipment of goods.

"For the moment, though, we're in something of a tight spot. Only about fifteen percent of the population of New Amsterdam is solidly on our side. The revolutionaries have perhaps thirty percent, and the rest just want to be left alone."

"It's not that bad, Mrs. Jefferson. A lot of the people here like what you're doing. I know some objected to your freeing the slaves, but not all of us. And, well, in all truth, the patroons needed to be taken down a peg or two. I think most folks here are willing to give you the benefit of the doubt."

Which, Anne guessed, was about all they could hope for.

Adam and Wolfert were having similar discussions at the considerably less than half-built Governor's Residence. "The tarps are going to be hard to replace, Governor, at least out of our own stocks. I know you brought automatic carders and spinning machines, but there aren't that many sheep. Not in the New Netherlands. We are going to need to ship in the cloth or the raw wool. And if we're going to ship anything from the Low Countries or anywhere in Europe, it might as well be finished cloth."

"His Majesty knows that, but sheep are self-replicating." When Wolfert blinked he added, "They make more sheep."

The look Wolfert gave him then wasn't respectful of his august rank.

"It's the up-timers," Adam said. "They have a habit of dressing up the most common of things in fancy words. But after you get used to it, it turns out it can be pretty useful."

"How's that?"

"It affects the way you think about things. Lets you see utility where you wouldn't automatically see it if you used the more common words."

"I'll take your word for it, Governor. I know the cheat sheets have been useful." Wolfert pointed at a set of troughs that were running along the bottom of the basement. "The new Governor's Residence is going to have indoor plumbing, and when we get that far, we'll be building tracks for electric lines and gas pipes into the building too. And the Governor's Residence isn't going to be the first building in New Amsterdam to have indoor plumbing."

They went on, Wolfert reaching up to scratch his face and being blocked by the eyepatch over his right eye. It had gotten the worst of the black powder and Anne had prescribed an eye patch to let the eye rest as it recovered. Whether Wolfert would get his full eyesight back or not was still an open question. The cornea over his right eye was scratched pretty badly, but that should heal given time and rest, but it might not.

"Do what you can about the Residence, but the urgent thing is to get the antenna tower rebuilt. There are a couple of reasons for that. First, and most important, is that it will let us talk to Brussels and Amsterdam, and order cloth and tarps. But it will also let us tell His Majesty about what's going on in the New Netherlands and about the weather."

"Why would His Majesty care about the weather here?" Wolfert looked confused.

"Because the weather here affects the weather there. And knowing the weather here can help the meteorologists in Brussels figure out what the weather there is going to be in a few days or weeks," Adam said. "Anne tells me that up-time the weather predictions were so good that people complained if they only had an eighty percent accuracy rate a week out."

"And we're lucky to guess for a day in advance," Wolfert agreed. "What about Admiral Tromp down south? He has a radio, doesn't he?"

"Yes, one of the Ferguson alternators," Adam said. "Ours will be better, once we get the thing working."

They still hadn't found the right tubes.

At the boarding house, Eduart was cleaning his Infante, while Nailah was watching not just Wolfert's two children, but three more who were from Everardus Bogardus' congregation. Setting one young scamp in the gaol for the crime of pulling hair, Nailah came over and sat next to Eduart. "Are you going to stay in the army?"

"I don't have much choice. I signed up for a three-year hitch."

"They'd let you out if you asked."

"Maybe. Do you want me to ask?"

Nailah considered. "Not unless you want to. I know it was hard for you, the killing."

"That's what scares me, Nailah. It wasn't hard, not really." Eduart took her hand and looked into her eyes. "Yes, I closed my eyes the first time I shot, and I threw up after. But on the second shot, my eyes were opened and I knew who I was shooting at. And I shot him as easy as I'd butcher a hog."

"Did you like it?"

"No. I was scared half to death."

"That's not what I meant. I mean the killing."

"No. Like I said, it was like butchering a hog or mucking out a stable. Just something that needed doing."

She leaned in then and kissed him, to the *oos* and giggles of the children. "You will be fine, my Eduart. As long as you don't take pleasure in the killing, you will still be you."

After giving the children a severe look, which only caused more giggles, she turned back to Eduart. "What about Wolfert? Is he going to ask her?"

Eduart rolled his eyes. Wolfert Dijkstra was a good man and a decent boss, but Eduart figured his first wife probably had to hit him over the head with a brick to get him to propose. Or would have, if the whole thing hadn't been arranged by their families. "He's still afraid that he and the children might be a burden on Brechtje."

"Well, talk to him, will you?"

"I have. You know I have."

"Find better words."

"I'm not a dominie, nor a matchmaker."

"That's it! We'll get Bogardus to do it."

What was it about women, Eduart wondered, that made them want to arrange everyone else's life?

Brechtje's boarding house, temporary Government House
November 23, 1636

There was a line around the block. The first snowfall of the year had started, but it looked to be a very light one. The weather didn't have any effect on the mood of the people in the line, though, one way or another. That was a line of very unhappy slave owners and of very happy slaves, and would have been in bright sunshine.

They weren't just there from New Amsterdam. Some were from settlements as far inland as West Point. The Emancipation Proclamation had made it very clear to whoever owned a slave that, as of dawn on December 1, the slaves were free. If the slave owners wanted to get any money at all out of the deal, they had to bring their slaves in before that day and time was running out. After the arrest, flogging and branding of the patroon Gijsbert van den Heuvel, followed by the quick suppression of the rebellion, nobody doubted that the operative part of Adam Olearius' title was *governor*.

The rich of the New Netherlands weren't happy, but it wasn't just the former slaves who were pleased by the new dispensation. So were quite a few of the middle people, the craftsmen and shopkeepers. Having to compete with slaves drove wages and profits down.

Brechtje Mulder had had enough. She knew perfectly well why Wolfert was hesitant about asking her to marry him, but his concern was, in her opinion, at best overblown. Wolfert had several contracts that would prove quite lucrative, and she had the boarding house. The logical thing was for them to get married and for him to sell the house on Cooper Street to one of the many people who were looking to buy a house. In fact, she knew just who he should sell it to. Bastien Dauvet had met a girl, a native who was familiar with the local plant life and they were interested in each other, but not ready to commit. To facilitate that interest, he needed his own home, and a place to make and store the drugs and other chemicals that he would be making. Dyes and priming powder, mostly, but other things as well.

Wolfert was feeling harassed, and everyone thought they knew the trouble. He'd just survived a half-hour lecture on the sin of pride, which, according to Dominie Everardus Bogardus, was why he was unwilling to move into Brechtje's boarding house and be her husband.

But all of them had it wrong. The truth was that Wolfert had never really believed that anyone would actually want him in that way. And he didn't want to push himself on someone unwilling. The rest of it was an excuse. But the truth was that Brechtje didn't need his income. She had her own. The governor's party filled her boarding house to overflowing, and, unlike Wouter van Twiller, he paid well and on time. By the time the Governor's Residence was finished, she would have a nice nest egg and an excellent reputation.

His income wouldn't hurt, but it was hardly necessary. And that was the thing that bothered Wolfert most. He couldn't figure out what he brought to the table that anyone in their right mind would want.

In spite of which, everyone around him seemed convinced that Brechtje did want him.

He was sitting in the dining room, playing with his bread pudding, as he thought about it all, when Brechtje came up. She was looking miffed, and he didn't know what he'd done.

And then he did.

They, all the people he knew, were correct.

She wanted him to ask.

Even now he didn't really believe it, but . . .

"Brechtje, will you marry me?" he asked.

Brechtje was done waiting. She was coming over here to take Wolfert back to her rooms and ask him to marry her. And was feeling quite annoyed that she was the one who would have to do the asking.

When right here, in front of the packed dining room, he blurted it out.

She was so surprised that she didn't know what to say.

Briefly. "Yes, you idiot. Of course I'll marry you."

There was a moment of silence, then most of the soldiers started cheering. Then a lot of the slaves joined in, and a few of the masters.

It took a few minutes for the people to get back around to the business at hand. But, shortly, they were back to going up to the governor's table, selling him their slaves, having the governor manumit them. Some of them hired their slaves to work for them. Some tried to hire their slaves to work for them and were refused.

One large black man looked at his former master and said, "You? No!" Then he turned and walked over to Wolfert. "I'm a cook, and if you're going to own this place, you're going to need one."

Wolfert shook his head. "Even after we're married, this will still be Brechtje's tavern and boarding house. If you want a job, apply to her."

The man turned to Brechtje. She looked him up and down, and considered. He was fat. He was also clean and he looked her straight in the eye. "Are you a good cook?"

"I am. That's why the master wanted to hire me when he doesn't like me any more than I like him."

"Lijsbeth!" Brechtje shouted, and a moment later Lijsbeth came out, along with a soldier who was a decent cook and had been acting as Lijsbeth's backup almost since the governor arrived.

"This man—What's your name?"

"Jacob."

"Jacob says he's a cook. Try him out. Jacob, I'll pay you for the day, and we'll see how it goes. Is that all right with you?"

He nodded. "You won't be sorry."

The Governor's Guard, too, was getting a lot of recruits from among the former slaves. That also didn't please a lot of the slave owners. Frankly, it didn't please a lot of the Dutch, in general. According to Anne, the level of prejudice against blacks in New Amsterdam didn't compare at all to the prejudice that was common up-time. But the Africans were still people who looked different and had strange accents and odd beliefs, so they weren't as trusted as other Dutch. And here Adam was, hiring a bunch of them for the Governor's Guard.

Adam was a bit ambivalent about that, but he knew that Captain de Kuiper wasn't. Johan liked the idea of a bunch of soldiers whose primary allegiance was to the governor, not to any of the locals, and former slaves fit the bill quite well. Not, perhaps, as well as a Spanish tercio or the Irish Wild Geese, but quite a bit better than hiring soldiers from, say, Karl Brouwer's church.

Adam, however, was a diplomat, not a soldier, and he didn't want the Guards looking like foreign oppressors. Well, at least he had Eduart as his token Counter-Remonstrant. But he would need to look into recruiting more of the local Dutch now that the resistance had been beaten down.

And that brought to mind what he was going to do with Dominie Karl Brouwer, Wouter van Twiller, and their cronies, religious and secular. A part of him really liked the decapitation idea. Those idiotic bastards had put Anne at risk. But, no. If he had a guillotine built, which was tempting, Anne would start talking about Robespierre and who knows what other up-time mass murderer. The up-timers seemed to have had a lot of them.

She wasn't all wrong, either. One of the points she made was that if he inflicted further punishment on the Counter-Remonstrants, now that they'd been defeated, they'd be filled with bitterness. That would make any relaxation of sectarian tensions even more difficult than it already was.

No. He needed a different solution. He had room for one, since the recognized ringleader of the assault on the hospital and the boarding house, Brouwer's cousin Diederik Hendrix, had been killed in the fighting. Although Brouwer certainly bore responsibility for it, he himself had not participated directly in the uprising. That allowed Adam to look the other way and did not require him to execute the man—which would have repercussions, given Brouwer's religious standing among the Counter-Remonstrants. Adam wanted to squelch a civil war, not cause it to burst into flames again.

So...

His thoughts were interrupted as a slave woman, on receiving her freedom, asked to join the Governor's Guard. Adam didn't immediately dismiss the idea. Anne had mentioned the lack of female guards. There were some wives of guards. Captain Johan de Kuiper was married to a bookkeeper who knew how to use the new aqualators they'd brought. She'd worked at the Brussels branch of the Wisselbank and was in charge of the New Amsterdam branch. But there were no female Guardsmen... Guardswomen? Guards.

He called Captain de Kuiper over. "Johan, what do you think? Don't reject the idea out of hand."

"I won't, Governor. The truth is she wouldn't be the first female soldier I've served with. They aren't common, but there are some. Usually dressed in men's clothes, and treated as men by their mates. It's not something that's talked about much, but it happens. Just not usually in elite units."

"In that case, run her through the same drill we used with Eduart, Oringo, and the other new recruits and see how she does."

"And the uniform?"

The ship that brought them had room for quite a few more

guns and uniforms than troops, especially since they'd brought more experts and specialists than soldiers. Recruiting locally was always part of the plan. So there were Infantes in the arms room here at the boarding house and uniforms in the warehouse next to the docks. However, there were no women's uniforms.

"I'll talk to Anne, and you talk to her. One thing I want to avoid is a fight over women wearing men's clothing." Anne wore a split skirt most of the time. It was a Grantville-developed garment that looked like a skirt, but had legs like pants, so it could be moved in. However, they didn't have any uniform split skirts. "If she works out, we'll think of something."

Captain de Kuiper took the freed slave woman to stand with the other recruits, and Adam went back to mulling over what to do with the prisoners.

Blast it! We need the big antenna for the radio. Their radio was powerful enough to cross the Atlantic and be picked up in the Low Countries, but to do that it needed a large specialized antenna, and it needed aqualators on both ends for encryption and decryption, as well as something his techs called checksum data checking.

They had the aqualators and had almost finished the big specialized antenna when Brouwer and his bunch had burned the thing to the ground. It was wire held in place by a wooden framework, and had proved quite flammable. Now they were going to have to start over, so it would be weeks before the antenna was rebuilt.

Dominie Everardus Bogardus' church
December 2, 1636

Everardus Bogardus spoke in a strong carrying voice to a packed house. The mix was predominantly European, but almost a third were African and there were some natives from nearby tribes as well. "Christ has moved the king in the Low Countries and showered His grace on that monarch, for he moved King Fernando to free all the slaves in the New Netherlands. And, like Moses of old, took his people, our people, out of bondage, for they are our people. It matters not which tribe they come from or even which continent, for we are all God's children and all of God's flock. So today we celebrate Our Savior for saving not just the African or natives who have been held in bondage, but even more for saving their masters from the mortal sin of slavery.

"And I assure you, it is a mortal sin. It partakes of greed, lust, and is an affront to God, in that it degrades His image, for we are all made in His image, whatever the color of our skin."

He went on in that vein for some time. It wasn't a ringing endorsement of King Fernando, more along the lines of a grudging acknowledgement that even a Catholic monarch could be moved to do the will of God when God puts out the effort.

Bogardus also threw in a prayer that God would save King Fernando and his queen from their Catholicism and bring them to the true faith. Calvinism, that was, since Bogardus was very much a Calvinist.

It was a sermon that Adam would have liked better if he was a Calvinist. The religious tensions between the Catholic king and the overwhelmingly Calvinist New Netherlands hadn't gone away just because he'd freed the slaves—most of whom were also Calvinists.

But it was better than nothing. It was a start, as his up-time wife liked to say.

Chapter 13

Antenna Rig
December 20, 1636

The antenna was up and the post amp was installed. Lidewij van der Kieij made the connection to the bank of lead acid batteries and watched as the large, thick glass tube glowed as the elements heated. This wasn't one of the little tubes that little radios used. This tube was a foot tall and six inches across. It allowed an alternating current to be amplified into the kilowatt range, and it was necessary both for transatlantic communications and the broadcast station for New Netherlands Radio, which would send music, educational and entertainment programs to crystal radio sets within a range of fifty miles from Manhattan Island.

Lidewij had studied in Grantville for almost a year, and had been involved in the design of this tube. They only had ten of them, and Lidewij hoped that would be enough to last until the next ship arrived from the Low Countries.

The output went out to a heavy copper cable, and from there to the antenna. This was the final signal booster. Once it was warmed and ready, she left, having more sense than to be anywhere near an alternating current in the kilowatt range.

"All right. Let's power it up." The radio station, except for this part of it, was located in New Amsterdam. The antenna farm was located just outside the city, connected to the radio station by heavy steel cables with a copper coating. The steel was for strength, and the copper for transmission.

There was a lot of snow on the ground now, enough to make

walking much slower than usual. By the time Lidewij got back to the station, they were up and running, putting out the first broadcast.

"How's the aqualator?" Lidewij asked.

The keyboard was a standard electric keyboard, but it activated valves that affected the flow into and through the aqualator. The screen was a combination of lights and liquid flow, affecting the position of tiny mirrors. It was three feet tall and four wide, and could display ten forty-character lines. And, as much as the tubes were Lidewij's babies, the aqualators were Giel Rolloos'.

"The Fifth interpreter is installed now." That was a reference to the computer language they were using. He looked at the screen as a series of numbers flowed across it. "We have encryption." Giel was a geek of the sort that worked in the early days of computers in the world that the up-timers came from. He worked and almost thought in machine language, in NANDs and NORs, and bit patterns.

"Loading the signal bounce routine now." That was the program that adjusted the precise frequency of the radio transmission within a range to let them get signal bounce even in this time of Maunder Minimum. He looked up at Lidewij. "Your end ready?"

"Radio is up and transmitting."

"Initiating handshake."

Again the electro-aqua-mechanical screen lit with numbers as the aqualator sent test signals to the radio in Amsterdam and waited for a return signal to send the checksum numbers to determine if the digital signal was getting through. It was, but with an unacceptable error rate. The frequency was adjusted slightly. Things got worse, not better. Adjusted again. Things got better. Gradually, the checksums started to indicate that they were getting a strong signal and weren't having to retransmit too often.

"Ready to send the mail," Giel said.

"Send it," Lidewij confirmed.

Giel hit a button and a queue of messages were sent to Amsterdam. First were messages to the government in Brussels, then came financial messages to the Wisselbank, and, finally, personal messages from anyone who had the money to send a telegram.

It took almost half an hour for the aqualator to get through all the messages, and then they started getting the messages that the Amsterdam station had in the queue for them. That took another hour. Not because they had more messages, but because there was greater atmospheric signal degradation, so more repetition was necessary. That was what the checksum was about. It let them know that the signal was corrupted and they needed to resend. It was all handled by the aqualators, and the aqualators were, in turn, watched on both ends by nervous techs like Giel.

Brechtje's boarding house

The stack of printouts was considerable. And these were just Adam's. Anne had her own stack. So did Lady Maria Amilia Alaveres, Captain Johan de Kuiper, Bastien Dauvet, and the rest of the group that came with the royal governor.

Adam's were essentially news from home, royal proclamations, acts of the States General, combined proclamations and acts, plus instructions on anything that the king or the States General thought he needed instructing on. There were a lot fewer from the king than from the States General. On the other hand, one of the king's was that, absent His Majesty's endorsement, the instructions from the States General were to be taken as advice, not orders. He still had to read through them all, though.

Near the bottom, the king informed Adam that he was a bit concerned about the continued silence, and had sent Admiral Tromp a request to check on him.

A "request," not a command, although the distinction was mostly a matter of diplomatic etiquette. In practice, Admiral Tromp served King Fernando as the commander of the Netherlands' naval forces in the western hemisphere. But formally he commanded an independent force, never having publicly given his allegiance to the new ruler of the Low Countries.

It was a complicated situation. In Europe, the King in the Netherlands maintained relations with his older brother the king of Spain which were cordial enough on the surface. Both of them wished to avoid any open conflict, for various reasons. But in the New World—*no peace beyond the line*, was the saying—the forces of the Netherlands were allied with those of the USE, and both were at war with Spain.

When Adam passed along the news to Captain de Kuiper after returning to the boardinghouse that still served as his informal headquarters, the man's response was swift and military.

"Let's hope Tromp comes through. With some reinforcements, we can round up the lot of them. Hang the leaders and exile the rest."

Adam didn't wince. There were times he viewed the matter not too differently from the captain. Although the rebellion had been suppressed, it would be going too far to say that the underlying conflict had been resolved. The population of New Amsterdam was still at least half made up of Counter-Remonstrants—and some were now migrating up the Hudson River to New Orange. To be sure, not all of them were adherents of Brouwer and his coterie, and the failure of the rebellion had made it easier for the more temperate-minded Gomarists to keep their distance from the fanatics.

That was the main reason, being honest about it, that Adam hadn't inflicted any punishment or penalties on the rebels, not even the ringleaders. The balance of forces favored him, certainly, but not by so much that he wanted to risk igniting another uprising.

Work site of the governor's compound

Wolfert looked at the roof. In spite of the weather, they had done it. Double brick walls with two feet of packed earth between them surrounded the building, which was two and a half stories tall. Besides the basements, the half story was an attic with a peaked roof to slough off the snow. Of course, the interior was just posts and supports at this point, but the shell was in place, so they would be able to do the rest of the work out of the weather. Wolfert figured he would have the governor and his party moved in by spring. Meanwhile the arrival of Tromp's ships had finally cowed the Gomarists. And now that they were cowed, the rest of the people were starting to stand up.

Wolfert hadn't realized how many of the people of New Amsterdam liked the idea of a king in the Low Countries who would let them worship as they chose and not let someone, whether they be Catholic or Counter-Remonstrant, tell them how they must pray.

Or, as with Wolfert, not pray. It wasn't that Wolfert doubted the existence of God. How could anyone know about the Ring of Fire and doubt the existence of God? But God hadn't saved his wife, so he would leave God to God's business and Wolfert would stick to his own.

His own. His own was his children and Brechtje. He continued his inspection and, in the back of his mind, he kept mulling over the situation. By now, several of the governor's party were moving out, buying or renting spaces in New Amsterdam. There was room for him, the kids, and Nailah to move into the ground floor of the boarding house, even for his office. He and Brechtje should set a date. And a date not that far off.

New Amsterdam
January 2, 1637

Tromp's ships arrived the day after the New Year. There were three of them, almost a flotilla. The first of the ships, which reached the harbor a few hours before the other two, was a Dutch jacht. By the time it docked, Adam Olearius and Captain de Kuiper were there to greet the new arrivals.

De Kuiper was disgruntled. "A jacht!" he grunted, frowning at the swift but rather small vessel. "Just what we don't need."

Adam shared his displeasure, but kept his face impassive. Jachts were fine ships for many naval purposes, but they weren't troop carriers—and that was what he'd been hoping for. A warship in the harbor able only to fire a broadside—not a big one, either—was of no real use to him.

But both he and the captain cheered up when the officer in command of the jacht came ashore. "Oh, we've more coming," explained Lieutenant Gysbert Wessels. "A galleon and a nao. Between them, we have close to three hundred soldiers."

De Kuiper's near-scowl was replaced by a smiling face. "Three hundred!" He looked at Adam. "That should do the trick nicely, Governor. What we ought to do—"

Adam held up a hand, forestalling whatever advice the captain had been about to provide, which would most likely have begun with *round up all the bastards* and ended with either firing squads or gallows. De Kuiper was an excellent military commander, but as a diplomat and statesman he ranked somewhere between badgers and bears.

"Yes, that will serve our needs very well." He looked up at the banners flying from the ship's masts. He didn't recognize the insignia but presumed they were ones chosen by Admiral Tromp to identify his naval force. But they weren't anything that indicated a connection with the King in the Netherlands. Someone, at least, was being a diplomat and a statesman.

Seeing the direction of his gaze, Lieutenant Wessels smiled. "This is officially just a visit from the *independent* naval forces of the Dutch Caribbean, you understand. Admiral Tromp asked me to convey his respects and see if our fellow Dutchmen might need any assistance of some kind."

Adam returned the smile. "I can think of something. Or two."

The first "something," when the galleon and the nao arrived, was to disembark most of the troops and stage a military parade to the boarding house. That took several hours, given the number of men involved, the limited width of the streets, and—best of all—the large number of onlookers who crowded alongside the route to watch. Fortunately, most of the snowfall that had taken place during the last week in December had already been cleared away, or the parade would have been all but impossible.

Once the parade was over, most of the soldiers returned to the ships in the harbor. Some remained at the boardinghouse but not more than a dozen or so. Officially, they were there to guard the small civilian delegation sent by Tromp. But their real purpose was just to keep reminding everyone that the royal governor now had a *lot* of troops at his beck and call.

The civilian delegation consisted of three men, led by Pieter Corselles, the Lieutenant Governor of St. Eustatia. That was the island in the Lesser Antilles that was the center of Tromp's naval power.

"How do you want to handle the situation?" he asked Adam, once they'd retired to a small chamber that Brechtje had set aside for the governor's use. Other than Adam himself, there was only room for Corselles, one of his aides and Captain de Kuiper. Even to clear aside that much space, they'd had to have the table Adam used for a desk shoved against a wall.

De Kuiper cleared his throat, but before he could say anything Adam spoke.

"I've got three factors I need to balance against each other," he said. He raised his hands to start counting off his fingers, starting with his left thumb.

"First, Brouwer and his diehard followers need to be eliminated. *From the city,*" he added hurriedly, just to make clear that the savage grin now on de Kuiper's face didn't indicate any bloodthirst on Adam's own part. "Actually, it would be better to get them out of the New Netherlands altogether. They'd be an even greater problem if we moved them to New Orange."

He brought up his forefinger. "Second, I want to split away as many of the Counter-Remonstrants as possible from Brouwer. At least half of them, by my estimate, would accept the situation even if they dislike it."

Corselles nodded. "I'm sure you're right. We have a fair number of Gomarists on St. Eustatia. Some of the hardcore may decide to resettle somewhere on the mainland, but the truth is they're driven more by economic grievances than religious ones. Most of them will stay in the islands." He smiled. "Of course, officially the Catholic King in the Netherlands does not rule there."

Adam smiled back. Then, counted off his middle finger. "And finally, as the royal governor I need to establish a reputation for being merciful as well as decisive. You can't govern effectively by fear alone. Not even mainly by fear, in fact."

Corselles leaned back in his chair, planted his hands on his thighs, and contemplated the wall across from him. Which had nothing on it but a small portrait of Anne Jefferson. He'd seen the portrait before, as it happened—that one and several others of the woman. The famous postage stamps that Anne Jefferson had modeled for had started making their appearance in Oranjestad.

Adam glanced back over his shoulder. "Yes, I suppose that's a fourth consideration. I need to stay on good terms with my wife, who is in some respects very up-time in her attitudes. She disapproves of headsmen."

Corselles chuckled. "I understand. What you are left with, it seems to me, is the option of resettlement. But where?"

Adam shrugged. "To be honest, I don't care—as long as it's several hundred miles from the New Netherlands."

The lieutenant governor pursed his lips. "That 'Charleston' place—whatever they wind up naming it—is perhaps five hundred miles away."

"Splendid."

"Too far to go by land, though, even if we weren't in mid-winter."

Adam shook his head. "I wouldn't drive them out in mid-winter anyway. They'll need at least a couple of months to put their affairs in order and make adequate preparations for such a relocation." He paused and cocked his head a little.

Understanding the unspoken question, Corselles said: "I shall raise the issue with the admiral. It shouldn't be a problem, though. We captured a number of naos from the Spanish when we seized La Flota. They're not particularly good warships, so we should be able to free up enough to transport Brouwer and his malcontents come the spring."

"Done, then." Adam rose to his feet. Then, looked at de Kuiper. "I think it would perhaps work best if you were the one to impart our decision to Dominie Brouwer, Captain."

De Kuiper was on his feet by the time Adam finished. The savage grin was back in place. "Oh, yes. I can explain the various alternatives to him, should he protest. Explain them in considerable and precise detail."

Chapter 14

Residence of Hansje de Lang
January 8, 1637

"What part of 'we might let you choose between a gallows and a headsman's block' did you not understand, Mijnheer Hartgers?" Dominie Brouwer tried to keep his tone simply sarcastic, but was pretty sure that the underlying anger—no, fury—was very close to the surface. Fine for Dirck Hartgers to be willing to chance the "justice" of the papist new governor, but Karl had no doubt at all that he'd be the first in line if a gallows were to be erected or a headsman's block be brought out into the city's square.

He rose to his feet, in order to add extra weight to his words. And then spent several seconds in silence, just gazing out over the small crowd gathered in the main room of de Lang's house and staring down anyone who tried to glare at him.

"We will accept the governor's proposal. As soon as the weather permits, we will sail to this 'Charleston' place in the south. It is by all accounts a more pleasant part of this continent to live in than the New Netherlands anyway. What's more important is that it will place hundreds of miles between us and these papists and their lackeys."

"But..." Hartgers hadn't given up yet. "By those same accounts, many of the people now infesting Charleston are no better. Worse, even. Some of them are pirates, they say."

By now, though, the Dominie had swung most opinions his way. One of the newly arrived colonists—Brouwer couldn't remember his name—stood up and said: "And so what if they

115

are? There are more than enough of us to deal with any such ruffians. I am with the Dominie."

"And I!"

"And I!"

Dominie Bogardus' church
January 10, 1637

It seemed natural to hold the wedding here, thought Wolfert, after all that had happened. As he stood waiting for Brechtje to make her entrance, he gave the area a quick check.

The wishing tree was on a table in a corner, already festooned with wishes written by the guests. Next to it was a wedding box, inside of which was a bottle of wine and letters which he and Brechtje had written to each other. The box would remain sealed until such time—perhaps, even hopefully, never—when they fell upon hard times and needed a reminder as to why they had gotten married.

"She's coming in," murmured Eduart. "Try not to make a fool of yourself."

That seemed...

Inappropriate and disrespectful, certainly, especially coming from a former employee. But he decided it was probably the best advice he'd gotten all year.

He looked, then. Dear God, the woman was beautiful.

The Brothers

Walter H. Hunt

28 August 1636
Don Estuban Miro
State of Thuringia-Franconia
United States of Europe

Most Esteemed Don Estuban:
   It has taken me some time to summarize our activities here in the New World, and you will have already received an account of our interactions with the Danish colony, New Amsterdam, Maryland and Virginia, as well as a brief description of our time in New England ... and it is there that I have been remiss, as I think you would put it.
   In June, I did hold a private interview with Governor Winthrop, and was called to speak before the Massachusetts assembly. Captain Thomas James briefed us on what's currently chafing the Puritans—and their allies the Pilgrims—a dispute over someone getting killed in the Connecticut Valley. What I didn't tell you, primarily because I wasn't sure how you'd take it, is what we decided to do about it.
   Pete was against it at first.

"You know," Pete said, "based on what you say, this is a situation that is beyond us. This isn't really about the French claims on English colonies at all. We should cut our losses and leave."

"I wish it was that easy."

"It *is* that easy, big bro. You wave to the nice little zealots on shore"—he waved again, making the same soldier scowl up, hand on his musket—"and you say sorry, we've got nothing, bye bye. Y'all come visit us if you're ever in Magdeburg."

"We might be condemning them to death."

"*We*? History is condemning them to death, Gord, if they don't change their attitudes. Not you. Not me. *Them*."

"I don't know how much we can do to stop it—except for one thing."

"Which is what?"

"Based on what I've read of history to come, the Massachusetts Bay and Plymouth colonies are within a few months of getting into a war against the Pequots. Once it gets started, whites and Indians will fight to a bloody conclusion that leaves lots of dead and lots of resentful survivors. It's only the first of a number of bloody wars that they'll fight—at least according to up-time history. Maybe it's something we can stop."

"Did you say the Pequots?"

"Yes."

"The casino guys?"

Gordon frowned for a moment, then smiled. "Yeah. The casino guys. In our time line, the soldiers from Massachusetts Bay and the Connecticut Valley massacre a whole pile of them in the spring of 1637, and what's left of the tribe gets swallowed up by its neighbors."

"I'm not clear about why we care. Aside from the whole casino thing, what does the Pequot tribe mean to us? Do you really think they're going to become USE allies?"

"I don't know."

"Did Miro give you any direction on this—or, better yet, Piazza?"

"Other than peeing in France's corn flakes, Estuban didn't give me much direction at all. Neither did Ed."

He chewed on his lip a moment, before continuing. "It's tricky, since we're officially in a state of peace with France and England. The Puritans have essentially declared independence—they have no interest in bowing to the French king; they were scarcely willing to bow to the English one. But I *do* know that this area stands a better chance of repelling a French invasion if the people here aren't fighting among themselves. The French have allies among the Indian tribes, and if they start arming them...I think that the big picture is bigger than anyone here will be able to see. If the Puritans and the Pequots don't go to war, maybe they can be allies."

"But you don't want to...*scare* them by flying a dirigible over their heads."

"No. Not really."

"I still think you're giving up a tactical advantage, big bro."

"All I can say is, we'd have to land sometime. I'd rather approach the colonists with open hands, even if it means giving up a 'tactical advantage.'"

Captain James wasn't in favor of it either. He thought we'd do better to get involved with technology by using the talents of Ingrid Skoglund, our expedition's doctor. They'd already had trouble from us about that; when I spoke before the assembly, I demanded that she be allowed in. They told her to shut up and sit down, but they let her in.

"There *is* something you *can* do for them."

"I'm all ears."

"They fear divine judgment, as we all do," James said. "And they fear the Indians. But there is something else they fear: disease. In the last few years the pox has ravaged the settlements along the Connecticut River, and has made the occasional visit here in Boston. From what I have heard, you up-timers have a solution for this problem.

"If you want to do something for these benighted Puritans, Chehab, you should send your doctor to them. You might not convince the most extreme zealots, but you'd win a lot of friends."

"Huh." Gordon leaned his head back against the wall behind him and looked up at the sky. Above, the great mast of Baltic fir framed the sky of deepening blue. "I hadn't thought of that."

James didn't answer. Gordon sat up straight and looked at James. "Is there a doctor here in Boston? Someone we could meet with?"

"None worth the title," James said. "They brought a chirurge—a poseur, I would not hesitate to characterize him—named Gager, the first year of the colony here, but he died. There was a doctor in Plymouth, though he has passed on as well; they may have replaced him. It is possible that you might speak with Richard Palgrave—he styles himself *Doctor*, as does old Oliver—but I do not have much faith in him. Thompson is something of an apothecary, but I do not think he leaves his island very often."

"Do you think any of them would be receptive to Ingrid Skoglund? And what about Winthrop and his advisors?"

"I cannot say."

In any case, Ingrid didn't think it would fly.

"They will never accept me. And even if they did, they would never consider the solution."

"They fear the smallpox more than the cure, Ingrid," Gordon said. "If you explained it . . ."

"I was afraid of the idea when I was studying medicine," she answered. "I resisted the inoculation at first—if I had not trusted James Nichols as I do, I might have caught the pox myself. You have no idea—"

"Hold on," Gordon interrupted. "Don't get started with the 'you up-timers' argument. I've been back in this century for almost five years, and I served as an army medic. I know what seventeenth-century medicine looks like.

"The people of Massachusetts Bay are terrified of smallpox, Ingrid. They might already know that we can solve it—and they might even know how. But that's not what they're afraid of. It's not what *you're* afraid of either. You're afraid they'll reject you because they do not hold with women doctors. When Governor Winthrop considers it, he'll weigh the natural bigotry of his constituents against the real possibility of saving them from contracting a painful, agonizing disease, and he'll come down on the side of accepting your help."

"You cannot be sure."

"No, not until I ask him tomorrow. Then we'll see."

The Puritans were suspicious. Instead of being in favor of the idea of us curing smallpox, they asked what our motives were, and what our price would be. I thought I had a pretty decent answer. They even let Ingrid explain it to them—how variolation would make them immune, and why that was good for everyone. But they didn't go for it immediately.

*They had bigger concerns, and asked us for our help.
They were dealing with the problem up on the Connecticut
River, in which the Pequots were refusing to surrender the
guys that killed Captain John Stone.*

*That's about the time we met John Endecott. He'd
already shown during the assembly what he thought of us,
and had asked that we be sent away because we had some
hidden motives that he didn't like. He basically called me
a liar, and I called him on it, and made him apologize. I
guess I'm less of a diplomat than I thought. But we weren't
done with him yet. He was all ready for the Puritans to
start a war. Fortunately, there were a few cooler heads,
like Thomas Dudley, the Deputy Governor.*

"Brother Dudley," Endecott said. "I have a question."

"Your servant."

"You are possessed of a trained and armed band of soldiers
at Sovereignty. Why did you not merely go to the Pequot and
demand that they turn over the villains who murdered Stone?"

"It would have been peremptory and provocative, Brother
Endecott. We are trying to prevent a war, not initiate one."

"They have no stomach for war," Endecott answered. "More
provocative acts than that have been committed, with no con-
sequence. Standish does not hesitate to make his presence felt
whenever he feels that Plymouth town is threatened."

"I do not wish to measure my acts by the standards of Captain Standish," Dudley answered.

"As Plymouth is our ally, he is on our side," Winthrop said.

"God guide and protect us nonetheless," Dudley replied. "I
make free to speak of him among the men of Massachusetts, but
he shall have to be informed of the outcome of our dealings—and
will likely suggest something similar. But on the river, even Winslow has no interest in provoking the ire of tribes that surround
us. It is a war we could win, but would cost many, many lives."

"Say on, Brother Dudley," Winthrop said. "What was the
outcome of your negotiations?"

"As I said, Governor—we were told that Sassacus would
return in due time and the matter would be continued. Winslow
remained, while Oldham and I departed our separate ways."

"Oldham?" Gordon said.

Dudley turned to face him, surprised to hear him speak. "'Mad Jack' Oldham. Yes, he had planned to depart shortly after I set sail."

"Is this man known to you, sir?" Winthrop said.

"Yes. I mean—no, I don't know him, but I know his name. He's a trader, a merchant of some kind."

"Correct," Dudley said. "He trades with various tribes. He was planning to go to Block Island to meet with the Niantics."

"He's in terrible danger. He's going to be killed there—and if history follows its course, it will bring you into war. It's in the up-time history: I was rereading it just yesterday. After he's killed, you"—he gestured toward Endecott—"will lead a war band that will commit genocide against the Pequots."

And that's when we became involved.

Gordon Chehab assumed that John Endecott, and others, were watching from the lookout point on Fort Hill as they laid out the canvas for the dirigible on what would someday be called Castle Island. He had wanted to go through the process on shore outside Boston, but Maartens, Thomas James and Pete set him straight—there was no reason, no reason at all, to make them vulnerable to the Puritan captain.

"See what they make of that," Pete said, looking back toward the shore.

"It's all part of the up-time magic show." Gordon sat down on the crate that had held the fan. "Damn it. Our first chance to do something to affect events, and things aren't playing out like the history books."

"There was no guarantee. So many things have changed. I don't think Winthrop, or any of the others, think we can make a difference. *It's several days' sail*, he told me. *I have a dirigible*, I told him. *We can be there before sundown.*" Gordon looked up; the afternoon sun was still high in the sky.

"Tactical advantage."

"Yeah. Whatever." Gordon glanced at the dirigible; it was just beginning to take shape as air was flowing into the bottom of the sack. In a few minutes, they'd have to start manipulating the control surfaces to assure an even distribution of air, and make sure that the whole thing didn't start drifting away. "I'd trade it for one of Jesse Wood's airplanes for *this* mission."

It took almost two hours to inflate the dirigible, attach the catenaries to the passenger car, and connect the control ropes and wires. *John Wayne* seemed almost eager to slip from its anchor and go aloft; and after weeks at sea, Gordon was eager to do so as well.

As they were preparing for liftoff, they saw a boat being rowed across the harbor from Boston. The late-afternoon sun reflected from the helmets and breastplates of some of the boat's occupants; without even being asked, Pete found himself a protected perch out of sight as Gordon stood and waited for the Puritan soldiers to come ashore.

They were led—unsurprisingly—by John Endecott. He had another, shorter man with him, who carried himself with the same proud martial air; Gordon could tell that the two were not particularly friendly.

The Puritan captain scowled at the huge form of *John Wayne*, inflated and almost ready to take off; then he turned his steely gaze on Gordon.

"These are the up-timers," he said to the other man. To Gordon he said, "May I present the representative of Plymouth plantation, Captain Standish."

"Standish?" Gordon said. "Myles Standish?"

"That is my name," the man said. He glared at Gordon.

"You mean, as in, 'Prithee, why do you not speak for yourself, John?'"

"Art thou mocking me, up-timer?" Standish said. He looked ready to draw his blade—which, Gordon noticed, was at least three or four inches shorter than any sword he'd seen.

"No—no," Gordon said. *I played you in a school play*, he thought to himself. *John Alden and Priscilla something or other. Longfellow. I got to stand off stage while Priscilla delivered that line to the boy who was playing John Alden—courting Priscilla for Myles Standish. For you.*

"You are going after Oldham," Endecott said, not sure precisely what was going on.

"We're going to try and warn him of the danger," Gordon said. "If the natives are waiting to ambush him—"

"He'll not listen to you, American," Endecott interrupted. "And neither will the savages."

"Indeed not," Standish agreed. "Mad Jack Oldham listens to no one."

"I'm willing to try."

"We are coming with you," Endecott said matter-of-factly. He gestured to Standish and the other two soldiers, then glanced again at *John Wayne*; Gordon heard nothing but bravado in his voice, but thought he saw a glint of fear in the Puritan's eyes. As for Standish, he seemed surprised by the remark, and didn't seem at all eager.

"You can't."

"Oh, I daresay we *can*," Endecott replied. His companions had muskets in their hands, and although they did not aim them at Gordon—or the dirigible—they seemed to grasp them a bit more firmly when their captain spoke the words.

"No," Gordon said levelly. "You *can't*. Not because I...not because I don't appreciate the offer of help: it's just that the craft can't lift that many people. Too much weight."

Endecott frowned. "I do not understand."

"I'll try to explain. The airship envelope is filled with hot air, which rises, and pulls the passenger gondola up with it. It's not magic—the dimensions of the envelope, and the continued flow of air into it, create a certain amount of lift, a measurable amount. It's designed to carry three—maybe four—people on board."

Endecott looked at his three fellow soldiers and back at Gordon, as if to say, *I don't see a problem here.*

"Someone has to pilot it. Preferably two or three people who know what they're doing. This dirigible is irreplaceable, at least here in the New World. I'm not taking any unnecessary risks. If I tried to lift with four extra men aboard, especially with all of the armor and gear, I'd probably make it thirty miles before I ran out of fuel. There's just too much weight. I can't do it."

"How many can you take?"

"One. Maybe one extra person. I could carry one of your men and three of my own—"

"You said that you only needed two pilots. Myself and one of my companions could accompany your two men."

"Captain Endecott, I am hard-pressed to understand why I would have *any* of your men accompany us. This is not a military mission, sir—we are hoping to help prevent men from being killed."

"It is a pointless mission," Standish said. "You should leave Oldham to his fate—and the savages to theirs. I do not understand why you have any interest in preserving him."

The dislike—perhaps even disgust—in his voice was palpable. There was clearly some history there that wasn't being discussed.

"Because this isn't about *Oldham*," Gordon said. "This is about Massachusetts Bay and Plymouth, and about whether you want every Native American—every Indian—as your enemy."

"They are already our enemies."

"No, they're *not*," Gordon said. "Maybe they're *your* enemy, Captain Standish, but they're not the enemy of your colony. Not yet. And but for the Indians, you—and your colony—wouldn't even be here. Isn't that right?"

"That was years ago," Standish growled, but he looked away, as if it wasn't a very convincing argument.

There was no answer for several moments, and Gordon wasn't sure if the encounter was about to become violent.

"You may choose your own course," Endecott said. "But if you seek alliance with Massachusetts Bay, and possibly with Plymouth as well, we should accompany you on this mission. We can be friends—or rivals."

"By which you mean 'enemies.'"

"I did not say that."

Is that a slow match in your holster, Gordon thought to himself, *or are you just happy to see me?* Despite the obvious tension of the situation, he had to resist laughing.

"If you are threatening me, Captain Endecott, I hope that you have thought it through."

Endecott gave one more glance to the dirigible, and then turned to his three soldiers and gestured to the boat; they walked back and climbed aboard.

Standish just stood there silently, his arms crossed over his chest.

"Very well. I shall accompany you alone," Endecott said.

If you had been standing there on that island, Don Estuban, I expect you'd have given me a long lecture about operational security. The number of things that could go wrong by bringing a loose cannon like John Endecott aboard the only dirigible in North America was a pretty long list. But I wasn't sure I had a choice—and even though Pete and Captain James and Captain Maartens and Ingrid all thought it was a pretty bad idea, I had strong feelings about it.

Without us, the war against the Pequots would go about as history had originally played out. Stubborn natives and hotheaded Puritans would fight, and in the end a lot of people would die. I wasn't about to stand by and watch, or sail away knowing I might be able to prevent it. With John Wayne we might be able to stop it all.

The ceiling for *John Wayne* was eighteen thousand feet, but Gordon had no intention of taking it up that high. Two thousand feet was plenty; it took only a few minutes to catch the wind with the inverted V-shaped tail and maneuver the dirigible into the air.

Pete was completely comfortable slouching in the back of the car, his rifle leaning on the seat beside him. Gordon stood at the front of the car with the yoke held loosely in his hands.

Endecott had likely never been much further in the air than the top of Fort Hill. At five hundred feet of altitude he held onto the side of the car and looked off into the distance as if he was viewing a pastoral scene—a Vermeer, perhaps. At one thousand feet he had stopped looking out but merely stood there, hands gripping the car hard enough for Pete to see white knuckles.

By the time they'd reached cruising altitude Endecott had found a seat in the middle of the car, holding on to handgrips with his eyes shut. Gordon looked over his shoulder and saw the tableau and smiled; Pete gave him a little wave.

"We'll be there in a few hours, Captain," Gordon said. "Nothing to worry about."

"If God had meant man to fly," Endecott said shakily, "He would have given him wings."

"I can't believe that you just said that," Pete said.

"You doubt my—" Endecott began.

"No," Pete said, laughing. "It's just that it's such a damn cliché." He leaned forward in his seat. "Where we came from, Captain," he added, "everybody but *everybody* says that, and it means nothing. We had airplanes, we had helicopters, we had dirigibles, we had freaking *gliders*. They all could fly. It had nothing to do with what the Lord God wanted us to have, or not have.

"You are in an *airship*, Captain Endecott, sir. You are two thousand feet in the air, give or take a hundred feet or so. Almost half a mile. Nothing but sweet air a foot under your feet, three hundred some-odd man-lengths to the ground. God protects you up here too, Puritan John, never fear."

Endecott opened his eyes and squinted at Pete. "If you were a member of the community of the Elect in Boston town, you would wind up in the bilboes with a bare back covered with lashes. You take the Lord's name in vain—"

"If you don't like the accommodations," Gordon said without turning around, "we can leave you off anywhere. I'm not sure, but I'd put us somewhere over what will be called Narragansett Bay."

Pete looked over the starboard side. "Long swim, especially in the armor."

Endecott gave Pete a murderous look, but didn't answer.

"Leave off him, Pete," Gordon said. "Captain Endecott, my brother is a blasphemer—among other things. He is not, however, a member of your community. Neither am I.

"You can make whatever judgments you want about our conduct, or our suitability for entry into Heaven, or whether we were meant to fly. But you can do it after we do what we're headed to do."

To his credit, John Endecott willed himself to stand and come to the bow end of the car as the day wound toward sunset, though he came no closer to the side than an arm's length. Gordon was not sure whether that meant that he only conditionally trusted in his God to be this high in the air, or if his will was only just strong enough; but he had to respect the Puritan captain's courage.

John Wayne was clear of the string of islands that separated Buzzards Bay from Vineyard Sound—names that belonged to a future that would never be, since these places would more than likely be named by Frenchmen. The island that Gordon's up-time map named as "Cuttyhunk" was off to starboard, and the long, sandy stretch of Martha's Vineyard lay to port; according to Endecott, that island was inhabited by Wampanoags, and had been considered by Massachusetts Bay as a likely site for a new settlement before King Charles had set them adrift. He did not recognize the name that appeared on Gordon's map—he called the place by its Wampanoag name, *Noepe*, "the land of the streams."

As they made their way across Vineyard Sound, half a mile in the air, Gordon wondered if there were any Wampanoags looking

up at the sky, wondering what was being lit by the orange light of
the setting sun. The same thought had occurred to him as they
came across the land west of Plymouth; perhaps some Pilgrim
farmer might have looked up in wonder from his plow. In any
case, no one tried to take a shot at the dirigible—not that there
was a weapon in North America with the range to hit it...at
least until it descended.

"I don't know very much about this Oldham," Gordon said.
He was beginning to consider where *John Wayne* might be putting in to land. They were nearly three hours into the flight,
and though the wind had been favorable enough that he had
been able to conserve fuel, they'd likely be spending the night
on Block Island, waiting for *Challenger* to catch up with them.

There had as yet been no sign of Oldham or his ship.

"What would you like to know?"

"Is he a friend?"

"Brother Oldham is brave enough," Endecott said. "It takes
a strong man to sail the coasts and to travel the Indian trails."

"That's not quite an answer, Captain."

"He is a member of the faith and a citizen of our com-
monwealth," Endecott answered. "He has been a member of the
general assembly."

"I get the impression that you don't personally like Oldham."

"I do not see how that has anything to do with this mission,
Chehab," he said. "We are not undertaking this journey because
John Oldham is a particular friend of mine."

"You call him brave and strong, but you don't call him a
friend. I get it. Why is he going to Block Island, anyway?"

"He is a trader, and a canny one. As we are cut off from
England, trade with the savages has become more important to
us. He...is very successful in his dealings with the tribes, particularly the Niantics, though some like him better than others."

"Why is that?"

"He may be brave and canny, but he is also quick to anger.
You know, of course, that Plymouth Colony exiled him?"

"Do tell."

"He drew a knife on Captain Standish and called him a
beggarly rascal. They put him and his pastor, John Lyford, on
trial and banished them. Oldham was forced to run a gauntlet

of muskets, where the men beat him with the butts of their weapons.

"But not everyone thought that Oldham was in the wrong—a fair number of Plymouth men chose to become Strangers and went to Nantasket, Oldham's settlement in exile. His personality makes its own trouble," Endecott added. "But he is a brave man and true to the faith. As for Standish...he is mischievous by design. He is William Bradford's catspaw, and if he tries to stir up trouble in Boston there will be a number of knives drawn on him, I daresay."

"About that," Gordon said, adjusting the direction of the dirigible slightly as he spoke. "Governor Winthrop indicated that your colony and Plymouth had entered into some sort of alliance."

"We have some irreconcilable differences of faith," Endecott answered. "Our alliance—if it can be called that—is for mutual protection, no more. I do not doubt that men from the 'Old Colony' will be working toward their own goals, just as we work toward ours."

"If you spend enough of your energy fighting each other, though, the French will have no trouble defeating you in turn. You—Plymouth—every Indian tribe—and everyone else." Gordon glanced over at Endecott, who didn't seem too happy with the conclusion. "Nobody wants that."

The last quarter moon was partway up in the sky, casting a rippling reflection on the ocean below, when he saw the first dark outline of Block Island to the south. He breathed a sigh of relief: *John Wayne* might, or might not, have enough fuel to keep itself aloft all the way to Long Island. Montauk Point, a long rugged finger of land, was somewhere off to the west, twenty or twenty-five miles away—assuming he didn't miss it entirely and go out to sea.

"We're going to have to make landfall on Block Island," Gordon said quietly. He couldn't read an expression on Endecott's face in the shadowed moonlight; but he suspected that Puritan John was disappointed—or perhaps frustrated that this had been a fool's errand.

But then Pete, who hadn't had ten words to say during the three-plus hours they'd been aloft, said, "Not so fast, big bro."

Gordon reached under the control yoke and drew out a spyglass. "You see something?"

"Two or three points to port," Pete said. "The sail catches the moonlight. It's a sloop all right, moving at a good clip. Fore-and-aft rigged."

Gordon looked where he'd been directed and saw it at once: a small sloop, smaller than a sloop-of-war, sailing close-hauled and heading south for Block Island. If there hadn't been as much of a moon to sail by, they would likely have waited until morning to cross the sound. They'd be on top of it in less than five minutes.

Not far away, cutting through the water with good speed, Gordon picked out four canoes making for the sloop. It wasn't clear that the canoes had been sighted yet.

"There's the ambush," Gordon said. "Pete, how close do you have to be to get a good rifle shot?"

"Two or three hundred yards," Pete said from the darkness in the back of the car. "You're going to have to lose some altitude."

"Once it's lost, it's gone until *Challenger* meets up with us."

"You were going to make landfall anyway."

"True enough." Gordon reached up and pulled on the cables attached to the control surfaces above; they could hear air beginning to vent. "You're going to have time for one, maybe two shots."

"From this distance?" Endecott said.

"He's a pretty good shot, Captain," Gordon answered without turning. "Even in moonlight."

They had dropped a few hundred feet during this conversation, and Gordon had turned *John Wayne* partially into the wind, slowing her down further. Through the spyglass, he could make out the four canoes; they were filled with men rowing for all they were worth.

"Captain," Gordon said. "Are your pistols primed?"

"Yes, but I couldn't hit anything at this range."

"You don't need to. I just want to get the attention of your pal Oldham. Let's make sure he knows we're here. Pete will handle the target shooting."

Endecott nodded and drew out a pistol. Gordon turned back to the business of piloting the dirigible, but a few moments later felt Pete standing directly next to him, his rifle held loosely.

"Something wrong, little brother?"

"Not so far," Pete said. "Just making sure that Puritan John's pistol is aimed in the right direction."

Endecott began to say something, but Gordon heard him hesitate, then he heard the sound of the pistol's mechanism being operated.

Gordon glanced at the altimeter. The *Duke* was down under a thousand feet, and had passed over Oldham's sloop: the shadow cast through the moonlight was running across the waves below. He wondered what the Indians must have thought they were seeing.

"Fire that pistol of yours, John," Pete said. "Aim high. I'll be aiming low."

Almost at once, two shots rang out: the click and boom of Endecott's wheellock pistol, and the crack of Pete's rifle. On the lead canoe, the frontmost Indian was thrown back into the lap of the man behind him. Their rowing stopped and they all began to whoop loudly.

They could hear shouting from Oldham's ship as they passed over it and left it astern.

"It's going to take me five minutes to maneuver back into position, assuming the wind is right at lower altitude. But it looks like they all know we're here now."

"Right," Pete said, ejecting the shell from his rifle. "What's the plan, big bro?"

"I didn't have one," Gordon answered. "I was just focusing on getting down here. I didn't expect to interrupt the ambush— that's pure blind luck."

"Or Divine Providence," Endecott said. Gordon didn't like the level tone that the Puritan captain used: it sounded a bit too fervent.

"Whatever it is, I'm not going to be able to stop them from carrying out their attack," Pete said. "I can't kill an Indian once every five minutes and expect to drive them off."

"The important thing is that Oldham has been warned," Gordon said, as he manipulated the steering controls, trying to catch a cross-breeze to bring them back toward the sloop and the oncoming canoes. "It looked like he hadn't known that they were coming. Now he knows."

"He should have no trouble dispatching the savages," Endecott said. He was working at reloading his pistol.

"*No*," Gordon answered. "No, damn it. That's not what should be happening at all."

"They were ready to kill him."

"And you'd do the same?" Gordon tugged on a catenary cable, losing some altitude. "You call them savages. What will that make all of you if you kill all of the attackers? Or, I don't know, take them as captives and sell them into slavery? You need to *make peace* with them. You need to make them allies."

"That's absurd," Endecott said quietly, emerging from the shadows, his pistol in his hand.

Gordon couldn't read Endecott's expression in the moonlight, but he was pretty sure he wouldn't like it if he could. The Puritan held the pistol loosely in his hand, not raising it—but in a few moments he could do that, and fire a shot at Gordon that would do a great deal of damage at short range.

And I'm the damn medic aboard, Gordon thought to himself. *Ingrid Skoglund is back in Boston, hopefully saving some lives.*

"This vehicle is the perfect weapon against these heathen natives," the Puritan said. "They'll be afraid of it, and they'll heed our wishes. The Lord of Hosts could not have provided better than He has done in sending you to us."

"Meaning what?"

"Meaning," Endecott said levelly, "that we will use your airship to make these natives—and all the rest of them, eventually—clients of God's Kingdom in Massachusetts Bay."

Gordon didn't answer for several seconds; there was silence in the car, until it was broken by the action on Pete's rifle.

"It's a long and lonely fall to the ocean, Puritan John," Pete said without emotion. "They'll never find your body."

It didn't take us long to find out Thomas Oldham was also a bit of a bastard. We made landfall on Block Island, near where Oldham's ship had anchored. Once we were down and secure, we were stuck there as well—at least until Challenger *showed up: there was nowhere near enough fuel to get us back to land. Oldham and Endecott had a sort of reunion.*

Oldham's ship had sent a launch to meet them, and when it pulled ashore with four men, Gordon got his first look at the Puritan adventurer.

He was of average size, and lanky—weather-beaten, really—but there wasn't too much that they could make of his features in the light of the waning moon. He had a musket in his hands and wore a metal helmet, but appeared to have left the breastplate behind. He had two young boys with him, who stayed well behind.

Gordon began to approach, but Endecott laid a hand on his arm. "Brother Oldham," the Puritan captain said into the darkness.

"Is that you, Brother Endecott? It sounds like your voice."

"It is. I am with up-timers. We have come on their airship, as you saw out to sea."

"Aye, and an impressive craft it is," Oldham said. "Scared the life out of those Indians. Good bit of work, Brother Endecott. I didn't know you were so solicitous of my welfare."

It was spoken with a sort of sneer that set Gordon's teeth on edge.

"The up-timers said that it was to happen, and they were right. Apparently your death in their future world caused quite a stir. They're here to make sure it doesn't happen again."

"Well, now." Oldham lowered his musket and smiled; if this had been a cheap movie, Gordon supposed, there would have been a telltale glint off the gold tooth in his mouth. But there were no gold teeth. "I suppose it's good to be remembered in history. Are those the up-timers with you?"

"Yes."

"And are they a part of the confession of the Faith?"

"No, Brother. They are not."

"Then it seems your duty is clear, is it not, Brother Endecott?"

"I would put those thoughts aside," Endecott said, glancing at Peter Chehab, standing beside him. "You are in the sights of an accurate firearm, and well within range."

Oldham seemed to squint toward where Endecott and the two Chehab brothers were standing. Evidently, even in moonlight, he could make out the three figures—and the rifle, held at aiming position.

"Peace," he said, leaning the butt of his musket against his leg and extending his hands outward. "Now, let's not be hasty here. I didn't mean them any harm at all."

"Are they *all* like you, Puritan John?" Pete whispered, not letting his rifle fall away.

Endecott didn't answer. They walked across the beach, and when they were a dozen yards away, Pete lowered his weapon.

"John Oldham," Endecott said by way of introduction. "Gordon and Peter Chehab, of . . . the up-timer kingdom in Europe. They are here on a trading mission, or so they say."

"My sons," Oldham said, gesturing to the boys. Then, back to Gordon, he said, "You're here to help us against the heathen Indians. A blessing."

"Not exactly," Gordon said. "I have come out here with the express permission of your Governor Winthrop. You are familiar with the Ring of Fire, and how our town has come back from our time to this one?"

"I cannot say I understand it, but yes."

"We don't completely understand it either, but that's neither here nor there. In any case, in the past we know, you—John Oldham—were attacked by the very people who were meant to seize your ship tonight. As a result of that attack, you were killed and your ship was plundered. That's how we know who you are.

"This incident touched off a campaign against the Pequots as well as the western Niantics, and resulted in a terrible slaughter. Hundreds, perhaps thousands, of natives were killed."

"Thus removing the threat to white settlers," Oldham said. "It seems we could have the best of both worlds: the threat removed, and *I* don't have to die for it."

"That's not the point."

"I don't *know* what the point is, up-timer. You say that the Pequots were killed? Or driven away? Good. They've been a thorn in the side of Massachusetts Bay ever since we began to settle in the Connecticut Valley. They always try to cheat us in trade, they intrigue with the Dutch; they know no law, and they're vicious and ill-tempered. They have refused to surrender the killers of John Stone, and they were apparently out to do me in as well. We put down dogs that behave less poorly."

That was the attitude. Pete was all for shooting him just out of spite, but cooler heads prevailed. I didn't know what to say, but I told him we weren't around to fight a war for him—the same as we'd told Endecott. Oldham wasn't happy to hear it, and he made a point of telling us that if it wasn't one thing, it was another: there'd be some other incident, and the war would happen anyway.

While we were cooling our heels on Block Island with Oldham, the natives showed up.

The brothers arrived on the scene to see Endecott, as well as Oldham and his crew, facing a group of natives who had just emerged from the trees. The natives did not have their weapons drawn, but their faces were painted with colored patterns. Gordon didn't know quite what to make of them, but assumed the worst: that they wore what Western movies used to call "war paint." There were at least a dozen of the natives, with a few still coming into view.

Neither side had said a word. Endecott was scowling; Oldham looked as if he could barely contain his anger. But no one had started shooting.

At last the natives were all assembled, in a sort of semicircle. One, taller and older than the rest, stepped forward. "Oldham, my brother. You do not greet us as we are used to hearing."

"My heart is not full of friendship, Chief," Oldham answered. "I do not greet men as brothers who seek to kill me."

"I do not understand," the man said, spreading his arms wide.

"Do not lie," Oldham said. "Your face speaks your thoughts. You tried to take my ship last night. You sought my death."

"There is no blood upon our hands."

"I have these men to thank for that," Oldham said, gesturing toward Endecott and Gordon and Peter.

"Ah," the native said. "Then we should prefer our suit to them. Blood of my people is upon *their* hands." He placed one hand upon his short-handled axe, tucked into his belt.

Pete looked at Gordon, then locked eyes with the chief. There was no attempt to dissemble or deny the charge.

"Last night," Oldham said, "your war canoes were bent on attacking my ship. A wise warrior does not wait until the bowman looses his shaft to make his own attack: so yes, an attack took place—but not against my ship."

"Arrows came from the sky-bird. These men—are they shamans? For this is evil medicine, friend Oldham. The sort of medicine your god forbids, is it not?"

"The Lord God was not specific about airships," Endecott growled. "You should feel fortunate, Chief, that any of you are here to speak today."

"What happened in darkness remains in darkness," the chief said, somewhat cryptically.

"I do not forgive so easily," Oldham snarled.

"But I do," Endecott said, stepping forward. "The chief is right, Brother Oldham. What happened last night should be a memory, no more. There are more important things to discuss."

They eventually made their deal. We were surprised at how much of a peacemaker Puritan John turned out to be, but Pete was pretty sure that he'd counted heads and figured out how outnumbered we were. As he always reminded me, up-timers could be killed by down-timer weapons just as easily as anybody else, and as long as we might be allies, Endecott wanted to make sure we survived.

Since he'd cheated the up-time history that killed him, Oldham wanted to know what we'd do next. And this is the next part of the story I hadn't told you. There was going to be a meeting at Fort Sovereignty in Connecticut, and I decided that we were going to be there. Endecott wasn't very happy with the idea of just letting Oldham sail away—after all, we were alone, the three of us, on an island where there were natives who were none too happy that we'd killed someone from above.

But I violated operational security—again—and showed Puritan John our radio.

With Endecott's help he moved a heavy box to the middle of the car. He unlatched it and pulled out a contraption that drew a curious glance from the captain: a metal disk mounted on a footing with pedals attached to either side. Two wires extended from a square block mounted on the top of the disk.

"What is this?"

"A little contraption invented for use in the Outback—a remote part of the world, up-time." He set it near another trunk and sat down. "Human powered. It generates the power to operate a communications device."

Endecott didn't answer; he watched intently as Gordon opened a black box secured to the deck of *John Wayne*. It was divided into two sections: on one side was a radio receiver, something apparently pulled from someone's old transistor box; on the other was a contraption consisting of four small wine bottles with bolts driven through their corks, attached to wires. Each bottle had a strip of silvery metal inside, attached to the bottom side of the bolt.

Endecott scowled at it, as if it personally offended him. "I don't understand this machine. What is it for?"

Gordon didn't answer. He connected an extension cord from the pedal block to a connector on the side of the black box. He closed the lid and secured it, then turned a knob on the side to a position labeled TRANSMIT.

"Pete, give me a hand with the antenna hookup."

"On it, big bro." Pete was stringing a length of wire from the catenaries to the radio rig.

"It's a radio," Gordon said at last to Endecott. "A communications device. We're going to talk to the ship."

"*Talk* to . . ."

"Is it hooked up, Pete?"

"Far as I can tell."

Gordon placed his feet on the pedals. They'd been taken from the remains of a beat-up bicycle that had been scrounged from somewhere in Grantville.

The only trick, he'd been told, *is not to pedal too hard.* There was a little dial on the top, with sections marked in green and red; he was to go hard enough to keep it in the green, and not so fast that it went into the red—that might be enough to short out the machine. He wasn't sure just how that might happen—*It's a black box, after all*, he thought to himself—but he took their word for it; with the main radio gone, this was all they had left.

He took a headset out of the pedal case, put it on his head, and plugged it into the side of the black box, and picked up a notepad and a pencil.

Then he began to pedal. The radio set slowly came to life, like television sets used to do when he was very small.

It would have been great if *Challenger* and *John Wayne* were equipped with wireless radio telephones, if only to see the look on John Endecott's face when he heard Maartens' or James' voice on the other end. But it would have cost almost as much as equipping the ship with everything else it was carrying for them to have had that technology. Instead, Gordon had had to spend a few weeks learning the most basic forms of radio communication: Morse code.

Now, somewhere out near Vineyard Sound, someone aboard *Challenger* would be picking up his slow, steady keying: CQ,

CQ, CQ—*calling anyone, please reply*. It was conceivable, though unlikely, that there was anyone else in range of the device that would be equipped to hear, actually listening, and able to reply; he wasn't expecting an answer from anyone except *Challenger*.

He moved the switch from TRANSMIT to RECEIVE. There was a long pause, then he heard Morse code signals in his headset: CH1 DE JW2 JW2 KN. CH1 was the agreed-upon identifier for *Challenger*; "JW2" for *John Wayne*, and the KN was an invitation for JW2 to reply.

He moved back to TRANSMIT and sent a greeting and their location: RST 577 NORTH SHORE BLOCK ISLAND. The "RST" numeric told them that the signal strength and tone was good. He appended another agreed-upon code—5X5—"five by five," which in radio parlance meant the best possible reception; but in this case was meant to indicate that they were not in danger. In the case where Gordon might be forced to transmit under threat, it was to reassure the folks aboard *Challenger* that they need not arrive ready to rescue the folks on the dirigible.

That last had been Pete's idea, and Gordon allowed that it was a good one.

DISTANCE 12 MI, 6 KNOTS, 2 HR TO LAND, *Challenger* reported. GOOD TO HEAR 5X5.

GOOD 2CUAGN, Gordon keyed back.

2 HR, the operator on *Challenger* replied, and then sent "SK"—signing off.

He let off the pedaling, and the lighted dials on the set dimmed and went dark.

"Well?" Endecott said.

"They'll be here in two hours," Gordon answered. "I told them everything is all right. Now let's see to getting *John Wayne* ready to fly again."

At midday, *Challenger* came in sight off the coast, and within an hour had anchored. A boat was sent ashore bearing Captain Thomas James and three men whom Gordon recognized from the pier in Boston. They were armed and looked wary.

"So much for my five-by-five," Gordon said, walking out to meet them.

"Ah, well," James said as the boat was rowed back toward *Challenger*, "Governor Winthrop was expecting trouble. When he learned

that we were intending to sail to Fort Sovereignty he suggested . . .
well, truly, he *insisted* that some of his own men accompany us."

"How many?"

"A dozen. These are just a part of the welcoming committee.
And another captain."

"A captain?"

"Yes," James said, his face showing distaste. "A man of . . .
small stature."

"Standish?"

Gordon's answer came from a glance toward the ship. He
could see the Pilgrim captain on the foredeck, waiting for the
boat to return.

"What does he expect to do with these soldiers? We're not
invading Pequot territory—we're trying to make peace with them.
That doesn't come out of the barrel of a snaphaunce musket."

"It's one of the things they best understand," Endecott said,
coming up to stand beside him. "Before you approach them open-
handed, Chehab, you'd better make sure you have their attention."

"And if they . . . fail to understand my message?"

"Then you're ready for their attack," James said. "I agree with
the captain, here. Injuries done to both sides cannot be resolved
in a single day."

"Does Captain Standish understand that as well?"

"He's along to represent Plymouth's interests." James looked
out to sea, at *Challenger* and beyond. "He understands that his
little colony, like Massachusetts Bay, is clinging to its land at
the edge of a hostile continent; that it's been abandoned by its
king and is surrounded by enemies. They've made an alliance
with people they despise only a little less, because of the threat
of people they hate even more.

"He wants to play the long game, Mr. Chehab. But he wants
to live long enough to play it. Now." He gestured to the soldiers,
who began to lift the fuel cylinders from the boat. "Let us see if
we can get your machine aloft again, shall we?"

*Pete had wanted us to show off as we approached Boston,
which we didn't do: it would have made the Puritans think we
were servants of the Devil. As we cruised up to Fort Sovereignty, I
decided on a different approach. Puritan John approved: not only
would we impress the natives, he said, we'd scare the Dutch. I'd*

approached this assuming that the Dutch and the English colonists were friendly rivals, not bitter enemies: I was schooled when we got to New Amsterdam, as you know. But Endecott was just the same.

"When did the Dutch become your enemy?"

Endecott turned to face Gordon, while still keeping a tight grip on the side of the car. "They have *always* been our enemy, Chehab. There is a vast land between the Hudson River and the river valleys in eastern Massachusetts, and their patent claims all of it—though they do not try to enforce their rights very far inland. There are too many deep forests, too many barrens and impassable swamps known only to the Pequots and the other heathen tribes.

"Three years ago Governor Bradford of Plymouth sent Edward Winslow, an undertaker—"

"An *undertaker*?" Pete interrupted.

"Yes," Endecott said. "An investor. One who has undertaken to seek profit in the New World."

"Please go on," Gordon said. *Undertaker. Best remember that one*, he thought.

"Edward Winslow is an undertaker for the Plymouth colony. He had just returned from England—and probably already knew about the plan by the king to sell away his claims, though he spoke nothing of it. Bradford sent him to Boston in order to persuade our people to join in a trading expedition to the Connecticut River to thwart the ambitions of the Dutch.

"A year or even six months earlier we would likely have turned him away—for we had enough to do trying to protect our inland settlements from the savages; but with the news of King Charles' arrangement with the French, we realized that we must make friends where we could."

"This is the basis for your alliance with Plymouth."

"Just so," Endecott said. "Oldham volunteered to lead a company, and he and Winslow went overland together and returned with specimens of furs and plants, as well as other items of interest to our colonies. He set up his trading post at Pyquag, and within a year all manner of persons who could not suffer the rule of the Elect were moving westward to settle. Now there are forts and posts of ours, and Dutch ones as well. They suppose us weak because our mother country has abandoned us, but they may soon find that it is not the case."

"Preparing for war, are you," Pete said.

"*Igitur qui desiderat pacem, praeparet bellum*," Endecott said. "Governor Winthrop quoted that to me."

"I don't know Latin," Gordon said. "Translation?"

"'Let him who desires peace, prepare for war,'" Endecott said. "It's from a book called *Rei Militaris*. I should like us to beat all our swords into plowshares, Chehab: but only once we are finished with them."

"What about Captain Standish? Will he lead Plymouth Colony to war with the Dutch over this as well?"

"I am not able to predict what that man might do. But in the former future that your people experienced, he carried out a murderous attack against the Indians, so he does not lack for ardor. How he might act against fellow Christians..."

"Haven't your colony and Plymouth Colony come close to war?"

"We have had our disputes, of course. But nothing like this. We are *rivals*, not enemies—and a real, open conflict with New Amsterdam would be yet different. They have the patronage and support of their own government—"

"I wouldn't be so sure of that."

"Indeed?" Endecott's right eyebrow went up. "They are willing to force a conflict without support from home?"

"I don't think they're forcing a conflict, Captain," Gordon said. "They simply believe that they have the right to these territories, and that—between hostile Indians and the act of King Charles of England—you're simply unable to do anything about it."

"There are certain...things that would change that balance of power."

Gordon looked away, surveying the dirigible's controls. "You need to remember who the enemy really is, Captain. And I think you'd better keep those swords sharp for a while longer."

When we reached the fort, Challenger was already docked. We took a little side trip up the valley, which gave me a chance to have a little chat with Puritan John. I don't mind telling you that it got me a little hot under the collar.

"This is amazing," Gordon said. They were drifting slowly northward, following the course of the Connecticut River. "You can't imagine what this looks like in the twentieth century. Or would, if..."

"I understand," Endecott said. "Or, let me say, I know what you mean. I do not think that any of us truly *understand*."

"Fair enough. But my point is that—well, this land is so *empty*. All I can see is hills and trees."

"As opposed to . . ."

"Towns. Roads. Farms and factories. This is Connecticut—it's heavily populated, sandwiched between Massachusetts and New York. Half Yankees fans and half Red Sox fans." Endecott looked puzzled. "Forget it. I'm just overwhelmed by the—wilderness."

"It is a testament to the savage nature of the natives, Chehab. They have not tamed the land. When we spread across it, this will all change."

"What about *them*?"

"What *about* them?" Endecott looked away from Gordon, shielding his eyes against the late-afternoon sun. "Are you asking me what I should do about natives' homes? I do not know why I should care at all. They will submit to civilization, or they will die. What does your history say about that?"

"I already told your governor. There are some Indians who took your religion—they called them 'praying Indians.' But many did not—and eventually their anger erupted into war—King Philip's War."

"'King Philip'?"

"The name taken by Metacomet, son of Massasoit."

"The Pokanoket sachem? He is a friend of the Plymouth Colony—he saved their lives when they first arrived. He has only one son, as far as I know: Wamsutta, who is only a boy—the name 'Metacomet' I do not know."

"He might not have been born yet; I'm not sure. He and his older brother—Wamsutta, I'd guess—took the names Philip and Alexander, but Alexander was killed. That was the last straw. Philip—Metacomet—waged war on all of the colonies in this part of the New World. He burned towns, killed civilians, women and children, and it took a year to pacify it all.

"Relations between natives and the colonists were never the same. They never trusted each other again . . . not here and not in other places. It was a terrible tragedy."

"But we have avoided it, have we not? Saving John Oldham avoids this future. We will not carry out our revenge attack on the Pequots."

"But that's just one thing, Captain Endecott. One event. One tragedy avoided. There will be other points of friction and other misunderstandings. Somewhere out there a great leader is waiting, maybe even now waiting to be born, who will want to undo all that you have done while it is still in his power to do so."

"A son of Massasoit, eh?" Endecott said. "Maybe we can strangle this 'great leader' in his cradle."

"God *damn* it," Gordon said, "will you listen to yourself?" He could see Endecott bristling at the blasphemy and decided he didn't care. "Listen to what you just said. If it isn't enough that strangling someone in his cradle is a violation of one of the ten fucking commandments, it's the same mistake King Charles made. *Yes*, if you kill Metacomet—King Philip—before he's old enough to make trouble for you, then *he* won't make trouble for you.

"But as long as you push against the Indians, cut down their trees and take away their hunting lands, cheat them with land transactions and kill them indiscriminately, you're adding fuel to the fire. Maybe in this time line it's *not* Metacomet. Maybe it's Wamsutta. Maybe it's Sassacus, or some other Pequot chief, who won't be killed because the raid on Mystic never happens. Maybe it's some great chief from further west armed by and in the pay of the French. Maybe it's someone we don't know yet.

"There's no way to know. And if you and the Plymouth colonists and the rest don't learn to get along with the natives, there'll be some kind of war and a lot of innocent people will die, and any chance of living in peace will be gone forever. In *this* time line you'll be weakened enough that the French will eat you alive."

"You paint a grim picture."

Gordon Chehab closed his eyes; in his mind's eye he could see the pictures he'd found in history books—woodcuts of the Mystic massacre, King Philip's War, and all the rest. In the time he'd come from, Indians were pictures in books, poor people on reservations, casino owners whose people's best days were no more than museums full of flint arrowheads and videos on *National Geographic*.

He didn't know if he could stop it all—but he knew that he could do something in this here and now. He knew he had to try.

"It can all be avoided," Gordon said, opening his eyes. "At least there's a chance."

Pete tells me that my idealism is out of place in this century, Don Estuban, and sometimes I agree with him. He rolls his eyes and talks about 'saving the whales'—I guess you can ask Mr. Piazza what he means by that. But I felt that we had a chance to change things for the better and not make the same mistakes that we made as down-timers. Hindsight has its uses, and maybe my twentieth-century idealism can do a little good.

While I was touring upstate with Puritan John, Pete was gathering intel. Apparently every tribe in southern New England had sent a group to this gathering. Imagine a whole group of little parties of natives, along with representatives from Plymouth and Massachusetts Bay, all ready to take their knives or muskets out and kill each other. I could make an up-time reference, but I think you get the idea. Captain Standish had already been talking with the captain of the fort and a guy named Stanton, who was serving as translator. He had a plan, as you'll see—but I went forward as if he didn't. Pete was skeptical; when he told me that everyone seemed scared, I told him that everyone had something to lose, and they had something to gain if they allied together. This was me playing high politics, I know: I expect you'd be ready to give me a smackdown for doing it. Pete asked me if we'd been sent to the New World "to save the red man from the white man," or if this was just for show; I told him it was our chance to make a difference.

He told me that they'd be at each other's throats as soon as we sailed away. He called it a "house of cards," even if we managed to get them to agree. He may wind up being right. But in the meanwhile, we had a chance to actually be diplomatic.

Gordon and Pete had become accustomed to waking with the sun, usually to the sound of the watch changing, or the calling of the soundings as the ship traveled through shallow waters. But this morning the situation was different: there was a commotion above-decks loud enough to wake them from their hammocks.

Pete had his rifle in hand by the time Gordon had his feet on the deck.

"Don't shoot, little bro."

"Not *you*, anyway." Pete laid his weapon beside him and pulled on his trousers. He picked it up again. "Let's see if there's anyone up top who needs shooting."

"Wait for me." Gordon reached for his own pants and a shirt, but Pete was already out of the cabin and headed up to the ladder, pulling his suspenders over his shoulders with one hand as he went.

By the time Gordon reached the deck he was more awake but the noise level hadn't died down. The scene before him was unusual: it had attracted the attention of most of the crew.

There were four natives on deck standing opposite Captain Maartens, who was flanked by two able seamen. Captain James stood nearby, leaning against the rail. Smoke from his pipe swirled away into the morning. Pete stood next to him, rifle held loosely in his hands.

In between natives and crewmen was a carcass of a very large animal. Gordon wasn't sure at first glance but concluded that it was a bear. It was apparently very dead.

"Chehab," Maartens said. "About time you got here."

"What seems to be the problem?"

Maartens looked about to erupt but managed to say, "I should think that would be obvious."

"The...bear."

"Yes, of course the *bear*. These four...visitors just hauled themselves on to my deck and dumped it here. I want it off my ship."

The natives scowled at this. One, a bit taller and more decorated than the others, stepped forward.

"You do not accept?"

"I don't—" Maartens began.

"Wait," Gordon said. "Friends," he said to the natives, "You have brought something to us. What is the meaning of this offering?"

"It is a gift," the native leader answered. "*Makwa*. The great hunter, awoken from his winter sleep and fattened by his spring hunting. You...do not wish it?"

"Of course we accept it," Gordon said. Maartens appeared ready to say something but Gordon immediately added, "You will take our thanks to your sachems, Great Warrior, and inform him that we will bring you a worthy gift in return."

The native leader did not answer for a moment; then he nodded, placing his hand over his heart.

"You speak with honor," he said, with a smile that showed all of his teeth. He paused to give Maartens a fierce look, placing his hand on the hilt of a small axe he wore tucked in his breechcloth.

Then he stepped back, and with his companions he climbed over the side of *Challenger* and down to the water. A minute or so later, Gordon could see them paddling away in a dugout canoe to the shore where the natives had camped.

After the natives had gone, Maartens approached the bear carcass and poked it with the toe of one boot.

"I hope you have room in your cabin for this, Chehab."

"I just wasn't going to turn it down."

Maartens grunted. "*Ach*, very well. I'm sure we'll find someplace to dump it over the side."

"You will do no such thing."

Ingrid had appeared from belowdecks. Unlike Pete or Gordon, she appeared fully dressed and ready for the day, as if she hadn't been sleeping at all.

"Eh?" Maartens managed before Ingrid arrived next to him. "I suppose you *intend* something."

"Indeed I do."

She knelt down and extended her hand to the bear's body, almost tenderly. She passed her hand over it, glancing up at Gordon. She looked sad, distant. "There is a pelt here, which has trade value. The bones can be used to make needles. And the meat—if properly and thoroughly cooked—will be good for stew. I shall have to instruct the cook."

"Bear meat," Maartens said. "I don't know..."

Ingrid stood up straight. "In northern Sweden, Captain, bear—and many other large animals—are delicacies. I am sure this fine animal will well provide." She looked at Gordon. "You know how to dress game, I assume?"

"This is a bit bigger than the sort of game I'm used to."

She looked more amused than disappointed. "I know what to do. I shall fetch my scalpels—but I think we may need carpenters' tools as well."

The damn thing must have weighed four hundred pounds,
but Ingrid took care of it. She claimed she'd learned how to

do that sort of thing in Salerno, where there's a big school for doctors. I expect you already knew that.

No one did much of anything for seven days; they were all waiting for the Pequots to turn up. Their chief, a man named Sassacus, was the most important, most influential chief of them all. From what I was told, he was like a king, but no one actually called him that. Captain James told me that it would have been far easier if he actually was a king—then there wouldn't have to be this great show.

But there was a show anyway.

Gordon was aboard *Challenger*, trying to work through his notes on Dutch and English settlements upriver, when Pete came into the cabin.

"He's coming," Pete said. He was out of breath, as if he'd been running all the way.

"Who? Sassacus?"

"Yes. Five canoes, apparently a half dozen sagamores and a good-sized warrior band. But we've got trouble."

"What sort of trouble?"

"Standish."

"Slow down. What sort of trouble is he causing?"

"I was at the fort," Pete said. He seemed to be gathering himself, as if he was making a report to an officer. "Standish was talking to John Mason. It would've been a funny scene, really, like that movie with Schwarzenegger and DeVito."

"*Twins.* Though why my brain is bothering to retain that five years on is beyond me. Go on."

"Yeah. *Twins.* Standish is like five-two, and Mason is built like a tall middle linebacker. Anyway, they were talking quietly, and I happened to overhear: they have plans for Sassacus."

"That doesn't sound good."

"It's not. It seems that the Pequots raided a settlement somewhere on the river within the last year and took two Plymouth girls as captives, and they haven't shown much interest in giving them back. They've also killed several settlers on the Connecticut and refused to give compensation."

"Have the colonists from Plymouth tried to negotiate?"

"As if. Their idea of negotiation is to demand that the killers be turned over and that the women be returned unharmed. They won't even talk about giving up warriors, and apparently the clan that grabbed the girls wants payment, and the governor of Plymouth has told them to go to hell. So Standish—and Mason, and a few others at the fort—are planning to grab Sassacus as soon as he sets foot on land, to trade him for the two girls. They apparently have someone on the inside of Sassacus' traveling party to help."

Gordon stood and remembered at the last minute to bow his head so as not to smack it against the ceiling beam. "*That* kind of trouble. Does Endecott know about this?"

"I wouldn't be surprised if Puritan John is in on it," Pete said. "Correct me if I'm wrong, but isn't all hell going to break loose if they try this—in front of all the Pequots, and all of the other Indians camped around here?"

"Yes," Gordon said. "All hell is going to break loose—unless we stop it."

Sassacus came with five canoes, crossing the north cove toward the beach near where *Challenger* was anchored. When Gordon and Pete came up on deck, they could see Standish and his men stalking through the high grass, muskets in their hands.

Gordon ran for the gangplank. When Pete made to follow, Gordon turned to his younger brother.

"Can you hit him from here?"

"Standish?"

"Standish."

"Not quite yet, but I can probably hit him over there"—he gestured toward the place where the canoes would come ashore—"if I stand near the bow."

"Lock and load," Gordon said. "And I'll do my best not to get shot." He ran down the gangplank to the wooden dock, not looking back.

"Are you—" *Crazy*, Pete wanted to say, but realized that he knew the answer to that. Of course his brother was crazy—the whole idea of being here was crazy.

Shoot Standish. Jesus, Pete thought. *That's no way to form an alliance.*

But right now it looked as if Myles Standish wasn't looking for an alliance—not with the USE, not with the Pequots. He was looking to demand, or maybe exact, justice. And if Standish and his men started shooting, there would be lots more of it.

He went back to the ladder and climbed down to grab his rifle.

Gordon ran along the dock and onto the open ground as if he were chasing a deep fly ball. He kept his eye on the Plymouth captain and his squad of men—their metal breastplates reflected the sun—and he could see the Pequot canoes coming closer to shore as they cut through the calm water.

The colonists were wearing armor and he was not, and he was willing to believe that they'd chased a lot fewer fly balls than he had. He headed for a spot in between the approaching Pequots and the advancing Pilgrims.

Sassacus and the other Indians hadn't noticed him, but Standish did, and raised his hand, halting the march.

"Chehab?" he shouted as Gordon came closer.

Gordon stopped running and glanced over his shoulder at the canoes. "What do you think you're doing, Captain?"

"The savage chief has to be apprehended, Chehab," Standish said. "His tribe holds two Christian women. I mean to get them back."

Gordon walked slowly toward Standish, keeping his hands visible. "Captain Standish," he said, "if you try to take Sassacus—or any of his men—there'll be a lot more shooting."

Standish stepped in front of his squad of men. "You don't understand them, up-timer. They respond to force: they will not fight. I will take their king in charge, and I will have my countrywomen returned."

"That's not why we're here."

"Oh, indeed." Standish scowled; his hand was still on his musket, though it did not appear to be aimed at Gordon—at least for the moment. "Why *are* we here, then? Have you not just come from an encounter with Indians who are subjects of this chief? It seems you have an argument with him as well."

"I'd rather find a way for him to become an ally."

"Of your United States of Europe?"

"No," Gordon said. "Of your colony—and Massachusetts Bay. You will benefit far more by having him as a friend than as an enemy."

"Benefit?" Standish laughed harshly. "*Benefit*? What have we gained by association with the Pequots? With the Pokanokets, perhaps—but the Pequots are liars and thieves.

"You saw it yourself. They killed Stone; they meant to kill

Oldham. 'Mad Jack,' as they quaintly call him, is a scoundrel, a man without honor, but he is yet withal a Christian and an Englishman—or whatever we have become in this new world.

"You do not *understand*," he repeated. "They are no friends of Plymouth. If the men of Massachusetts Bay think they can be friends, they are deluded—or, worse yet for them, they have become soft and indulgent. If that is what they believe, they cannot survive what is to come."

Gordon had walked close enough to stand a dozen feet from Myles Standish, and could see the righteous expression on his face. It seemed illuminated by zealous fire; he'd seen a little of that from Endecott, and suspected that it might have come out under the right circumstances. What was happening now was just that for the Plymouth captain.

"And what is to come?"

"A great cleansing," Standish said. "Here, in the Connecticut Valley, and in all the Pequot lands to the east. All of this will be ours, because *God wills it*. He granted us dominion over all of the earth and all that dwells upon it, and through His Grace we were able to survive the harshness of our first few years in the New Jerusalem. These Pequots will submit—or die."

"I'm asking you to reconsider."

"And if I refuse?"

"Then I'll have my brother change the course of history," Gordon said, gesturing toward *Challenger*. They could all see Pete, standing at the bow, his rifle aimed and ready.

Standish looked from Pete to Gordon, anger in his eyes.

"I could shoot you where you stand."

"I imagine you could," Gordon said, hoping it didn't come to that. "But I expect that Pete could drop you before you put slow match to flashpan. And, of course, you'd make an enemy of the USE.

"The French are already looking forward to rubbing Plymouth off the map. How do you think Governor Bradford would feel about having two enemies?"

And this is where I find out if I'm a complete moron for reasoning with this extreme lunatic, he thought. If Pete sneezed, or the rifle jammed, or any of a dozen other things happened, the only person for whom the course of history would change would be *him*.

Standish waited a few more seconds, which were the longest seconds of Gordon's life.

"Very well," he said at last. "I will accede to your wishes. For now."

I realized later what a very, very stupid move that was: not because of what I achieved, but because I was betting that Pete actually could drop him before he shot me. We hadn't come to North America to get me shot, or to kill Myles Standish either. Sometimes you play poker; sometimes you play Russian roulette. I got lucky.

I should take a minute to describe Sassacus. He reminded me of a weird combination of Nelson Mandela and Samuel L. Jackson—sorry, Mr. Piazza will have to explain that to you. But he brought quite a crew with him. He didn't speak, and no one else spoke either—from the moment he put his foot on the shore he was the man in charge.

I made my pitch to all of them—but I was mostly talking to Sassacus.

Sassacus bent down and touched the earth with his right hand, then brought it to his nose and mouth and took a breath. Then he stood erect and looked at Standish and his men, scowled, and turned his glance to Gordon.

"You are the one who crossed the great water in the sky ship," he said.

"I am the visitor here," Gordon said. He decided that it wasn't time to correct the Pequot sachem on the details.

"My shaman tells me a story," Sassacus said. "He says that you are also come from the time-to-come. Some great work of the higher powers that we do not understand. Is this true?"

"It is true, Great Sachem." Gordon looked at Standish, who looked angrily back. "We do not know how, or why, but we were brought to this time. But we are here."

Sassacus made a gesture, and the other Pequots began to disembark behind him.

"Do you now speak for the Englishmen?"

"I speak only for my brothers across the great water," Gordon said. "The Englishmen"—he again decided not to sweat the details—"speak for themselves."

"The Englishmen speak much," Sassacus said, "but say little." He gestured to some of his companions; they began to unload bundles from the canoes. "We will take our place here, in the shadow of the great English house. When all is ready, we will speak again."

Gordon wasn't sure how to respond to that, but didn't have a chance; the great Pequot chief turned away from him and began speaking rapidly in his native tongue with another younger man, similarly attired, standing behind him.

Within a few minutes, Gordon was joined by his brother and Thomas Stanton, who surveyed the scene and said, "Chief Sassacus is making a statement, no doubt."

The Pequots were assembling a long, low tent from skins and wooden poles they had brought along for the purpose. Sassacus—who had not spoken another word to Gordon or any of the English—was watching the progress while standing, motionless, with his arms crossed in front of him; it was like a woodcut from an old book.

The man he had originally spoken to, by comparison, was taking a more hands-on approach; he also seemed to be glancing in every direction—but particularly toward the spot where Standish and his men were now sitting, and where Gordon and Pete and the English interpreter stood. Stanton nodded to him—they seemed to be acquainted.

"Friend of yours?" Gordon asked.

"I would not term it thus, but we know each other. That is the sachem Uncas, who has at times been a friend to the English. He is in . . . a precarious position at the moment."

"Do tell."

"A few years ago after the death of Sassacus' father, he made a move for the top position and rebelled—but received little support among his people or his allies in the Narragansett people. He had to flee, and could only return after humbling himself before the great chief."

"How old is Sassacus?" Pete said, looking at the Pequot sachem. The man was clearly old, but looked as if he could handle himself in a melee.

"No one is quite sure," Stanton said. "But based on what I have been told, he is no younger than seventy-five."

Pete whistled. "You're joking. He could probably kick anyone's ass in sight, including Captain Standish."

"I would not underestimate that one," Stanton said; he looked as if he was resisting the urge to glance over. "But I suspect that Sassacus is still a match for most warriors. As long as that is the case, Uncas is powerless. But no one lives forever, and eventually there will be a struggle for control. Captain Mason would prefer that Uncas be the one to win that struggle—but there are no guarantees."

It was dim and smoky inside the long tent. There was a fire—which Gordon considered entirely unnecessary, given the balmy temperature of the evening outside—and the tent had been constructed in such a way that it vented directly up and out. The smoke came from tobacco, which was being consumed by the many Indians that had gathered within. Belts of wampum were hung along the main supports of the tent. From what Gordon had been told, together it amounted to a small fortune.

Standish and one of his men sat uncomfortably near the entrance; Stanton, John Mason and Endecott were more at ease, finding comfortable places on blankets spread near the fire.

All of the natives were watching Sassacus, who sat perched on a low stool near the fire, sucking smoke from a long clay pipe.

Gordon and Pete had found a spot opposite. Pete was more at ease than his older brother. *Don't worry*, he said; *if things go sideways, it'll be just like a rumble at a biker bar.* Gordon knew he could take care of himself in a fight, but wasn't completely sure that this was that kind of fight, and wasn't eager to find out.

It all had the feel of the sort of drama he'd been forced to read in high school English. Sassacus was drawing it out, waiting for the right moment to speak. Gordon wanted to tell him to *get on with it*, but he was fairly sure that even if he said so it would do no good.

Okay, tough guy, he thought, looking at the great Pequot sachem. *It's your play.*

Sassacus finally handed the pipe to one of the other natives and placed his hands on his knees.

"I am Sassacus. All men in all tribes know me to be fierce to my enemies, generous to my friends." He cast a glance at Uncas, who reclined nearby, his face partially in shadow. "Our clans have roamed the fields and forests of this land for many suns, long before the newcomers arrived.

"There was a time that we rejoiced in the coming of the new people from across the great water: they brought us tools and fine weapons and asked only for small places to build their houses. In the time of the great sachem Tatobem, they observed the laws of sky and earth and took only what they needed.

"But like children who have been given all that they want, they became greedy, and their greed grew like a snake twisting inside them. They were not content." Above the murmuring, he repeated, "They were not *content*. I have come to think: Is there any amount of land that is enough for these strangers? Is there any limit to their greed or does the snake grow and grow?"

The great tent was quiet now as Sassacus looked from face to face in the firelight.

"What do you have to say to us, Englishmen?"

Gordon looked at Standish and then at Endecott; the little Plymouth captain looked eager to reply, while the Massachusetts man made the smallest of gestures. *Go ahead*, he seemed to say. *Say your piece, up-timer.*

"I am not an Englishman," Gordon said, "but I would answer you."

"We are all listening," Sassacus said, gesturing with each hand in turn to the many natives sitting to either side.

"I come from another time," Gordon began. "It is not the time to come, for the time to come for this place will not be the world where I was born. That world may no longer exist.

"Almost five years ago my home, and the land around it, was brought to this time by some means I cannot explain. Our... shamans have no idea how, or why: but it happened, and we are here now. *This* is our time now. We have tried to make the best of it; our presence has changed history so much that the path we all walk will never lead back to the time when I was born."

He looked around at the audience; there were many furrowed brows. *You're losing them, you moron*, he thought.

"You know that we have books in our town that came back with us. There is knowledge there of many things—about Captain Standish and his Plymouth town, about Massachusetts Bay, about the French and the Dutch and the English. There is even knowledge of you, Great Sassacus."

The Indian sachem made a gesture. "What do these books say of me?"

"I . . . cannot tell you exactly," Gordon said, "but I do know that the Pequot nation—in our time line—came to blows with the English, and suffered a great defeat so that its people were scattered. Your brothers and sisters, Great Sachem, died, or were exiled, or were made slaves—and the lands were given over to the English colonies."

"Did we not fight?"

"Yes. You fought. All of you"—Gordon swept his hand in a circle, indicating the many warriors in the tent, now murmuring to themselves—"all of you fought. The many wars between whites and natives cost untold lives and brought immeasurable misery. Indians were used as pawns in the wars between Europeans, and rarely did well by it. In the time from which I come, their lands had been shrunk to nearly nothing and their pride was crushed by poverty.

"*That* is the legacy of wars with Europeans. If all else had remained the same, there would be little possibility of avoiding it, and little chance that anything could be done to change it.

"But something *has* changed, Great Chief. The great king of England has abandoned his children in the New World, and another king—the king of France—has claimed all of these lands as his own: not just the English colonies, but the Dutch territories as well, and all of the native lands.

"The French king is an enemy of my people. True, there is no state of war at the moment, but his goals run counter to ours. We seek to be your friend, and a friend to the Englishmen who have made their home here, and even a friend to the Dutch of New Amsterdam if they will accept us as such. But there is a price: we seek to have you be friends with *each other*."

"We want nothing else," Sassacus said mildly, his face relaxing into a slight smile. "We would live in peace with the Englishmen."

"How?" Standish said at once. "By killing our people? By *kidnapping* them? What do you say to that, Great Sachem? How do you answer for these crimes?"

"You call them *crimes*," Sassacus said. "What of your greed, Englishman? You make treaties with one hand and hide your other behind your back. Your people made a solemn promise about settlements here on the great river, and then sent my people away when you wanted more land. You cut down and clear the forest so that we must travel further afield for game. You cheat us at bargains, and try to trick us with your teachings about the world in the sky.

"There should be enough land, enough trees, enough game for all. But you will not rest until you have your portion and *our* portion as well."

Standish looked ready to reply, but Gordon cut him off. "There are faults on both sides," he said. "But it doesn't have to reach the point of bloody war. You have much to gain by being friends and allies, and much to lose if you don't. You can avoid the mistakes that were made in my time line, but it requires trust on both sides."

"How will we ever reach this trust?"

The question came out of the dimness from Captain John Mason, who had not spoken a word during the entire proceeding. Mason, Gordon knew, had a foot in many camps: he was a Massachusetts man, a Connecticut settler, a devout Puritan, but a one-time friend to the rebel sagamore Uncas. Somewhere in that tangle of beliefs, loyalties and commitments were motivations about which Gordon couldn't be sure.

Gordon glanced at his brother for a moment, remembering Pete's comment. *It's a house of cards.*

"You need someone to guarantee it," he said. "Ultimately it will be up to settlers and natives to make sure peace is maintained, especially in the face of the threat from the French and their Indian allies. But in the long run, the guarantor can be the USE."

Gordon was going way out on a limb here. He didn't have the authority to commit even the State of Thuringia-Franconia to such a diplomatic position, much less the entire United States of Europe. But he figured the old biblical axiom applied here: *Sufficient is the evil unto the day thereof.* If he could help keep the peace in North America, he'd worry about covering his ass later.

Sassacus did not immediately respond. He stared at Gordon for several moments, the firelight flickering in his deep-set eyes.

Then he turned aside and whispered something to Uncas, who leaned forward to hear and respond. Gordon looked at Thomas Stanton, who sat, frowning, trying to make it out.

"We should trust an invisible people from across the sea," Sassacus said at last, "to keep the Englishmen here from killing us and taking our land."

"And *we* should trust—whoever you might be," Standish said almost immediately, "to protect us from devil savages who kill and kidnap our people?"

"*In the long run*," Gordon said. "Yes, that's what I'm saying. *In the long run* you trust us to guarantee peace between you. If you can keep from going at each other's throats, both settlers and natives can benefit from what my government—and my people— have to offer. But I can't offer it myself. This is about the future, Great Sachem. This is about *survival*, Captain Standish, Captain Mason, Captain Endecott."

"Kumbaya," Pete said under his breath, smirking.

Gordon wanted to smack his little brother, but decided instead to ignore him.

"So?" Gordon said at last. "What do you have to say?"

You'll be relieved to know, Don Estuban, that they didn't *really have much to say. Sassacus didn't give in; Standish and Endecott left empty-handed. As far as I know, there's been no war to exterminate the Pequots, and there might not be. But it would be ironic if the French decided to send an expedition to New England to take the colonies there and no one was at home because they were carrying out a crusade against natives who they thought were no better than dogs.*

It's taken me a while to put this all down for you. Despite our intention to just gather information, I actually made them offers—to ward off smallpox, to be an honest broker against a common enemy, to...I don't know, to save the whales. To this moment they haven't accepted any of it, at least as far as I am aware. The USE has not been committed, so you can rest easy on that account.

As Pete told me when we left Boston, they were "a bunch of useless assholes." That's about what we found in New Amsterdam as well. When the French arrive—and they will, even if there's no Cardinal Richelieu to direct them—all of these colonies, and all of these tribes, will be easy pickings.

I still hope to get back to the USE by Christmas. From here I'll have to go back to Virginia to pick up Pete, unless he's completely gone native. I'm entrusting this letter to what I believe to be a trustworthy courier. I wanted to make sure you had the full story, even if it involved me going out of bounds. I hope I've represented the USE—and the twentieth century—with honor and integrity. It matters to me, even if all the whales can't be saved.

With respect,
Gordon Chehab

The People from the Sky

Eric S. Brown and Robert E. Waters

Near modern-day Rhode Island
Summer, 1636

Fast as Lightning's spirit lifted as he stepped into Sun Rising's longhouse. The aged Narragansett sachem was still alive. *Praise the Red God*, Fast thought as he took a few steps toward the fire pit. The flames were low, but hot. Fresh kindling was tossed in the smoldering ash. The fire quickened in a pop of sparks and smoke. Without a word, Sun Rising offered up his pipe. Fast accepted it quickly to help hide the incessant shaking of the old man's hand from family members who stood away from the fire, but close enough to observe. The expression on their faces was clear.

Sun Rising is dying...

"Come," the old sachem said coughing, "and sit. Let us talk."

Fast sat and drew a long draft of smoke. He had smoked with Sun Rising before, the most recent occasion being just two winters ago. Then, he and Speaks His Mind, sagamore and son of a Montaukett sachem, had sat inside this very longhouse, around this same fire pit, and discussed securing peace with Raging Wolf and his Mohegan warriors. A peace necessary to stand against the coming of the up-timers, the people from the future, and the terrifying changes that they might bring. But that peace had been broken when Raging Wolf ambushed them in the deep snow, killing Sun Rising's nephew, Good Hawk, and

159

badly wounding Speaks His Mind. Since then, there had been
no peace between the Mohegans and the Narragansett, and Fast
wondered if there ever would be again.

Sun Rising drew generously from his pipe. He let tendrils
of smoke leach out of his dry, thin mouth like coiled snakes.
He coughed, winced in pain, and said, "They say you killed the
Black Tooth."

Fast nodded. "Yes, Sun Rising. It was necessary to protect the
Narragansett from future attacks. Plus, he threatened the lives of
Raging Wolf's children."

Sun Rising smoked again, and smiled. It was good to see that.
"And yet, the Mohegans have not recognized your sacrifice to
their people, protecting their future sachem from certain death.
They continue to raid our villages."

"Yes, they do. It is Uncas who feeds their anger and distrust."

Sun Rising handed over the pipe. "Uncas' anger is with Sassacus and his own standing among the Pequot. He is taking his
frustrations out on us and trying to assert an authority he does
not have." Sun Rising straightened his back and slowly crossed his
legs. The fresh leather of his leggings and breechcloth held clean
streaks of red-and-white clay. "Killing the Black Tooth, though,
caught his attention. No small task for a simple Narragansett
warrior like yourself."

Fast smoked and shrugged. "The Red God kept me safe."

"Ah, yes, your up-time Manitou." Sun Rising coughed again.
"Someday, you will have to introduce me to this red god of the
sky."

Fast remembered the moment that he had discovered the
up-time Red God. Then, he had been known as Runs Like Deer
and had been a member of the Deer Clan. But inside the satchel
of an Englishman who had died of a snake bite, he had found a
brightly colored book. On its cover was the depiction of a man
dressed in red. He wore a symbol that could only represent
lightning, brightly emblazoned on the skintight red armor that
covered him head to toe. Smaller lightning bolts were affixed to
the sides of the mask that left only his eyes and his nose and
mouth exposed.

Being unable to read the book's words did not stop him from
going through the book page by page, examining everything
carefully. The story within seemed to be told by drawings as

much as by the words in the white circles and boxes that broke up the pictures. It was clear the man—if he *was* a man—was a great warrior among his people. There was one drawing where the man in red was confronted by half a dozen other white men in odd clothing. The others all had the loud weapons of the white men pointed at him. In the next drawing, they fired at the man in red, but he moved so fast that death could not catch him. Swerving among their shots, he raced toward them. As the story continued, he took their weapons, throwing them aside. The man in red swept in to defeat the others with only his speed and bare hands.

It was to Fast an *epiphany*, as a Christian colonist might say. He felt an immediate connection with this man, this *god*, and from that day forward, Runs Like Deer was Fast as Lightning, and he would be so until his final day.

"Someday, my friend, I will tell you," Fast said politely, but knew that that day would never come. He could hardly take time to explain now, nor would there be time later. But they smoked and shared the lie together and spoke of other pleasantries until Sun Rising's dog, Kitchi, came through a small gap in the long-house wall and rested his panting snout on Sun Rising's thigh.

Kitchi brought joy to Sun Rising. He patted and rubbed the dog's sides and boney spine. He leaned over and placed a small kiss on its head. He seemed most happy in the presence of his pet. But was that a tear brimming at the bottom of his left eye? Was his lip quivering?

"Sun Rising," Fast said, leaning closer, "why have you called me here? What is wrong?"

The sachem blinked away his tear and said, "The time of change has finally come. The up-timers have arrived."

Breath caught in Fast's throat. Those were the words he had been expecting, anticipating, for a long time. He had been north and west, moving from one Narragansett village to another, help-ing to keep them safe from Uncas and the Mohegans. He had heard, and seen, nothing of this.

"Are you certain?"

Sun Rising nodded. "Both the Niantic and the Wampanoag have seen a flying ship, one that floats on the clouds as easily as a canoe on the river. It is a big ship, they say, and it bristles with life and color. Tiny men are seen on its deck. It is moving from one white settlement to another. There is no doubt what it is. The up-timers have come, and they mean to make war on us all." Sun Rising sighed, fought back the pain that gripped his expression, and said, "Everything that comes from Europe is a poison."

Fast was shocked at such words. Certainly, Sun Rising did not believe that, since he was good friends with William Bradford from Plymouth Colony. The Englishman had personally helped Fast during the Black Tooth incident. Bradford was no poison. But looking at Sun Rising now, so close to the end of his life, perhaps his anger, his defeated words, stemmed from a life of missed opportunities. Fast shot glances around the longhouse. War clubs, bows, arrows, and a small leather cord of teeth from vanquished Mohegan and Pequot foe hung from a post nearby. Signs and symbols of war in the home of a man who had always prided himself as a peacemaker.

"What can I do?"

Sun Rising made a *chi-chi-chi* sound with his tongue, and Kitchi jumped into his lap. He was a modest-sized dog. Brown-and-black fur. Part wolf and another breed that William Bradford had brought with him from England years ago. He was a good dog, loyal and obedient, and one of Sun Rising's favorites.

"I ask that you take Kitchi to Ninigret and offer him as a gift. He has always admired my dogs, so I will give him one. I fear that my desire to find peace with Uncas and the Mohegans is no longer possible. So be it. Let them live or die at the hands of white Europeans and up-timers as they may. But I wish to ensure that the Narragansett and the Niantic maintain their good relations so that *we*, together, can survive the coming storm. Go to Ninigret and reaffirm my friendship, and his commitment to our alliance, with this gift."

Now, Fast understood where the sachem's tears had come from. To give away Kitchi, to give away any of his dogs, was more painful than death. To do so, then, would be seen as the highest honor. For Ninigret to refuse...well, what if he did? Fast did not know what to do in that situation, but he'd figure it out when and if the time came. The Red God had given him the power to think quickly and efficiently under stressful, uncertain situations.

He nodded. "Very well. I will take your gift to Ninigret and secure his commitment to us. But I must confess, Great Sachem: dogs do not like me."

Sun Rising forced a laugh and patted Kitchi's head. "Then take Little Bear with you. He is more than capable of helping if you run into trouble." He smiled. "And he loves my dogs."

Fast took his leave. He paused outside the longhouse and looked into the sky. A storm cloud was forming, thick and black. Rain would fall soon. But there was no up-time sky ship to be seen.

Despite his name, Little Bear was a brute of a man. He was tall and stocky, almost twice as wide as Fast, and three times as strong. Sun Rising was wise to recommend him for this journey. If things did go poorly, Little Bear would be a great benefit.

They walked through the woods with Kitchi between them. The dog was in good humor. The chill of the coming night filled Kitchi with energy. Fast felt much the same. The up-timers from Europe had finally arrived. He hoped very much to catch a glimpse of their flying ship, as Sun Rising had described it. He hoped even more that, during the course of their journey, the Red God might bless him with the chance to speak to an up-timer. In his heart and mind were questions about the Red God that he *knew* only the up-timers could answer. But the skies remained clear, save for storm clouds. Rain had been falling on and off throughout the day.

Little Bear pulled him out of his thoughts. "We should make camp soon. I am soaked to my bones."

"You are right," Fast sighed, his excitement suddenly dampened by memories of Sun Rising. The old chief would almost certainly have passed on by the time they returned home. His spirit had been barely clinging to his old and sickly body when they had departed. Sun Rising had been a fair and wise leader. Fast respected the old man, and his loss would hurt their people.

Finding a spot suitable for the night, Fast built a fire. Kitchi huddled with them as the sun set. The dog chewed generously on the remains of a squirrel that Little Bear had shot out of a tree. The dog seemed content.

"Kitchi," Little Bear spoke loudly, "would you honor us with a story to help pass the night?"

Fast stared at Little Bear with a smirk on his face. "What are you doing?"

"I am trying to get Kitchi to tell us a story. I thought it might help you take your mind off your troubles for a time. Give you some peace."

"Dogs cannot speak." Fast laughed.

"They did once."

Fast grunted and shifted into a more comfortable position at the fire's edge. Its warmth felt nice and was already drying parts of his breechclout and leggings.

"You don't believe me?" Little Bear frowned.

"I have heard the story," Fast said, "but I don't believe it."

"It is true, though. Dogs once spoke as we do. Do you not know the legend?"

"Go on then," Fast urged Little Bear on, seeing that his friend desperately wanted to tell it. "Give us the story."

"Long ago, dogs spoke just as we do," Little Bear began. "Dogs lived side by side with Man as they do now, and back then it was their sacred duty to warn us of approaching strangers. They, too, would search the forests for game and tell us where it could be found. In this time, there were evil spirits that dwelt beneath the earth in the dark belly of the ground. These spirits, these creatures, were foul and mischievous things. They were our enemies."

"Have we not enough of those," Fast asked, "in our own lives? We do not need evil spirits to—"

"Are you going to let me tell this story or not?"

"I am sorry. Please, continue." Fast motioned for Little Bear to get on with it.

"These imps from beneath the earth..." Little Bear started.

"I thought you said they were evil spirits?"

"Does it matter?" Little Bear gritted his teeth in frustration.

"I suppose not. It's your story. Tell how you want."

"These spirits came to the dogs one day, offering wondrous treats and much more. The dogs were so overcome by what was given and promised that, in their greed, they forgot to warn the village about the spirits.

"Late that night, the spirits... those foul imps... crept into the village and took away everything they could carry. The village was left with nothing of what they had stored to get them through the coming winter. The dogs never once issued a warning. They slept, content and full, by the fires, never raising their voices."

"And they lost their voices for it?" Fast asked, pushing Little Bear's story along.

"I am getting to that." Little Bear grimaced, annoyed by yet another interruption of his tale.

It was not Fast who interrupted the young warrior this time, however. It was Kitchi.

The dog's ears perked up at something neither of them had heard from the surrounding dark wood. A low growl came from the dog as it rose up from where it lay near Little Bear.

Hearing the distant twang of bowstrings, Fast launched himself up and over the fire at Little Bear. His friend grunted as Fast's weight hit him, taking him down. An arrow thudded into the ground a few feet from where they lay. Another slammed into the fire itself, sending embers soaring. Fast rolled away from Little Bear, both of them scrambling to their feet as war cries rang out among the trees.

A painted warrior came bounding into their camp. His face was slicked with red-and-black clay. The sweeping, upwards angle of the clay that marred the warrior's cheeks in two black streaks with a bright red line in the center of each was a pattern that Fast recognized immediately. The burly warrior, with a four-foot war club held ready to swing, was a Mohegan. There were a pair of other warriors behind him, racing toward the camp. They had cast aside their bows, one drawing fierce knives, the other hoisting a heavy war club from where it had bounced on a cord at his waist. The blade of the knife gleamed in the light of the fire as they entered the camp. The war club waved dangerously in the smoky air.

Fast thanked the Red God for the speed that had saved himself and Little Bear from the arrows of their enemies many times in the past. That speed, unfortunately, wasn't enough this time to avoid the war club that was swung violently toward his head. It was Kitchi who saved him.

The dog leaped at the enraged warrior, teeth sinking into the soft flesh of his thigh. The Mohegan screamed as Kitchi tore a chunk of meat from his leg. Fast yanked his tomahawk free from where it hung on his belt. The warrior in front of him was reeling from the wound in his leg and hadn't yet recovered enough to bring his war club to bear again. Fast took advantage of the enemy's painful hesitation, burying the blade of his tomahawk in the center of the Mohegan's chest. The Mohegan's eyes went wide. He opened his mouth as if to curse Fast, but only blood poured over his chest in stark contrast to the streaks of war clay that covered his bare skin. Fast ripped his tomahawk free from the collapsing Mohegan. His two conspirators were in the camp now. Kitchi confronted one of them, Little Bear the other.

Little Bear flashed a knife. It was a poor weapon against a war club, and as he raced toward the snarling Mohegan, he took a blow to the side of his face that sent him sprawling onto the dirt. He did not get up.

Kitchi was faring better. The dog leapt through the air at the other Mohegan who had lost footing. Its teeth closed around his neck. The Mohegan slashed at the dog, cutting a long but thin gash along its body as he tried defending himself. His effort was fruitless. Kitchi's teeth had already torn out a chunk of throat. Kitchi yelped, darting away from the Mohegan as the warrior fell to his knees, hands clasping at the bleeding red meat of his throat.

The Mohegan who had downed Little Bear moved quickly against Fast. Standing his ground, Fast let the warrior approach. His tomahawk lashed out to meet the warrior's knife hand as the Mohegan thrust it forward. The Mohegan cried out and withdrew his bleeding hand as his knife fell from his grasp. Fast finished him, chopping away half his face in a single swing of his tomahawk.

The night fell silent, save for the horrid, wet gasping of the Mohegan as he bled out. Fast stepped forward and buried the blade of his tomahawk in the top of the Mohegan's skull.

Little Bear groaned where he lay. Relief washed over Fast as he saw that his friend was alive. He mumbled a prayer of thanks to the Red God as he moved to kneel next to Little Bear.

"Come on. Get up," Fast said.

"Give me a moment," Little Bear said, touching the bleeding wound on the side of his head. He seemed embarrassed that he had been bested by one club swing. "I took a war club to the head."

Fast grunted and waved off any concern that Little Bear might have had about his weak effort. "You are lucky it is intact. Thank the Red God for that hard head of yours."

Little Bear accepted Fast's hand and allowed himself to be pulled to his feet.

"Who were...?"

"Black Tooth's men," Fast said. "They were not seeking coup this night. They were seeking revenge for what I did to him."

Little Bear frowned. "Do they come at you often?"

Fast nodded. "From time to time. They will succeed eventually I am sure, Red God or no."

Little Bear nodded. "Thankfully, they did not succeed tonight."

Kitchi, wounded but alive, joined them near the fire. Little Bear leaned over carefully and patted the dog's back. Kitchi licked Little Bear's dirty, bloody hand. "I did not finish my story."

Fast snorted as he motioned to one of the dead Mohegans. He grabbed the man's arms, Little Bear his legs. As they pulled him toward the edge of the wood and away from the fire, Fast said, "That is fine, Little Bear. Dogs may not be able to talk anymore, but we should be most thankful that they can still growl."

The clouds opened, the sun shone bright, and there it was. Fast as Lighting felt both elation and fear. He had never seen anything like it. Nothing like it had ever existed in all the world. How was it possible? And yet, there it was.

It was wooden like a canoe, but larger. Its hull was painted a dull yellow. It did not have a rudder, but it had three circular blades that rotated on its sides and at its rear, like the weather vanes he had seen in Plymouth Colony. It looked like it had satchels of some sort hanging off its sides, and beneath it rested what looked like steel arms or legs. Above it all, tethered to a wooden frame and wrapped with some kind of rope, sat a large bladder, all puffed out and full with . . . what? Air? Spirits? Smoke? It must be lighter than air, Fast figured, for how could it just float there, moving slowly but deliberately, up the coast toward the same place that they were traveling? *How could this be?*

They moved into Niantic territory, keeping close to the coastline, but far enough back from the water so as not to be seen by the tiny little men who moved about on the sky ship's deck. Fast tried many times to steal a better view of what they looked like, but it was too far away. In time, the sky ship lifted into the clouds and was gone.

They arrived at Ninigret's village soon thereafter. The young sachem was not in his wigwam. He was standing quietly in the middle of his village, bare-chested save for a red vest that a European colonist had given him as a gift. Some of its brass buttons were missing, but it was clear to Fast that Ninigret gloried in the look. His long, dark hair fell over the shoulders of the vest. He looked proud and powerful.

Ninigret greeted Fast warmly. He then frowned, looking at their wounds and dishevelment. "You've had trouble."

Fast as Lighting nodded. "Black Tooth's men."

Ninigret sighed and shook his head. "The Mohegan would have us all killed." He pointed to the sky. "You have seen the ship?"

"Yes. We followed it for a while. I believe it is coming this way."

Ninigret's expression turned cold. He reached over and laid his hand on the head of a young boy standing beside him. "I do not fear these up-timers as others do. I do not believe that they would come here and fly like birds above us, exposing their bellies to our arrows, if they intended to do us harm. Nevertheless, I am concerned. I fear trouble is coming."

Having seen the sky ship himself, Fast doubted that any arrows could bring it down, though perhaps striking its bladder might do so. "What do you fear?"

Ninigret pulled Fast aside while children played with Kitchi. Little Bear did not follow, content to stay and talk with the young girls who had come out to greet them. They introduced him to a bowl of boiled maize, kidney beans, and shad. It smelled wonderful.

When they were alone, Ninigret grabbed Fast's arm and squeezed. "Our brother Niantics near the Connecticut River have been heavily influenced by the Pequot. They live in the shadow of Sassacus. They feud with white settlers far too often. Too much blood has been shed, and this has caused a rift between my people. Something is being planned. I do not know what it is, but I fear that my Western brothers are leading us to war."

"Ninigret," Fast said, standing tall, "Sun Rising has sent me here to gain your pledge to the Narragansett people. As his show of loyalty to you, I have brought Kitchi"—he gestured toward the dog—"as a gift. Please accept this gift and honor me with your pledge so that I may give Sun Rising peace in these times of trouble."

Ninigret watched Kitchi play with the children. He smiled. "Kitchi is a good dog. I accept Sun Rising's gift. You may tell him that he has my loyalty now until my end comes. But you must do something for me first. You must go to Mentotopha and my Western brothers and put a stop to their plans."

Fast stepped back. "I am honored by your faith in my negotiation skills, but it is not my place to—"

"It is, and you must," Ninigret said, stepping forward. "I cannot go. I am not afraid of the up-timers, but many of my people are. I must be with them now, to keep them calm in the shadow of this ship that floats in the sky like the hawk. You must speak with Mentotopha and keep him from bringing death to us all."

"What about your father, Sassious?" Fast asked. "Can he not speak to Mentotopha?"

Ninigret shook his head. "He has important matters to attend elsewhere."

Fast as Lighting felt trapped, like a beaver in a snare. He did not want to do this. He wanted to return to Sun Rising and give him the news before he passed from this world. Yet, seeing the sky ship himself, confirming its existence with his own eyes, did make the situation more urgent. Like Ninigret, he did not fear the up-timers, but perhaps he should fear what their arrival might bring.

Fast sighed and nodded. "Very well, Ninigret. I will go and speak for you."

The sun was approaching its zenith as Fast and Little Bear reached the outskirts of the Western Niantic village. A pair of warriors, carrying bows and war clubs, greeted them.

"Hold," one of the warriors warned, holding up his hand.

Fast stepped forward. "I am Fast as Lightning. I come in peace to address Mentotopha."

The two warriors exchanged glances. One nodded to the other.

"Come." The smaller warrior motioned both Fast and Little Bear to follow, and he led them through the village. Children were playing, and the Niantic women worked at various tasks. All of them stole glances at the two newly arrived strangers. All through the village, young warriors were readying themselves for a fight.

"They are preparing for something," Little Bear whispered. "Something very big."

Fast frowned and nodded. "Then let us hope we have arrived in time to stop them."

They were taken to a wigwam in the center of the village. The young warriors opened its flap to allow them entrance. Inside, a man sat near a small fire, smoking a pipe.

"These men have come to see you, Mentotopha," the young warrior said as he introduced them to his leader.

"Sit," Mentotopha ordered, gesturing toward the small fire. "I welcome you to my home."

Fast and Little Bear sat. Little Bear accepted the pipe and drew slowly, his young lungs still weak against the strong smoke swirling through them. Fast hid his amusement and worked to stay serious in the presence of a man who sat like stone in the flickering light of the fire.

Mentotopha, Four Bears, was a sagamore. He was a bright, fiery man, full of life and ideology. Fast had met him only once in passing, but had held him in high regard. Back then, however, the relationship between the Niantic and the white settlers had been more pleasant. Now, Fast could see a quiet anger on Mentotopha's face, a face now streaked with the dark clay of war.

"Most honored Mentotopha, we have been sent by Sachem Ninigret," Fast spoke, accepting the pipe from Little Bear. He held it, but did not draw.

Mentotopha looked them over, then frowned. "You are not Niantic."

Fast nodded. "We are Narragansett, but we are your brothers. We speak on Ninigret's behalf."

Mentotopha worked the muscles in his jaw. "Young Ninigret does not understand the deceits of the white European. He seeks to live in peace with them. That is folly and cowardice. His father understands this, but is too old to do anything about it. Ninigret does not see that we must strike at the white man now. If you have come to broker a peace, to convince me not to do what must be done, then your journey has been pointless."

"What do you intend to do, O great *sagamore*?" Fast asked, making sure to accentuate the fact that Mentotopha was no sachem.

Mentotopha ignored the insult, clenched his teeth, and said, "A white man by the name of Mad Jack Oldham is anchored near Block Island. He has brought upon us many privations, and so he will pay for them now before he and his up-time allies can join against us. We will row out to his ship in the dark of night, ambush him there, and his wooden decks will run red with his blood. Then the white men will see that we will not allow them to continue treating us like this world is no longer ours."

There was venom in Mentotopha's words. Little Bear had gone pale from the violence in the sagamore's voice.

"The strength of your arms is great." Fast nodded, remembering the number of warriors preparing outside the wigwam. "You would indeed kill many. Yet, is this a wise course to take, Great Sagamore, when it is clear that the up-timers have arrived and can fly through the sky like birds? Do you not think that they have ways of stopping such an attack?"

Mentotopha leaned forward and glared. "Are you afraid of the white men too, Fast as Lightning?"

"No. Their Red God protects me in all things. I have no fear of them or of any other white men. But the up-timers have arrived, as you know, and so perhaps it is best to show restraint and wait and see what they will do."

Mentotopha shook his head. "Blood will be answered with blood. We will tolerate the white men's presence in our lands no longer... up-timers or no."

It was clear that Mentotopha's mind was set. He had already streaked his body with clay, and this pipe he smoked was one of war, not peace. They could go round and round this dwindling pit fire forever, and nothing would move the sagamore from his decision. Fast did not have time to find a Niantic sachem to order Mentotopha to stop. Whatever was going to happen, was about to, and what could he do about it?

He thought quickly. "Then if I cannot talk you out of this course of action, then perhaps I and the Red God will join you."

Little Bear started to speak up, but Fast stopped him, reaching over to place his hand on the worried boy's knee.

"As you said, we are not Niantic," Fast continued, "but we too have had our issues with the white men. If you will not be convinced to heed Ninigret's urgings, then I will join you in your fight. The problem of the white men is one that must be dealt with and we have traveled too far to do nothing. I will fight with you... if you will so honor me."

Mentotopha grunted approval. "Very well. And let us hope that you are as fierce in battle as you look right now. Go join my warriors in their preparations, and may *Gitchi Manitou* guide you."

"Thank you, Mentotopha."

As soon as they were out of the wigwam, Little Bear grabbed Fast by the arm.

"What are you up to?" Little Bear asked. "I thought we were supposed to be stopping these people from starting a war, not joining up with them."

"Mentotopha will not be made to see reason," Fast explained. "His path is set. By going with them, and perhaps with the help of the Red God, I can at least mitigate the damage they will inflict upon this Mad Jack Oldham and his ship. Maybe I can even find a way to stop it before it happens."

"That sounds very risky to me," Little Bear sulked. "I would prefer it not be our blood that gets spilled."

"It won't be your blood, Little Bear," Fast said, placing his hand on the young man's shoulder. "You are not going."

Little Bear was angry that he was not given the opportunity to go and redeem himself for his poor showing against Black Tooth's men, but Fast was adamant. If things went afoul and he did not return, he needed Little Bear to warn Sun Rising of what had happened on Block Island, for the aftermath would surely cause grief to the Narragansett people. "How can you stop it?" Little Bear had asked. "I do not know," Fast had answered as he climbed into the war canoe to sit behind Mentotopha. "The Red God will guide me."

Block Island was not far off the coast, but there was need for haste in order to reach their rendezvous point with the Niantics waiting there quietly in the wooded shadows of the shoreline. The Niantic sagamore on the island was Mentotopha's good friend and blood brother. They had planned this ambush together, and now it was finally going to happen. Fast assisted in the rowing of the canoe whenever he could, not content to just be a bystander. It was his duty to pitch in, and it also gave the Niantic warriors around him the belief that he was one of them and that he shared in their struggle. He did on some level, but not when it came to killing a white captain and his men on his own ship. Nothing, *nothing* good would come from such an attack.

They met the two other canoes filled with warriors just as the sun was setting. The Block Island Niantics were dressed and streaked with clay in similar fashion to those that had come from shore, and they had muskets, which they hid beneath a fold of deerskin in the bottoms of their canoes. They shared a few with Mentotopha. The guns would remain hidden until they got close to Oldham's sloop, and perhaps they would not even be needed. In the cover of darkness, perhaps club, spear, and bow would suffice, and they would cause less stir and alarm for any of Oldham's men belowdecks when the attack occurred. Speed and silence would bring them onto the deck of the ship; victory would follow. Fast had the speed, but he hoped to use it to stop the attack, not participate in its success.

The canoes moved quietly through the calm water. The poor weather of the past couple days had not stirred the ocean, and they moved quickly toward Oldham's sloop with a slight breeze assisting. Fast's mind worked to figure out what to do, when to try to stop the attack. Now, or wait until they reached the ship itself? By then it might be too late.

In front of him, Mentotopha took up his war club and stood, readying himself for the assault. Fast prayed to the Red God for wisdom, calling upon his Manitou for speed of thought, and he found his hand moving toward the knife at his waist. He lifted his head and stared into Mentotopha's exposed back, in the small space right above the seamline of his breechclout, the place where a blade could strike death quickly. Yes, that was the best way to do this: remove Mentotopha and take over the attack. The other Niantic sagamore would be angry, but if Fast could force the retreat of at least his own two war canoes, then perhaps the other two would relent and retreat as well. Yes, there was a chance.

Fast drew his knife and stood.

A long shadow fell across the water. It was as if the moon itself had died. Fast looked up and there it was, the up-time sky ship, moving lower than he had seen it earlier, so low as to almost be in the water itself. Even as a dark shadow it was majestic, powerful, and it covered their approach in complete darkness.

Fast took an unbalanced step backwards. A shot rang out.

Two shots, in fact. Or perhaps three, perhaps four. The echo of each was strong. Fast as Lighting looked up and saw just a simple blink of fire from where one of the shots had rung out. Then he heard a moist *thunk!* as Mentotopha yelped, and then fell backwards with a spray of blood bursting from his back. The shot went straight through his body and splintered wood in the canoe side.

Fast dropped his knife and caught Mentotopha as he fell dead. The sky ship moved on, and the Niantic warriors began to shout in confusion and fear.

The ruckus alerted the men on Oldham's ship, and they fired a few shots themselves toward the canoes. In the darkness, none hit, none like the one the sky ship had fired. All four canoes were now flailing chaotically, as men took up paddles and began rowing in many directions. The Block Island sagamore called for a retreat and slowly, slowly, they obeyed and turned the canoes around.

The ambush had failed. Fast was pleased.

But sorrowful as well. In his arms lay Mentotopha, bleeding his life into the canoe hull. And all it took was one shot from the sky ship—in total darkness—and a prayer to the Red God. *Was it my prayer that had brought on the wrath of the sky ship?* Fast did not know for sure, but if it were true, it was the most terrifying, exhilarating thing that had ever happened to him.

What if the Red God is on the sky ship? What if he has come to meet me?

Questions swirled in his mind as the men behind him rowed their canoe toward Block Island.

Fast held Mentotopha tightly, watched him die, and sang a warrior's song.

It was Fast's obligation to deliver Mentotopha's body to his people. He wanted to stay on Block Island, for the sky ship had touched down near the shore and its occupants were having a meeting with the very men who had participated in the ambush. It was not fair that he had to depart immediately, but what could he do? He had decided to leave Little Bear behind in safety. The young man could easily have been the one to deliver Mentotopha to his people, and Fast could have stayed behind and spoken with the up-timers, to finally meet them face to face. But that was not the decision he had made, and there was no changing the course of fate.

He and Little Bear stayed with Mentotopha's people to aid them in their preparations to ensure their sagamore's spirit would not roam the earth and to prepare him for his continued life in the spirit world. It was a sad time, but Fast enjoyed his stay with them. It was clear that these people were afraid. They felt trapped between the Pequot and the Mohegans further west and their Niantic brothers and Narragansett cousins to the north and east. What would the future hold for these simple coastal folk? If one bullet from an up-time sky ship could take away their sagamore, how many were needed to destroy their entire way of life? Despite what had happened, Fast still did not believe that the up-timers had come here to harm anyone, but it was hard to look these anxious people in the eye and convince them of that. The subtle, awesome power of the sky ship had definitely convinced Fast of one thing: all people everywhere, all the tribes, must join together to stand against whatever the future may bring. But how could he make this happen?

Two days later, Niantic men from Block Island arrived with word that a large gathering of people would occur at Fort Sovereignty near the mouth of the Connecticut River. Everyone was going to be there, including the up-timers and their sky ship.

"That is where we are going, Little Bear," Fast said, as he tucked away Mentotopha's pipe that had been given to him as a gift. "And I will finally speak with these up-timers myself."

Fort Sovereignty
At the mouth of the Connecticut River

There were Paugussets, Wangunks, and Hockanum Podunks. Quinnipiacs, Wampanoags, and Mattabesics. Other Niantic and Narragansett tribes had sent people as well, though Sun Rising and Ninigret and his father Sassious were not among them. There were Nipmucks and Mohegans and, of course, many Pequot. All camped along the banks of the Connecticut River. It was the largest gathering of people that Fast had ever seen, and his heart rejoiced. Rejoiced... until the sky skip arrived.

It touched down, as light as air, resting comfortably on steel arms that supported its weight. Up closer, it seemed no bigger now than a small boat, almost canoe-like, though it was much wider than a canoe, and certainly had more of an *elegant*—wasn't that the English term for it?—construction than one. *Oh, what it must be like to be flying like a hawk among the clouds...*

"What are you doing?" Little Bear asked him late one evening as they camped near a Narragansett fire.

Fast dipped his fingers into yellow clay, and then ran it across his bare chest in a pattern of the jagged lightning bolt he saw in the dead Englishman's book. It was not as even or as beautiful as the picture he had seen, but it would do. "Preparing myself."

"For what?" Little Bear asked.

"To meet the Red God."

The sky ship was guarded. The large bladder, which had been all puffed out and prominent in flight, was now deflated, still and limp, and it sagged down onto the hull's structure like the bark covering of a tipi. In its current state, the sky ship did not look so impressive; and yet, Fast could not think of any other place to be but on its deck.

The guards were white, but were they up-timers? They looked like Englishmen from this distance. He could not tell, but one thing was certain: they were lazy, complacent, and too confident in the muskets that they held. Fast looked past them and toward his target. All he needed now was for the moon to drop behind the clouds and then...

He moved quickly, just as the Red God had shown him in the book, unburdened now by anything but a thin breechclout. His bare feet were silent among the dry tufts of grass and weeds and small pebbles that lined his approach. He jumped straight over a tiny hillock, landed, rolled, and waited. The guard closest to him sniffed, turned as if he had heard something, paused a moment, sniffed again, cleared his throat, then returned to his post at the prow.

Fast crawled through the wet grass, worried that it would smear the yellow clay on his chest. But he kept crawling until he put his hand out and touched the hull of the sky ship.

It was dry to the touch. Its dull yellow sides felt no different than any other piece of wood he had felt. With his other hand he touched its steel leg. It was cold and smooth, smoother than anything he had ever felt in his life, save for perhaps the top of a lake or the cold rush of creek water. He was close enough to reach out and touch one of its circular blades, but was afraid to do so. What if they were sharp and cut him? What if they were poison? There was also fear that touching too much would awaken the great ship, and then what would happen? Was he fast enough to get away then?

He ignored his concern and all the questions in his mind and pulled himself close to the ship. He wriggled himself underneath the limp folds of the ship's bladder. The guards were talking quietly near the prow, and there did not seem to be anyone else on guard. Fast raised himself up slowly, pushing against the heavy bladder. Light from the moon, which had now cleared the clouds, shone into the small gap that his pushing had created, and it spread across the deck of the sleeping sky ship.

"O Red God," Fast whispered, "Are you there? I have come to meet you. I am your servant, Fast as Light—"

But all he heard was the loud, uncontrollable snoring of a white man whose bearded, sweaty face shown in the moonlight. The man suddenly awoke, blinked many times, and raised his head. His breath was foul. "Who are you?"

Fast was gone. He dropped to a crouch and ran headlong toward a patch of trees where Little Bear awaited him. He could hear the guards calling after him, threatening him to stop, but they made no attempt at firing their muskets, nor would it have worked. No one ran faster than he.

"Did you see the Red God?" Little Bear asked him as he reached their hiding place. "Did you speak to him?"

What should I tell him? Breathing hard, he shook his head, and said, "No, I did not speak with him. He was . . . sleeping."

Three days later, the man everyone was waiting for arrived.

The great Pequot sachem, Sassacus, had seen well over seventy suns, and yet he still held the attention and loyalty of many sagamores and sachems from other tribes. He was considered by many to be the greatest chief to have ever lived. Fast had never met him, but immediately understood the sentiment. Sassacus had a way of walking, a way of holding himself upright which revealed his inner strength, his courage. Fast watched the Pequot sachem as he and his entourage passed by and wondered how the Red God might manifest itself through a man such as Sassacus.

Powerful . . .

Sassacus and the other tribe leaders gathered in a longhouse hastily constructed for their meeting with the up-timers. Englishmen Standish, Mason, and Endecott were there as well, along with the Mohegan sachem Uncas, who had tried to seize power when Sassacus' father had passed. But that bit of rebellion had failed, and thus, Uncas had pledged his allegiance to the Pequot leader. Under duress, Fast had no doubt, but in the shifting alliances and motivations of the Algonquian people, a public display of support was sufficient.

Due to his status among the Narragansett, Fast was allowed inside the tent, though he was not as close to the up-timers as he would have liked. He did not object, however, for his heart was beating so fast that if he had been nearer, he might have passed out. Weak behavior by a true Narragansett warrior and a follower of the Red God, but there it was. He was finally, at long last, going to *see* an up-timer.

Introductions came first, and then the passing of a pipe. Sassacus introduced himself. The other sachems in attendance came next. The Englishmen did the same. The up-timers were last. Gordon and Peter Chehab. Interesting names. Interesting faces. Not much different than English faces. Perhaps Peter had been the one Fast had seen the other night sleeping in the sky ship? It was hard to know for sure. Both he and Gordon looked similar. They spoke English well, but had a different tone and inflection than the Englishmen. Fast could understand neither very well, but certain words were clear. The tone of the conversation was *very* clear: a sachem, an English king, had sold the British colonies to the French.

The French were coming.

And it did not appear that, despite all their power, the up-timer Chehab brothers were in a position to do anything about it. Not right away, at least.

Up-timer Gordon was calling for all the Algonquian tribes and the English colonists to set aside their differences, to unite against the mutual threat that the French posed. He implored, in fact. But looking around the room, Fast could see skepticism in everyone's eyes. All present did not doubt the danger that the French might pose, but why were they any different than any other European power that had made promises to them in the past? The English. The Dutch. The French. There was little difference between them in the eyes, and memories, of all in attendance. Sassacus seemed willing to discuss the future and the unification of all the tribes... under his control, of course. For him, such a unification was beneficial. For Uncas, who sat near the Pequot sachem in silence, such an agreement was offensive. Uncas' face was calm and stoic, but Fast could see the boil of rage below the surface.

They broke the meeting with a promise to continue their talks in the afternoon. As people filed out, Fast stood tall and thrust his chest forward so that the Chehab brothers could steal a glimpse of the yellow lightning bolt on his skin. For a long while, they did not look his way. *Look at me... look at me! Do you not see your Red God's totem on my skin? Do you not see the blaze of his fire in my eyes? See me, and talk to me. I can help forge the path forward...*

Peter Chehab did finally look his way. The up-timer paused, stared deeply into Fast's eyes, then glanced down at the faded yellow lightning bolt on his chest. He seemed to study it, then shrugged, and stepped away.

Uncas pushed his way out of the tent, and Fast followed.

Fast emerged from the tent. Uncas wasn't far away. He had stopped to speak with one of his warriors, a lean, muscled fellow with a long knife at his waist, a quiver of arrows on his back, a bow in his hand. Uncas hadn't noticed Fast follow him out of the tent. Fast stood where he was, staring up at the sky, but his ears were focused on what Uncas was saying to the warrior. Fast couldn't understand exactly what was being said in their muffled tones. It was obvious, however, that Uncas was telling him something about Sassacus. The warrior nodded generously, smiled, and gripped his bow. Then they walked away. Fast, having heard what he needed, watched them leave and then went to fetch Little Bear.

He found Little Bear and said simply, "Follow me."

Little Bear, confused, nodded and followed.

They left the camp, tracking the warrior that Uncas had been speaking to. They held back far enough not to be seen, but close enough to know where he was headed. Little Bear, despite his size, was very good at moving quietly, even better than Fast in many ways. They watched and followed, watched and followed, until they came to the edge of the wood.

Sassacus had left the meeting with a lone guard and had wandered through the woods to this clearing, likely to have time alone so that he could collect his thoughts and ready himself for the afternoon smoke and discussion. Sassacus came upon a quiet spot near the tree line and stopped. Uncas' warrior scampered up a tree with the bow in his hand. He climbed up with great care to keep quiet and his presence unknown to Sassacus and his guard. Once he had reached a good position in the tree, he readied his bow and aimed it at the Pequot sachem's back.

"Coward!" Little Bear whispered and spit. "He is going to shoot him in the back. Coward!"

Fast nodded. He looked around, studied the approach. The distance between them and the warrior's tree was great.

"No," Fast muttered, pushing Little Bear aside. "He won't."

Saying a prayer to the Red God and touching the yellow lightning bolt smeared on his chest, Fast broke into a run. He focused all of his energy into his legs. Only the Red God's power could save Sassacus now, and Fast dug his feet into the soft ground, gaining speed with each stride. The warrior in the tree was so focused on Sassacus that he didn't see Fast coming.

Fast threw himself into the air toward the tree. He slammed into its trunk just below the warrior's position, giving no shout, no yelp of pain to reveal his presence. With his left hand he held onto a branch; with his right, the warrior's ankle. The warrior's bowstring sounded, but the arrow flew off target. It thudded into a tree between them and where Sassacus stood. Neither the Pequot sachem, nor his guard, moved.

Fast's tug at the warrior's leg rocked the man off balance. The warrior toppled from the tree, crashing to the forest floor. Little Bear came up quickly as the warrior tried regaining his feet. The warrior opened his mouth to shout. Little Bear's war club struck the man's head and knocked him unconscious. Little Bear then pulled leather cord from his waist and tied the man's hands behind his back.

Fast jumped from the tree. "Quiet!" he hissed, as he held Little Bear down behind foliage and waited until Sassacus and his guard walked away. Little Bear then finished his binding.

Together, they hoisted the man up and onto Little Bear's shoulder. Fast then slapped his friend on the back. "You did well, Little Bear. Thank you."

"It is you I should be thanking," Little Bear said, securing the unconscious man on his shoulder. "I've never seen anyone move as fast as you just did."

Fat shook his head. "Do not thank me. Thank the Red God... and thank the up-timers for bringing him to us." Fast checked to make sure the man's bindings were secure. "Now, bring him. We have much to discuss with Uncas."

They walked right into the center of Uncas' camp, with no fear or concern on their faces. Fast was clenching his teeth for sure, knowing that at any moment, several Mohegan warriors could reveal their weapons and attack, and would he and Little Bear survive such an assault? Up to this moment, the Red God had favored them with his gifts of life, speed, and vitality. Would he continue to do so? Was his patience with Fast infinite? He did not know, nor was he willing to test such a thing. But they walked, unfettered, up to Uncas anyway, letting the Mohegan warriors around them see their lack of fear.

Little Bear dropped the unconscious man at Uncas' feet. Uncas, his eyes never leaving Fast's stern face, knelt beside his man and studied the large, bloody knot on his head. He then turned his attention to Little Bear. "You did this?"

Little Bear nodded. "Yes, and I will do it to any man who tries to draw near."

Fast put up his hand to end the conversation before it spiraled out of control. "We are here in peace, Uncas. We come as brothers."

"Brothers?" Uncas stood and spit the word back at Fast. "You come in peace, and yet, you bring a great Mohegan warrior, bloodied and beaten, and drop him at my feet. How dare you speak of—"

"A great Mohegan warrior who was about to put a shaft into Sassacus' back. Sounds more like a coward to me."

Uncas raged, stepped forward, and put his face a mere inch from Fast's clenching jaw. Little Bear reached for his club. The Mohegan warriors pressing in reached for their weapons. Uncas, his eyes wide, puffed his foul breath onto Fast's chin. For his part, Fast stood like stone, never blinking, never wavering, though his heart was beating very fast.

Finally, Uncas relented, stepped back, took a deep breath. "What do you want, Fast as Lightning?"

"I saved your life, Great Sachem Uncas. *Konchi Manto* was watching over you today." He pointed at the bloodied warrior at their feet. "Had this man put his arrow into Sassacus' back, and if the attack had failed—which was likely given how powerful, how mighty, he is—the truth of your involvement would have been discovered. This man would have died, and so would you, slowly too, at the end of Sassacus' own knife."

Uncas shook his head. "I know nothing of this man's actions."

"Do not lie to me, Uncas." Fast raised his voice. More than he wanted to, but enough to send the message. "I saw you speaking with this man right after the meeting ended. I then followed him. He did not wander from his path. He spoke to you, and then he climbed a tree to his killing spot—"

"And Fast stopped the attack," Little Bear interrupted, "by

moving faster than any man I have ever seen. No man, anywhere, can move as fast as he."

Fast breathed deeply, letting his chest expand to reveal the lightning bolt. "The up-time Red God gives me powers that you cannot believe, Uncas. I walked into Raging Wolf's own long-house and counted coup against him. I then saved his children from the Black Tooth. I then killed the Black Tooth, something that no Mohegan warrior was ever able to do.

"I can catch an arrow flying. I can snatch a single raindrop falling from the sky and hold it gently between two fingers. I touched the sky ship—"

"I saw him do that," Little Bear confirmed.

"—when everyone else was afraid to go near it. And I walked right into your camp with no fear and laid a coward at your feet. These things and more have I done, and can do, Uncas. And so hear me, when I ask you for an agreement."

Uncas raised his brow. "What kind of agreement?"

Fast paused, then: "The war between the Narragansett and the Mohegans must end. You have heard the words from the up-time Chehab brothers yourself: the French are coming. And if we are killing each other, then they will easily take our lands, scatter and kill our people. We must unite, now, so that we may stand against them and anything else the Europeans may bring to our shores."

Uncas huffed. "And if I refuse to agree?"

"Then I will tell Sassacus of your attempt against his life. And he will believe it too, for he sees, like I do, the anger and resentment on your face. You are not the leader of the Mohegans and Pequot nations, but you wish it. You wish it so badly that you are willing to risk this man's life and your own for a chance to see the great Sassacus dead. If you do not agree, he will learn of your deceit, and he will watch you die slowly, in disgrace, and your spirit will roam the earth forever, with pain and suffering."

Uncas struggled to find a response in his own heart. It was clear to Fast that the sachem was confused, uncertain as to the right answer. To help, Fast added, "And if you agree . . . then I will support your desire to be made great sachem. Sassacus will not live forever. He will die, normally, in good time. When that day comes, I will support your claim to lead the Pequot and the Mohegans. I can think of no better man than you."

"You give me your word?" Uncas asked.

"I do."

"What will Sun Rising say of this?"

Fast swallowed. "It saddens me to confess it, but he will be dead soon, if not already. He will not express an opinion."

"What about Canonicus?" Uncas asked, folding his arms across his chest. "I do not think he will happily accept your authority. He has authority of his own."

"Canonicus is a great man," Fast said, "and if the world were the same today as it was yesterday, I would follow him gladly. But the up-timers have arrived, in sky ships that can fire lightning bolts from their decks.

"I saw this myself. You have heard the stories by now, I am sure. I was behind Mentotopha in the canoe when the up-time sky ship struck him with lightning. I have seen their power up close, Uncas, and I have survived it. I thrive in it." Fast preened again to ensure Uncas saw the lightning bolt on his chest. "I understand it better than anyone. Better than Sun Rising. Better than Canonicus. Better than you.

"The French are coming...and then what after them? More sky ships? Fleets of them? We cannot hope to survive the relentless coming of the Europeans and the up-timers without joining together and defending what we have. So I ask you again...shall we stop this war before we are consumed by it?"

Uncas stepped away, turned, his arms still crossed. "This is something we should discuss over smoke."

"We do not have time," Fast urged. "We must agree now, before the meeting continues. I have given you my offer. I now give you my word: I will support your claim to great sachem when Sassacus dies if you agree to end your attacks against my people, forever and always. Do you agree?"

Uncas considered a little longer. Then he turned and nodded. "I agree. We will keep all of this quiet for now. But the time will come, Fast as Lightning, when I shall expect you to publicly declare your support."

"I will."

Uncas flicked his wrist as if he were swatting a fly. "Go, now, before there is talk. The war between the Mohegan and the Narragansett has concluded. And I pray to *Konchi Manto* that you keep your word, Fast as Lightning. For if it is broken, then no two warriors shall ever clash with such blood and sorrow as we. That is my warning to you. Remember it."

Uncas walked away.

Fast and Little Bear left the camp. As they walked back to their own encampment, Little Bear said, "That was a deadly threat. Do you think he meant it?"

Fast shook his head. "I am not worried. We embarrassed him today by walking unafraid into his camp and throwing his assassin at his feet. He needed to save face in front of his men. We will let him boast, but he will keep his word. His thirst for power is too great, and my endorsement of him too important."

Little Bear looked at Fast in surprise. "Are you going to declare yourself sachem when Sun Rising dies?"

Fast shrugged. "I do not want to. But what I said to Uncas was true. I may be the only one of our people to understand the up-timers and what they may bring to our shores. But first, we must deal with the French. The French first, then the up-timers. And I will do what I have to do to ensure that our people survive them both."

They reached their camp. A strong smell of roasting fish and boiled maize and beans struck Fast as he walked past a fire.

As they sat and ate and prepared for the afternoon's meeting with the Englishmen and the Chehab brothers, Little Bear asked, "Was Mentotopha struck by lightning? You said it was a ball from a rifle."

"No lightning. I lied to Uncas about that one."

"And raindrops. Can you really catch a raindrop falling from the sky and hold it between your fingers?"

Fast looked up. A few clouds, but no rain. It was a pleasant day, and he had accomplished a lot on their journey for Sun Rising. The sun was not rising. It was falling, but it was warm and pleasant. He was alive, and life was wonderful. For now, anyway.

Through the Red God, I can do anything.

"Can I catch a raindrop?" Fast asked. He leaned toward Little Bear and smiled. "What do you think, my friend?"

Remember Plymouth

Bjorn Hasseler

Plymouth town, Plymouth Plantations colony
Saturday, May 9, 1637

"The French will be here soon," Governor William Bradford stated. The governor was a healthy, physically fit man whose neatly trimmed mustache and goatee contributed to his sense of presence and dignity. He glanced at the sails in the bay, then at the men who stood beside him in the middle of Plymouth, their backs to the wind. It was a damp and chilly spring day, mostly overcast with a dark cloudbank on the horizon.

After a moment Bradford spoke again. "John Winthrop's letter outpaced them. He is no longer the governor of Massachusetts Bay—no Englishman is—but I think we can rely on his account of the French landings in Boston and Salem last month."

Elder William Brewster nodded firmly. He was no longer the pastor of Plymouth—in fact, he lived in Duxbury now. But if the French were coming to take possession of the colony, he was the spiritual leader everyone wanted present. Brewster was aging, his white hair and narrow face giving him a monk-like appearance. Now he spoke up. "I am sure his warning will prove accurate and insightful. There's been little violence, and some of that accidental. Small comfort to the families of those killed, of course. And the French have not, as yet, interfered with the Puritan congregations."

Captain Myles Standish snorted. "Yet. They will wait until after they have gained control of all our towns. How many men does Winthrop say they have?"

Bradford was meticulous. He brought the letter out from under his cloak and checked it, even though the numbers had to be fixed in his mind. "Some few hundreds. Ten ships. One man-of-war with thirty or forty guns and two men-of-war with twenty to thirty guns. The rest are merchant ships carrying troops and colonists. A few guns and swivels, of course."

Standish pointed toward the bay. "Four sail yonder, so perhaps two hundred men. But...colonists, you say?"

"Farmers, a smith, a cooper, a chandler, and so on," Bradford summarized. "A governor and subordinate officials. That means..."

"That we have no leverage." Standish sighed. "They do not need any of us for their colony to survive."

"Not so." The only Native American in the group spoke up in English. He was a tough, well-muscled man who wore tunic and trousers while he was in Plymouth town. "These French follow a new king called Gaston. They have not heard the words of their great chief Champlain who would counsel them to avoid the mistakes you yourselves made at first. Nor will they speak with Massasoit Ousamequin." He pronounced the title *Mas-SA-so-eet*.

None of the four white men bristled at that statement, not even the often-irascible Myles Standish. It was simply the truth.

"We thank you—*I* thank you, Hobbamock—for rescuing us from those mistakes." William Bradford's words were sincere.

Hobbamock nodded gravely to Governor Bradford. "Edward here did likewise for Massasoit Ousamequin in turn."

Hobbamock had lived with the Pilgrims for several months in those disastrous first two years. Had been assigned to them by Massasoit Ousamequin wasn't too strong a way to characterize it. Later, Hobbamock had worked with and sometimes against Squanto, but when he'd been the one to bring word to the Pilgrims that Squanto had been captured by another tribe, Standish had led the rescue party.

And that, Hobbamock reflected, was odd. For all that Myles Standish did not respect the Wampanoag or the Massachusett or any other tribe—he'd nearly started a war with Sassacus, the great sachem of the Pequot, just last year—he *had* gone to Squanto's aid. And Standish and Hobbamock were not precisely friends, but something close to it.

"Did the French governor actually refuse to meet with Massasoit Ousamequin?" the fourth Englishman asked. Edward Winslow was Governor Bradford's right-hand man, had explored the Connecticut and Kennebec Rivers, established trading posts, and was a personal friend of Massasoit Ousamequin. He and Susanna White had even been the first Pilgrims to marry in Plymouth. Each had lost a previous spouse in the terrible first winter.

"The governor said he would summon him at leisure. *Summon*." Hobbamock shook his head in disgust.

"That would be a grave mistake," Winslow stated.

"Perhaps, once the formalities are over, I might speak with the new governor or his designate..."

"The French are lowering boats," Standish announced.

"Very well," Governor Bradford stated. "Allow us to meet them. In a solemn manner—all Plymouth is watching."

An hour later, the five men were waiting by the gate nearest the bay. They had seen to it that the gates were open, and both the blockhouse at the far end of Plymouth and the stockade in the middle of the town were unmanned.

An irregular line of eight boats was struggling through the wind-driven chop toward shore. Each held several soldiers, muskets or pikes held upright between their knees. Behind them, several sailors rowed. A couple of the central boats held one or two men who appeared to be dressed in finer clothes.

One of those boats finally grounded on the beach. The soldiers leapt over the side at once. The Plymouth men heard shouts, and the soldiers formed into rank. Within a couple minutes, most of the other boats reached land. Their soldiers added themselves to the formation, pikes in the center and muskets on the flanks.

"Fools," Standish muttered.

"How so?" Winslow asked.

"The gate lies open, no colors are flying, and not a soul is near the cannon. Anyone ought to see that we wait in greeting. If they cannot discern that, why then, forming into a single mass is the worst of all. Were the guns loaded, two charges of grape would down half of them."

"I appreciate it offends your professional art." William Bradford's tone was dry. "But, please, enough."

At a crisp command, the formation of French troops marched forward. A second command brought the pikes down. A third brought the formation to a halt with the blades a few intimidating yards away. Then a voice called out from behind the formation, and two soldiers stepped up to the Plymouth men. One held a musket, the other a sergeant's half-pike.

"Give us your weapons!" one of them barked in English.

Myles Standish shrugged. "A sword would do little against your numbers, but if you are determined..." He unbuckled his sword belt and handed it to the French sergeant.

The other soldier glared at Hobbamock and held out his hand.

Hobbamock gazed at him, then glanced down to where he had a knife sheathed at his waist. He looked up at the sergeant's half-pike and held his hands a few inches apart.

"Give the knife to me," the soldier insisted. "No weapons." He spoke slowly.

"I am truly a skilled warrior, but I have more sense than to attack fifty men. If the Wampanoag desired war, we would have attacked you on the beach. Instead Massasoit Ousamequin sent me as his ambassador."

"Ambassador!" The sergeant looked like he was about to spit. "Tell your tame Indian..."

"*Pniese* Hobbamock of the Pokanoket tribe." Standish spoke angrily. "He does, in fact, speak for Ousamequin, Massasoit of the Pokanoket and all the Wampanoag and has proven trustworthy since the earliest days of the colony."

The Plymouth men heard a snort as one of the civilians approached. "I am Capitaine Choublet, sent by Colonel Desormiers, military governor of Nouvelle Lorraine, to take possession of this... village. The Indians will wait. Colonel Desormiers will summon them at an appropriate time, and then they will appear before him."

"If I may, Captain?" William Bradford asked. He gestured to the man beside him. "Elder William Brewster, Edward Winslow, and Captain Myles Standish. I am William Brad—"

"I do not care who any of you are," Capitaine Choublet stated. "I am in command here, and you will obey my orders. Disobedience is treason against France and will be dealt with harshly. Take us within the walls."

Bradford put a restraining hand on Standish's arm while simultaneously exchanging glances with Brewster and Winslow. Brewster shrugged, as if he were asking, *What choice have we?* The five men started toward the open gate. Thunder rumbled in the distance.

"*Arrêtez!*"

The Plymouth men stopped because of the sergeant's tone, not because they understood the word.

"The knife." The French sergeant held out his hand.

Hobbamock handed it to him and watched with amusement as the sergeant tried to carry his own half-pike, Standish's sword belt, and Hobbamock's knife without dropping any of them. Then he turned and followed the four colonists into Plymouth. The French sergeant and the musketeer were at his heels, with the rest of the French soldiers shifting formation to enter the gate.

As soon as Hobbamock passed the heavy, sturdy palisade, he saw that the inhabitants of Plymouth were quietly watching events unfold. He saw William Bradford motion outward with his hands, indicating they should back up and make space for the French. Bradford led the way toward the central intersection, near a small stockade.

"*Arrêtez!*"

Everyone stopped. Capitaine Choublet came forward, this time accompanied by the other man in expensive clothing. He was younger and carried a rolled-up document. Choublet held out his hand, and his aide handed it to him.

"Gaston, by the Grace of God, Most Christian King of France and Navarre, etc., claims possession of New France, all territory in North America north of the Viceroyalty of New Spain save the possessions of the Netherlands. The lands east of the Hudson River extending north and east to Acadia are nearby designated Nouvelle Lorraine...."

Once he had read the entire proclamation, the captain stated, "Colonel Desormiers has given me command of this village. Therefore, I order all previous inhabitants to remove themselves outside the walls."

Gasps came from the residents gathered around.

"*Oui!*"

"Captain," Edward Winslow began, "some here have dwelt inside the palisade for fifteen years. Would you seize all they have built—"

"*Oui*, I would and I do. I will not tolerate complaints. Dissent will be treated as treason against France, and traitors will be executed!"

Again, there were gasps, and this time Elder Brewster held out his hands as if to curtail them. "We shall build anew. We have done so before. Houses, a meetinghouse—"

"No meetinghouse," Capitaine Choublet barked. "Your heretical practices will not be tolerated in public."

Hobbamock heard a shrill sound. A woman's voice, he realized, and a cry of triumph, not dismay. He spotted Eleanor Billington, one of only four adult women who had survived the colony's first winter. The Billingtons were strangers, not Separatists, and had caused all sorts of trouble.

Hobbamock saw faces in the crowd darken, some in dismay, others in anger. Then William Brewster gave an exaggerated shrug and spoke.

"We had no meetinghouse at first. I am sure we can make do."

"Then get your belongings and get out."

Brewster and Bradford exchanged glances. Then Bradford raised his voice.

"Everyone, please begin moving your belongings."

Some grumbled, but with Capitaine Choublet glowering at them and fifty soldiers right there, most moved to comply.

Hobbamock kept an impassive expression on his face over the next several minutes. He noted that Standish was scowling, and Bradford, Brewster, and Winslow all had concerned looks. That was no surprise. The English would have to build houses and plant crops. It would have to be nearby but not—

"*Mousquet!*" The sudden shout in French rang out, followed immediately by the deep *whoom* of a musket firing.

Hobbamock whirled around as a second musket fired. He immediately saw what had happened and knew it was already too late.

One of the Englishmen had come out of a nearby house carrying an armload of his possessions, a musket and an axe among them. Both would be critical in starting over, but one of the French musketeers—white smoke was still wafting from his musket barrel—had seen the barrel precede the man out the door and fired. He'd missed, but the soldier next to him hadn't. The Plymouth man was sprawled in his doorway. His musket lay in the dirt, and his ax had fallen across his body.

"No!" Elder William Brewster cried out in horror. He dashed several steps forward, raising his hands in a gesture to stop.

At the same time, the first Plymouth man to reach the man who'd been shot shoved the ax away.

Someone shouted in French, and two more musketeers immediately fired.

"Stop!" Brewster cried. "It is a mista—"

Capitaine Choublet drew his sword and ran William Brewster through.

With shouts of horror and anger, several Plymouth men surged forward.

"*Apprêtez-vos armes!*" the French sergeant called out. "*Joue!*"

The French soldiers' muskets came up, and their pikes came down.

Myles Standish leapt forward and caught the sergeant in the throat with a rock-hard fist. The Frenchman made a choking noise and fell to his knees. His half-pike, Standish's sword belt, and Hobbamock's knife fell away in separate directions.

"*Feu!*" Capitaine Choublet ordered.

The musket volley crashed out, twelve shots from the left side and only six from the right. Edward Doty, Henry Samson, and William Latham all went down. Then Myles Standish caught up the sergeant's half-pike and thrust it into the nearest musketeer.

Hobbamock drew a second knife from a sheath inside his trousers and leapt on the musketeer who had originally come forward with the sergeant. That man went down, his throat cut, and now Hobbamock held his unfired musket.

"Charge! Kill them!" Capitaine Choublet shouted.

Hobbamock jerked the trigger back, the slow match dipped into the black powder in the pan, and he shot the capitaine in the back.

The pikes surged forward as the musketeers frantically reloaded. If he had a dozen warriors *right now*...

"Allerton!" Standish bellowed. "The musketeers!"

Hobbamock saw Francis Billington and Samuel Hopkins wrestle one of the musketeers to the ground. Another butt-stroked Bradford, but then Edward Winslow crashed into him.

Standish shot by, half-pike gripped firmly in both hands. Hobbamock realized his goal immediately—to keep the musketeers on the right side of the formation from firing again. He was two steps behind Standish when the short captain speared the first one.

Hobbamock knifed one, spun away from a short sword. He grabbed the man's musket from him, landed a blow to the knee, and spun left again. He was behind them now, and these white men were *slow*.

Another volley boomed out, entirely from the left. Hobbamock heard running feet. He smashed a Frenchman in the back of the head, and then he and Standish finished the last one. One glance told the Pokanoket that the pikemen were butchering anyone who couldn't outrun them. Another glance showed him the French boats were landing a second group of soldiers.

"Standish! More soldiers!"

Standish swung the half-pike and laid out the capitaine's aide. "Allerton! Quickly! Men, take these matchlocks!"

"*Apprêtez-vos armes!*"

Hobbamock whirled and saw the dozen musketeers on the left had reloaded.

"*Joue!*"

Hobbamock felt rain on his face, and, for an instant, he thought the boom from above was thunder. When he saw the musketeers' line had been blown apart, he understood. The English had small cannons, what they called *patereros*, at the top of the stockade.

"Follow Hobbamock and finish them!" Standish ordered. He turned away to holler at a different group of men. "Stop! You cannot stop those pikemen yourselves! Women and children to those houses there! A few of you brace those doors from the inside! The rest of you men, pick up these matchlocks and fall in!"

The next few minutes were a blur. Hobbamock led a dozen Plymouth men in a charge against the remaining musketeers. In the end, they swarmed them under, but lost two of their own. He heard a ragged volley as Standish's townspeople fired into the pikemen. Bodies lay seemingly everywhere. Fifty more Frenchmen poured through the eastern gate.

Another paterero fired, spraying nails and broken bits of metal into the new arrivals. They drove forward stubbornly, trying to gain the door of the stockade. A second paterero struck down the back of the column, and then they were so close the cannons could not depress far enough to reach them.

But they were caught in a crossfire.

One volley crashed out from Standish's line. Hobbamock cared not for the manual of arms. "Shoot!" he ordered.

The ragged series of pops seemed almost pathetic, but it was fire from a third angle, and that broke the charge. Musketeers and pikemen withdrew. Not all the way to the gate; they took cover behind the last few houses.

Standish called to him.

"Hopkins, take charge." Hobbamock loped over to where the initial confrontation had taken place. *Did I just give Englishmen orders?*

It was sprinkling steadily now. "We are going to have to flee Plymouth," Myles Standish stated without preamble. "We have some twenty French firelocks. Perhaps ten of our own—if we can get to them. The pikemen from the first body will come for us some enough. The survivors of the second band and the whole of the third will make eighty men. We must get the women and children out into the woods."

"Why?" someone demanded.

The first French cannon fired.

"That is why," Edward Winslow stated. He held a cloth to where blood was dripping down his scalp. "They've cannon, bigger than ours."

"Make for Aquidneck Island," Standish ordered. "Move the wounded if you can, but do not delay everyone to await them lest all perish. The French *will* come to Duxbury and our other towns, and they *will* take or burn them. Gather everyone and flee. Governor Bradford?"

"Head injury." Winslow's voice was grim.

"Elder Brewster?"

Winslow shook his head sadly.

"He is with Keihtánit now," Hobbamock realized. "I will mourn him later."

"Hobbamock has the right of it," Standish stated. "Quickly now!"

As if to underscore his words, two booms sounded out in the bay. One cannonball thudded into the palisade. The other missed, either short or wide of its mark.

"Allerton!" Standish shouted at the stockade. "Send me your best assistant!"

The man emerged in seconds. "You and"—Standish turned and

pointed to several of the Plymouth men who now had muskets and then several who did not—"you men, come with me. Hobbamock, hold here."

"Where are they going?"

"The blockhouse," Hobbamock answered. "Allerton's man and the others to fire cannon back at the ship. Standish and those with muskets to keep those pikemen at bay. You, you, and you, pick up every pike here."

"Why?"

Hobbamock wiped rain from his brow and flicked his fingers at the man. "Because wet gunpowder does not burn."

The French ship continued firing, and it found the range. Cannonballs plunged into two houses. One cannon, then another, began firing back from the blockhouse up on the hill. But they were only four-pounders, and their crews were far from expert.

A servant boy ran up to Hobbamock. "Master Hobbamock, Master Winslow says he will have one hundred fifty ready in five minutes."

Hobbamock thanked him and wondered where Standish was. Then he realized he'd spoken in his own language. "Thank you."

Another messenger ran up. "Master Hobbamock! Master Hopkins says there are French with pikes outside the south gate!"

The French had another capitaine, Hobbamock realized, and he was a good one.

"Quick! Run toward the north gate! Do not get too close. Come back and tell me if the French are there, too."

As soon as the messenger was off, Hobbamock shouted up at the stockade. "Allerton! Allerton!"

A face looked over the edge.

Hobbamock pointed with both hands. "Pikes to either side! Aim your cannons!"

"They will withdraw out of sight!" Allerton protested.

The white man's way of war is complicated. But Hobbamock was a *pniese* and knew how to lure an enemy.

"The first time the ship's cannons hit the stockade, you must feign defeat! Load your cannons but wait."

"Yes, sir!"

If I survive this day, I shall make use of "Master" and "sir."

Gunfire sounded. The French musketeers were forming up. And there were more marching through the gate. Hobbamock understood. The new French capitaine had sent his pikes to block the north and south gates. He would simply drive forward with his musketeers. If the Plymouth men wanted to charge him, he would accept it. *Because it is a trap.*

A house one street over was hit, and this shot did considerable damage to the roof.

Hobbamock spread his musketeers out in pairs, holding the seven pikemen in reserve. "One man fire, and the other waits until he is half reloaded," he instructed.

The rain was light but steady now, and he was not surprised when two of the first four muskets did not fire.

The French ship finally found its mark, and a cannonball crashed into the stockade. It struck halfway up the wall and splintered the wood. No one was hurt by it. But it was a matter of time now.

Myles Standish ran up a couple minutes later.

"Hobbamock! What is the situation here?"

Hobbamock sketched the situation.

"We defeated those pikes," Standish stated. "But Edward's group must run at once."

A volley of musket fire kicked up dirt all around, and one of the Plymouth men went down.

Hobbamock heard a voice say, "John, get your mother and the rest of the family to safety." Then Francis Cooke took up the fallen man's musket and cartridge box.

"Pikes!" came the shout from atop the stockade.

"Well executed," Standish murmured. A double row of pikemen appeared at the north and south gates.

"I've two patereros laid on them to the south!" Allerton shouted down to them.

"Cooke, you men hold here," Standish ordered. "Pikes with me. Edward Winslow!"

"Captain Standish." Winslow hurried over. "It looks as though we are too late."

"You'll leave by the south gate. Start now. We will clear the street for you." Standish turned to Hobbamock.

"Well done. I could not ask for better. When we force the gate, run. Run for Duxbury."

"I will fight beside you," Hobbamock declared.

"You must survive to tell Massasoit Ousamequin what happened here. Sassacus, too, if he will listen. Tell them all the up-timer Chehab was right. We will hold as long as we can to give Edward's group time to escape."

Hobbamock nodded gravely. He and Standish clasped forearms.

"Warn Duxbury. Warn my family and the Aldens."

"I will see they reach safety."

Standish signaled Winslow, and those inhabitants of Plymouth he'd been able to gather started for the gate. It sucked the French pikemen in nicely, Hobbamock observed. Their own pikes—all seven of them—started toward them.

The French formation gave a great shout and came forward.

Two patereros boomed. One charge missed entirely and splattered into the palisade.

The other hit the formation dead center.

"Forward!" Standish ordered.

The French hurriedly dressed their formation, stepping over the dead and wounded. They came on with pikes lowered.

Plymouth's pikes faltered. But then Samuel Hopkins' musketeers fired from nearly point-blank range. Four Frenchmen went down.

"Charge!" Standish led the charge himself. He'd recovered his sword at some point. Standish evaded a pike, closed in, and slashed the man. He was on to the next.

Hobbamock rolled under a pair of pikes, knifed one, and made for the gate. A junior officer lunged at him with a sword.

A body flew into him from the side, knocking him to the ground. The other man took the blade.

Hobbamock scrambled to his feet and saw that it was Standish. Plymouth's captain came to his feet, too, his breastplate now bearing a long scrape. The French officer lunged again, and Standish parried.

"Run!"

Hobbamock ran. He looked back once, and saw the first townspeople emerging.

"Keihtánit, the Son, and the Holy Manitou protect thee, Myles," he whispered. Then he picked up his pace. Duxbury was nine miles away, and he wanted to be there in what the English called one hour.

Hobbamock lost track of time. He ran through the rain, and he was sure he had never run faster. Finally, he saw the first house ahead. He started shouting.

"The French are coming! The French attacked Plymouth town!"

Duxbury, Plymouth Plantations colony

Priscilla Alden was spinning and singing the hundredth Psalm. More precisely, she was teaching her oldest daughter Elisabeth, thirteen, a more advanced technique while Sarah, nine, played with little David.

The door opened. Joseph, ten, and Jonathan, five, burst into the house.

"Boys!"

"Mother, an Indian is running through town, shouting that the French attack!" Joseph delivered that news in a breathless voice.

"An Indian? A Pokanoket?" *I will discuss manners later. This could be important—or it could be folly.*

John, fourteen, came in, remembering to take off his hat and wipe his feet. "Mother, I think it's Hobbamock."

Priscilla rose at once and went to the door.

"See?" Jonathan asked.

"I do see an Indian at the Standishes. And Mistress Standish looks distressed, even from here." Priscilla raised her voice. "John, run to your father, and tell him to come quickly."

Young John took off like a shot.

"What is it, Mother?" Elisabeth asked. She came to her mother's side.

"Hobbamock is one of Massasoit's mightiest warriors and a wise advisor. The first year in Plymouth, Massasoit sent him to help us. Remain here with the younger children. Joseph, come with me."

With that, Priscilla Alden hurried toward the Standish house. As she drew closer, she realized that Barbara Standish was indeed in tears.

"Oh, Priscilla! Myles is dead!" she cried.

Priscilla gasped.

"He was not dead when he ordered me to run for Duxbury." The Indian delivered the words with a gravity that caused Priscilla to believe him.

"Hobbamock, what happened in Plymouth?" she asked.

"The French arrived—in four ships, all larger than the *Mayflower*. They landed in boats, fifty or so men each time. The capitaine of the first group said he would brook no dissent, and ordered everyone out of their houses. They were beginning to carry armloads of belongings out when a man came out of his house carrying a musket. A French soldier shot him. Elder Brewster stepped forward to try to stop it, and the capitaine ran him through."

Priscilla and Barbara both gasped.

"Then the battle started," Hobbamock continued. "Many died. Men who survived your first winter here. Women and children, too.

"Edward Winslow gathered all he could find. Myles ordered him to make for Aquidneck Island. Myles, Samuel Hopkins, Francis Cooke, and others forced a way out for them. They were still fighting. Myles ordered me to warn you to flee Duxbury before the French come here."

Other townspeople were beginning to gather around now. Priscilla looked for her husband John and saw him and Young John coming at a run.

"Hobbamock!" John Alden cried. "Greetings! What brings you to Duxbury?"

"The French have attacked Plymouth town." Hobbamock repeated what he'd just said.

"Might the Lord give us victory?" John asked.

"It seems unlikely. We defeated the first band, pushed back the second, but the third came from three directions. Isaac Allerton still fired the cannons on the stockade."

"We must march to Plymouth's relief!" one of the Duxbury men cried out. His words were met with a rumble of approval.

Alden raised a hand to quiet the crowd. "What did Myles say?" he asked Hobbamock.

"That Plymouth was lost, and Duxbury and the other towns, too. He commanded me to tell you to flee to Aquidneck Island."

"Could we fight the French?"

Hobbamock was shaking his head before Alden finished asking the question. "No. Not now. They would have taken us at the first rush but we were in among them. Powder and shot for the small cannons were at hand. Governor Bradford ordered the platform clear and the guns unloaded, and Myles obeyed. But he must have made private plans with Allerton, should an attack come to pass." He paused. "I saw women and children killed."

"We've no cannons or patereros here," Alden noted. "Nor a palisade. We must not tarry. We leave for Aquidneck within the hour. If the situation changes, we can return."

Alden pointed to two young men.

"Lads, you are single, fast, and sober-minded. Run to Marsh-field, and then on to Scituate. Tell them to evacuate and meet at Aquidneck. Bring their guns, their seed, as much food as they can carry. Gather your own and be on your way. Meet us at Aquidneck."

The two young men nodded and left immediately.

"I will guide you as far as I can," Hobbamock stated. "But I must warn Massasoit Ousamequin."

"Of course," Alden agreed. He raised his voice. "What I told the lads. Gather your guns, seed, food, and anything you might carry. But it is several days' journey."

"The cows?" The question came from the back of the crowd.

"Aye, cows and sheep and goats, too. We will not be traveling fast. Warn every house. Tell everyone come, but if they choose to stay, do not get caught with them. Now go!"

Alden turned to his wife and Barbara Standish. "I would rather march on Plymouth now, but it would be the wrong decision."

Hobbamock nodded his agreement. "The capitaine who came with the third band of Frenchmen is a skilled soldier. You would need every man and still might not defeat him because he could set his fourth band in ambush for you. Some *must* guard the women and children until they are far enough to sunset that a French scout cannot overtake them." He named a Pokanoket village. "Nemasket."

"That is wisdom." John Alden turned to his wife. "Dearest, tell young John what he and Elisabeth should direct the other children to gather."

"You mean for me to stay with Barbara for a while. Will you be helping the Standishes, too?"

"No," John told his wife. "I will stop William Holmes from charging off to Plymouth with men who are needed here."

Roughly an hour later

With the assistance of Hobbamock and George Soule, John Alden restrained William Holmes and a band of like-minded men from marching to Plymouth town.

"Standish and the others fight to give you time," Hobbamock stated flatly. "Not so you are slaughtered, too."

Priscilla helped the Standish family pack for the journey. Other women spelled her so that she could return to the Alden household where young John and Elisabeth were doing their best.

By the time men started shouting for the inhabitants of Duxbury to assemble, the Aldens were more or less ready. They'd carry what they could. Young John was leading their cow, Elisabeth held David, and Joseph, Jonathan, and Sarah each had something to carry. Priscilla ran her hand over the spinning wheel, regretting that she had to leave it behind. Then she made a final check of the house, hefted her own burden, and walked out the door. The rain had settled into a light mist.

"Children, we will travel with the Standishes. Be a comfort to them," she told her children.

Her husband had the heaviest pack on his back and carried his old matchlock musket. He was trying to get the townspeople moving. Some of them wanted to begin with prayer—*long* prayers.

Hobbamock rolled his eyes. He remembered what he'd prayed for Standish and spoke up loudly. "Keihtánit, the Son, and the Holy Manitou protect us." Then he started walking.

John Alden stepped up to a man who'd about choked at that prayer. "Follow that Pokanoket. You may teach him doctrine along the way."

Most, but not all, of the inhabitants of Duxbury went with them. Hobbamock and John Alden took the lead. But after their first break, Alden let the whole column pass by. He grouped households together into bands numbering a couple of dozen. "Count all your members each time we stop and each time we set out," he instructed.

Priscilla smiled to herself, very proud of her husband. But by the second stop, she was becoming worn—not from the walk itself but because the younger children were growing tired and cranky.

They stopped about sunset and made camp for the night. Alden joined his family once all the stragglers had arrived.

"I am sorry to be late."

Priscilla waved it away. "We have a fire to cook and to dry us. How far is this village Nemasket? Will we reach it tomorrow?"

"About fifteen miles from Plymouth," John told her. "Somewhat more from Duxbury. We should reach it tomorrow. I do not think we should impose on Nemasket longer than one night. It is twice or even thrice as far from there to Aquidneck."

"Do you think anyone will join us from Plymouth town?" Priscilla asked softly.

"I pray so. Hobbamock believes that Edward's band escaped."

"And Myles?"

John lowered his voice. "I believe Myles and Isaac resolved to fight to the last to gain time for Edward and for us."

Priscilla nodded. She did not trust her voice just now, and she did not want tears where Barbara Standish might see them.

"Hobbamock will ask the Pokanoket in Nemasket to send out scouts," John continued. "They may find Edward's band." He rose. "I must organize the watches."

Priscilla realized something. "John, tomorrow is the Sabbath."

Her husband looked troubled. "Aye, 'tis. We've a dozen or so miles to Nemasket. That will trouble some, but we dare not remain here else our flight be in vain."

The watch kept the fires burning for warmth. With many children and the occasional cow lowing and sheep baaing, their camp was already conspicuous. Having fires lit wasn't going to make them any more obvious than they already were. Warmth was more important on this damp night.

A forest, Plymouth Colony
Sunday, May 10, 1637

Priscilla awoke (again) when little David awoke with the dawn. Another few nights of this, and she knew she'd begin to look back fondly on the months spent in the cramped Mayflower. She resolutely set that thought aside. She'd not think just now of how much she missed her parents and brother who had all died that first terrible winter. That was...half her life ago, she realized. Since then, she and John had made a life first in Plymouth town and then, after the division of land, in Duxbury. It hurt to give up everything they'd built. They were "strangers and pilgrims on the earth" again.

Priscilla thought the writer of Hebrews probably meant that the Old Testament believers were both strangers and pilgrims. Here, though, in Plymouth Colony, Strangers and Pilgrims were two different groups, as they soon proved this Sabbath morning.

The Strangers were, by and large, Anglican. They tended to be less observant than the Pilgrims.

"Mother?" Elisabeth asked. "Did Jesus not journey through the fields on the Sabbath and His disciples pick grain?"

Of course, there was a lull in conversation just then, and the thirteen-year-old's voice carried. Several Pilgrims shot her disapproving glances.

Priscilla returned their gazes. Elisabeth had a point, a good one.

"Smoke! Smoke!"

Everyone looked for whomever was shouting. Eleven-year-old Alexander Standish slid partway down a nearby tree trunk and dropped to the ground.

"There's smoke coming from the east!" he announced.

"Plymouth town." John Alden pointed to one of the well-respected men. "Please lead us in prayer. We will set out and then pause at noon to worship the Lord."

Afterwards, Priscilla murmured to her husband, "That was well done."

John's eyes warmed, losing their worried look for a few moments.

"How do you and the children fare?"

"We will persevere."

By afternoon, Priscilla Alden was less sure of that. They had all hoped—perhaps unreasonably—to encounter survivors from Plymouth. As the day passed with nothing but more trees, and the occasional clearing and small brook, the adults grew fretful. The children grew tired, and the two fed one another.

John set William Holmes and the men following him as their rear guard. Each time they stopped, a man or boy climbed a tree. By now, they could no longer see any smoke from Plymouth town.

It was almost sunset when someone hailed the column. Hobbamock answered in Wampanoag. After a couple of minutes, the other Wampanoag and Hobbamock were deep in conversation. When the Alden and Standish families caught up, Priscilla suddenly realized that John had had more than one reason to make Holmes and his men the rear guard.

The Wampanoag of Nemasket came out to greet the refugees of Duxbury. But they indicated that they should camp outside the village.

John Alden nodded vigorously when Hobbamock translated that. They had exchanged gifts, but the group from Duxbury was at least half the size of the Wampanoag village.

Later, as Priscilla was settling the children to bed, Joseph asked, "Do the Indians not like us?"

Priscilla bit her lip. "Joseph, there are many Indians. Plymouth Colony is friendly with some and less so with others. Sometimes, both we and the Indians have made bad decisions. Nemasket is one of the places that happened, and this village does not trust us."

"But they should," Joseph insisted.

Nemasket, Wampanoag Confederation (up-time Middleborough, Massachusetts) Monday, May 11, 1637

In the morning, more Wampanoag came to their camp.

"They have given us food," John told Priscilla. "We have given them some, too."

She nodded her understanding.

"More importantly, they have sent scouts east, toward Plymouth town. I am torn whether to await their return this evening or press onward toward Aquidneck."

Priscilla did not know which was more important, so she said nothing, and let John work it out himself.

"If Edward and his band are nearby, the Wampanoag will find them and direct them here. If he is pursued by the French, uniting our band with his adds men of fighting age but slows the whole. Hobbamock is most anxious to report to Massasoit Ousamequin, who will certainly send men in search of Edward if those of Nemasket do not find him first." John looked up. "It would lift our hearts to meet Edward's band, but every other reason says we should move on today. If they indeed escaped, we will meet at Aquidneck if not before."

Priscilla put a hand on his arm. "I will inform the women. John, I know you do not seek to lead, but you do it well."

John gave her a brief smile.

As they resumed their journey, the Wampanoag of Nemasket saw them off, a few children watching them curiously. Suddenly, Jonathan Alden broke away and ran up to a Wampanoag boy who looked like he was also about five years old. Jonathan hugged him.

"Friends?"

The Wampanoag boy said something that might have been "*Nétop.*"

Priscilla spotted the concerned-looking Wampanoag woman who had to be the boy's mother. They exchanged tentative smiles.

Throughout the day, Priscilla took strength from that incident and from the look in her husband's eyes that morning. The third day's journey was even harder. They took turns carrying David Alden and Josiah and Charles Standish. Barbara was fraying, and Priscilla increasingly found herself keeping track of twelve children.

They made camp in a clearing that night. Many of the younger children were worn out and cried at every small provocation. Many of the adults were equally worn out and short-tempered as well. Priscilla recognized the problem, but she had her hands full—usually quite literally. Somehow, they got the littlest changed, food cooked, and everyone bedded down.

John came by as she and the oldest children were cleaning up. He looked as tired as she felt.

"John, take a moment to eat," she urged.

"Thank you, dearest. I have been trying to assure everyone." He sighed. "Tempers are short. It was the right decision to press on today. One more day, and we should reach Montaup, perhaps even Aquidneck. I know not how to get there, but Hobbamock does. He says that Massasoit Ousamequin's men will encounter us on the morrow."

Once he had eaten, John checked the watch, and then all but fell on his blanket. Priscilla snuggled close and pulled her blanket over both of them.

A clearing, Wampanoag Confederation
Tuesday, May 12, 1637

Enough young children were up at dawn that most of the other Duxbury folk were awakened. A few still slept deeply. John Alden was up and circling the camp, though he was far from fully alert himself. He saw the state of the watch—awake but not truly alert—and gave thanks he'd not given the order to tarry at Nemasket another day. If a French patrol had happened across them . . .

"One more day, and you can rest at Montaup," came Hobbamock's voice. "You have pushed on hard."

"Thank you, Hobbamock. If not for your guiding . . ."

Hobbamock completed the circuit of the camp with John.

They arrived back where the Aldens and Standishes were to find Priscilla comforting Barbara Standish. After a few minutes, Priscilla came over to John and explained quietly. "Loara asked if we could all go home today. She is five. She doesn't understand."

John bowed his head and held his wife for a few minutes. Then he took a deep breath and got them started on that day's journey.

About noon, Hobbamock signaled a halt. He gave an odd whistle, and suddenly there were a lot more Wampanoag just ahead of them.

John couldn't understand them, but from the occasional English word, he realized the other Wampanoag had asked Hobbamock what had happened.

One Wampanoag stepped forward, and the others immediately made way for him. His face was painted a darker red than the others', and he wore a necklace of white beads. Beyond that, nothing distinguished him from the others.

"Massasoit Ousamequin!"

A serious but fast conversation between Massasoit Ousamequin and Hobbamock followed. Then the sachem turned to John Alden.

"Edward . . . danger?"

John nodded. "Yes."

"We find him. You go with Hobbamock. Sowams, not Aquidneck. Food. Safety."

"Thank you."

"Wampanoag . . . Plymouth . . . nétop. I go find Edward."

Massasoit Ousamequin and most of the other Wampanoags strode east. John watched them go, saw how they split into three groups, weapons at the ready.

"Come," Hobbamock said.

It was another long, exhausting day. But one worry was gone. The French would not overtake them without encountering the Wampanoag first. They reached Sowams in good order while there was still daylight. Wampanoag women were waiting for them and showed them where to camp.

Priscilla Alden worked alongside Pokanoket women preparing the camp and a meal.

"They expect you to make a speech," Priscilla prompted John.

He gave her a rueful look. "I know little of what to say."

But he stood. "We from Duxbury thank the Pokanoket of

the Wampanoag for your hospitality, for coming to our rescue again. May this day be a celebration of deliverance and friendship between us."

Heads nodded in approval.

Sowams (up-time Bristol, Rhode Island)
Thursday, May 14

"They're coming!"

Priscilla shook her head. Somehow the children could already communicate with the Wampanoag children. It might be slow and halting, but they were well ahead of the adults.

"Who is coming, Joseph?"

"Massasoit and his warriors and more Englishmen."

"Well done."

Priscilla quickly found John and Hobbamock. They reached Sowams just as a long, ragged column began to emerge from the forest. Massasoit Ousamequin and Edward Winslow were at its head.

"Edward!" John and Priscilla rushed up to him.

"John and Priscilla Alden! How do you happen to be here?"

"Hobbamock warned us. Most of Duxbury is here."

"Thank the Lord," Winslow murmured. "Some of us are wounded, and we've had little to eat since fleeing Plymouth."

"We will have food ready in a few minutes," Priscilla promised.

"Myles?" John's question was quiet.

Edward Winslow shook his head. "When I last saw Myles, he and Samuel Hopkins and Francis Cooke still held the line, but the French pressed them hard. One of Allerton's patereros fired for a while, but then we saw the stockade in flames."

Meanwhile, Massasoit Ousamequin spoke to several of his warriors.

"Tell the other tribes what has happened." He pointed to each in turn, assigning a particular tribe. Then he pointed to the last two. "Tell Sassacus. Tell the Dutch."

Grantville, State of Thuringia-Franconia, USE
Sunday, May 24, 1637

Nona Dobbs was spending a lazy Sunday evening in front of the television. She'd graduated from high school yesterday, and tomorrow was the sixth anniversary of the Ring of Fire. The news was mostly full of speculation about the upcoming elections, but once that was finally over, she could watch the Sunday night movie.

Someone actually dashed onto the set to hand the anchor a story. Nona was amused until the woman glanced it over and visibly paled.

"A radio transmission from North America has been received in the Kingdom of the Low Countries. A French flotilla landed in Massachusetts Bay in April and took control of Boston and Salem. On May 9, it arrived in Plymouth Colony. French troops entered Plymouth town. Fighting broke out immediately. Many were killed by French troops. Parts of Plymouth were on fire. Governor Bradford is missing. Captain Myles Standish was last seen in command of men holding the south gate open so that the residents of Plymouth could escape. At least two groups of Pilgrims had reached safety by the time this report was sent."

Nona gasped. Then she ran for the phone.

"Alicia? Did you see the news?" Nona quickly related the story. "We have to do something!"

Grantville, SoTF, USE
Monday, May 25, 1637

The *Times* carried Ring of Fire Day as its headline story, but "Battle in Plymouth" was also above the fold. The *Freie Presse* didn't have Plymouth on the front page at all. But the *Daily News'* secondary headline was "Plymouth Massacre."

It was weird, Nona thought. Down-timers had been through a lot of battles and massacres in the past twenty years. One more, and this one far away in North America, made little difference to them. She understood why. And there were up-timers who, after six years, were pretty well-adapted and understood that history wasn't going to replay itself.

But there were also those who studied history and knew the significance of Plymouth. Grantville's Committee of Correspondence was angry. Some of the older up-timers were furious. She'd already seen one pamphlet broadside today whose headline read REMEMBER PLYMOUTH!

"I can't believe they killed the *Pilgrims!*" she hissed to Alicia as they made their way through the crowded streets.

"I know! But the papers say there are survivors."

"Oh! They'll need help. Food, shelter...Is there a way to send help?"

Alicia pointed. "I see Mayor Carstairs. I bet she'd know."

They hurried over.

"Mayor Carstairs?" Alicia was tentative at first.

"What can I do for you, girls?"

"Everyone remembers what they were doing when the Ring of Fire happened," Alicia said. "Some of the older folks remember the night the Gulf War started, or the *Challenger*, or the Kennedy assassination, or Pearl Harbor."

Liz Carstairs nodded.

"We heard about Plymouth yesterday," Nona said. "How can we help?"

Long Island Sound
Tuesday, August 18, 1637

The *Griffin* was nine weeks out of Hamburg, to the day, when the lookout spotted the Connecticut River. Captain Gallop had been beside the tiller since they entered Long Island Sound. He passed his orders in a calm voice, suppressing the tension he felt.

They'd made a fast passage. His greatest worry had been encountering French ships, especially here in Long Island Sound. As they drew closer, it became clear to all why the *Griffin* had not seen any French ships. They had already come and gone. Fort Sovereignty was a charred ruin.

He considered turning back, or at least diverting elsewhere. But he was under contract. The *Griffin* had sailed from England to Boston each year since 1633. Each year, fewer Puritans decided to remove themselves to Massachusetts. This year, to fill out the complement of passengers, he'd sailed to the Low Countries to see if any more of the Leiden community wished to go to Plymouth.

Instead, he'd received a well-paying charter to load goods in Hamburg and take them to the mouth of the Connecticut River. Half the offer came in hard currency up front and very good charts indeed. So, the *Griffin* would unload, quickly, and be off back to Europe again before the French took notice.

Dorchester (up-time Windsor, Connecticut)
Friday, August 21, 1637

Priscilla Alden hummed to herself as she prepared dinner. It was a more substantial dinner than they'd become accustomed to. Messengers had come from Sovereignty earlier in the afternoon with news that a ship had arrived. She was the *Griffin*, which had brought Puritans to Massachusetts Bay each of the last four years. But this year she carried mostly food, and much of that food was on its way to Dorchester. That meant they'd survive and not starve.

She thanked God for the good news. Since fleeing Plymouth Colony, their lives had been filled with wild swings from mountaintops of blessing to valleys of despair and back again.

Other bands of Pilgrims from Marshfield and Scituate, and even a number of Puritans from Massachusetts Bay, had arrived at Aquidneck in May. Some had wanted to plant crops on Aquidneck Island, but the area was becoming overcrowded and taxing the ability of Sowams and Montaup to provide for them. Moreover, it was too close to Plymouth.

Massasoit's warriors had kept Plymouth town under observation. The stockade and the blockhouse were gone, presumably burned, for the smell of smoke still clung to the town. Under cover of night, they'd approached a patch of turned earth outside the palisade and found it was a mass grave. If the Wampanoags' estimates were accurate, anyone who had not fled Plymouth with Edward Winslow's band was dead.

John, Edward Winslow, Hobbamock, and Massasoit Ousamequin all felt that the Pokanoket would be safe enough by themselves, but if the French learned of the gathering of a few hundred Europeans, they would certainly try to attack. Moreover, the Narragansett were looking at any European activity on Aquidneck Island very suspiciously. So, they had sent envoys to the Connecticut River towns, who had invited them to settle there. John had volunteered the Duxbury band to go first.

It had been another long, difficult journey through the forests. Not fearing pursuit, they'd moved more slowly. Still, it was hard on small children. They'd veered too far north.

And then Robert had found them. He hadn't said much about himself, but John and Priscilla thought him a Puritan. He'd gotten them back on course, and they'd arrived at Dorchester safely.

At that point, the leaders of the river towns had sent fishing boats to Sowams. It had taken multiple trips, but they'd brought all the Pilgrims and Puritans in the vicinity of Sowams to the Connecticut River Valley.

The French had seen them. The Sovereignty men thought a ship they'd glimpsed off Block Island was one of the French flotilla. In July, several French ships appeared in Long Island Sound. They'd bombarded Fort Sovereignty, doing heavy damage. Then they'd landed troops. Most of the inhabitants of Sovereignty had fled.

The French force—barely a hundred men—had started to push up the Connecticut Valley. But one of the men from Sovereignty, Colonel George Fenwick, had rallied Puritans, Pilgrims, and even Dutch from the trading post on the river. Sassacus, Uncas, and Wequash Cook had arrived with Pequots, Mohegans, and Niantics. No one fully trusted each other, but after some light skirmishing, the French had turned back to their ships.

When the inhabitants of Sovereignty returned, they found the charred ruins of the fort and village—and the bodies of those who hadn't escaped. They'd been executed.

Some had talked of fleeing further, but New Netherlands was to the west. They had nowhere to go. And their crops were in the ground. They couldn't flee. The arrival of the *Griffin* changed all that. Messengers had reached Dorchester earlier in the day, and already rumors were flying. Some of the more outlandish ones even said the ship carried weapons.

"Mother!" Young John stuck his head in the door. "Father asks if you would come to Council Hall."

Priscilla looked surprised. "Of course. John, help Elisabeth prepare supper. If I am delayed, please feed everyone."

"Yes, Mother."

Council Hall was what they'd taken to calling a building in the center of Dorchester where representatives of the river towns and the various bands of refugees met. There was an open area nearby where the Indians were currently meeting.

"Dorchester is neutral ground," John had explained. "Massasoit Ousamequin, Sassacus, and others can talk here, and no one has the advantage."

As soon as she entered the building, John and another man approached. John introduced him as one of the messengers from Sovereignty.

"Goodwife Alden, the *Griffin* carried packages. Some of them are addressed to leading men like Edward Winslow and John Winthrop. Others are addressed to Indians." The messenger mangled the names, but Priscilla understood whom he meant. Massasoit Ousamequin, Sassacus, Samoset, Uncas.

"And there's one for you. Priscilla Alden."

"Why?" Priscilla asked.

The messenger shrugged.

Priscilla looked to John. He shrugged, too. She carried the package to a table and carefully pried the seal away, then opened it. It was full of booklets, with a letter on top.

Dear Priscilla Alden,

You don't know me, but I wrote a report about you in school. My name is Nona Dobbs. I am eighteen years old and an up-timer. My friend Alicia and I will always remember what we were doing when the Ring of Fire happened, and we'll always remember where we were when we heard Plymouth had been attacked. We hope you and John and your kids escaped from Plymouth.

Priscilla looked up at John in confusion. Why did up-timers know their names? But yet, these two girls seemed to think they lived in Plymouth town.

We figure you aren't just sitting at your spinning wheel.

Priscilla's eyes widened. How did they know *that*?

That's in the poem, "The Courtship of Miles Standish." It's by Henry Wadsworth Longfellow, who was one of your descendants in our timeline. But according to the poem, you're a perceptive lady, and we thought at least one of these packets should go to a woman.

Priscilla read their description of "The Courtship of Miles Standish" and didn't know whether to be indignant or amused. John was reading over her shoulder, and he laughed. She glared up at him.

"Have you not been urging me to speak up all summer?"

John's innocent tone was too much, and Priscilla giggled.

Once she had herself under control, Priscilla pointed to the letter. "John, we seem to be part of their history. Plymouth is a place of import to them."

Please read the booklets and pass them around.

Priscilla and John examined the stack. *Farming Methods. Sanitation. Medicine. Pilgrims, Puritans, and Colonial History. A Short History of the Up-Time United States of America. The Native Americans. The Ring of Fire. The Gospel and Missions. Interpreting the Holy Scriptures. The Salem Witch Trials.*
Ten booklets.

Most of these are research papers from the State Library. We wrote The Gospel and Missions. *Some friends of ours wrote* Interpreting the Holy Scriptures.
We cannot tell you what to do. We are not there. Alicia and I hope to be, someday. But there's something in The Gospel and Missions *you need to show the other Pilgrims—and any Puritans you meet.*
When Protestant churches started sending out missionaries all over the world, the missionaries from Europe and America often stayed in charge of the new congregations for as long as they were there. So when the missionaries got killed or expelled, the congregations foundered. Up-time, some were starting to emphasize indigenous leadership, that missionaries should teach local leaders, like Paul did. Except that we didn't start doing that because that's what Paul did. We did it because that's how the Special Forces operated, and we saw that it worked. It seems to us that this ought to be an important principle in how Europeans interact with the Native American tribes. You can see from the booklets that we didn't do a good job of that in our timeline. The Native Americans are people. They're adults. They just see the world differently.
We were told that anything we sent you had to be ready very quickly. We couldn't find much about the Special Forces in the time we had. But we included a few pages of information we found at almost the last minute.
We're praying for you. So is the prayer watch. The Anabaptists who have come to Grantville take one-hour

shifts so that all day and all night someone is praying.
You are on their list.

Nona Dobbs
Alicia Rice

Priscilla turned so that she could look up at John.

"Most remarkable."

"Yes. Edward's packet held these same ten booklets. So did Thomas Hooker's. Another was intended for John Winthrop, who is still in Massachusetts Bay. We—the representatives of the towns and Massachusetts and Plymouth bands—have agreed his son who is governor of Sovereignty Colony ought to open it. It was the same as the others. Moreover, the messengers carried packages for several Indians. I venture theirs are the same. Each package has a short letter, but not like yours."

Priscilla considered that for a moment and then set the letter aside. The next sheet bore a title at the top:

Rogers' Rangers Standing Orders

Priscilla read the page, and John continued to read over her shoulder.

"This appears to be a collection of military proverbs," she observed. She set it aside as well.

The next two pages were... different.

"This appears to be written in English, but I understand little of it," she confessed.

John reached out and tapped the page with the orders. "This is from their world, but a time near ours. The circumstances are different, but one may understand it." His finger tapped the other pages. "This must be later. It is what the girls who wrote the letter to you mean when they saw that the Church of their day began to imitate how this force conducted itself." He shook his head. "I have no idea if it works."

"How they treated those they trained?" Priscilla asked. At his nod, she suggested, "Go and ask Hobbamock what he thinks."

She saw that look in his eyes again as he left.

Priscilla looked down again to see that there was one last page. She read it and found her eyes were watering.

✧   ✧   ✧

John Alden approached Hobbamock during a break in the tribes' discussions.

"John Alden."

"Hobbamock."

"Have you a bundle of books, too?" Hobbamock swept his arm around. The gesture encompassed several stacks of booklets that lay on blankets.

"Yes. May I?" At Hobbamock's nod, Alden stepped closer and peered down at the nearest booklets. *The Native Americans* was on top, with *Pilgrims, Puritans, and Colonial History* laying askew beneath it.

John straightened. "Yes, it looks like the same set of ten booklets. That is why I am here. Did any of you receive a letter along with them?"

In answer, Hobbamock picked up a single folded sheet of paper and handed it to Alden, who opened it and read.

"The others are like it," Hobbamock told him. "We suspect that the Ring of Fire people sent the letters to the people their stories speak about. Massasoit Ousamequin, Sassacus, Samoset, Uncas."

John thought about how to respond to that. "I am certain they did not mean to slight anyone else."

Hobbamock laughed. "Oh, most of us understand that. A few of us were either proud or jealous at first until one of your English lads read the letter to Uncas aloud. They said plainly that they know some of their stories about him are wrong. It is no surprise that they do not know many of us."

"Did your packages contain anything else?" Alden's voice was almost urgent.

"Nay. Each had a letter to the individual. All four suggested the tribes form a league or confederation." Hobbamock shrugged. "We were already discussing how that might be done."

"Ours—I have seen the letters to Edward Winslow and John Winthrop—caution us to 'treat the Native Americans better this time' and 'learn from our mistakes.'" Alden frowned. "They say nothing about an alliance of tribes."

"Truly? So they did not favor you?"

"Truly," Alden confirmed. "I think it plain to all here that we must work together lest the French conquer us one by one."

Hobbamock nodded emphatically.

"One of the packets came to Priscilla," John stated. He held up the letter and began reading. Hobbamock listened with interest. When John started reading *Rogers' Rangers Standing Orders*, he started snickering. As John kept reading, Hobbamock laughed out loud and eventually beckoned another Native American over.

"Samoset," he managed. "You must hear this. John, please read these orders again."

Alden complied. By the time he was done, Samoset was all but doubled over with laughter.

"What?" John asked.

"Any of our warriors could have said this," Samoset finally explained. "We have heard of the wars in Europe. Is this not how white men fight?"

"No," John told him. "It is not. Hobbamock described how the French fought at Plymouth."

Samoset's eyes widened. "I thought that was because they were inside Plymouth town. They would do the same in the forest?"

"Aye. But there is more here." Alden began reading the pages about the Special Forces.

Partway through, Hobbamock stopped him with an upraised hand. "John, you must read this to the sachems." He looked at Samoset. "You hear what they intend, do you not?"

Samoset nodded. "I believe so. I will find the sachems."

Hobbamock looked to Alden. "Please summon Edward Winslow, John Winthrop the younger, George Fenwick, and William Holmes."

Monday, August 24
Dorchester

Food from *Griffin* began to arrive three days later. With it came five rectangular wooden crates, about six feet long, two feet across, and a foot deep. Two were labeled PILGRIMS-PURITANS-CONNECTICUT. The other three were labeled ALGONQUIAN CONFEDERATION. A smaller square crate accompanied each.

All were opened carefully. The most outlandish rumors of *Griffin*'s cargo were true. Each crate held ten firearms and instructions. These were not matchlocks nor flintlocks. They were something called *shotguns*, and each had a single moving part. The barrel slammed back against the rest of it and fired the shell. Each barrel had a leather handgrip fitted around it and was attached to the rest of the weapon by a strip of leather.

Naturally, people got upset. Some of the Pilgrims, William Holmes among them, didn't like the fact that the Indians had more shotguns than the English. Sassacus realized very quickly that the supply of shotgun shells was finite.

"Hear my words!" John Alden shouted down the growing hubbub. "Hear my words!"

He had enough respect among Englishman and Native American alike that most quieted down.

"I have read to the tribes and to all the varied English the letter to my wife Priscilla Alden." Alden pointed at the colonists' crates with one forefinger and at the tribes' crates with the other. "This is what the letter talks about. They do not order us about. They expect us to do the right thing."

"Like parents," William Holmes muttered. Several Pilgrims and Puritans laughed. Once the remark was translated, so did the Native Americans.

"I hear," Massasoit Ousamequin said into the pause that followed the laughter. "Your twenty guns are not enough to face the French. Our thirty are not enough. If we do not unite, three for each tribe? Three warriors, powerful for a day. If we unite, powerful for many days, guns or no guns."

"With all fifty we could attack the French."

Alden shook his head. Holmes didn't understand yet.

"No," Hobbamock stated. "I saw how the French fought in Plymouth town. So did Edward. That is not what the Ring of Fire sent us. The up-timers sent us the story of their men who fought like we do. Their girls write of sharing their God but us keeping our ways and manner of dress. I do not think they ask us to fight a great battle but to fight our way."

Everyone considered that for a few moments.

"You leave something out," Sassacus said. "They write words that say if they send more shotguns, they will send some to the Haudenosaunee as well."

"We can make more," George Fenwick blurted out.

"What?"

"I showed one to our blacksmith. He said that now he has seen it, he can make more. Maybe not as fine, but serviceable."

Sassacus waited for the translation.

"We need blacksmiths," the Pequot sachem declared.

John Alden sensed this was a turning point, the last point where the English could choose to exert control.

"Send men who want to learn to work metal," Edward Winslow offered.

Sassacus shook his head. Hobbamock translated. "He says it is properly women's work."

The Pilgrims and Puritans were dumbfounded.

Massasoit Ousamequin stood. "Let us decide whom we send. Gunpowder."

"That is a problem for us, too," Winslow agreed. "We can make small amounts, but it is not very good gunpowder."

The council descended into details, from *Will we?* to *How will we?*

Dorchester
Monday, August 31, 1637

A week later, the Algonquians and the colonists sent the team forth: the Massachusett sachem Kuchamakin, Wequash Cook of the Niantic, Hobbamock of the Wampanoag, the Abenaki sagamore Samoset, a Narragansett, a Pequot, a Mohican, a Mohegan, a Puritan, a man from Dorchester, and—and John Alden.

Priscilla was not happy about that. At all.

On the other hand, one of the team's goals was to make sure that any Pilgrim or Puritan still in Plymouth or Massachusetts Bay who wanted to reach the river towns could do so. They doubted the French would simply let them into the towns to tell everyone that—or let everyone leave. But Priscilla had found something in *A Short History of the Up-Time United States of America*. In their world, word had been passed by means of song to African slaves who wanted to escape slavery. One of the songs was included. Priscilla had no idea what the tune was supposed to be, but she had rewritten the words.

Samoset and Hobbamock were chanting them now.

> *When the Hebrew month starts and the first owl calls,*
> > *Carry your drinking gourd.*
> *Band of twelve waiting to lead you on to Canaan,*
> > *Carry your drinking gourd.*

Hold it off to your right and journey on,
*   Carry your drinking gourd,*
Go with the wind that parted the Red Sea.
*   Carry your drinking gourd,*
Band of twelve waiting to lead you on to Canaan,
*   Carry your drinking gourd.*
On to William and down the tidal river,
*   Away from your drinking gourd.*

Holding the Big Dipper on their right as they journeyed west should bring them to the team. If they missed them, continuing west to William Pynchon's Agawam Plantation on the Connecticut River and then following the river south would bring them to relative safety in the river towns.

John left the other men and came over to Priscilla and the children. He embraced each of them.

"Can we come?" ten-year-old Joseph asked.

"No. We go to scout and find any other English who might join us here. Children, obey your mother, you hear?"

A chorus of ayes answered. Priscilla and John traded an amused look.

"Be careful, John," she told him.

"I will. Worry not."

Priscilla forced a smile. *Easier said than done.*

Hobbamock called. John kissed Priscilla and turned to join the other men.

Priscilla remembered the last page in her packet. It was a second letter she hadn't shown anyone but John.

Dear Priscilla Alden,

*   If I were in your place, I would wonder if I could trust all this information. Alicia Rice and Nona Dobbs are fine, God-fearing young women. They put this together as soon as they heard about Plymouth. They have been told that there is a way to get all this to you, that it will be included with some other things being sent to help you.*

*   If you are there, if you made it out, I suppose your people are at war. So are mine. My husband is with our army. It's the fourth time he has been away. It is hard. On him, on me, on the children. "For our struggle is not*

against flesh and blood, but against the rulers, against the powers, against the world forces of this darkness, against the spiritual forces of wickedness in the heavenly places." (Eph 6:12)

The United States of Europe is at war with the Ottoman Empire, Poland, and Spain. So we cannot send whole armies. But we're sending what we can. We remember Plymouth.

Kathy Sue Burroughs

I Will Walk This Path Again

John Deakins

1

Grantville texts knew a great deal about many things, but they knew nothing about butterflies. The searing storm over the Sahara's Massif de l'Aïr rolled down its slopes and raced toward the Atlantic, but some distant air-pressure fluctuation caused a sand dune in its path to slip. That stole only a pinch of the wind's energy, but enough.

It nursed at the warm ocean's breast off Africa. Any watcher from space would have seen it swell into a hurricane. In the year 1635, however, there were no human watchers in space. Offspring of desert heat and warm water, it should have blossomed hugely, and it did grow, only a trifle stunted. It would never have been a Category 5, but its destiny should have been to spread its cloudy wings into a Category 3 hurricane. It was meant to own a name—The Great Colonial Hurricane of 1635—a contender among champion storms, but for that one sand dune...

It lacked that final strength to slam Long Island and to rake New England with destroying, windy fingers. Its unstoppable breath should have killed, toppled forests, and sent ships to watery graves. Instead, the cooler Atlantic waters turned it toward New Jersey's thinly settled shore. It would have to be satisfied with raining millions of gallons onto the Hudson Valley, dragging its tattered skirts across land, dying slowly, clawing toward the parent

221

ocean. It was still a storm, but it didn't send humans fleeing in terror: only hunching their shoulders against the downpour, eyeing swollen rivers, and frowning skyward.

It could expect resurrection. The African Sahara had grown no cooler; its mountains were no less steep; its hostility to humanity remained unweakened. Warm equatorial waters continued to nurse its countless siblings, but in that year, it could only spew curses, sinking into the chill Atlantic, merging again with worldwide waters.

2

"John Eliot! Quit mooning in the doorway. You don't need to make the walk to the meetinghouse! It's raining, and you'd be soaked before you arrived. Look at that sky! It's going to rain more; it shows no signs of letting up. We live on a little hill. It's never going to flood here. Our roof doesn't leak. There's no need for you to walk to that church building, just to write on some silly book that will never see the light of day. Where are you going to find a publisher here? Books are published in London, not Boston. You're never returning to England as long as Charles sits the throne. Now, close the door." Anna's voice softened as she approached, slipped her arms around his chest, and laid her head on his back.

"We can't afford to be burning candles in the daytime. You'll wait until you can use the church's candles. Is it such a chore to spend a rainy day with me?" That wasn't a fair question, and she knew it. In their three years married, she'd never doubted that he loved her.

"John, I tire of old biddies looking at my belly, and seeing it as flat as it was when we married. Three years, John, and I haven't conceived." He turned to speak, but she placed two fingers to his lips. "No, you haven't neglected me." She stood on tiptoes and kissed him briefly.

"Nevertheless, husband, I've been thinking about something better to do on this eternally soggy day than listen to rain slapping our walls." Other wives had warned her that sometimes men were slow to unravel a hint. A more direct approach... She reached up, unfolded his cravat, and pulled it from around his neck. Keeping herself pressed against him, she unbuttoned first the top button and then the second button of his stiff, gray shirt. His eyes were as round as saucers. She turned, leaning back against him.

"Would you help me with the buttons down the back of this dress? They're always so hard for me to reach." He stuttered; his hands fumbled at the buttons. "Do hurry!" He was nearly incapable of hurrying by the time she turned toward him again.

"But, Anna—It's the middle of the day: broad daylight!"

"But, John, it's ever so dark outside, and there's no one in the house but us." She threw her arms up around his neck and kissed him again: not just a simple brushing of the lips as earlier. If she'd chosen the slowest man in the entire Massachusetts Bay Colony, by that time, even he'd have lacked any doubt about her intentions for them.

Thus it was, as a hurricane died, a child was conceived. John Eliot, Jr., would be born in May 1636, instead of August 1636, confusing New England's old-line history even further.

3

"John, they should let you speak. There should've been more voices raised that say that the Indians are the children of God as much as we are."

"I'm afraid I'm not that important, Anna. I was only an assistant at First Church, and now that I'm at Roxbury, the powerful Boston men don't want to listen to me. I may complete those final drafts about converting the natives *someday*, but right now, even those aren't ready." He smiled.

"Come, my dear. Bring the baby so that someday we may be able to tell him that he saw the first airship in the New World. We shall use that as an excuse, as we're craning our own neck to get a good look. It's hard to believe that men could rise so high."

"I choose not to be impressed," she said, sniffing. "They may rise high *physically*, but my husband is higher *spiritually* than any bunch of bloodthirsty war-pushers like Endecott. *He* got to talk to the men from that wondrous foreign place, and you didn't."

"How could I not love a woman who defends me so? Let's

just go look at the airship, and then be about our business. I can't see how these visiting strangers could have the slightest effect on us." She frowned, but agreed.

4

It was the commotion that attracted everyone, not the violence. Ships—many ships—had entered the springtime harbor before anyone realized that anything untoward was happening. The ships were launching boatloads of men as soon as their anchors dropped. Others were unloading directly onto the wharves. The men, forming into organized dockside groups, all bore bayoneted muskets. It was too late to fire the harbor's defensive cannons.

An April breeze straightened a ship's flag atop a mast. Three golden fleurs-de-lis on a blue field flapped in the wind. John Eliot stared at the newcomers from outside the Roxbury church door.

"French!" That meaning was uncertain. A pirate flag would be obvious. Charles I's British flag would have identified enemies just as certainly as a French or Spanish flag. Dutch flags, Swedish flags, or Danish flags on a flotilla would have meant more mystery than danger. There was only one certainty: he needed to get to his family. He could hear the pop-pop-pop of distant musketry, but there was no way to identify its origin. His legs were running almost before he commanded them.

Anna had exited onto the hill's crest with John, Jr., watching the spectacle. Her husband raced up to stand beside her, winded. Some militia were swarming out of their houses and shops, muskets in hand. The French troops were still milling around, organizing into companies. A frontal squad pointed muskets at the advancing militiamen. A second troop line had their weapons angled upward, ready to step forward if the front line couldn't handle their task.

The French musketeers' volley went off with a roar and a cloud of yellow smoke. One musketeer hadn't been shouldering his weapon properly. He staggered backwards into the man behind him, whose angled musket went off prematurely.

Only God's hand could be that quick, or Satan's. There was a thump next to John. Anna looked suddenly startled. She turned and handed the baby to him. Then, she looked down at her own chest. A central red stain was spreading rapidly. Her mouth worked, but bright red blood came out instead of words. The spent musket ball from the startled musketeer had torn through a lung and the great vessel next to the heart. She held out a hand to her husband, but then folded to her knees; then to one hip, and then supine.

"No!" he screamed. "No!" The baby began to cry. His father was careful not to drop him as he knelt beside his wife. Her legs were still pawing at the ground, and there was an awful stench. Her half-open eyes stared at the sky, never to see her husband or child again.

Neighbors began to arrive; one of the women lifted the crying baby from his arms. He still repeatedly choked out his denial. He held his dead wife's head in his lap, careless of the blood; sobs shook him; tears flowed like a summer storm. Memory of another watery storm rose in his mind, and he wept all the more. More neighbors arrived: the women crying; the men talking quietly among themselves. Some left to return with someone's shutter. Another man returned with a squat, brown bottle. They pressured John to drink some, and he couldn't fight them. His strength was gone. A non-drinker, John quickly entered throat-burning, blurry unconsciousness. With one eye toward the advancing French, the neighbors agreed: unconsciousness was the preferred state at that moment.

5

John Eliot woke to a dim, painful world, filed with horrible memory. He raised his head. A voice spoke to him from the gloom.

"John, my son, I'm here for you."

"Mmm... Mother Mumford?" His head hurt too badly for him to remember exactly why his mother-in-law might be there.

"The baby's asleep right now." Then, he remembered.

"Where—?"

"She's at the undertakers. Your neighbors took her. The undertakers are very busy. The best we can hope for is a simple pine box, and a grave we dig ourselves. The French swine killed a dozen when they came ashore. Who knows how many more they killed across the bay? There was musket and cannon fire there." He didn't want to wake up; he didn't want to think, but it was going to happen, whatever he preferred.

"Wait: What about your health, Mrs. Mumford? I know it hasn't been good. How can you—?"

"You were always the politest young man who ever courted my daughter. I think it's time that I was 'Abigail' instead of 'Mrs. Mumford.' And, lad . . . If you bring up my health again while I'm caring for you and for my grandson, I'll catch you on the side of the head with a skillet. *Do you understand?*"

"Yes, ma'am."

"As soon as the baby's awake, we'll go and make arrangements."

The undertaker had indeed manufactured only a pine box, for which Eliot could afford to pay immediately. With a borrowed shovel, he dug a grave at the cemetery's rear margin, tears sticking more dirt to his face than did sweat. Neighbors came by and offered to help, but he'd accept none. The stone would be just that: a stone, with the letter "E" carved by his own hand and the name "Anna Eliot" painted on. Someday he'd be able to afford more.

The farewell group was small. Anna's father was himself gone; her brothers and sisters, even her sister Mary, were scattered, forbidden by the French to travel. The cemetery was dotted with other groups in black, weeping and tossing handfuls of dirt into amateur graves. Puritans were said to be cold and stiff, but the world's evil had crushed them together. A surprising number of strangers had gathered with each mourning family. Some of the down-turned faces already showed anger against the indifferent papist invaders. Patrolling soldiers would allow only groups in black to walk as far as the graveyard.

6

A stranger to John Eliot left another mourning group and walked toward him. The distraught husband and father barely noticed him until he was an arm's length away.

"Brother Eliot?"

"Eh? Yes?"

"I was aboard that Dutch ship with more brothers and sisters, the one that the French just seized in the harbor. I'd really meant to seek you at your house. Have you heard of the strange city that arrived in Germany? Grantville?"

"Yes, but what—?"

"Their library brought back some peculiar knowledge. Someone—I don't know who—found a reference to you in that library. Whoever it was knew that there were Puritans in the Netherlands. You were there yourself, for a while, I think." John shook his head. "It's only one page. When it didn't find you there, one of the elders gave it to me, knowing that I was leaving for Massachusetts. O brother, I never meant to deliver this at a time like this! Take its message as the voice of God. He wants to tell you something, even in this moment. I'm so sorry!" He fished inside his vest and pulled out a rumpled, folded paper. He handed it to John and departed, wiping tears from his face. The mourning widower didn't remember to ask his name: "angels unaware."

7

He tucked away the paper, later to be forgotten, laid on a table's corner. At home, he held his son and crooned to him. He had to be careful not to hug him so hard that he hurt the baby. In his empty home, white-haired Abigail Mountford fed and changed the child. She prepared their food. If he ate it, he didn't taste it.

The sun refused to stop shining, despite the French occupation. The invaders confiscated whatever supplies they wanted, robbing Puritan coin and food at gunpoint. Eliot was little affected; as a poor minister, he had very little that they wanted. They'd already robbed him of his most beloved treasure. His greatest future struggle would be to forgive and not to hate; to love and not to take vengeance. He could foresee no personal future except as a destroyed husk of a man. The sun still refused to stop shining.

His mother-in-law couldn't understand why he wouldn't burn candles in order to read inside his house. Candles were expensive, but it was more than that. He wouldn't walk to the church building to write, though it was only two miles. The blood flow to his spirit had dried up like a dead tree's sap. He wouldn't make the long walk to write anything, because he *couldn't* write anymore.

He could read, he supposed, and there were still good books in the town. Everything else was restricted by the occupiers. Outside, on his house's north side, with the light from the sky, he could read. He began with a book he'd gotten in England. He read it, but he didn't remember it. His eyes traced the letters, but the words refused to settle in his soul. He set it aside and went looking for some other printed word to stir himself. He considered that a hopeless task.

The rumpled paper still lay on the table. Mrs. Mumford, unsure of its significance, had left it there and cleaned around it. Her eyes were too far gone to read it herself. He picked it up and went outside, to rest against the small house's wall. There were no clouds; there was no thunder; yet, lightning struck through to every limb's tip as the words seared home.

8

"JOHN ELIOT: APOSTLE TO THE INDIANS."

That mystery-sourced paper named him an apostle: "one who is sent." He could no more have stopped reading than he could've stopped breathing. It told how he'd been Thomas Hooker's follower, only to see him driven to Holland. He'd later left for the New World himself, to avoid persecution. He'd already experienced all that. It told how he'd married Anna Mountford in 1632. He knew that, too. Oh, how he knew that!

Then, that one paper page shredded his life apart as if he'd been thrown into a meat grinder. On the back, it spoke of the Great Colonial Hurricane of 1635. There'd been no Great Colonial Hurricane of 1635. It spoke of how his son John, Jr., was born in August 1636, when the baby asleep within his house had been born in May 1636. It didn't speak of the French at all.

He sat there: clutching it; stretching it, as if to reveal more words; trying not to tear it. Words like a storm surge smashed into his life. Denying them had no more effect than holding up his hands would have had on a tidal wave. Somewhere, *somewhen*, they spoke of how he'd written the first book published in the New World: a Bible in the Wampanoag language. He also seemed to have written the first book authored in America: the first book to be banned by the government there.

The miraculous paper named his and Anna's six children, listing their birth dates and some of their future. Somewhere, he'd raised two fine sons to the ministry. He'd married a daughter into one of the most important New England families. That was the cruelest literature: Anna would have no more children.

He read how he'd established town after town for Christian Indians, the Caughnawaga, around the Bay Colony. He read how he'd stood for Indian rights in Puritan courts. He read how he'd fought for Indian literacy: their right to read the Word; how he'd trained native preachers to go to their own people, the Praying Indians. At last, he read why his life had been cruelly twisted from its course.

The Puritans had been frightened by King Phillip's War's bloodshed, a war of which he'd never heard (and never would, it seemed). They'd treacherously turned on the Caughnawaga: imprisoning them in their villages; starving them; denying any chance to work their fields; destroying villages; dragging them away to be walled in; finally bribing them to go far away, so that their remnant wouldn't forever embarrass their persecutors.

So that was it.

He *had* been sent, and he'd gone. Isaiah had said, "Here am I, Lord. Send me." The John Eliot that he'd never meet had said the same, only to see his apostleship wasted and erased. He leaned against the clapboards with the tears washing his face, for his spiritual children, whom he'd never meet. God hadn't given up on them or John, but there'd been a satanic price extracted for his new apostleship. A stone with the hand-carved letter "E" rose before his mind's eye. The French had had to arrive, to shake him from his life in Boston and Roxbury. The works that he'd have once done wouldn't have been enough. He shot to his feet.

"Not this time! Not this time, Lord!" he shouted to the sky.

He paced back and forth, too excited to read more, his feet itching to be on the road. *Which* road remained a matter of conjecture. He finally settled and began to read again.

He'd been helped in his first Wampanoag translations by a Pequot slave named Cockone of Long Island, captured by the Puritans during the Pequot War. What? There'd been no Pequot War. The USE ship and its miraculous airship had intervened, and an uneasy peace had held until the French arrived. Cockone must still be on Long Island! And he'd thought that the impossible American flying ship hadn't touched his life!

"Abigail! Abigail!" He raced around to his front door. His mother-in-law met him inside, wiping flour from her hands. "Abigail, I know what I must do!"

"John, for the love of God! What's gotten into you?"

"The Spirit of God's gotten into me. I didn't see any 'cloven tongues of fire,' but It came just the same. I must go to Long Island, and Junior will be going with me. He'll be a great minister someday, himself." Abigail's face turned brick red; then white.

"You'll do *what* again? Long Island?" She sat down on a chair—hard.

"I'm called by the Spirit. I must go to Long Island, to find a man named 'Cockone.' I've seen my future, and I've also seen Junior's future. I have a work to do for God, and Junior will follow me. Cockone is part of that."

9

It couldn't be said that Abigail didn't try to argue him out of his journey. She made him sit in her kitchen. Was his mind, perhaps, disarrayed by Anna's death? Could an evil spirit, not from God, be launching him in the wrong direction? Might he not be killed by the dangerous Indians along his path or by those on Long Island? Might he or the baby not be struck by disease on such a hard journey among strangers? Might he not starve, without a congregation to support him?

He listened politely, because he loved her. He embraced her and patted her back, but he made it absolutely clear that he and Junior were going. In Abigail's mind, John's journey instantly became "our" journey. Then, it became his turn to argue. That had just as much effect for turning the elderly woman from their path as her arguments had had diverting him. He started to use the word "health," but her hand closed instantly on a skillet handle. He stopped and tried to work around the problem indirectly; he made no headway.

"We'll leave as soon as possible, in the midst of a week. I won't tell the congregation Sunday. With so many ears listening, the word might reach the French. I don't want us as dead as the Pilgrims. The French don't want another valuable slave—all right: *two* more valuable slaves—leaving Massachusetts. I know that some fled overland to the Connecticut Valley when the French came. We'll find help there, and that'll put us that much closer to Long Island." Abigail ignored him and went on packing, only necessary things.

The next day, she disappeared back to her own house, taking the baby with her. John would rather have left that day, but she delayed too long. They'd leave the next morning.

"Exactly where were you?"

"Well, there were certain things that I valued. It's not as if I'd be coming back for them, and I don't want the French to have them. So, I gathered them, and Junior and I walked around to visit the members of your congregation."

"My—"

"Hush! What do I need with a silver tea set, and what do they need with money that the French will steal from them anyway? You're a man full of spirit; on fire with the Spirit; with no more practicality than a baby bird. We'll need money, and you had very little. If an Italian shawl or a set of Dutch carving knives will give us the coin with which to eat later, what good are those things to me? My legs are too old, and the time is too short for me to get rid of everything, but perhaps now we'll have enough money to eat on. I kept his grandfather's ring for Junior to have someday. He couldn't wear it anyway because of its showiness. I kept my ruby broach for the same reason. I know that it will— Never mind.

"I sent word by a boy, whom the French would never think to stop, to Anna's brothers and sisters. I hope that Mary can make it to our houses and clear them of everything valuable before the French thieves get their hands on them." He didn't dare argue with the fire in her eye. The partial cataract in one gave her a sinister look.

10

When he saw the weight that they'd carry, John himself added another day. He created a handcart: used wheels, a broken boat body, and some oars—beneath a tarp, which they'd also need. They rolled out an hour before sundown Friday, generally toward the Roxbury church. In the twilight, they kept on past the meetinghouse, on the roads southwest, until the track began to play out. The cart allowed them to carry blankets and cooking gear; they wouldn't be too uncomfortable.

The following morning, they still found partial roads. A few dozen Puritans had fled the French incursion, fearful for their future. Some had cleared a trail. Open, it wasn't; better than underbrush, it was. John wouldn't let Abigail near the cart handles, no matter how tough the going. He could tell that simply marching, sometimes holding Junior's toddler hand, was exhausting her. She insisted on cooking for her men. They'd have to travel the next day, Sabbath or not. They were more than thirty miles from home when they met the Indians.

John suspected that they were Mohicans. Two men simply stepped out of the brush beside the trail and stared at them. He raised his hand in a friendly gesture; he had neither pistol nor musket. They only crossed their arms and continued to stare. Though each had a knife and a tomahawk slung at his belt, neither was painted. A woman in a buckskin dress also stepped from the trees to watch. Two older children joined her, and another pair of dark eyes peered from among the trunks. John rolled the handcart along, sweating from more than the heat. Abigail made sure that all watching eyes saw baby Junior.

They took no more precautions that night than any other night. If Indians had wanted to kill them, they'd have been dead already. Abigail thought John unnaturally confident that God would protect them, especially from Indians, but there was precious little either could do about the danger.

Toward midday of the sixth day, Abigail collapsed. As much as she wanted to walk independently, she couldn't. As much as John didn't want to pull her extra weight, there wasn't much choice there, either.

Near midmorning on the seventh day, one of the Mohican men, whom they'd previously passed, stepped from the forest. By gesture, he indicated that he'd manage an oar shaft. He pulled half the load all day, disappearing at twilight. John was able to feed the baby some thin corn mush and molasses, but he ate little himself. Abigail could eat nothing at all.

An hour into the eighth day, they saw the first farm on Newtowne's outskirts. When the crude fort rolled into sight, Abigail kissed the baby. She hugged John's neck and kissed him on the cheek, without speaking. She died that afternoon, living the Grandmother's Code to the last.

11

He'd buried Abigail in the Newtowne cemetery. That was already too full; frontier life wasn't easy. He'd marked her simple stone with an "E" for "Eliot," because of what she'd been to his family, and an "M" for her own family. Someday, Junior would return and mark the grave properly.

And then . . . and then . . . nothing.

The fort was filled with activity, people cycling through continually: Puritans, Dutch, and natives from Algonquian tribes. Some white men had so adapted to Indian ways that they were hard to distinguish from tribesmen. Some natives had spent so much time around white men (or perhaps around white man's liquor) that they, too, had lost tribal identity. In such a menagerie, it should have been easy for John to find a way to Long Island. It was only a few miles down the river and ten miles across a quiet bay.

Carrying Junior on one hip, he asked anyone he thought might speak English. None seemed interested. He suspected that the Pequot, known for their fierceness, were currently an unknown quantity. He heard that the Pequot had driven every other tribe from Long Island, making it a Pequot (and only Pequot) hunting ground. If they didn't like someone disturbing them—native or white—that person might reach Long Island, and simply disappear. John was determined to carry his son with him, and none wanted to be responsible for a child's death at cruel hands. The French appearance had made the Pequot uneasy: they were dangerous when uneasy.

John had camped outside the fort, near a grove where he could find firewood. On some days, certain farm women baked bread; others kept milk cows. Junior was thriving on mush, with occasional bread and milk, toddling here and there. After his son was bedded down one night, a scarred Indian stepped into his firelight.

"Tell me, white man, why you want go across the water."

John was startled to hear English. "Well, I . . . I won't lie to you. I must find a Pequot named Cockone."

The Indian grunted. "I know this man, whose name you say wrong. Why must you find him?"

There was no point dissembling. "The Great Spirit has called me to find him. We have a great work that should be done together: the two of us. I need someone to help me find him, and to help me speak to him." Again, the native grunted. He crouched beside the fire.

"I can take you to him, but you will pay me first. I do not want white man's money. It too easy to cheat using money that only white men understand."

"Very well. What do you want?"

"I want your cart. There is old *nokomis*, a grandmother to whom I owe a debt. She grows feeble and cannot drag wood. With your cart, she can haul wood from far away. Some longhouse will give her a shelf on which to sleep and food to eat, so that they may use her cart. That will get you to Cockone."

"And to speak to Cockone...?"

"More."

"Have you seen something that you want?" John suspected that the Indian had been watching him continually.

"I see nothing that I want, but I want something. Your own journey gear...you will need again. We take all in my canoe. It must be something else, something special."

"I have no— Wait." He knew exactly where he'd stored Junior's inherited ring. With it...

"I will give you this. It is very valuable to both white men and to your people." He held up the ruby broach. (How had Abigail known? Was it something about her approaching death? He shook his head.) The Indian examined it closely, smiling to himself.

"Return it, please. It shall be yours when you have assisted me in speaking to Cockone for three days. That man and I will speak further, but at three days you will have earned your payment." The Indian handed it back with obvious reluctance.

"I am Black Turtle. Be at the river tomorrow when the sun is one hand above the horizon. Have your things and your son ready to travel in canoe. Have your cart ready to be empty. I am Mohican. I heard of you, from my tribe. They like me not, but some of them will speak to me. They told me of your determination, but they cannot tell me of your honesty. Do not cheat me, or you will never return from across water." He unfolded from his crouch. Like a shadow, he was gone.

12

John packed everything, trying not to bump or clank and wake Junior. He didn't want to discard Abigail's traveling clothes. There wasn't time to find a proper recipient among the fort's women. Then he remembered that Black Turtle was going to transfer the cart to an old woman. She might accept another older woman's clothing.

He slept poorly that night. With the dawn, he approached the river, after feeding Junior. Black Turtle was already there, accompanied by a bent, white-haired woman. John pulled his pack from the cart and lifted the baby down. The toothless woman exclaimed over his son. The Grandmother's Code crossed every boundary.

"Tell her, Black Turtle, that I have given her a clothing gift in the cart because of my son." The Mohican look over the clothing, frowned, and shook his head.

"You have made this *nokomis* a rich woman. The longhouses will fight to have her stay with any one of them." He snorted and laughed to himself. "Together we load your gear. As I tie it down, be prepared to sit in front of canoe. I will be in back, ready to paddle. Push us off, and jump in immediately with your son. You would be in my way if you try to paddle."

Eventually, John sat (wet) in the canoe's prow, rocking (dry) Junior. The trio headed downriver.

13

A stick two-and-a-half feet long stuck up from the canoe's prow, with a half dozen white bead strings hanging from it, easily visible. Black Turtle pushed the canoe to the river's center, where the current was strongest, making only an occasional strike with his paddle. The Connecticut would grow wider as they approached the ocean.

An hour into the journey, Junior woke up. John fed him mashed berries, cold mush, and molasses. After John had washed out a dirty diaper and swaddled him in a dry cloth, he seemed perfectly happy to watch the scenery pass, standing between his father's legs or dozing with the canoe's rocking.

There was some river traffic, mostly canoes. They saw a few flat-bottomed boats being poled near the bank. Once they had to move aside for a schooner headed upstream; twice they passed anchored ships. Every native canoe tended to veer toward their canoe. Sharp eyes would note a man holding a baby and a native without war paint. They also looked carefully at the white strings hung at the bow.

It was thirty or forty miles down the Connecticut to the ocean. Black Turtle moved closer to the bank; he worked harder when the tide changed against them. The native wasn't one for conversation. It was a day of new scenes for John and Junior, but not new information.

They camped that night on a sandbank close to the river's mouth. Black Turtle, who carried no cooking gear, appreciated the frying pan that John had brought. He caught two fish, and they ate well, with a little bear grease to slick the pan. John tried a pinch of cooked fish on Junior, and the boy ate happily. Mashed thoroughly, no fish's bones reached his son's mouth.

With the dawn, from a tall dune, they could see a low-lying point across the water. When the tide turned, the river gave them a shove out to sea. They set out as before, with everything tied down thoroughly. Black Turtle got no relief from paddling, but the distance was shorter. As they approached the sandy point, the Mohican bore off to the right.

"No villages there. Too flat. Storms hit too hard there. Cock-one lives down the coast."

"Black Turtle, what are these white strings that hang here in front of me? I have seen many look at them."

"White wampum. We come in peace, like traders."

"Oh. Why didn't we stop at Fort Sovereignty?"

"Not safe. I have no friends there." Two hours later, they saw a substantial village, with two dozen canoes pulled up on the strand.

"Cockone's village." The Mohican paddled directly in.

Warriors hurried down to the water, weapons in hand, but the defense was only half-hearted. One canoe was unlikely to be a war party. Two men and a baby certainly weren't. The white wampum of negotiation hung prominently at the canoe's prow.

"Come," Black Turtle called. "We will see chief. Then, we speak with Cockone."

14

An important-looking man came out to talk to Black Turtle, frowning. The Mohican was probably seldom greeted by smiles anywhere. He spoke at length and gestured, pointing both toward John and toward the village. He gave the chief one white wampum string. The chief finally agreed to whatever Black Turtle had requested. The Pequot turned away with a dismissive gesture. John believed that what the chief had agreed to was indifference. If his man didn't want to talk to two interlopers, he didn't have to.

As soon as the warriors had let the pair ascend the beach, the village children and dogs began noisily circling, some barking and some yelling. As soon as the chief released them into the village, a dozen running children began orbiting them. The dogs didn't try to get close, but they did bark continually. The commotion couldn't help but attract Cockone. He stepped from his longhouse, an impressive figure even without war regalia.

Black Turtle spoke to him at length, obviously requesting an interview, inside (away from children and dogs). Junior had been so entertained that he hadn't fussed at all. Once inside the dark interior, the toddler began to cry. Cockone shook his head lightly and clapped his hands. A woman came from the other end of the longhouse and held out her hands to take Junior. The chief spoke kindly to John, and Black Turtle translated.

"He says that this is first wife. She has had many children. She will care for your son with great tenderness. He is probably only hungry." It was a test, and John knew it. If he was to become the apostle to the Indians, he couldn't dodge becoming close to them, but this was his son! His hands were almost knotted with tension as he passed the baby to Cockone's wife.

The Pequot warrior gestured them toward an open area near the longhouse's center. He crouched on one side of a barely smoking fire; they would take the other side. He spoke briefly. Black Turtle translated.

"He says for you to begin. Tell him what you came to say." John cleared his throat. Sweat popped from every pore. If the internal prayer he uttered had been spoken aloud, it would have blown away longhouse walls with its intensity.

"I bring you the words of the Great Spirit, spoken by white

man's letters on this piece of paper." Cockone's eyebrows rose until a person could see the whites of his eyes. "Do you remember when the great flying thing appeared in the sky? This paper was created by the same men who built the great flying thing. They come from a place of events that *might have been*. Those events were not always for the good. It is clear: they have come to this place to change things, so that they will no longer be as things *might have been*." Black Turtle had to speak for more than a minute. Some back-and-forth was required before the warrior agreed that he understood.

"The Great Spirit sent this paper to me, to tell me of things that *might have been* in my own life. Those things were not perfect: not as I wished. He has told me to try again, to make them as they should be. I will tell you what this paper says about my own life: how it is right; how it is wrong." He read the title. "It says that I am to be sent as a messenger to those who are not white men. I knew nothing of this. This is about things that were to happen when I was older. Until a few days ago, I did not know that I would be this messenger." He read aloud then about his past life and marriage.

"This is all the truth. The same events happened in this world as happened in the world that only might have been."

Sometimes when he preached, John Eliot felt the Spirit of God on himself: signs in his own body; the rapt attention of his audience to his words. Here, he had an audience of one, but he could feel the Spirit falling on him like a cloak and see the fascination in the Pequot's eyes.

"I brought my son to your longhouse, so that you might see him. The other side of the paper told about a great storm that happened months ago. You and I had our eyes open. *There was no such great storm.* Already, something has changed. The paper says that my son was born at the hottest part of summer. It is not true: a change has happened. My son was born in the spring, not long after the ice broke up. The strangers who came in the great flying thing have begun to change the world. *They are not the only ones who can change it!*" He rose and paced.

"Those things were nothing to me. The paper named the year that I was married. It was truth. The paper told of the six children my wife would bear. It was a lie! The day the French came, a French musket killed my wife. She had the one son, but she will have no more." He stopped, flustered, as Black Turtle translated.

"This paper tells me all the great things I will do: great things that I have not done yet. The Evil One speaks to me and says, 'See. This message lies. Your wife lies dead and will bear no more children. You cannot do these great things, because they are certain to be lies, also.' I will listen to the Great Spirit instead! He says to me, 'Go,' and I must go. There are many things to be done at the Great Spirit's command, first by me and later by my son. When they were done the first time, I did not do them alone. I had the help of a great Pequot. His name and his story are on this paper also." Cockone blinked several times before he spoke.

"Who is this warrior of wonder among the Pequot?"

John Eliot stood to his full height. "His name is Cockone!" His eyes rolled up into his head, and the preacher fainted.

15

John Eliot woke from sleep on a Pequot longhouse's shelf, wrapped in a deerskin. Black Turtle was close at hand, sitting on another shelf.

"I told them what the Mohicans told me. You had fled many days from your enemies with your child and your grandmother. You pulled a heavy load all day, every day, caring for those you love. At the last, you were carrying it all, and the Mohicans could not stand to watch you. They helped, but you never stopped. I know that you have eaten almost nothing, as you buried your grandmother. You made sure that your child had food in his belly. One small fish? Pah! None were surprised when you fell under the spirit-load that you had been given. Tonight you will speak again to Cockone and the elders of the Pequot. Now, you must eat something, or your strength will fail you again." He called something in the Pequot dialect.

A young woman was there immediately with a bark bowl of corn, bean and squash stew, with bits of wild turkey in it. Though he had only his fingers to use, he ate it all. She brought more food later in the day.

He meditated and prayed throughout the day. Cockone's wife brought Junior, to show that all was well, and then departed again. That night, he was summoned to a council in the chief's longhouse.

"They wish you to tell them about the great deeds that the Great Spirit has set before you."

"I am ready. I will tell them about the great things that I might have done. About things that failed—things that I will never do now. I will tell them about the great things that I plan in this life.

"In my life that never was, that never will be, others helped me to translate the Word of the Great Spirit and His Son into language that you could understand. It will not be the same now. I held too tightly to my own language and left it to others to learn yours. In this life, I will learn to speak as you speak. As quickly as I learn, I will reveal the words of the Great Spirit. I will make a letter Book in your language of those words and teach you to read it.

"In that spirit life, I helped build villages for people like you who came to believe in the Great Spirit and His Son. I will not do that again! In that life, my own white men destroyed believers like you. This time I will build no villages. I will *convert* villages so that good people of the Great Spirit live among their own. In that life, I taught many like you to become prophets, to speak the words of the Great Spirit and His Son. I will do that again, with all my heart." His palm stumped his chest.

"In that life that never was, I defended your people against the white people who would use words to rob you. At the last, I failed. *I will not fail you in this life!*" The Pequot seemed stunned by what they'd heard. The chief rose and spoke; Black Turtle translated.

"They would speak among themselves of the things that you have told them. What of the warrior Cockone? What do you say of him?"

"When they have talked among themselves, tomorrow night I will speak to Cockone and tell him what the magic paper said of his life."

16

With the third night, Eliot discovered that so many wanted to hear him that they once again had to gather in the chief's longhouse.

"I have told you before how the strangers in the great flying thing came to change how things would have been. This paper of mistakes tells me about the warrior Cockone. It tells me how he was a slave." The longhouse erupted in noise. Cockone jumped to his feet.

"I am no slave!" He slammed his fist against his chest. John had to wait for the noise to die down.

"No, you are no slave *in the here and now*. In that other time that might have been, you were captured during the Pequot War and made a slave to the white men. You learned to speak English. Do not be astounded. *There was no Pequot War!* The men from the great flying thing stopped the war before it could happen. Hundreds of the Pequot were supposed to die. Cockone was supposed to be captured. Do you not see? The men from this other time have come to change the things that went wrong. They do not even know their own destiny.

"In that different time, you became my friend. You helped me with the words I needed in your language, to bring the Great Spirit's Word to your people. Even as a slave, you became a great leader of those who believe in the Father and the Son. This paper told me of you. It gave me your name. I am sent by the Great Spirit to find you, that you might help me to set things right for your people. You know what I plan. I want you to help me. I want you to walk my path with me again." John Eliot folded his arms. He would say no more. His three days of speech were ended. He let Black Turtle lead him back to Cockone's longhouse.

17

When he awoke the next morning, Black Turtle was still present.

"I thought—" The Mohican held up his hand.

"You are a man too interesting to leave. I will stay until you are interesting no longer."

"Cockone...?"

"He has built himself a medicine lodge, a *midewigaan*. He will let it purify him until he has an answer." There was a cry from the village edge and the distant sound of running feet. "Ho! I think that Cockone has his answer. Come." They hurried toward the ocean's margin with the rest of the village. Steam was still trailing from the ruptured *midewigaan*. Cockone was emerging, dripping, from the ocean water. He stood tall and strode straight to John Eliot. He embraced the Puritan preacher. He spoke, and Black Turtle was eager to translate.

"He says, 'I will walk this path again!'"

The First Conductor

Michael Lockwood

Mohican Village
Near present-day Greenfield, Massachusetts

Robert Lockwood's knees hurt from kneeling in front of the firepit in the middle of the wigwam.

His hands hurt, knuckles painfully white, from being tightly clasped in prayer for hours.

His eyes hurt from the smoke that lingered in the wigwam rather than rising through the hole in the top.

But, mostly, his soul hurt. He spent most of his time in prayer. Whether it was for patience, forgiveness, vengeance, strength or even an end to all of this. Perhaps it was a prayer for all of those things. His prayers had long since ceased to be ones of words and conscious, coherent thoughts. His "prayers," such as they were, were streams of raw emotions and carnal appeal for assistance. Pleading for something other than this feeling of hurt.

But, all he felt was a silence. It wasn't an emptiness; that would have pushed him over the edge of despair. It was simply a silence of waiting, as though the Almighty had given instructions and He was waiting on Robert to fulfill those instructions.

The problem was that Robert didn't know what those instructions were. Had he missed some sign? Some pointer of where he was to go? He didn't know and Robert felt all the more lost for it.

Elinor had taken the children into the village after their sick

243

time was over. Thankfully, they had been clean and accepted safely behind the walls.

But, Robert couldn't allow himself to leave the wigwam that had been his home for the last few weeks. He couldn't return to civilization, any form of it, even as rural as a Mohican village, in this way. He didn't feel as though he had control of his body, his mind, or his emotions well enough to rejoin other humans. The quiet of the wigwam allowed him to think, both of vengeance and duty. Eventually he hoped the wigwam would allow him to find closure.

The flap that served as the door to the wigwam was raised and a cool blast of air entered. The smoke swirled from the new currents. Machk looked at the kneeling man and grunted.

"Has your god answered your prayers?" he asked with a sneer.

Robert didn't feel the need to answer. Such a comment was typical of the large Mohican. Their vow of a few weeks ago seemed to have encouraged a sense of openness in the man, a view into a soul far more bitter than Robert's. Robert, at least, had the dubious comfort of striking out against a real enemy that had taken his Susannah from him. Machk had none of that. The disease may have been brought by a Frenchman, but Machk knew deep inside that the French merchant had been just as much a casualty of the disease as his wife and infant son. Hating the French was a justification for a real hatred, the Almighty Himself.

Instead, Robert stood, ignoring protesting back and knees. He looked around the wigwam to see if he had forgotten to pack anything for their trip. He spied his worn Bible and picked it up. Defiantly, he placed the book in his satchel and looked at Machk, daring the big Mohican to say anything. For his own part, Machk simply snorted and let the flap close.

Robert took a moment to dump dirt from a crude bucket onto the smoldering embers. He would need to dig the firepit out when he returned, but for now there would be no hot ashes to catch the little wigwam on fire. He took a stout stick, brought for this purpose, and stirred the soil into the ashes, smothering them.

He stepped out of the wigwam and noticed the fog which blanketed the field. It was thicker in the dips of the land and thinner on the rises where tall grass poked through here and there. It was morning. He had lost track of time and spent the night in prayer. No wonder his knees and back ached. He had knelt soon after the sun had set to begin his vigil, breaking only to put more wood on the fire before returning to prayer.

Robert took a few moments to adjust his equipment. Unlike Machk, Robert did not carry a bow. While he had gained some proficiency with the ball-headed club, the simple bow and arrow eluded him. Even Machk had finally given up.

Instead, Robert adjusted a pistol and ammunition at his belt. It was the same gun that had taken his Susannah's life, taken from Jean-Marc Crevier's cold, dead hand. Luckily, the Frenchman had included a full pouch of lead conical bullets and a powder horn full of gunpowder. It wasn't going to last forever, but it had allowed Robert to practice with the unfamiliar weapon. To his surprise, he proved to be quite capable with the pistol, though he had little experience with firearms. The pistol was well made and forgiving for a novice marksman.

Machk had sneered at the weapon but said nothing. Robert would only have one shot from the pistol before it became a smaller version of the club in his main hand. He wouldn't have time to reload in the heat of battle. That would just have to do.

They set off at a trot, heading south to follow the river. The plan was to follow the river to the Puritan settlement at Agawam Plantation. Hopefully, Robert could bargain for some ammunition and gunpowder. If not, he could always take some from the first French village they raided.

Machk set a blistering pace and Robert soon found himself completely focused on making sure his feet didn't catch on sticks, roots and rocks.

Agawam Plantation
Near modern-day Springfield, Massachusetts

It was late in the day when Robert and Machk topped the final rise to the wide valley where Agawam Plantation resided. There were two settlements here. One was a small homestead: a main manor house, a warehouse, some longhouses and a sizable sty for pigs. A short wooden fence surrounded the buildings, meant to keep wild animals out.

To the south, atop the largest hill, a new palisade was being erected around temporary wigwams. Robert could hear the noises of tools and laboring men even from the top of the hill.

He looked at Machk and nodded before taking a step toward the settlement. Machk simply shook his head and followed.

A pair of men stood as they approached. The older one on the right was familiar. Bryan Pendleton had been a neighbor in Watertown and one of the more respected leaders for both his leadership and his wealth. He had shared the same parcel of land with Robert and the two men were on friendly terms.

"Robert!" Pendleton exclaimed and dropped his tools.

"Bryan," Robert said. "How are you?"

"As well as I can be..." Bryan said with a smile that quickly soured as he sensed something in Robert's face. "Robert? What has happened? Where's your family?"

Even months later, Robert still shied away from the memory of Susannah's cold corpse.

"Johnathan and Deborah are well and staying with Elizabeth." Robert's hand gripped Jean-Marc's pistol tighter. "Susannah has gone to sit with our Lord."

"My condolences, Robert," Bryan said. "I shall offer prayers for her soul."

"And yours, Bryan? How do they fare?" Robert asked.

"Very well," Brian replied. "We arrived here a week ago and William was gracious enough to grant us shelter. Eleanor left with the children the next day and took them to Dorchester, down the river. I've stayed with William to help with erecting this wall."

"I am happy they are well," Robert said. "But I was not aware that events have warranted building a palisade."

Bryan shrugged. "This isn't Watertown and William faces dangers that we did not." He turned to talk with Machk. "I mean no offense, my native friend."

Machk responded with a gaze that was chilly, bordering on hostile. Bryan wasn't one to back down from a hostile person, regardless of race, but Robert was glad when he returned his attention to Robert.

"After you left, we saw Jean-Marc Crevier with a large bruise on his face riding one of the best horses the new comte had. He nearly rode a few of our brothers and sisters down in his haste." Bryan sighed. "We were afraid that he was connected to you and your family missing."

The silence hung between them with the unasked question.

"I was responsible," Robert said. "That evening, I accosted

Jean-Marc and stole some papers from him. He was going to simply kill me, but De—" Robert shook his head. "Something startled him and he shot Susannah."

"Then the fault is his, Robert. Not yours. He will face God's judgment in the Lord's own time."

"He is facing His judgment as we speak." Robert drew the pistol from his belt, careful to keep the barrel facing the ground. "I ensured that this weapon would be the last he ever fired."

Bryan merely nodded and motioned for Robert and Machk to follow him.

"I will take you to talk with William," Bryan said. "We can talk on the way there."

Robert nodded and stepped to his side. He heard an irritated grunt behind him but ignored it. Machk would either follow him and Bryan or not. Robert spared no further thought.

"As I said, after you left, the new comte began his reign of abuse," Bryan said. "I have never known a human being with such a childish soul in a grown man."

"How so?" Machk asked, finally showing a flicker of interest.

"He became obsessed with enemies all around him," Bryan said. "The day after Jean-Marc left, the comte gathered all of us in the square. He had the guards in full armor and weapons and the wheel had been rolled out."

Robert stiffened. Machk's keen eyes noticed this. "There is some significance I'm missing?"

"Aye, Robert's brother, Edmund was arrested and chained to that wheel," Bryan stopped. "Jean-Marc systematically broke each and every bone in his arms, legs, hands and feet as well as a number of ribs. Edmund couldn't stand to give his arms relief nor could he hang to let his legs rest."

"Edmund spent three days in agony before the Lord showed him mercy," Robert said quietly.

"You did not tell me of this," Machk said with a strange note of accusation in his voice. He then let the silence hang for a few moments. "You have more than enough cause to hate the French as I do."

"Not the French, my friend," Bryan said. "One man committed these acts and he has paid the price with his own life. We cannot ask for more."

"We can demand more from the French," Machk snapped.

"This man was a Frenchman and had all of the evils that race possesses. Your new Frenchman shows that the French soul is corrupted."

"Jean-Marc and the comte are two different creatures. For all of his ills, Jean-Marc was a man of integrity."

"He was a murderer!" Robert snapped.

"Undoubtedly," Bryan replied calmly. "But, in your honest heart, Robert, you know that what Jean-Marc did was motivated by his devotion to France, not from his own little soul."

Robert nodded against his will. Bryan nodded and turned to continue.

"The comte made a speech, a paranoid speech about how Jean-Marc had allowed treason to fester. He fully intended to expunge this and said he would take whatever measures were necessary."

Machk grunted. "I know of sachems who behave much like this."

"How does your tribe handle such men?"

Machk shrugged. "They are removed and a new sachem is chosen."

"If it were only that simple for us as it is for your kind," Bryan sighed.

Robert glanced at Machk and saw the indignation in his eyes. Robert silently willed Machk to be silent and let it drop. Bryan hadn't meant it as an insult, simply as a way of making a comparison. But, after spending time with the Mohican, Robert knew that the process of removing a sachem and replacing him with a new one was anything but simple. Matrilineal lines had to be traced and evaluated so that the next sachem would be legitimate.

Yet, Robert also knew Machk well enough to recognize the look in the large Mohican's eyes. Machk wasn't going to let this perceived slight go unchallenged.

"Bryan is only referring to the clarity of action that the Mohican shows in removing a sachem who is unfit," Robert said. "He wasn't speaking to the process of removal and replacement."

Bryan nodded agreement and Machk looked somewhat mollified. It was hard to tell with the big Mohican. He was a man who found insult in anything that a white man might say, regardless of how innocent. Machk was a wise man, but all too often let his own anger cloud his view on the world.

The rest of the journey was short but passed in silence. Bryan appeared to be unwilling to risk the chance of insult that his previous comment seemed to have excited. For his own part, Robert was glad for the quiet that let him regain his composure after talking about Jean-Marc.

Bryan had a point; Jean-Marc was a zealot. Not for God, but for France itself. What he did was for the glory of France, not for his own ego. Before Jean-Marc had murdered Edmund at the wheel, certainly before he shot Susannah, Robert had felt a detached wariness toward the man who had been assigned to advise Watertown on how to integrate into French society. One was always careful about what they said around Jean-Marc, but there was no animosity between him and the people of Watertown.

That is, until Edmund had a little too much to drink at the public house and spoke his mind too blatantly where Jean-Marc could hear it. Of course, Edmund hadn't known that Jean-Marc was in the common room, but that made the talk no less foolish.

If Jean-Marc's aim had been to punish sedition, a quick, relatively painless hanging or beheading would have been sufficient unto the task. No, Jean-Marc had wanted to make a statement. Make a violent, bloody, horrific example now and, perhaps, scare the rest of the Puritans into behavior that wasn't contrary to French goals.

But, Jean-Marc had misjudged the Puritans, only succeeding in driving the open talk of dissatisfaction into the quiet hidden holes and family homes. Puritans were used to oppression and, as long as no sedition was expressed, Jean-Marc was content to let them go on as they wished.

But, what about Susannah's death at the man's hand? Robert didn't want to revisit that memory, and not simply because of the pain that memory held. He didn't want to examine it too much lest he come to a different conclusion than the hate. But, he couldn't help himself. His mind opened itself up and he found himself reliving that night.

Susannah's death hadn't been an accident. Jean-Marc had come to their campsite with murder in his heart. It was Robert who was to die, of that he was certain. Jean-Marc had no interest in Susannah and the children other than their leverage over Robert himself. Robert had seen the hate and betrayal in Jean-Marc's eyes as the Frenchman raised the pistol.

Deborah's cry had startled him and he turned toward what

he thought was danger. His shot into the dark was a defense against his fears. There had been nothing except reflex in Jean-Marc's actions.

Of course, it didn't mean that Robert had to like the man. Try as he might, pray as he might, Robert couldn't bring himself to forgive Jean-Marc's ghost. He hoped God would understand, if anybody could, the pain and anger at his heart. But, Robert's ingrained integrity wouldn't let his anger cloud reality. He still hated the man, but he could also see where Jean-Marc was simply a man doing what he thought was best for France.

Robert marveled at the depths of cruelty a man would go when he followed his heart and not his head. The heart was blind when it was invested in a cause. For Jean-Marc, that was the good of France.

Then, what did that say about Machk? Was his Mohican companion any different from Jean-Marc? Ironically, they were both motivated by France. Jean-Marc to protect and advance her, and Machk to destroy any works, or blood, of her. But, the mindset was the same. It was the same, single-minded focus. Both men overwhelmed by a single, solitary object of motivation.

And what did that say about Robert himself? He had already come to worry about Machk, but in the depths of his heart, he was sure the same rage and single-minded purpose lurked. The Robert Lockwood of a month ago would have embraced it. However, the Robert Lockwood of now wasn't so sure.

Agawam Plantation
Near modern-day Springfield, Massachusetts

William Pynchon was cut from a far different cloth than Bryan Pendleton was. By no means was it a lesser cloth, simply a different one. Bryan would lead from the front, expecting, and often getting, others to follow his example.

William, on the other hand, was the weaver himself. He pulled the threads about him to shape the tapestry of the world he lived in. Each man, woman and child had their place in God's creation, and William seemed to understand where that place was. Where Bryan would pull and heave to encourage, William would shape and nudge the best of all around him.

Robert knew and respected William. They had both come

across with Governor Winthrop's fleet in 1630. Robert and his brother Edmund had elected to move west along the northern bank of the Charles River to settle in Watertown and Cambridge. William and his family had moved to a town they called Roxbury just southwest of Boston proper.

He knew that William was a very intelligent man and shrewd in the ways of business. His town of Roxbury was set astride an isthmus of land that separated Boston from the mainland. That made Roxbury something of a funneling point. You had to go through Roxbury to get to Boston, with all of the economic benefits that came with it.

Yet, William had grown restless in Roxbury. His first wife, Anne, had died in the first year, leaving behind four children. He married Frances about a year later, but the ghost of Anne must have haunted him.

The rocks of Roxbury probably contributed to his desire to move west. The land, while fertile, was also full of rocks that made tending it a chore. Rumors had circulated that William had sent explorers west to find more easily arable land. Robert didn't know if William had found it, but shortly after the news of French possession arrived in Boston, William, his family and a few close friends left Roxbury to settle on the Connecticut River. Robert hadn't known where, or how, William's new home was agreeing with him.

However, now that Robert watched William approach, he could see that the large tract of land was quite agreeable. William looked content. His lively eyes darted this way and that powered by a mind that was constantly busy.

"Robert?" William squinted as though his eyes were deceiving him.

"Aye, William," Robert responded with a ready smile. He and William had always gotten along well together. He, Susannah, Edmund and Elizabeth, Edmund's widow, had traveled to Roxbury to attend Anne Pynchon's funeral. "You are well, I see."

"With the Good Lord's blessing," William embraced Robert. The easy familiarity was typical of William. "Frances will be happy to see you. How fares Susannah and the kids?"

How many times am I going to have to relive this memory? Robert prayed silently to the Lord.

"The children are well," Robert responded. "They are with

Elizabeth in a Mohican village on the river north of here. Susannah is resting with God."

William nodded understanding. He too had buried a wife and understood some of Robert's pain. Robert saw that in William's eyes.

If he knew how Susannah had died, would he still be able to understand the pain? Robert mused to himself.

"My flesh and my heart faileth: but God is the strength of my heart, and my portion forever," William quoted Psalms 73:26. "Have faith in Him. That is the only way to live."

"Amen," Robert said. "And thank you."

"And let me offer my condolences for Edmund's death. Bryan told me of it when he arrived a week ago," William continued. "It seems as though this Jean-Marc has much to answer for."

"Thank you, William," Robert said. "Jean-Marc is dead."

"I see," William said thoughtfully. "Indeed, I see."

"Robert, I was simply giving noteworthy news to William." Bryan sounded uncertain.

"Think nothing of it," Robert said. "Truly, it is no secret and you betray no trust."

"Thank you, Robert."

William turned and beckoned the three men into the house.

"Please come. I believe that Frances may have something for dinner and you are all welcome to join us."

"Robert!" Frances exclaimed. "I haven't seen you in far too long!"

Robert smiled and bobbed his head in recognition and some warmth.

"Thank you, Frances," Robert said. "You are looking well."

"I am. Where are Susannah and the children?"

"The children are in a native village north of here," Robert said. "Susannah is no longer with us."

"How?" She paused as she caught her husband's expression and the shake of his head. "Never mind that. Have you eaten?"

"Not since breaking our fast on the trail."

"Then, please, join us," she invited. "We are just about to sit down for our midday meal."

"Absolutely!" William said with gusto. "And is that fresh bread that I'm sinfully smelling?"

"William Pynchon," she said sternly. "Are you implying that my cooking is demonic?"

William's mouth opened and closed a few times while his mind raced to find a way out of the corner that he now found himself in.

"Of course not, Goodwife!" Bryan came to William's rescue. "Only that your cooking is so divine that it is fit only for our Lord. Our mortal mouths sin against the Almighty by sampling what is rightfully His, and His alone."

Frances chuckled. "One day, Goodman Pendleton, that silken tongue of yours will land you in trouble."

"Not if Eleanor can keep me in line," Bryan responded. "Granted, that is a monumental chore in the best of times."

They settled around a rough, yet stout, table that had been polished from care and use. Frances moved about the kitchen, setting plates for the midday meal. It was simple, in the manner of all Puritan things: bread, some pork and a hard cheese. This was washed down with mugs full of clean, cold water from a well behind the house. William said a simple, yet devout grace and the meal began in earnest.

"Regarding Eleanor," William said. "Is it not time for you to continue to Dorchester to rejoin your family?"

"There is much more work to be done here, William," Bryan said. "I can't, in good conscience, leave your home undefended."

"We will be fine," William said. "We are friendly with the noble natives here, and they have much in the way of honor, so we are not overly concerned with an attack from them." He lifted his cup and tipped it in salute to Machk. Machk barely looked up and acknowledged the compliment.

"I'm more concerned with the French, William. I know you are as well."

"That is true," William nodded. "However, the news that you have brought me convinces me that France will be more occupied oppressing our Puritan brethren and the Pilgrims than they are going to be with pushing west into the frontier." William stopped and took a bite.

"We cannot forget that we know nothing of how the French in Quebec are going to behave. If they aren't on friendly terms with those in Boston, then the Boston French will have even more on their plates than harassing us in the west. We have plenty of time to finish the wall ourselves, Bryan."

"William…" Bryan tried to speak but William cut him off.

"A man's place is with his family," William said firmly. "We've already taken you away from them for too long. These are tough, difficult times for all of us. A family must have their father with them to be a foundation that they can rely upon against the waves being sent against us. In these troubled times, I refuse to keep you away from your family."

A piece of bread threatened to lodge itself in Robert's throat and he was forced to reach for the mug of water before he choked. William's comment hit him entirely too close to the heart. He had actively avoided saying goodbye to his children. Johnathan and Deborah were living in the Mohican village with their aunts, Elinor and Elisabeth, and their families.

"Are you trying to be rid of me?" Bryan smiled.

"Of course not!" William said. "Any peace-loving man, whether they be Puritan or native, is welcome here. We will offer what assistance we can and help them along to Dorchester if that is what they need or desire."

"I understand, William," Bryan said, obviously not happy about the situation. "We have a section that is currently raising up. I will stay until that is complete and then take my leave."

"That is welcome news," William said and then turned toward Robert. "And what of you, Robert? Are you to return to your children? Without their mother, they are in even more need of your strength and guidance."

"I am not a fit father, William," Robert said.

"Posh!" William snorted. "If you are not a fit father, then the rest of the world is sadly lacking as well. Which may explain most of our trials and tribulations."

Robert felt his lips curl against his will as William's humor chipped away at the discomfort in the room.

"What I mean is that I have too much hate in my heart," Robert said. "I don't think Jonathan or Deborah need to learn about hate this early in their lives."

"Perhaps," William shrugged. "But, you understand your limitations. I would argue that you are more able to avoid that pitfall in parenting, teaching your children to hate."

"I will think about what you have said," Robert promised.

"Then I can hardly ask for more. Is there anything I can provide you with?"

"If you have some powder and shot for my pistol, I would be willing to barter with you for it," Robert said.

"Alas, that is the one thing that I cannot part with." William shook his head. "We have little enough as it is. And, even though I assured Bryan as to our safety, I would be remiss to not have some ability to protect ourselves from the unforeseen."

Disappointment flared in Robert's breast and he didn't have to look at Machk to see the anger in the man's eyes. Should he press? He was sure that he could talk William into providing a small store of powder and shot. But, would Robert be able to live with himself to accept them knowing that William needed it more than Robert did? To what extent was he willing to live with his decisions?

"I see," he said. "Then may we impose upon your pantry?"

"By all means," William said and waved expansively about the kitchen. "I'm quite sure that Frances can gather enough foodstuffs and such to keep you well fed for a few days."

Machk opened his mouth to say something, but Robert grabbed his wrist. Machk's eyes flared with shocked rage. He jerked his hand away from Robert and abruptly stood. Gathering his belongings, he stormed out the door.

"Perhaps we could spare a little powder," William said with uncharacteristic uncertainty in the uncomfortable silence.

"No, William," Robert said. "You are quite correct, you need what you have to ensure that you and your family are safe."

"Very well. Will you and your friend stay the night with us?"

Robert shook his head. "I don't believe that would be wise. Machk is a valued friend and I can't ask him to stay here."

Robert found Machk just outside of the incomplete palisade, still angry.

"Robert!" he said. "Have you forgotten our oath to the other?" The tone was accusatory.

"I have not, Machk," Robert said. "I simply don't wish to place others in danger to get my revenge."

"Danger?" Machk scoffed. "From who? The Pocumtuc? Better to be afraid of the deer than with one of those mewling kittens."

"'Yea, mine own familiar friend, in whom I trusted, which did eat of my bread, hath lifted up his heel against me,'" Robert said.

"Another of your Bible verse nonsense?"

"Psalms 41:9, Machk. It reminds us that even the closest of

ours can turn against us. We love others as we love ourselves, more so, but we must be aware of the dangers that even the most friendly of others can lift their hands against us."

"You need a book to tell you what is common wisdom to a child?" Machk sneered. "I hardly need your scribbles to tell me that there is betrayal in the world."

"I am glad to hear that," Robert said. "Where do we go from here? We still have a few hours before darkness."

"I assume that you still wish for powder and shot for that absurd firearm?"

"You would be correct, my friend. We'll need to find another homestead or town to get it."

"More time away from our vengeance?" Machk asked. "We should go and take the powder and shot tonight so that we can stop with this delay."

"Are you a Mohawk now, Machk?" The large Mohican jerked as if Robert had physically punched him. Shock turned to rage as Robert continued. "Have you lost your honor that you would sneak about like a thief to take what is not given?"

"We will take what we wish from the white man," Machk grated. He wasn't thinking clearly.

"We will take from the French for they are our enemy," Robert said firmly. "They are the ones who have taken our loved ones from us. We will take what we wish in an honorable raid, matching blood for blood. I will not allow English blood to be spilt unless they have done us wrong."

"You are weak, Robert."

"I am practical. We need to have friends here that we can work with, and shelter with, when the French begin to hunt us down." Robert paused.

"Do you wish for tales to travel that you and I are raiding anyone we choose? That will make it difficult for us."

"We can shelter with the other tribes," Machk retorted, but he knew that his heart wasn't in it.

"No Machk, we can't and you know that," Robert said gently. "The other tribes are as hard-pressed as the Mohican, and the diseases the white man brings ravages whole villages."

Machk glared at Robert for a long moment and then sharply turned and began the distance-eating trot that had brought them to Agawam.

Ten miles south-southeast of Agawam Plantation

Machk had been blessedly silent since they had departed the Pynchon homestead in earnest. For his part, Robert was happy for the silence. It was a sullen, rebellious silence, but silence nonetheless and it let Robert think about both his footing and the thoughts in his mind.

Something William said had struck a chord in Robert. He couldn't narrow it down, what exactly William had said, but it burned inside of him. Perhaps it was what William had not said. His comment of any "peace-loving man, Puritan or native" made Robert feel as though he had a piece of grizzle between his teeth that no amount of prying was going to dislodge.

If there was a more generous man than William Pynchon, Robert didn't know him. He had no doubts whatsoever that if a man should arrive on his porch, William would take the man inside, give him food, water and comfort. But, could Robert impose upon that kindness? Could he vouchsafe William's hospitality knowing that such a promise would strain William's resources?

"Do you see anything over there?"

Robert started at the voice that sounded so near him.

"No," another voice replied disgustedly from further away. "It must have been a deer or the like."

"That is still something to investigate. Some venison would be welcome around the camp."

Robert thought furiously. Instinct had frozen him in place after the initial shock. A part of him wanted to bolt, but he brutally forced that instinct to the back of his mind. He recognized the accent if not the voices themselves. Those were English accents, comfortably familiar. Unless he missed his guess completely, those were Pilgrim voices from around Plymouth. He relaxed and stood.

"Hello!" He kept his voice cheerful and friendly. Still the men turned to him and instinctively raised their muskets at him. "You are from Plymouth?"

They lowered their weapons and Robert could see them clearly. He recognized the men, but only their faces. He didn't know their names. They were people to whom he had said a brief welcome during his travels to Plymouth on occasions they required his service as a carpenter. One of them would order a piece of furniture or such and he would deliver to the colony.

"Aye, and who might you be?"

Robert felt safe enough to emerge completely and approach the men.

"Robert Lockwood," he introduced himself. "Lately of Watertown. I have a friend who is also in these woods. A Mohican by the name of Machk. Please do not be alarmed should he approach."

"I am George Soule and this is William Holmes, both of Duxbury."

Robert nodded welcome.

"Thank you for your warning," George said. "Our nerves have been somewhat frayed as of late."

"Your village…" Robert jumped as Machk stepped out from the tree line. "The one you call Duxbury is far from here to the east. What brings you to lands which are not yours?"

Robert shot a look at Machk. There was no need for the hostility and suspicion. However, neither man seemed to mind. George even laughed aloud.

"What are we doing?" William asked. "Being lost is what we are doing."

Robert thought there was a ghost of a smile from the big Mohican. For that, Robert was thankful. There was still a ghost of humanity left in the man.

"It seems as though you have an idea of where we are," George said. "May we impose upon you for assistance, friend?"

"Where do you wish to go?"

"We are bound for Dorchester and should have arrived already."

Machk nodded. "You are far north of that village. About three days travel for a party your size."

"Party?" Robert asked.

"Yes," Machk said. "I heard their passage an hour or so before."

"You didn't tell me you had heard them."

Machk shrugged. "There was no need. I had hoped to pass without meeting them. We have other tasks that require our attention."

"Might I ask what that business is?" William asked.

"To punish the French for taking our loved ones away."

"Machk's wife was killed by a sickness brought by a Frenchman," Robert clarified. "For myself, I lost my wife and brother."

"Brother?" George seemed to remember something. "Edmund

Lockwood was your brother? The one the French tortured a few months back?"

"Yes."

"Ghastly business that," William shuddered. "We heard some of the details, but not all of it. Enough to give a man fear enough."

"That was Jean-Marc Crevier's intention," Robert said.

"We will ask no more details. Barbara would certainly agree with you."

"Barbara?"

"Barbara Standish," George said. "We have not seen nor heard from her husband Myles since Plymouth fell. We fear him dead as well."

"Plymouth has fallen?" Robert felt like one of those birds that he had heard of that mimicked human speech. He just couldn't form more coherent thought. Things were moving too quickly and his mind was racing to catch up.

"In early May," William said. "The only one to reach us before we left Duxbury was an Indian named Hobbamock. He spoke to John Alden and John organized our party."

"But the rest of the story is for John to tell," George said. "He spoke directly to Hobbamock and will have more to say."

Robert didn't know John Alden personally, but he was a well-known figure in both the Plymouth and Massachusetts Bay colonies.

Robert and Machk followed George and William to the camp among the trees that held the refugees from Duxbury. William moved ahead while George fetched some water and hardtack to nibble on while they waited. The wait was only a few minutes and John Alden joined them.

"Hello, Goodman Lockwood," John said and then turned to Machk. "And friend Machk. William has told me of you and your tasks."

Machk nodded politely.

"And we have heard that you are lost," Machk said bluntly, and John chuckled.

"A rather succinct way of putting it," John replied. "But, don't let our wives know that. No need to encourage them, I think."

John took a deep breath and returned to serious matters.

"But yes, we are quite turned about in these thick woods. William says that you would be able to assist us. We would be eternally grateful."

"You are, perhaps, a day's march from the great river that you call the Connecticut," Machk said. "You could follow the river, but I don't recommend that."

"I'm not doubting your words," John said. "I would be interested in hearing why?"

"The banks of the river are not suitable for travel and you would not be able to build rafts and still bring your animals and carts with you."

"What choice do we have?"

"I know of a way through these mountains," Machk said. "It is a rough path for carts and animals. However, I don't judge it as impossible."

"That would be welcome assistance indeed, my friend."

Robert looked at Machk with surprise on his face.

"I am not a Mohawk," Machk said, then turned and walked away.

Dorchester
Present-day Windsor, Connecticut

"Might I join you, Goodman Lockwood?"

Robert looked up from his task to see John Alden standing at the doorway to the improvised woodshop that he had set up to pass the time more than anything else. There was always furniture to be made and repaired, and Robert was happy to lend his skills.

"Of course, John," Robert nodded and lay down his mallet and chisel. The piece before him was a simple chair, nothing fancy. The smell of the walnut shavings hung in the air, heightened by the pine burning in the lone firepot.

John leaned against the door frame and crossed his arms.

"How are you faring here in Dorchester?" he asked.

"Well enough," Robert replied. "I have enough tasks to keep my hands busy and out of mischief. I thank you for asking."

"And your family? Will you send word for them to join us here?"

Robert paused for a few seconds before answering.

"Eventually," he said. "There are some issues that I need to come to grips with before I subject my children to them."

"I'm not a confessor, Robert," John said. "But, if you need to talk, you only have to buy the drinks."

Robert returned the grin. It felt good to smile again, to appreciate humor that wasn't dark and bloodthirsty.

"You did not come only to ask how I am doing," Robert said. "I can see it in your face that you have another matter you wish to discuss."

"Yes," John replied, shifting slightly into a more comfortable position. "That is correct. I've come to ask you for assistance."

"By all means," Robert nodded. "Any assistance I can provide is freely given."

"Hear me out on this one first, Robert. I'm not asking you to mend a chair. Let me first explain before you pledge yourself to such an endeavor."

"Very well."

"As you know, the *Griffin* arrived a few days ago." John moved to a chair and sat. "Other than supplies and tools, she carried crates and crates of books and letters. We've made no secret that they arrived. However, we've also kept them to the elders until we can fully digest what they contain. To be frank, some of the letters are disturbing."

"What do they contain?" Robert asked.

"Visions of the future. Of a future that would have existed had these Americans not arrived into our time. It's confusing to think of our future as their past, and one thing the letters warn us of is to not expect the exact letter of their histories to follow. They acknowledge that their arrival has changed things and will continue to change things that will muddle anything they can document from their history beyond recognition.

"However, they also stress that the mistakes their ancestors made were the results of trends in the process of history that were doomed to occur unless we learned from them now and worked to prevent them."

"I'm curious," Robert said. "I can understand why their arrival changes things, but I'm not sure I grasp this idea of trends."

"Completely understandable," John nodded. "It took us leaders a few hours to understand it ourselves. After that, it became clear. In fact, it almost caused a schism in our ranks."

"Why?"

"History isn't kind to the natives of this land. You're familiar with how innocent they are to our diseases?"

"Yes," Robert replied. "The Mohican village that Machk comes from was ravaged by smallpox."

"Exactly. However, imagine that effect on all the natives of this land from Quebec to the tip of Spanish Florida and west."

Robert's eyes widened and John nodded.

"You now begin to understand. Diseases we've brought over already have or will kill a great number of the natives of this land. For that and other reasons, the fate of the native tribes here in North America and elsewhere in the New World, is not favorable. They are too weak to resist the efforts of our descendants to expand their own land.

"Most of this was accidental, we could not have known about the specter of death that we harbored aboard the colony ships. Yet, there is the story of British soldiers using smallpox as a weapon against the natives. At a place called Fort Pitt, just over one hundred years from now, a British officer would gift blankets and linens to the natives. These were taken from the sick ward of the fort from patients suffering from smallpox."

"That's disgusting, John," Robert said.

"It is, indeed," John agreed. "Thankfully, this appears to have been an isolated incident, but, in honesty, it is the only one that the American books had available. And I shall say nothing of the Indian Removal Act which led to what the natives of the future call the 'Trail of Tears.'

"But, even knowing what we do now, we couldn't stop the death of millions of natives by staying away. The sicknesses we've brought are out there already.

"I'm digressing," John said. "I came here to recruit you for a project, and adventure, if you will."

"I've already said that I will volunteer," Robert said.

"Yes, but you have not heard of what you have volunteered for."

"Indeed, please continue."

"I was particularly struck by a notion brought by the books." John leaned forward in the chair, propping his elbows on his thighs. "In its history, the nation these Americans hail from would experience only one civil war. For decades prior, the nation was split between states where slavery was permitted and those in which slavery was prohibited. In the decades that would lead to their civil war, there was a system by which slaves from the states that permitted slavery could escape to the states that did not permit it."

"They called this system the 'Underground Railroad.' A group of slaves would be led by a guide, often an escaped slave themselves, through the dangers of slave hunters. Along the way, the slaves would have stops in which to hide to rest and eat.

"They called these guides 'conductors.'"

"And, you want me to be one of these conductors?" Robert asked.

"In a word, yes. I plan on creating an 'underground railroad' for anybody who wishes to be free of the French in Boston. It doesn't matter whether they are Pilgrim, Puritan, native or slave, this railroad will be for anybody who wishes assistance and guidance."

Robert leaned back in his chair to think and John gave him time for his thoughts.

Just how plausible was this idea? This "underground railroad"? It sounded so easy. You walk into a town, find out who wants to leave and lead them away. But, Robert knew it would be far from easy. Perhaps the first few groups would have the easiest time. The French wouldn't be expecting something like this. But, once they noticed their English subjects were disappearing, that ease would disappear just as quickly. The countryside would become dangerous from French patrols seeking to return those settlers to their towns. Not to mention executing the "conductor" in question.

And what about the stops? There was a distinct dearth of white settlements between the outskirts of Boston and the Connecticut River. An obvious stop would be William Pynchon's Agawam Plantation, but that was at least three days, more realistically four to five days with a laden group of townsfolk unused to the strange wilderness. Add the need for caution and stealth from searching parties and the trip could easily take a week.

But, still, the idea held a certain amount of charm and a certain amount of daring. He would be doing something other than mending chairs. As important as the mundane task was, Robert felt that he would be of better use actively helping his fellow Puritans escape from the French.

But, then, what of Machk and their oath to each other? The

big Mohican would not take kindly to this. The idea of any activity that did not result in dead Frenchmen would offend the man, and the killing of Frenchmen would be counterproductive to this endeavor.

That was one bridge he would have to cross when it came to it. This was now and Robert had a decision to make. His oath, solemn word, or rejecting honor to help others.

Dorchester
Present-day Windsor, Connecticut

Machk stopped short as he caught sight of a small boy. Something he couldn't express, let alone explain, held him. There was nothing outwardly remarkable about the boy. He was young, barely more than an infant, not yet walking. Certainly younger than his own little boy would have been. The child before him had blond hair; his son's hair was a raven black fuzz that had just begun to grow in earnest the last time that Machk had held him.

It was the eyes, Machk decided. They weren't identical; the boy's were blue while his son's were so dark as to appear black. But, he knew those eyes. And most importantly, those eyes knew him. They remembered times before his birth. They recalled the evenings that Machk had held him with his mother by his side. He remembered playful afternoons in the spring grass. He remembered fear as his mother smothered him to keep him from dying of the sickness that was consuming her or the hunger that would follow after her death.

In those eyes, Machk saw disappointment. He saw betrayal. Not at his own death. The world was what it was and there was no point in being angry in the natural course of things. What Machk saw in those eyes was sadness, not for himself, but for Machk. Sadness and disappointment that the man those eyes had known and loved could have let himself be taken by grief and hatred as to let his own light dim. Machk had fallen from worthiness in those eyes.

It was that sad disappointment that Machk was completely unarmored against. When his boy had been born, Machk had promised his son safety. To himself, Machk promised that he would never be anything less than someone his son could look up to. That promise had driven Machk into depths of madness and self-hatred. Depths that he hadn't found the strength to drag himself from. Not until the blue eyes of a young boy that Machk had never met remembered a man far greater than what Machk had allowed himself to become.

A spear of pure white light pierced Machk. It wasn't visible; no eye could discern it. But, it shone nonetheless and shoved aside the perpetual red haze of hatred, anger and pain that Machk had lived with for almost a year. He could not, would not continue the path that he had been on. He was not a man that his son would have been proud of. No child would be proud of a father whose only thought morning, noon and many sleepless nights was of killing. Of a man who wasted away his strength of mind, body and talents. A man who threw away the ability to love. That was a promise that Machk refused to break now that he knew the eyes of his son still judged him, even from beyond his short life.

Calm washed over him as the light expanded, filling his soul. Call it the Great Spirit, God or any thousands of names attributed to the great supreme being in the heavens, Machk had finally found his master in this life, and in the next. Without the bloodthirst, Machk was left without a tiller to guide him. He clung desperately to the inner peace within him as a man who is tossed upon a raging sea will rely on anything that floats to keep his head above water.

Was this the feeling that his wife and his friend Edward had felt praying to their god? One of calm serenity and the sense that you were no longer alone in this world? Machk hoped so. Yet, he was still too stubborn to admit himself into the halls of whatever transformation was washing over him.

He opened eyes that he didn't remember closing and found the child again. Those eyes smiled. It was a self-satisfied smile, content in the knowledge that the world was returning once more to its proper alignment. Things were finally righting itself. That his father had found something within himself that even he didn't know he had.

The child and his parents turned a corner and disappeared behind a house. Those eyes had their own journeys, separate from the path that Machk had been set upon. But, Machk would always remember those eyes and the soul that they possessed. In his heart he heard a soft voice whisper to him. *Safe journeys, Nooch. I will see you again.*

"I will do my best, little one," Machk promised the soul of his boy. "Kiss your mother and wait for me."

Robert sat on a fallen tree trunk and watched the Standish children playing under Barbara's watchful gaze. She was everything that Robert had expected after talking to John Alden on the trek across the wilderness to Dorchester. Robert could see pain in her eyes as she went on about her day. The uncertainty of Myles' death haunted her. Like everybody else, she assumed that he was dead, but a stubborn part of her refused to believe that. She wanted to believe, against all reason, that her stubborn, irascible lout of a husband was still alive and simply unkind enough to show his face in Dorchester.

At least, that's what Robert saw in her face. A stubborn set of the mouth and furrow of the brow when he first made his acquaintance and offered his condolences for her loss. She had accepted them gracefully, but Robert could tell she didn't quite believe it necessary yet. She still hoped and that hope etched against Robert's soul. She needed the closure of death, of an eyewitness who had seen her husband fall, or a story from an eyewitness.

Robert had decided that she deserved that closure. Any person needed to know whether or not their loved one was alive or dead. It was cruel to live in the purgatory of the unknowing.

And not just for her, but for all of those living in Dorchester, or wherever they may be. Each woman and child, and even some men, deserved to know what the fate of their loved one was.

And, if they were still among the living, they deserved the company of their loved one. After all, what William Pynchon had said was true; a family needed their father. If Robert could bring these families together again, he would. It would be something that Susannah would have wanted. It was something that he could, perhaps, redeem himself in his own eyes for abandoning his own children.

Perhaps.

He felt more than saw Machk approach. Uncomfortable silence had been the normal state of their relationship since leaving Agawam. The two had hardly exchanged more words than necessary, and only then short, curt and coldly.

But, this was different. Something had changed, Robert could feel it. The air was still cool, but not frigid.

The log rocked slightly as Machk sat. The large Mohican was unusually quiet, unusually hesitant. It was as though an internal struggle coursed through the man. Perhaps that was what disturbed Robert so very much. Machk had always been a rock. A homicidal rock, but a solid foundation that refused to budge whatever life may throw at it. Robert was surprised by how much he had depended on that strength, the sense of purpose. Finding that sense of purpose gone was unexpectedly disturbing.

"Tell me of your god, Robert," Machk said.

Robert's world stopped. It was quite literally the last thing that he had expected from the man. He would have more readily expected Machk to grow horns, a tail and hooves and announce himself as Satan himself. For Machk to speak the name of the Lord without malice, let alone with something almost like reverence, was unthinkable.

"I would be happy too, Machk," Robert responded. "I must say that this is unexpected from you, my friend."

"Yes, it is," Machk replied and his face split in one of the most serene, satisfied smiles that Robert had seen in many years. "Something has happened that I'm at a loss to explain, even unto myself. But, one thing is for certain; I can't continue on the path that I had set myself upon."

Robert didn't press any further. Instead, he paused for a few moments to gather his thoughts. He opened his mouth to speak, but nothing came out. Any child could have detailed the tenets of the Puritan faith; yet, Robert found himself unable to at this moment.

His mind returned to a quiet evening, soon after they had arrived at the Mohican village, when he and his sister, Elinor, spoke about faith. The seeds that Nicholas had planted before he left for France had begun to sprout and were in full root. What answer *did* he tell Machk? That God had already chosen His own and Machk wasn't welcome? No, that was neither correct nor charitable, Robert mentally reprimanded himself. The Lord would choose His people, and Elinor was right. Who was he to judge who was a member of the Elect?

A new thought came to Robert. What if the Elect was a destination and not the journey itself? If it didn't matter *how* a soul got to the foot of God, but only whether he was destined to get there. If that were the case, then how could Robert, being honest with himself, insist that the path that he found himself on was the only path?

Robert was still a Puritan and he knew in his heart that the path that he was following was the one laid down by Scripture and His own holy Word. That was as unshakeable as the mountains around him. But, what he had lost was the hubris, the overweening pride, in the certainty of his path. He believed in it and would encourage others to follow his example, but he could no longer find it in his heart and soul to judge any man as condemned in the eyes of the Almighty. He could no longer shun others.

Inside, Robert felt a flutter in the silence of his soul. The quiet stillness of God's Word awaiting stirred, just a bit and just for a moment. But, that quiver gave Robert peace that he hadn't felt in a long time. The Lord was still with him and He felt that Robert was still worthy. It was going to be a journey to full revitalization, but Robert was now sure that the joy would come again and with it, profound serenity.

"I don't know how to answer that, Machk," he said. "I know what He means to me, but I don't know how He's going to speak to you. I'm afraid that no man or woman would be able to answer that."

Machk was silent for a few moments before replying.

"A fair answer, Robert. What does he mean to you?"

"Still, that is a difficult question to answer. I know you tired of Bible verses, but that is often how we frame our conceptions of God. Perhaps you can bear a few?"

Robert saw Machk's eye instinctively twitch as they wished to roll, but forced themselves to behave. Instead he gave a nod for Robert to continue.

"Exodus 3:14 reads: God said to Moses, 'I Am who I Am.' And he said, 'Say this to the people of Israel, *I Am has sent me to you.*'"

"That makes little sense, Robert," Machk said.

"I agree; however, it encapsulates God Himself. Words fail when talking to each other about Him.

"Revelations 1:8: 'I am the Alpha and the Omega,' says the Lord God, 'who is and who was and who is to come, the Almighty.'

"Alpha and Omega mean that he was the first, Alpha, and the last, Omega," Robert explained. "We believe that there was nothing before Him and will be nothing after Him. He is all there will ever be."

"These are verses in your Bible?"

"Yes, I can obtain you one, if you wish," Robert offered.

"I cannot read your language."

"That is not something that will stop us; I can work with you on reading."

Machk nodded and another silence fell. Robert was reluctant to broach the topic, but it couldn't wait any longer.

"Machk," he said. "I can no longer honor our oath. I can no longer find it within myself to indiscriminately murder the French."

"Neither can I, Robert," Machk replied. "I don't believe that our loved ones, my wife and child and your wife, would approve of us if we did so."

Robert nodded and Machk's face split in the first honest, warm smile that Robert had seen from the big Mohican.

"Besides, I don't think we would enjoy this Heaven you claim to be if our loved ones were to have an eternity of recriminations."

Robert laughed and another weight slid from him.

"I don't think that we need to hate the French," Robert said. "However, I will not be overly concerned if a few of them were to fall beneath our clubs."

"Indeed," Machk nodded.

"John Alden has asked me to return to Massachusetts Bay and Plymouth to see if any of our brethren have survived. I would ask that you join us. Your knowledge of these woods would be valuable."

"Not of these woods, Robert," Machk replied. "I know of the woods along this river and to the west. To the east remains a mystery that I have not had the leisure to explore."

"Then come as my friend. Let us become the brothers that pledged to be. Not from blood, but from purpose."

Machk paused to think. "My wife died because she thought it was worthy of her to risk herself to care for others. How could I fail to follow that example?"

"So help us, God." Machk and Robert clasped hands again.

Confederation

Bjorn Hasseler

Grantville
March 1635

"Thanks. You all have it under control here." Garland Alcom spoke loudly as he emerged from the office. He retrieved his own bag lunch and looked for a seat at one of the tables in the front room, noting some smiles and pleased looks. The workers at one table waved him to an open seat.

"*Herr* Alcom."

"Just Garland is fine. How are you all doing?" he asked in Amideutsch. Garland learned names and shook hands all around before sitting down.

After a few minutes of small talk, Garland said, "How is work going here?"

"*Gut.*" Fine. The rest of the answers were variations on that theme.

"Anything you want to know?"

Garland answered three or four questions about the company, which was doing fine. He was troubled that there weren't more. Most veteran employees would have given management the third degree. But those who took jobs making percussion caps were often down on their luck and hesitant to make waves. Garland had a lot of experience with employees like that since the Ring of Fire and had learned to recognize them. He couldn't put all

271

of it into words, but many of these men and women had that look about them.

One man with a deep tan sitting at the next table did not. While Garland considered how to draw him into conversation, the lunch table discussion began to return to what he supposed was its normal level. The assassination of Mayor Dreeson and Reverent Wiley, the riots, and the crash of the vice president's plane were the primary topics.

"Who is the Vice President?" That was Johann Lämmerhirt.

"We just voted a month ago, *dummkopf!* It is Helene Gundelfinger." Garland remembered that speaker's name was Willi Friederaun.

"Who is she?"

"Some businesswoman. Married to an up-timer, I think."

Eyes turned to Garland. He shrugged. "Yeah, she married Walter Goodluck. I've met him a couple times, but I don't really know him. He was from out of town, just working on a construction project in Grantville when the Ring of Fire hit." He shook his head. "Not such good luck, if you ask me. But Walter seems like a stand-up guy. He's an Indian, you know. Navajo, I think."

"A what?"

"Navajo. They're one of the Indian tribes in North America."

He had everyone's attention, including the man he'd been intending to draw into a conversation.

A bell rang. It sounded like an honest-to-goodness school bell, and everyone quickly got up from the table. Garland watched them go.

"Stop." He pointed to the man whom he'd been studying. "*Komm her, bitte.*"

The other workers, especially those Garland had tentatively pegged as down on their luck, quickly left the front room. They were pretty enthusiastic about going back to work. Garland suspected they wanted to get out of the line of fire if the big boss had a problem with somebody.

The man approached Garland with no apprehension visible in his face or in his eyes. But something was off about how he moved.

"Please walk to the end of the next table and back," Garland requested.

The man's eyebrows may have lifted a fraction, but he complied.

"*Herr* . . ." Garland had lost the man's name.

"Weston."

"*Herr* Weston, you are sliding around in your boots. You could slip. That's dangerous when you're making percussion caps."

Weston grimaced. "These new boots premade to standard sizes do not fit me. They are tight in the toes and wide in the heel."

"Oh." Garland remembered hearing that before. Where was it? Oh, back up-time. A fellow mail carrier over in Fairmont...

Garland Alcom slapped himself in the forehead. Here he was, trying to read the company's employees, and he'd missed the obvious. That wasn't a tan....

"You're an Indian, aren't you, Weston?"

"I assure you, I was not born in India." There might have been the faintest hint of a smile on Weston's face.

"Native American, then."

"I am Sakaweston of the Wampanoag."

"Where do you live?"

"What you call Massachusetts." Weston pronounced the name a little differently than Garland was used to. "But that is a different tribe."

Garland blurted out his next question. "What are you doing in Europe?"

"I was abducted."

"What?"

"In 1611, the English captain Edward Harlow sailed along the coast and seized us one, two, three at a time. Twenty-nine, all together. I lived in England for many years. Some of the others went back. I joined an English regiment and fought in Bohemia."

Garland Alcom shook his head. "Have you been fighting your way across Europe ever since?"

"Until Alte Veste."

"What are you doing now?"

"Learning how to make percussion caps."

"Oh. Wow." Garland literally rocked back on his heels.

"How did you know I am Wampanoag? What you call Indian."

"I used to deliver mail. I knew one of the carriers over in Fairmont. He had to order custom shoes because his heels slid around just like yours do. He was Cherokee." Alcom shook his head. "So...percussion caps. Are you planning to take that home?"

Sakaweston did not answer.

"Because percussion caps are too advanced for North America

right now. One cap, one shot. Use a flintlock. The flint will be good for a hundred shots. But you're going to need gunpowder, too."

Sakaweston's eyebrows raised.

"You know what I plan, and you offer advice?"

"Yeah. What else do you need?"

"I need to talk with Walter Goodluck."

Bamberg
Sunday, May 24, 1637

Spring had arrived, and Walter Goodluck felt a need to be outside. After Sunday services—while Seventh-Day Adventist himself, he felt a responsibility to accompany his wife to the Lutheran church on Sundays—he'd left the city for a walk in the countryside. It was still cool to his thinking, but he'd grown up on the reservation in Arizona.

When he returned to the family's townhouse, Walter greeted the mounted constable at the door in Amideutsch.

"*Gut tag*, Franz."

"*Gut tag*, Herr Goodluck. The children are inside, but your wife was called to the communications center."

Walter raised an eyebrow at that. Helene tried to avoid government business on Sundays.

"*Dank*, Franz. I'll head over there."

Walter quickened his pace. Helene probably had to talk to either Grantville or Magdeburg or both about some new crisis. He supposed it could have something to do with the Ottoman War. Or the Polish War.

One of the SoTF National Guardsmen at the door of the communication center checked with someone inside and then held the door for Walter.

He found his wife and a couple of officers seated at a table surrounded by chaos. At least a third of the radio operators spaced around the perimeter of the room were frantically scribbling down what they heard over their crude earpieces. Another third or so tapped away at their keys, sending replies back out. Two aides collected the transcribed messages and handed operators the replies to send. Another attempted to keep all the printed message forms in front of Helene and the officers in order.

"Walter!" his wife exclaimed. "The French have attacked the Plymouth Colony."

"The Pilgrims?" he blurted out. "When?"

"May ninth."

Walter Goodluck froze. Barely more than two weeks ago.

"There's a radio in North America?" he demanded.

"Dutch. New Amsterdam. Here is the interesting part. It may mean more to you than it did to me. The message originated with Massasoit."

"Ousamequin." Walter's correction came automatically. "Massasoit is his title. Great sachem." He stressed the second syllable and pronounced the last vowel as a long *e*.

The President of the State of Thuringia-Franconia nodded her understanding. "He sent a runner to New Amsterdam. Two, running together. One stopped to brief..." She struggled with the name. "Sassacus. Sassacus allowed the other to continue to New Amsterdam."

"Whoa," Walter breathed.

"Why is that significant?"

"Eastern Woodlands isn't my area," Walter warned his wife. "We were all Native Americans, but they're Algonquians. I'm Diné. But Sakaweston told me what things were like in 1611. The Wampanoag and the Pequot weren't allies. They're rivals. It's not that different from the *adel*."

"So if... Sassacus is helping Mas—Ousamequin..." The President shook her head. "New Amsterdam radioed Vlissingen. Vlissingen sent to Magdeburg, Magdeburg to Grantville, and Grantville to us. Word will be getting out."

"How soon?"

"The evening news in Grantville." Helene sounded annoyed at that.

Walter smirked, just a little. He couldn't help it. "Just like up-time."

"Thank you very much."

"What are the USE and the SoTF going to do?" Walter asked.

"I am talking to Ed and Estuban. There is not much we *can* do. We do not have enough information about what is happening, and we certainly do not have forces we can send." Helene Gundelfinger looked at her husband strangely. "Why?"

"Some of the Pilgrims are dead, and as much as I'm Diné, I'm an American, too. I'll arrange for an acting manager at work and a train ticket. It could take a few days. I need to talk with Sakaweston."

Ruins of Fort Sovereignty
(up-time Fort Saybrook, Connecticut)
Tuesday, August 18, 1637

George Fenwick grabbed one end of another board that could be salvaged from a mostly burned house in what had been the Sovereignty settlement. The river towns, refugees, and tribes had joined forces long enough to turn back the French when a few dozen of them had ventured upriver. But they'd lost the fort and most of the settlement and too many people who hadn't evacuated in time. Now the survivors were salvaging what they could.

A faint yell came from down by the water. Fenwick listened carefully but couldn't make out the words. One of the lookouts came pounding up the path to where the survivors were working.

"Sail! Sail!"

George Fenwick dropped the board he was carrying. "French? Get your weapons!"

The two dozen or so men working with him raced for the muskets leaning against trees or unburned fences not far away. Then they took up positions near the shore.

A lookout reported to Colonel Fenwick and Governor John Winthrop the Younger.

"She's a big one—and I know that fishing boat that's with her. That's the boat Richard More's been using to bring in people from Sowams. But she raised colors I've never seen before. Red-and-white stripes. Blue in one corner."

Fenwick exchanged glances with Winthrop and shrugged.

Soon the ship was close enough to lower a boat. When the boat touched bottom, four men quickly hopped out and splashed the last few steps to shore. The boat's crew quickly shoved off and began rowing back to their ship.

The four new arrivals headed unerringly toward Winthrop and Fenwick.

"Hallo!"

"That's far enough!" Fenwick called out. He'd seen that two of the men had muskets slung over their shoulders. Now he saw something at one man's hip that had to be a small firearm of some sort. The other two, however...

"You two!"

The two men approached Fenwick and Winthrop.

"Good day," one of them said. "I am the Reverend Thomas Shepard. This is my colleague, the Reverend John Wheelwright."

"Good day to you both. Colonel George Fenwick. This is Governor John Winthrop the Younger."

Once the greetings were completed, Shepard's eyes cut toward the burned fort. "The French?"

"Aye, but let us meet your two companions first. Are they friend or foe?"

"Would-be friends to us English," Wheelwright replied.

"If we still call ourselves English..." Winthrop muttered.

"Governor!" Wheelwright exclaimed.

The two men came forward, neither touching a weapon. One of Fenwick's nearby men exclaimed, "You've brought us two *more* Indians! Why?"

"Say rather, they brought us," Shepard said. He nodded to the two.

"I am Sakaweston of the Wampanoag, taken from Nohono—what you call Nantucket—in 1611 by the English captain Edward Harlow. I have fought in the European wars, and I return to my people."

"I am Walter Goodluck of the Diné. I was born in the desert two thousand miles southwest of here in the year of our Lord 1966... up-time."

Dorchester (up-time Windsor, Connecticut) Thursday, August 20, 1637

Edward Winslow leaned back as men continued to squabble. All wanted to have their say. Well, that was reasonable, he supposed. What was not was almost everyone's tendency to revisit ground that had already been covered.

John Mason was finally winding up his speech. "In any alliance to march upon the French, Dorchester must be the senior partner."

True enough, Edward thought, if by Dorchester one meant everyone gathered along the Connecticut River. But if one meant just the initial party led by Robert Ludlow and Reverend John Warham... well, the band of refugees Edward himself had led out of Plymouth town outnumbered them. So did John Alden's Duxbury band. The Scituate and Marshfield bands were smaller. Then there was the Stiles party that had come soon after Ludlow and Warham, more recent Puritan refugees, the other river towns, and even the Dutchmen in Fort Hope a few miles downriver. Moreover, a decision ought not to be made without the men from Sovereignty who had already paid such a steep price.

Sure enough, Reverend Thomas Hooker rose to defend Newtowne, a new settlement downriver by Fort Hope. John Oldham would be next, asserting the primacy of Watertown, Winslow thought sardonically.

The door to Council Hall—as people had begun calling the building—unexpectedly opened, and Thomas Stiles entered.

Hooker paused, and Henry Stiles addressed his younger brother. "Thomas?"

"If it please the assembly, the ship *Griffin* has arrived from Europe. With passengers. Governor Winthrop and Colonel Fenwick brought them here."

He stepped aside, and Governor John Winthrop the Younger entered Council Hall.

"I apologize for interrupting the deliberations." Winthrop's words were smooth and polished. "We have a guest from Europe. I think we should hear what he has to say."

Captain John Mason stood. "Is Chehab back?"

"No." As Winthrop found a seat, another man entered Council Hall. He was tall, dark-complected, and wore the same strange clothing a few of them had seen the Chehabs wear the previous year. He strode to the front of the room.

"My name is Walter Goodluck. I come here from the United States of Europe."

"Do you bring aid?"

"Yes. The *Griffin* is at the mouth of the Connecticut River, unloading food and supplies. We'll need men to help move that food here."

"Sir, we are in your debt." Edward Winslow rose to his feet. "I will find men at once."

"I will see to it, Edward." Another man rose to his feet. "I'll ask for volunteers."

"Thank you, John."

"John?" Goodluck asked. "May I ask your surname?"

The man had already been moving toward the door. He stopped and faced the newcomer. "I'm John Alden."

"After you have organized the volunteers, would you stay, sir? You are one of the men I am charged to speak with."

"I had thought to carry grain myself, but...certainly. I am merely a cooper turned farmer. No one important."

"Please, if you would remain in Dorchester yourself."

Alden considered Goodluck for a moment and then nodded slowly. "I will stay."

Captain Mason spoke up. "Goodluck, you say you represent this United States of Europe, but you look like an Indian yourself."

Goodluck smiled. "There is a reason for that. I am of the Diné tribe, whom white men call the Navajo."

"Never heard of them."

"We live two thousand miles away, in the desert to the southwest. I was working in Grantville when the Ring of Fire hit."

"Why can you speak for this United States of Europe when Chehab could not?"

"In part because the USE now has Chehab's report and a better idea of what is happening here. We know about the battle in Plymouth. Massasoit Ousamequin sent a runner to the Dutch in New Amsterdam."

"That's right," John Alden recalled.

"The Dutch sent a radio message to Europe. We sailed three weeks later." Walter Goodluck took a moment to consider how he was going to say the next part. "The Chehabs were scouting for President Piazza of the State of Thuringia-Franconia. Since then we have had elections, and Edward Piazza is now the prime minister of the United States of Europe. Circumstances give us a few more options than the Chehabs had."

"What we need are troops to throw the French out!" That was Thomas Hooker again.

"Be careful what you wish for." Goodluck smiled. "Oh, it *sounds* like a good idea. But it was done up-time. The English and the French struggled for control of this part of North America. There were four wars, and in the fourth, the English drove the French from the continent. Your colonies were bigger then, and there were thirteen of them. The English taxed them to pay for those troops. The colonies had no representatives in Parliament and had been left more or less on their own up to that point. One thing led to another, and the colonies declared independence and formed the United States of America."

"This sounds like a good idea to me!"

"Forgive me, sir. I don't know everyone yet."

"John Endecott. England has abandoned us. I say we make our own way."

"You will all have to work together." Goodluck took a deep breath. "We want something from you, of course."

"What is that?" Endecott demanded, although half a dozen other voices were no more than a beat behind him.

"Don't drive out the tribes and take their land this time."

A hubbub of protests began immediately.

Endecott's was perhaps the loudest. "We have a God-given right—!"

"No, you don't." Walter Goodluck spoke over him in a harsher manner than he had intended. "I stand before you as a Christian and a Native American—an Indian—and I tell you that your power did not bring very many of us to God. Those of us who believe did so because people came and shared God with us. You know, like the New Testament says to." Walter held up a hand, as much to remind himself to tone down the sarcasm as to quiet anyone else. More softly, he said, "Are John Eliot and Thomas Mayhew here? I would speak with them about this."

A few minutes of mutual checking established that those two men had not come to Dorchester.

"We need them," Goodluck stated. "*You* need them."

Edward Winslow rose. "We need time to absorb this, sir. But I must ask. Do the Indians know?"

Thomas Shepard spoke up. "They are learning right now, I should think. This United States of Europe sent two Indians."

"Sakaweston made his own decision to return," Goodluck said. "He was abducted from Nantucket in 1611 and taken to England. From there he went to mainland Europe and fought in the Thirty Years' War. I met him in Grantville in 1635. We agreed he would speak to the tribes, and I would speak to you. No favoritism."

He let that hang in the air for a moment. Then he said, "I think all of you should discuss this. I will make myself available if you have questions."

A couple of lads showed Sakaweston to the Indian camp.

"Which tribe?" one of the them asked.

The white one, Sakaweston noted. That was interesting. "Wampanoag."

"Massasoit Ousamequin is there," the native lad said. "We will take you."

"My thanks."

Sakaweston was aware they passed warriors in the tree line. When he had just glimpsed the camp, two more stepped in his way.

"Who are you?"

"I am Sakaweston, taken from Nohono many years ago. I have returned from Europe and would tell Massasoit Ousamequin and his *pniesesok* what I saw there."

One of the men nodded toward the rifle Sakaweston had slung over his shoulder. "Your weapon?"

"An example of their weapons."

One of the men led him to a longhouse. The other trailed him. Sakaweston noted with approval that two other warriors took their places without needing to be told.

Inside, a number of warriors gathered around the second of three stone hearths. Several were seated on blankets. The central figure appeared middle-aged and powerfully built. His face was painted a dark red, and a string of white beads hung around his neck.

"Massasoit Ousamequin."

The great sachem looked at him in surprise.

"Massasoit Ousamequin, I am Sakaweston. You may not know me personally—"

A Wampanoag seated not far to Massasoit Ousamequin's left held up his hand. "I recognize you, Sakaweston."

"Epenow!"

The other man, as powerfully built as Massasoit Ousamequin, smiled broadly. "So, you have found your way back from England."

"No. I went to the wars in Europe. Years later, I came to Grantville, the town from the future."

"The People from the Sky."

Sakaweston frowned. "I do not know them by that name. They called themselves Americans or West Virginians, for their town was west of the English colony Virginia. All others call them up-timers." He inclined his head to Massasoit Ousamequin. "Great Sachem, their leaders give you their thanks. The messenger you sent to the Dutch reached New Amsterdam where there is a powerful radio—a machine that can send messages across the sea. They knew of the French attack on Plymouth town sixteen days after it took place."

"It is as that Narragansett said," said the Wampanoag to Massasoit Ousamequin's right. A single glance told Sakaweston this man was a fearsome warrior and probably a *pniese*.

"Did they send you?" Massasoit Ousamequin asked.

"They contacted me because they knew I would want to return now. The ship they call *Griffin* brings a few more Puritans every year." He paused as heads wearing grim expressions nodded. "It has a few more this year, too. But the up-timers hired the ship and sent food and information."

Sakaweston paused for effect.

"They sent two of us. The other man is Diné, a tribe I never heard of that lives in the lands far to the southwest, where the Spanish are. He is an up-timer."

Massasoit Ousamequin stopped him there. "One of the People from the Sky is one of us? Just one? Or more?"

"A man from this town Grantville went away to the southwest. It is a hot, dry place, and the tribes there live differently than we do. He married a Diné woman. They returned to his home in Grantville and had three children. She told her family there was work, and her cousin came to the town. He was working there when Grantville came to our time. She died the year after. I have not met her children, although I am told the son is a good soldier and the younger daughter is a skilled maker of white men's machines.

"Many people from our time went to Grantville. It is not as big as London—Epenow, you know what I say—but I was just one more. No one knew I was Wampanoag until two years ago. He kept silent at my request, but arranged for me to speak with the woman's cousin. His name is Walter Goodluck."

"A white man's name," the Wampanoag beside Massasoit Ousamequin said.

"Yes."

"Is he important?"

"His wife is the *president* of their state. She is from our time. Massasoit Ousamequin, this president is roughly as powerful as you or Canonicus or Tatobem."

One of the other seated Wampanoags surged to his feet. "Massasoit Ousamequin is the greatest of all the—!"

Massasoit Ousamequin stopped him with a raised hand. "That

is good of you to say. But Tatobem is dead, killed by the Dutch. Sassacus is great sachem of the Pequot now."

Sakaweston inclined his head. "I have been away many years."

Epenow laughed. Then so did the Wampanoag to Massasoit Ousamequin's right. Sakaweston noted that he had *not* risen to his feet. But now when he was done laughing, he stood.

"The Patuxet are no more. Disease came to their villages. The last was Tisquantum." He paused, evidently waiting to see if Sakaweston recognized the name.

"I knew Tisquantum in England," Sakaweston stated. He looked around. "Is he well?"

"He died two or three years after the white men called Pilgrims came," Massasoit Ousamequin answered. "I sent him and Hobbamock here"—he indicated the man to his right—"to Plymouth town. I came to mistrust Tisquantum. Maybe I was right to do so. Maybe I was wrong."

The great sachem stared intently at Sakaweston. "What do the People from the Sky say about us?"

"Their children know that you, Tisquantum, and a man named Samoset helped the Pilgrims. They say Massasoit wrongly and do not realize it is not your name. Tisquantum they call Squanto." He turned to Hobbamock. "I did not hear your name. But understand that while Grantville is now a center of white man's learning, it was not so in their own time. You will hear tomorrow that they sent information that they acknowledge is incomplete."

"Can we trust them?" Massasoit Ousamequin's words were urgent.

Sakaweston knew this question was coming. "Yes. They admitted they mistreated our people and wish to do better."

"That is easy to say."

"I am told two of them came here last year and said the same thing."

"We have heard. A few Wampanoags were there. It was mostly Pequots, Mohegan, Narragansetts, and Niantics they spoke to."

"They say all the Algonquian peoples should work together."

"Now that is interesting," Hobbamock said. "That is the same thing that Fast as Lightning says."

"You must find out tomorrow why he does not like you," Massasoit Ousamequin commanded. "I already speak with Winslow about how we must ally against the French."

Friday, August 21, 1637

Hobbamock was awake before dawn. He prepared himself and then strode to the Narragansett camp.

Two warriors met him. They, along with three more he saw but chose not to acknowledge, were on watch.

"I would speak to Fast as Lightning."

"Why?"

"That is between him and me."

"You are armed." The Narragansett held out his hand.

Hobbamock rolled his eyes and handed the man his knife. "If I need one, I will take it from someone."

One of the Narragansetts left to find Fast as Lightning. He returned in a few minutes, with another Narragansett beside him. This man's chest was painted red with a yellow bolt of lightning.

"Fast as Lightning, I am Hobbamock, *pniese* of the Wampanoag. Let us speak together."

Fast as Lightning's expression did not change. A mixture of curiosity and challenge, Hobbamock thought. The younger man waved the other Narragansetts off.

"You have said that all our people must stand together when the People from the Sky come."

"Yes, I have," Fast as Lightning acknowledged.

"You have half persuaded Canonicus and Awashaw."

"It may be."

"What have I done to you?" Hobbamock held up a hand. "Yes, I raided the Narragansett as they raided us Wampanoag. But I have no interest in war between us."

Fast as Lightning appeared to study him carefully. "It is your name," he finally said. "Not that word you go to war often causes warriors to settle their differences before you arrive. That is well known." He hesitated. "Last spring, before the People from the Sky came, I fought the Mohegan Black Tooth. He was said to be possessed by Hobomok."

"And you ask if I am possessed by the same spirit?" Hobbamock paused to order his thoughts. "Years ago, I would have taken offense. Now... Much has changed." He pointed. "You follow the Red God but warn us of the *up-timers*."

"Yes."

"A Wampanoag has returned from their land. He will speak today. Hear him."

"I will. I have heard that you fought beside the Pilgrims in Plymouth town."

"I did."

"That you called on their God, Keihtánit's Son, for protection."

"It was a time for flight, and they would have prayed all day if I let them. I told them what I told Standish. 'Keihtánit, the Son, and the Holy Manitou protect.'"

"Thank you ... Hobbamock." Fast as Lightning still looked grave, but relieved. "I do not think the actual Hobomok would call on Keihtánit."

"It seems unlikely," Hobbamock agreed.

"When does this warrior speak?"

Today it was the Nipmucks' turn to build and maintain the fire. Who and how many they chose for that duty was up to them. Since they were a collection of scattered bands, one man from each band was chosen. The fire was purely ceremonial; the August day was warm, and only the first circle of sachems could feel its heat anyway.

Massasoit Ousamequin rose. "I ask we all hear a Wampanoag tell us about the People from the Sky."

"It should be a Pequot," Sassacus objected.

Sakaweston stood. "Great Sachem, no Pequots were among those taken to England so there are none who can tell this story. Count yourselves fortunate that none of you were captured."

Sassacus shook his head slowly. "Fair," he acknowledged. "Speak."

"Twenty-nine of us were captured and taken to England." Sakaweston reeled off the names he remembered. "Epenow tricked the English into bringing him back and escaped. I stayed in England many years. I saw no chance of return and had no way to be a warrior. But the English were sending soldiers to a war in a far-off place called Bohemia. Great armies fought in the open, not as we do here. The fighting moved to the Germanies, and then the People from the Sky came. Five years ago, an army went to war with almost one hundred thousand men." Sakaweston paused and turned in place, looking at all the men gathered around. "The People from the Sky think that there may be eighty thousand if all our peoples south of the Huron and east of the Mohawk are added together. This army was more, and it was all in one place.

Its enemy was much smaller, but included the People from the Sky and their weapons. They destroyed the larger army.

"Many others have joined the People from the Sky. Three years ago, the names we hear from white men—England, France, and Spain—were all against them. The People from the Sky and their allies were victorious. They still face many enemies, and they are not coming here in strength. But many others use their tools.

"They are from the future. They look back and say they did not treat us fairly. They have chosen not to build their own colonies here, but they will not necessarily stop others from doing so. They offer friendship and tools. But they want something, too."

"Of course. Everyone wants something." That was Uncas, sachem of the Mohegan.

"Freedom. An end to slavery. Many kinds. *Serfdom* is what it is called in parts of Europe."

"Surely they do not mean we must give up our captives."

Hobbamock, seated nearby, murmured a name to Sakaweston.

"No, Wequash Cook, they do not." Sakaweston smiled. "They would prefer we did, but they acknowledge that we often return captives after a time or adopt them into the tribe." He sketched out what the People from the Sky did not want.

"They urge us to work together. One of the People from the Sky returned with me. I ask you to hear him this afternoon. He is an up-timer, but one of us. Not from here but from far away. He will tell you what happened to us between now and when the People from the Sky came." Sakaweston paused. "That future will not happen. I do not understand. I do not think they understand. But in their past, there was a great war here"—he swept a hand around him—"last year and this year. But it has not happened. I am told there were two People from the Sky here last year, and they stopped the attack on the Englishman Oldham. You heard their words, and you stopped the war. They believe we can do this again."

Sakaweston saw satisfaction on many faces and felt some of his own. Others looked skeptical, and that was only natural.

"They saw our best hope is to work together, so that when English or French or Spanish come, they must deal with all of us." He bent and picked up thick packets at his feet. "They sent these. Sassacus, Massasoit Ousamequin, Uncas, Samoset. They know only a few of us."

Sassacus accepted the packet, carefully opened it, and pulled out a thick stack of paper. He looked at Sakaweston in bewilderment. "What is this?"

"Information."

"I *speak* English," the Abenaki sagamore Samoset said. "I do not *read*."

"We could ask some of the English boys to read them for us," Sakaweston said. "I can read a little. Not this much."

Uncas looked up from the papers in his hands. "How do we know they will speak truly?"

"You have four packets," Sakaweston said. "Right now, Walter Goodluck is giving the English four packets. He and I did not read them, but we probably know much of what they say. Let English lads from different colonies read them aloud. The story will be as strange to them as it is to us. There will not be time to make a lie. Why not hear the words of the People from the Sky? Make sure what I tell you matches."

After a few minutes of discussion, messengers were sent. An hour later, several English boys had established that each packet held the same ten booklets and a personal letter.

Sassacus guffawed when the letter to Uncas was read. "Last of the *Mohicans*? Ha! Say rather, would-be first of the *Mohegans*."

Uncas started to take offense, then saw the humor in it. "At least they know they are wrong. But chasing after a white girl? If I meet this man James Fenimore Cooper, I shall surely challenge him."

That afternoon, Sakaweston and Walter Goodluck switched places.

"We do not know the Diné," Uncas said. It wasn't quite a challenge.

"You know the Iroquois, the Five Nations," Goodluck began. "Beyond them are the Great Lakes. Past the farthest are the Sioux." He paused as Hobbamock translated, then waited some more as the words were clarified in various Algonquian dialects. "In this time, I think they live at the edge of what people in my past called the Great American Desert. The Great Plains. But it is not really a desert. In my time, much of it was very productive farmland. Beyond the plains is the true desert. That is where the Pueblo, Hopi, Zuni, Apache, and Diné live."

One of the oldest medicine men present spoke up. "I have heard stories."

"The desert is hot and dry and few plants grow there. We live differently than you do. On the reservation—"

Goodluck was interrupted by hisses. He smiled. That had taken not more than a few hours. Good.

For the rest of the day, he told them of the Indian Wars. The Battle of the Greasy Grass. The reservations. The Mohawk steel walkers. His own tribe's code talkers. Joe Medicine Crow, the last of the Plains tribes' war chiefs, who met the four requirements in Germany during World War II.

"Well told," the Narragansett diplomat Awashaw said when Goodluck was finished. "In your world, we lost."

"Yes."

"Do you really believe we can win in our world?" Awashaw stared him down.

Walter Goodluck realized others were awaiting his answer. Massasoit Ousamequin. Sassacus. Canonicus.

"I hope so." Goodluck turned slowly in place, looking at each man. "Up-time we were outnumbered." He waved a hand toward Dorchester. "Dorchester and Boston and Plymouth town are not much now. In my time, more people lived in Boston than live in London now. New Amsterdam filled Manhattan Island and spread onto other islands and the mainland. Ten million people or so. In this time, the English are not coming in big numbers. That is important. No one power will control all of North America.

"But that is France's plan. That is why France bought the colonies from England."

"The French oppose the Iroquois," Sassacus pointed out. "So they have been closer to a friend than an enemy. All say the great captain Champlain is a man of honor."

"I believe the same about Champlain," Goodluck agreed. "The French who came to Plymouth town and Boston are not the same. They serve a different king. But what we must do—what *you* must do, because it does not matter if *I* do it—is unite. If the French—or the English or the Spanish or the Danes—set Wampanoag against Narragansett, Pequot against Mohegan, Nipmuck against Mohican, they will conquer. That is what England has done in Scotland and Ireland. That is what happened up-time."

"So you say we must combine. Stop being Pequot and Nipmuck and Massachusett," Sassacus said.

"Who won up-time?" Goodluck asked. When no one answered,

he said, "The English. But they did not stay English. Massachusetts and Connecticut and New Amsterdam after the English conquered it and Virginia worked together while remaining themselves."

"You mean a federation." Samoset's voice was flat. "Like the Iroquois. I have listened to the English boys reading. Such a complicated government!"

"You do not have to copy the whole thing," Goodluck replied. "Follow the principles. Adapt the forms."

That took longer than usual to translate.

Canonicus spoke for the first time. "A great council. But..."

"Who would be the great sachem?" Awashaw asked the question for him.

Men called out names. But Goodluck noticed that they all came from the back rows. The sachems and medicine men were silent.

Saturday, August 22, 1637

After the Montaukett lit the fire, Massasoit Ousamequin began the proceedings.

"You forgot something, Person of the Sky."

Walter Goodluck kept a straight face. He'd heard rumors. "What have I forgotten, Great Sachem?"

"The women's council. Do not the Women of the Sky have a say?"

Goodluck grinned. "Oh, yes. They most certainly do. They vote in the same elections that we men vote in."

"How much influence do they have? Do any serve in this *Parliament*?"

"Yes."

"Who?"

"Amalie of Hesse-Kassel is regent of Hesse-Kassel for her young son. She is Hesse-Kassel's acting senator. Charlotte rules Jülich-Berg. Charlotte Kienitz represents a district in Mecklenburg and is far more influential than that suggests. Rebecca Abrabanel resigned as a delegate to serve as secretary of state. That is similar to what Awashaw does for Canonicus."

"And in your...*state*?" Massasoit Ousamequin pressed.

"My wife Helene Gundelfinger is the President of the State of Thuringia-Franconia. That is... There are differences, you understand? But president is like great sachem."

Sunday, August 23, 1637

Neither the Pilgrims nor the Puritans nor even the Anglicans would hold a political council on Sunday, so both Goodluck and Sakaweston joined the tribes' council. They listened as the Algonquians discussed whether they wanted great councils.

Monday, August 24, 1637

On the following day, boats carrying food from the *Griffin* began arriving at Dorchester, Newtowne, Watertowne, and Fort Hope. The refugees from Plymouth and Massachusetts Bay would not starve. But even the food that would help them through the coming winter was second to the other cargo: fifty shotguns, the new Evans Slamfires out of Nuremberg.

The guns were tangible proof that they had to cooperate. If they went their separate ways, two or three or four guns would make almost no difference.

But together...

For the first time, Sassacus, Canonicus, and Massasoit Ousamequin gathered off to one side. After a few minutes, they called for Sakaweston and Goodluck.

"We are rivals," Sassacus stated. "But we must fight together against the French. Perhaps against others. We cannot have one great sachem."

"Nor can we have one from every tribe and band," Canonicus said.

"I am content to hear the great council on most matters," Ousamequin told them. "But sometimes we must act swiftly and will not be able to remain in council lest our enemies overrun us."

"You have both used weapons like this," Sassacus said to Sakaweston and Goodluck. "How would you use them? Not how do you fire one—I watched you earlier. I believe I could fire one myself. But when I send warriors to battle, they do not fight each alone."

"The Algonquian tribes need an army." Walter Goodluck's words were blunt. "Not a large one, because a standing army causes its own problems. But you need warriors who can use these weapons when you need them. Not two here and three there, all trying to find each other. Not all fifty stored in one location with everyone hurrying toward it."

"Goodluck," Canonicus spoke. "I have had battles with less than thirty men. Thirty men with these weapons would be a tribe of their own."

"We discussed this as we sailed," Walter Goodluck stated. "Sakaweston and I. We did not tell the Puritans."

"We know. We saw their faces when they learned the boxes held guns."

Sakaweston spoke. "Give them a name. Set them apart from the tribes. Let them serve for a time, and then others take their turn. But while they carry a shotgun, they serve the Algonquian as a whole, not their own tribe."

"You have heard the letter to Priscilla Alden," Goodluck reminded them. "Not even Sakaweston and I knew about the letters."

"Those are truly written by English girls?" Massasoit Ousamequin asked.

"American, but yes."

"These . . . teams?" The great sachem shook his head. "Those with green hats? Begin with one. If it is successful, add more."

Sassacus gave a single, sharp nod. "One warrior from each tribe. They must practice but use as little ammunition as possible."

"But not us," Canonicus warned. "We must find a way for the tribes to work together." He spread his hands. "There have always been raids. But these new weapons should not be used against other tribes. Perhaps against the Iroquois. But these men who are set apart, they must not be part of any raids."

"This is wisdom," Massasoit Ousamequin stated.

Sassacus simply nodded again.

Walter remembered the information the girls had added to the packet addressed to Priscilla Alden. "I cannot give you the esprit de corps . . . the morale and the purpose that they had up-time. They must work together and become your elite warriors. I do not think telling them they are eleven Bravos and Charlies and Deltas would mean anything."

Sakaweston laughed and then translated for the others.

"Your letters and numbers will mean nothing to us," Massasoit Ousamequin agreed. "But we saw the pictures . . . ."

Goodluck nodded. He wasn't sure if Grantville still had

working photocopiers, but if so, the girls hadn't had access to one. They'd drawn uniforms and unit badges and colored them with crayons.

"The coat of arms that is red, white, black, and yellow. That is all people. That is what you People from the Sky seek."

Walter Goodluck shook his head. "I do not think that was the intention."

Massasoit Ousamequin smiled. "But it fits. Three? . . . Four years ago, some of my warriors encountered a blackamoor in the forest for the first time."

Sassacus took over. "The *railroad* in your history was a way for blackamoors to escape. It is what the Mohican Machk and the Puritan Robert Lockwood are already doing. It is what Massasoit Ousamequin led warriors to do, to rescue Winslow and his people from Plymouth town."

Canonicus nodded in agreement. "That is what the warriors with the *shotguns* will do. Be the *railroad* for all the people of the shield."

"You did say that your up-time leaders seek to end slavery and serfdom," Ousamequin stated. "Massasoit Sassacus and Massasoit Canonicus speak well."

Walter realized the sachems had just recognized each other's authority.

"Make the *team*," Canonicus said. "Walter Goodluck of the Diné and the Thuringians, we need more ammunition. I remember other things we need. Blacksmiths. Doctors. Teachers. The white men need food."

Sakaweston translated.

"The up-time girls are correct," Canonicus continued. "They offer to share their God but let us remain Algonquian rather than becoming white men. It must be this way with the rest."

"Yes. We will have a women's great council instead of your representatives," Massasoit Ousamequin said. "It cannot be otherwise."

Walter simply nodded.

Sassacus sighed. "The forests shall stand. But for some of what Canonicus asks for, there must be buildings. Can you build them?"

Walter blinked in surprise. "That is what I do. I work for a company that builds. But it should not be just my company. I am not here for that."

"That is why we trust you," Massasoit Ousamequin told him. "You are up-timer and"—he undeniably smirked—"*Indian*. You make no secret you are caught between."

Walter sighed. "All my life."

"We have not spoken of it, but you will return to Europe."

"Yes."

"Massasoit Sassacus, Massasoit Canonicus, Goodluck should be our ambassador to the United States of Europe."

"I build things." Walter Goodluck spoke firmly.

"Yes. Yes, you do," Sassacus agreed.

Tuesday, August 25, 1637

Walter Goodluck went back to the colonists on Tuesday. The tribes needed to pick their men and agree how their team would work. Then he and Sakaweston could train them.

"The Indians are allying against us!" John Endecott was speaking before he was even completely on his feet.

"They are allying against any power that seeks to do what was done up-time," Walter corrected. "It does not have to be against *you*. In fact, you should ally *with* them. Some of you already have agreements with individual tribes."

"Absolutely not!"

Debate raged most of the morning. Walter passed through annoyance, anger, and boredom. Judging from how the sun had stopped coming directly through the windows, it must have been approaching noon when the door flew open. A Puritan woman entered Council Hall.

"If it please the assembly, when will we establish *our* women's council?"

Thomas Hooker shot to his feet. "Anne Hutchinson! Leave this assembly at once!"

Walter Goodluck spoke over other voices raised in agreement. "My wife would agree that women ought to be represented. How you do that..."

Endecott whirled on Goodluck. "How can you say that?"

Walter shrugged. "My wife is the President of the State of Thuringia-Franconia."

He waited for the hubbub to die down. "Look, you have to organize your own society. But you might want to remember that the Algonquians are going to have a men's council and a women's council. Whatever leaders you choose are going to have to work with whatever leaders they choose. You're going to talk to each other. If the Algonquian women are represented and the English women aren't, you might have problems."

"English law—!"

"Charles sold you out." Goodluck glared at the speaker. "I am so sick of hearing about English common law and Charlemagne's law and Justinian's code. Stop treating them like Scripture. Are you Pilgrims and Puritans or not?"

Walter Goodluck was not invited to the assembly's afternoon session. So he checked with Sakaweston.

"It is just as well," Sakaweston said. "The tribes are choosing. You can begin training us."

"Me?"

"You have fired modern weapons much more than I have."

Goodluck's mouth quirked. He wasn't sure if it was at the seventeenth-century Wampanoag's quick adoption of the term "modern weapons" or that someone would consider the slamfire shotguns state-of-the-art weapons.

"I've never been in the army, Sakaweston. Not even right after the Ring of Fire. They wanted anyone who could build doing that. I can't teach anyone how to fight."

"They do not need to learn that, Walter." Sakaweston's grin was feral. "Hobbamock and Samoset laughed because we already know your Rangers' orders. Just teach us the weapons."

"I can do that. I thought to join the team myself."

"No." Sakaweston held up both hands. "You must speak for us in Europe."

"But . . ."

"Teach your son the ways of the Diné. One day, one of you will reach them."

Walter swallowed. "I'd like that."

"We will fight beside the Diné anytime," Sakaweston continued. "But we must fight together without up-timers."

Walter laughed.

"You are not offended?"

"No, not at all. They have the same debate in Europe, with a newspaper on either side."

"Speak for us, Walter. You have Canonicus' list. More shotgun shells. Then come back and build the shops."

"We need to talk about having goods to sell to Europe," Walter reminded him. "Not just beaver pelts."

"Most of what we have thought of so far is plants. We need more."

Walter shook his head. "I don't have all the answers, Sakaweston. I just know we—you—can't remain hunter-gatherers indefinitely. But I will not force you to my vision of what should be. It has to be your vision."

Sakaweston nodded, a very serious expression on his face. Then he clapped Walter on the shoulder. "We cannot fix everything this afternoon. Let us find the men the tribes have selected."

Walter laughed.

"What?"

"You say 'men,' but I see a woman of the tribes approaching us."

Sakaweston turned in place. He saw a man and a woman. "Niantic. Married," he whispered to Goodluck. But he had no chance to explain how he'd observed that.

"I am Quaiapen, daughter of Saccious, sachem of the Niantic. This is my husband Mexanno."

Sakaweston translated that for Goodluck. Immediately after they had exchanged greetings, Quaiapen spoke. "Walter Goodluck of the Diné, I understand your wife is a powerful sachem across the sea."

"It is not quite the same thing, but the essence of what you say is true."

"We hear the People from the Sky sent the story of their past to a few of us. We hear those were the only names they knew. But the story was sent to some of the English, too, and one of them is a woman."

When Sakaweston finished translating, Goodluck said, "Yes, that is so."

"We also hear the English woman Anne Hutchinson demanded a women's council."

"She requested that women be represented in the assembly... council... however they decide to organize it. The Europeans think differently than we do, and it would not occur to them to have a separate women's council."

"But she was not the woman who received the story."

"No, that is Priscilla Alden."

"I have met the wife of Hobbamock. She speaks well of Priscilla Alden. May I meet her?"

Wednesday, August 26, 1637

"Are there so many of you that you *need* a bicameral legislature?" Walter Goodluck asked the colonists. "No. A bicameral legislature is a compromise. In the up-time United States of America, between the large states who wanted representation by population and the small states who wanted equal representation by state. In the down-time United States of Europe, for similar reasons.

"If you must guarantee Puritan representation and Pilgrim representation and Anglican representation—and Dutch representation—then go ahead. You would do better not to have a religious test for office, even if you reserve seats for each group."

Thomas Hooker surged to his feet. "The Halfway Covenant was—will be—a travesty! God brought us here to establish a new order—"

"A shining city on a hill," Goodluck interrupted. "We know Governor Winthrop's phrase. It was famous in my time, and it is a worthy goal, to be that city. I thought about it, talked with Sakaweston about it, on the voyage from Europe. There were those who criticized it because people did not always live up to it. That is foolish. We are agreed that mankind is fallen. It is not surprising that people don't live up to it. It is better to encourage each other to strive to live up to it."

Edward Winslow stood. "If I may, Friend Goodluck, you are about to exhort us to be that city for everyone, to include women and Indians and Moors. To cut a straight path through the woods that you wandered around in up-time."

Goodluck smiled. "You know me well, Friend Winslow."

"The Indians are already creating a league—"

John Endecott was on his feet. "If all the tribes ally together, we cannot stand against them! We must choose carefully..."

"Divide and conquer." Goodluck's words were flat. "Sakaweston and I already told the tribes about that. Look, you have to stand together to survive against the French. You have to have peace with the Algonquian tribes to do that."

"They cannot be trusted!"

The door burst open. Sakaweston entered, his face painted in quadrants: black, red, white, and yellow.

"The French have landed again in Sovereignty. Yesterday. Colonel Fenwick's work crews evacuated the area without loss. They stayed nearby long enough to see the French burn what was salvaged for rebuilding. Then they rowed all night to get here."

"The *Griffin*?" Walter Goodluck asked quickly.

"Sighted the French before Sovereignty did. She fired a gun to call her boats back and ran for New Amsterdam. One of the French ships went after her but the Sovereignty men say the French will not catch her. Not with Richard More aboard as her pilot."

"We need to stop them below Watertowne." Captain John Endecott's words were firm.

"He's right," Captain John Mason declared. "We have to protect the three towns."

"Algonquian warriors will set out at noon. As many as we have canoes for. The rest will stay here to protect the camps and the river towns." Sakaweston paused. "We need twelve on the team. We have ten."

A burly Dorchester man stood. "Is this the team with the shotguns?"

"Aye."

"Count me in. If I am to build more, I would see how they fare in battle."

John Alden stood. "What other colonists do you have?"

"Robert of the Puritans," Sakaweston answered.

"Someone from the Old Colony should go." Alden started for the door.

Sakaweston held up a hand and addressed the assembly. "They need three of your shotguns."

"I'm coming, too," Walter Goodluck declared.

Sakaweston frowned. But all he said was, "We welcome the Diné."

Algonquian encampment outside Dorchester

A few minutes later, fourteen men gathered near the Algonquian encampments. Sakaweston pointed at a straw man on a post. The rags were barely holding the straw in.

"Those were our targets yesterday. The children put one back together as best they could.

"The Evans shotgun is a very simple weapon." He pointed at the one John Alden held. It had a barrel, a stock, and no trigger. The barrel had a long leather sleeve several inches wide partway down its length. One end of a leather thong was woven into the sleeve, and the other end tied around the small of the stock.

"Left hand on the leather strap around the barrel. Now, pull."

Alden did so, and the barrel slid clear of the weapon.

"The *shell* goes here. Then you slam the barrel into the shell, and it fires. So you have to aim and then hold it steady while you slam the barrel. This is not a precision weapon like the SRG rifles that Walter and I carry. This a weapon for fighting an enemy that fights in formation or bunches up. It would be less effective against our warriors."

"Convenient," one of the warriors stated. "A *manitou* is looking out for us."

"Sachem Kuchamakin of the Massachusetts." Sakaweston identified the speaker when he translated the remark to English.

"Or Keihtánit. Or the white man's God," said another.

"Wequash Cook of the Western Niantic," Sakaweston added in English.

"Or Hobomok. Or the Red God," Samoset added. "This team has as many religions as the white men!" He translated it to English himself.

All the Algonquians laughed uproariously. Pomeroy scowled, while Lockwood and Alden exchanged glances.

"And you, Walter Goodluck?"

Walter smiled. "Seventh-Day Adventist. A Christian denomination that started up-time."

"Why that one?" Samoset asked. "Why not Puritan or Pilgrim or Anglican?"

"Adventist missionaries came to the reservation."

Sakaweston held out three shotgun shells. They had metal bases and heavy paper walls.

All three of them missed their first shots. Pomeroy sprayed straw from one side of the target with his second. Lockwood and Alden aimed too high.

"This is not like a musket," Sakaweston told them. "You keep a loaded musket pointed up in the air, yes?"

"Aye."

"Not a slamfire. Once you place the shell, you mean to shoot. Keep it straight and level after that."

Pomeroy's third shot blew through the center of the target. Lockwood took off its "head." Then Alden stepped up and actually shot low, hitting about where the upper legs would be.

"Good," Hobbamock said. "Now we are twelve."

He pointed to each man in turn. "Sachems Kuchamakin of the Massachusett and Wequash Cook of the Niantic command. Samoset and I can speak to all. Fast as Lightning of the Narragansett and Machk of the Mohican are our best scouts. Sawseunck of the Quinnipiac knows something of healing. Kiswas of the Pequot, Wawequa of the Mohegan, and Robert Lockwood of the Puritans know all the factions. Eltweed Pomeroy of the river towns is a blacksmith, and John Alden of the Puritans is a cooper."

Kuchamakin spoke. Hobbamock translated. "We go ahead of the rest in canoes. But not fast. Let the French come. They will have farther to flee."

Quinnehtukqut (the Connecticut River, near up-time Middletown and Portland)

At dusk, Wequash Cook and Kuchamakin directed the men to shore. John Alden was only too happy to comply. They'd paddled down the Connecticut River all day and were nearly to the big bend. In the stern, Hobbamock showed no sign of fatigue.

They had no more than posted a watch and pulled the canoes out of the water when voices called out.

Sawseunck called back to them.

Two men appeared from the woods. Their relief at seeing the team was obvious. Hobbamock kept up a running translation for Alden, Lockwood, and Pomeroy.

"The French are in boats. Twelve of them. They landed from four ships in two trips." Hobbamock interjected something in Wampanoag. "At Plymouth town they used eight boats to land fifty men at a time. Say one hundred twenty here. Two trips could be two hundred forty, with half of them still at Sovereignty."

"I heard tell the French had ten ships at Boston," Robert Lockwood put in. "About five hundred soldiers total seems about right. Two hundred here. A hundred in Plymouth or dead there. Two hundred between Boston, Salem, and the smaller villages."

The two messengers gave additional information. Samoset summarized for the English-speakers. "The French surprised the Wangunk village Cockaponet. The French have taken prisoners—guides to help them and hostages to keep the rest of the Wangunk from attacking them. These scouts were sent to the great council in Dorchester to seek aid from Wawaloam. She is the sister of the sachem and married to Canonicus' nephew."

Wequash Cook spoke. Hobbamock translated. "If we defeat this force, the French will be hard-pressed to make raids. But it must be done in such a way that the boats do not reach Cockaponet before we do. Coming by boat is a much better plan than earlier in the summer when they walked along the river and gave us time to confront them."

"Get behind them," Kuchamakin suggested.

"There is an island a short distance ahead," Kiswas said.

"Mattabesset." One of the Wangunk scouts supplied the name, pronouncing it as though it ended with a K. "Sowheage and his people have already fled into the woods."

Kuchamakin and Wequash Cook held a quick discussion.

"Kiswas, Wawequa, can you guide us to Mattabesset?" Kuchamakin asked.

"Yes."

"We will go now and try to find Sowheage," Kuchamakin said. He shot Walter Goodluck a sly look. "This is what the green hats from your time would do, yes? Join us with the *indigenous forces*?"

The Massachusett sachem had slaughtered the pronunciation, but Goodluck grinned back.

Samoset stumbled through the word, too. "*Indigenous.* That means us 'Indians,' yes?"

"I don't think it's from the same word." Goodluck's words were cautious. "I would have to look it up in a book."

"Heh. For now, that is what we will do," Kuchamakin said. "But we must row hard before it is full dark to make sure we arrive at Mattabesset before the French."

Mattabesset (up-time Middletown, Connecticut)

Kiswas waved the seven canoes ashore as the sky darkened. They dragged the canoes into the forest and set off to approach Mattabesset from the inland side.

The Pequot Kiswas was in the lead, with Wawequa of the Mohegan, Sawseunck of the Quinnipiac, and Wequash Cook of the Niantic close behind. Samoset followed them, relaying important observations to Kuchamakin. Hobbamock had Pomeroy, Lockwood, and Alden together, simply because it was easier to translate for all of them at once.

Machk and Fast as Lightning returned from opposite directions.

"The French boats are on the shore with only a few guards," the Mohican reported. "They have patrols, but they are lazy and not watching inland."

"The Wangunk hostages are in the middle of the village," Fast as Lightning added. "I believe that *wetu* must be Sowheage's. Some of the French are stealing, but most are cooking food."

Walter Goodluck moved up from the back of the column. "Tomorrow, if our armies face each other, will the French threaten to kill the hostages if we do not back down?"

Hobbamock spat. "Not if they have honor. We have heard stories of the great captain Champlain. He would not. But you say these French serve a foolish king."

That seemed an accurate and concise description of Gaston. "Yes."

"They might."

"We cannot back down," Wequash Cook said after Hobbamock translated the conversation.

"What if we rescued the hostages tonight?" Goodluck asked.

"The French outnumber us badly," Kuchamakin hissed. "Ten to one, or close enough. It is clear they do not expect an attack. But someone must say it. If we all die tonight, our peoples and the English may not form another team."

"It is even more important that Sakaweston and Walter Goodluck survive," Hobbamock pointed out.

"Is the French sachem with the hostages?" Wequash Cook asked. "If these weapons are as powerful as we think, our attack may break their spirit. If their sachem is killed..."

"...our united tribes and colonies will find it easier to prevail tomorrow," Kuchamakin finished. "I agree, but Goodluck and Sakaweston must stay here."

"We have rifles," Goodluck agreed. "We will be long-range cover."

Sakaweston settled in behind a tree. Goodluck chose another some fifteen yards away. He brushed away sticks and leaves and settled to the ground.

Fast as Lightning and Machk set off in separate directions. The rest of the team divided evenly behind them. Goodluck tracked Fast as Lightning, watching the shadows ahead and to either side. The Narragansett was fast and silent. So were the five men behind him. Within a couple minutes, they were nearby out of sight.

Then Goodluck heard voices. He turned his head to the right and saw a French patrol was finally sweeping along the inland edge of Mattabesset. No, "patrol" was too formal for what this was: four soldiers tromping along the tree line.

The four of them stopped. Goodluck did not understand French, but the body language was clear. One of them, probably a sergeant or corporal, was posting a sentry. That man stayed while the other three continued on.

They walked right past the tree Sakaweston was behind. Goodluck had long since frozen in place behind his tree. The three passed by without even a glance and continued off to the north.

Once Goodluck dared risk turning his head, he saw that the sentry had begun pacing. He stopped short of Sakaweston's tree and then turned back. Goodluck peered into the village and saw nothing. He looked back to his right, and the French sentry was coming their way again.

This time he did not stop. He passed Sakaweston's tree. Now he was ten yards away. Five. Two. The man stopped directly in Walter Goodluck's line of fire, to all appearances unaware that a rifleman was on the other side of the tree.

Goodluck ever so slowly turned his head. Sakaweston was perfectly still, focused on his sights. That made up Goodluck's mind. If Sakaweston had a possible shot, he'd be needed, too. The sentry had to go.

Goodluck left his rifle on the ground as he rose. No branch or leaf betrayed his presence. His right hand went to his hip, and he drew the nine-millimeter. He eased it up, little by little. It was shoulder high when the sentry finally began to turn.

Goodluck swung overhand, bringing the pistol barrel crashing down on the Frenchman's neck. The impact seemed deafeningly loud. Goodluck caught the man and dragged him back into the tree line, easing him to the ground a couple trees deep. Walter quickly resumed his position. He noted that Sakaweston was still peering through his sights.

Goodluck could not see anyone in the village. He could *hear* some of the French, but they seemed to be mostly inside the dwellings.

Then he heard something else. A scraping or scuffling. It was followed by a distinct thump.

Seconds later, a shotgun blast thundered in the center of the village. Sakaweston's SRG cracked before the echoes died away.

A figure entered his vision, running left to right. Goodluck identified him as a French soldier, led slightly, and pulled the trigger. The bullet knocked the man off his feet. Goodluck was up now, reloading the rifle.

Figures emerged from a *wetu*, distinct against the birchbark house even in the dark. Sakaweston took several steps in Goodluck's direction. Goodluck saw a glint of light from a blade. Somehow Sakaweston had already fixed his bayonet.

"Ready?"

"Ready."

"Take the one on the left. Fire."

The two riflemen fired, and both dropped their targets. Immediately they heard an owl call.

"That is the team! Let's go!" Sakaweston directed.

Goodluck took off after the Wampanoag. Three men were still bunched up in front of the door of the *wetu*. Shotgun blasts sounded, and they all went down. More shotguns roared, somewhere on the other side of the central *wetu* they thought was Sowheage's.

A figure appeared from between two *wetus*. Sakaweston smoothly bayoneted him. Goodluck skirted around them and smashed into someone. He staggered, regained his footing, and swung hard with a clubbed rifle. The butt of the weapon caught the other man in the ribs.

Another! His rifle was tangled up. Goodluck grabbed the sword out of the falling Frenchman's hand and drove it at the newcomer. The man twisted out of the way. Off-balance, he couldn't immediately aim a blow at Goodluck.

Walter dropped the unfamiliar sword and drew the pistol he knew and practiced with. Two shots, both center of mass.

He saw Sakaweston had bayoneted another Frenchman. There were two more. Goodluck shot them both with the nine-millimeter, then snatched up his rifle with his other hand. He and Sakaweston ran.

The shotgun fire was now a continuous thunder.

"Goodluck! Sakaweston!" That was Hobbamock's voice.

"Here!"

"Good. We have to leave now!"

Goodluck slowed. He saw that most of the team was firing the Evans shotguns as fast as they could load, and many Frenchmen were down. The Quinnipiac and Mohegan members of the team had gathered the hostages. Sawseunck shouted something to Wequash Cook.

Wequash Cook shouted something back as he put another shotgun shell in place. Samoset translated. "Upstream! There are too many!"

A couple booms rolled through the village. Goodluck recognized them as musket shots, but he did not see anyone get hit.

But Wequash Cook was right. There were too many French soldiers. If they fell back to the canoes, it would be a running battle. The hostages would slow them. The French would rush them as they pushed off. Then follow...

"Boats!" Goodluck shouted. "Take the French boats!"

He ran toward the boats and heard a couple others behind him. He saw men silhouetted against the boats, about a squad or so. One began to level a musket.

Goodluck fired two shots. The man fell to the ground. He saw the next closest man, on the other side of the same boat. He was reloading. Goodluck fired and missed. The man hit the ground. Goodluck jumped into the ship's boat. It rocked a bit as he crossed its width in two quick strides. Goodluck held the pistol out over the side and fired twice more. The man on the ground did not get up.

He turned and saw Hobbamock blast a French soldier to the ground. Another charged him, and the Wampanoag *pniese* swung the detached shotgun barrel like a club. It struck his sword arm, and the blade fell to the ground. Two more quick blows to the head, and the man was down.

Goodluck checked the other direction. Fast as Lightning eluded one Frenchman and engaged the man behind him. As the first Frenchman whirled around in confusion, Goodluck shot him.

The shotgun blasts were nearer now. Goodluck saw team members approaching, with the hostages running along between them. Goodluck jumped out of the boat. They needed to get it completely into the water.

John Alden arrived first. He immediately put his shoulder against the bow and shoved. Two men, apparently Wangunk hostages, quickly did the same. By the time half a dozen of them were pushing, the bow of the ship's boat slipped into the water. "On board!"

Alden pulled himself over the side. He dropped into the boat, popped up, and immediately opened fire with his shotgun, firing one round after another off to the left. The Wangunks boarded. As soon as a couple more team members were aboard and firing, Alden ceased fire and found the sweeps.

The Quinnipiac shouted something. Hobbamock shouted something back. Other members of the team raced up: Machk and Lockwood, Samoset, Pomeroy.

"On the boat!"

Goodluck left organizing the rowers to Alden. He reloaded the SRG, then inserted a fresh magazine into the nine-millimeter pistol. Kuchamakin, Wequash Cook, and Wawequa came running toward the shore, and someone had rallied a couple dozen French soldiers in pursuit.

Sakaweston fired first, and a figure at the forefront of the French charge went down. Goodluck paused for a moment, waiting for someone to take his place. Someone did. Goodluck shot him.

Kuchamakin stumbled at the water line. He leapt for the boat and missed. He was back to his feet before the splash settled. Others pulled him aboard. Wequash Cook was the last man onto the boat.

"Stroke!" Alden called out. He was at the last sweep on the starboard side. It took a minute to get the boat swung around, and the shotgun fire temporarily ceased. At least two musket balls thudded into the hull. The oncoming French charged into the water.

"Fire!" Wequash Cook gave the order, and shotgun blasts shredded the charge. A couple men moved to the stern and continued shooting as the longboat pulled away from Mattabesset.

Sawseunck was soon busy tending wounds. Kuchamakin had taken a sword slash to the leg. It was messy but not deep. Others, including a couple of the hostages, had minor wounds.

"Now what?" Eltweed Pomeroy asked.

"We find the rest of our army." Goodluck's answer was automatic.

"Our army?" Samoset asked. Then he translated.

Kuchamakin grunted. "We will find out who and how many when we find them."

The team kept a sharp lookout, both ahead and astern. But there did not seem to be a pursuit.

A couple hours later, Machk sighted boats. A long row of canoes and small boats were lined up on the shore.

As the boat drew closer, Goodluck could see that someone had mounted a heavy guard. A couple dozen men were on guard, and they'd clearly spotted the longboat already.

"One of you, fire a shotgun to port, then reload and fire again." John Alden's words were calm and sure. "Firing away from the disengaged side is a sign of surrender. Some of the colonists will know that."

Samoset did so. A couple hours removed from the battle, the blasts were painfully loud. But no one on shore fired back.

By the time the longboat nosed into the riverbank, dozens of Native Americans and English colonists had gathered around. Within a few minutes, Sassacus, Massasoit Ousamequin, Canonicus, Colonel George Fenwick, Captain John Mason, Lieutenant William Holmes, and Edward Winslow arrived.

"The French camp in Mattabesset," Kuchamakin told them. "We raided them. Rescued the Wangunk they took hostage. Stole a boat."

"It went well?" Canonicus asked.

"The team works," Kuchamakin stated. "We saved each other's lives a number of times."

"Who struck first?" That came from the gathered warriors.

"Walter Goodluck," Sakaweston said. "I saw a sentry almost step on him, a couple minutes before the first shot. He hit him with his pistol and dragged him into the woods."

Many of the warriors looked at Goodluck with newfound respect.

Then Sakaweston laughed. He turned to Goodluck. "You said that the team should rescue the hostages while we provided cover fire with our rifles. And I saw you strike that Frenchman down with the butt of your rifle, then take his sword. You directed us to steal the boat."

"It seemed like a good idea at the time." Goodluck frowned. "I dropped the sword and shot the second one with my pistol as soon as I could."

"And the third one. And the fourth one."

Kuchamakin's eyes widened. "You planned the raid, Walter Goodluck. You stole a boat. You touched an enemy in combat without killing him. And you took a weapon from an enemy's hands."

Goodluck blinked. "That wasn't really much of a plan . . ."

"But it was successful. The hostages are safe. The French commander is dead. I saw Hobbamock kill him." He smiled. "Do you not hear? The four tests you spoke of, when you told the story of Joe Medicine Crow."

"What?" Goodluck stared at him. "No. It's steal a *horse*."

When Hobbamock translated, Kuchamakin shrugged. "What good is a horse here? It carries a man in the dry places. Here we use boats. I say you fulfilled the four requirements." He turned. "How say you, Wequash Cook?"

Wequash Cook nodded gravely. "All four." He said something else.

"The Algonquian will send a sign with you," Hobbamock translated. "Someday, when you reach the Diné, they will recognize you are a war chief."

Quinnehtukqut (the Connecticut River), east of Willow Island
Thursday, August 27, 1637

Walter Goodluck was bleary-eyed when the Algonquians and the colonists launched their canoes and boats before dawn.

"'Don't sleep past dawn. Dawn's when the French and Indians attack,'" Hobbamock quoted.

Goodluck shook his head. Not only was the older man ridiculously fit, he apparently didn't need sleep, either. And he could quote Rogers' Rangers Standing Orders after hearing it . . . well, as much as he and Samoset had been laughing over it, they'd probably told the whole story to their fellow warriors at least a few times. But still—!

By the time it was truly light, most of the English boats lay between an island covered with willow trees and the eastern riverbank. They were moving very slowly south. The Algonquian canoes were not in sight.

A couple hours later, the French boats came into sight. On board the captured longboat, Colonel George Fenwick gave the order.

"Signal the fleet. Set course upstream."

Only a handful of the boats had masts. But as scraps of blue cloth were waved from boat to boat, any with sails furled them and used sweeps or even oars to put about.

"That's blue," Fenwick muttered to himself. He had only two other orders he could give. Red to attack and drab to land. He glanced at the next boat, a longboat nearly the same size as the captured French one. Half a dozen men were on the sweeps, and a sergeant and eight Dutch soldiers were in the bow. Those were the veterans, the men he was counting on to remain steady...

...which was a ridiculous thing to be thinking about a battle on the river. Control of New England might hinge on a naval battle this far inland. It was a strange notion, perhaps too strange for Captain John Endecott and his men. Their boats were getting a bit separated. Fenwick nudged the man directing the sweeps and gave a very unnautical order by jerking a thumb to his left. "More that way."

As the colonists' boats tightened up on Endecott's, the French increased their speed. Single sails were raised, and the men at the sweeps redoubled their efforts.

Fenwick wished they'd had enough cloth to add a signal for "go faster." The French were gaining, the more skillfully crewed boats pulling ahead.

It sucked them north between the island of willows and the eastern bank very nicely.

Quinnehtukqut (the Connecticut River), west of Willow Island

"Attack!" Sassacus ordered.

The plan had almost worked. The Algonquians were in their canoes between the island of willows and the western bank, waiting for lookouts on the island to signal that the French boats had passed so they could fall on them from behind. The way Willow Island lay in the big bend of the Quinnehtukqut, a stretch of the western channel could not be seen from either upstream or downstream.

But the new French commander was smart. He'd sent one longboat up the western channel.

Dozens of canoes surged forward. Some carried only the two

warriors paddling. Others were larger and carried one, two, or even three passengers. The rush looked like chaos—but it was anything but. Groups of canoes stayed together. The team built on the stories sent by the People from the Sky led the way. Other warriors paddled those canoes while those on the team waited with their shotguns. Sassacus' Pequots were right behind them, with Uncas' Mohegans beside them. Nipmucks, Wangunks, Niantics, Narragansetts, Wampanoags and others followed.

The French longboat tried to put about. The sail lost what little wind there was. Without sweeps, it would have been in irons. But it got around and started south.

The canoes continued closing in.

In the lead canoe, Wequash Cook shouted his orders. "If it flees, let it go! If it turns upstream around the island, attack!"

The longboat attempted to circle around the southern tip of Willow Island. The turn began smoothly enough. As soon as the longboat broke into the channel east of the island, a number of muskets discharged at once. Only a couple were aimed at the Algonquian canoes. A few of the men in the lead canoes saw a small splash well short of them.

Then the longboat veered to starboard. This was evidently a harder maneuver. The craft came close to shore before steadying out on a course downriver. The Algonquian canoes closed within two hundred yards. The longboat fired an ineffective handful of musket shots. A few canoes started after the longboat, but Uncas recalled them with a sharp order.

The team's canoes slowed, the fourteen of them forming a staggered line across the eastern channel. As more canoes rounded the tip of the island, they began paddling upstream.

Machk shouted something. Goodluck didn't know the words, but it was obviously a warning that the rest of the French boats had seen them. A couple of the rearmost vessels were already beginning to come about.

Wequash Cook gave an order. The warriors paddling the canoes stopped doing anything but making an occasional stroke to keep the canoes pointed in the right direction.

A shout went up somewhere off to the right. Word passed from canoe to canoe. The English boats were turning around.

For a few minutes, the French longboats continued to close with the English. Then boats began swerving aside. Goodluck was sure there was a proper nautical term for it. But right now, all that mattered was that at least some of those boats were going to try to crash through the canoes.

Four, as far as he could see. Two and then two more a ways behind them. Others might be behind those, but Goodluck couldn't see past them. They ought to . . . No, this was not going to be a battle of timely orders aimed at precise opportunities. It was his job to shoot French officers.

It took forever to close. Goodluck waited. When he thought the nearest French boat was one hundred fifty yards away, he fired his rifle. Clean miss. Goodluck reloaded as quickly as he could—which wasn't very fast at all while seated in a canoe.

French muskets began firing at seventy yards. They would be effective at that range on land, but even the relatively smooth water of the Quinnehtukqut was enough to spoil their aim. The nearer of the two French boats was on course to pass to the right of Goodluck's canoe. Very carefully, he turned so that he was facing backwards. That let him fire to his left instead of to his right, always a good thing with a flintlock. Then he waited.

At thirty yards, Goodluck steadied his SRG, picked out a Frenchman who appeared to be almost reloaded, and pulled the trigger. The man dropped out of sight. Goodluck thought he'd hit him, but . . .

The two warriors paddling were angling for the longboat. From other canoes came the thunder of shotgun blasts. Goodluck saw two more French soldiers drop as well as a couple of the sailors manning the sweeps.

Then as his canoe reached point-blank range, he realized the Algonquian and English attack was all wrong. Those with shotguns shouldn't be trying to board. But telling the Algonquians . . .

Goodluck drew his pistol. At ten yards, he systematically shot every man at the starboard sweeps. He was sure it took too many bullets, but slammed in a full magazine. When the bow of the canoe bumped into the longboat, the warrior in the bow leapt aboard, knife in hand. Goodluck was right behind him. He shot a French soldier, then realized that Algonquians were already boarding from the other side. Everyone was already too jumbled together. He had no shot.

Instead he turned to the stern, where three sailors quickly let go of the port sweeps and raised their hands. He pointed at the deck—or whatever the bottom of an open boat was called. The three understood at once and lay down.

A quick glance to his right revealed Algonquian warriors boarding the second French longboat. He couldn't identify individuals, but at least two of them wore the team's warpaint of yellow, red, black, and white quadrants.

The third French longboat was attempting to sail right between the two that were already engaged. The first wave—the team, the Pequots, and the Mohegans—were already committed. Goodluck checked behind him. The Algonquians were winning the fight in the bow.

He reloaded the SRG, knelt. With the barrel on the gunwale, he waited for the roll of the boat to bring him on target.

The SRG cracked, and a sailor at the starboard sweeps of the third boat went down. Goodluck reloaded.

One of the sailors he'd captured lurched to his feet. Goodluck laid him out with the butt of the SRG, then finished ramming. He knelt and laid the barrel across the gunwale again. Another crack, and a second sailor was down. The third one let go of his sweep. Good enough. Goodluck reloaded.

The longboat slewed. For a moment, Goodluck thought its crew might intend to come alongside the boat he was on. But then he realized that the sailors were still working the port sweeps. The boat was about fifty yards off, and soldiers in the boat leveled their muskets.

Then there was a crack, and one of them pitched into the river. That had to be Sakaweston. Goodluck was too busy reloading to look for him.

He spotted something out of the corner of his eye. More canoes. The remaining Algonquians were paddling hard, bypassing the first two longboats. The French soldiers fired, and Goodluck saw at least two men were hit.

But now the canoes were within fifty yards themselves. Goodluck saw bow paddlers drop flat in the several canoes. In each case, a passenger fired one of the precious shotguns. And fired again a couple seconds later. And again. Other canoes passed them, but their fire had hit a few men and forced others to take cover. Canoes came alongside, and a mixture of Wampanoags and Narragansetts flooded onto the longboat.

"Goodluck! Goodluck!"

He whirled. Hobbamock came toward him. He was covered

with gore, but the way he was moving, most of it had to be other people's blood.

"We have this one. And the next."

"And the third."

"Look!" Hobbamock pointed. "One is headed ashore!"

The Wampanoag *pniese* turned. "Team! Paddlers! Back in the canoes!"

That took a couple minutes. Warriors who were armed with knives and clubs jumped into the river and chased down canoes that had drifted away. They brought them alongside.

"Goodluck!"

Walter climbed over the side into a canoe.

"Stop!" Hobbamock ordered the paddlers. "We attack together! Not one at a time!"

Goodluck recognized the wisdom in that order, but time seemed to drag as they got organized. Finally the order came.

"Go!"

Eight canoes set off. They carried Goodluck, several members of the team, Sassacus, and a dozen other warriors.

"The rest are making for shore!" Alden shouted to Goodluck.

Goodluck looked where Alden was pointing. Three more French longboats appeared to be angling for a clearing on the eastern bank, inside the great curve of the river.

Goodluck tracked the leading longboat, but did not fire. The canoe wasn't stable enough for such a long-range shot. When the longboat grounded, men jumped out and splashed ashore. He wasn't sure exactly how many there were. More than twelve but less than twenty.

Other canoes were visible to their right. A few had broken off from the second longboat and were on a converging course with Goodluck's group. Others were coming from downstream.

The French soldiers assembled into a line.

"Paddlers down!"

The French delivered a crisp volley and amazingly hit two men. A shotgunner in one canoe went down, mortally wounded. A warrior in the stern of another canoe was hit in the side, although not badly.

The Algonquian shotgunners immediately returned fire without any orders. The first shots were wildly inaccurate. Team members corrected. A couple Frenchmen went down.

The first canoes grounded, and Algonquian warriors leapt out. This was no careful assault with shotgunners softening up the target before men with knives and clubs closed in. It was a chaotic scramble.

"French on the left!"

That bellow was in English. Goodluck immediately turned in that direction and saw a longboat almost to shore.

"Shotguns! Shotgun the longboats!" He had lost track of Hobbamock. Lacking a translator, he simply grabbed an Algonquian who carried a shotgun. He wasn't part of the team, but Goodluck bodily aimed him in the right direction. A moment later, the man shouted his own warning in one of the Algonquian languages.

The Puritan Robert Lockwood was at Goodluck's side now. He and the Algonquian opened fire. Goodluck loaded the SRG. The longboats grounded. French soldiers jumped out and charged.

Goodluck shot the man leading the charge—so that the rest would see him fall. Lockwood and the Algonquian fired as fast as they could put shotgun shells in position and slam the barrels home. Goodluck drew his pistol and emptied a magazine in seconds.

The French scattered. Several were down. Goodluck saw a few run north along the riverbank. Other Algonquians newly arrived on shore surged forward.

Someone shouted in Algonquian. Goodluck didn't understand the words, but the Algonquians around him slowed.

"Drop your weapons! Drop your weapons!" That was Hobbamock, coming from further inland, off to Goodluck's right. The rest he didn't understand.

About twenty French soldiers formed rank. The dozen or so sailors formed up with them. They appeared to be armed with swords and knives.

"*Apprêtez-vos armes!*" The French readied their flintlocks.

"Fire!" Hobbamock ordered.

Several shotguns discharged in a ragged volley. At least three French soldiers and a sailor fell.

"*Joue!*" The barrels of the French muskets came down. But this time, Goodluck spotted the man giving the order.

A second shotgun volley tore into them. Goodluck fired three pistol shots. At least one hit the French commander.

"Surrender! On the ground!" Hobbamock roared.

A few of the sailors dropped their weapons and got down.

"*Feu!*" a noncommissioned officer roared.

Both sides fired. The French volley was a thunderclap in the midst of individual shotgun blasts. Men screamed and fell.

The shotgunners reloaded and fired again. And again. And again.

"Cease fire! Cease fire! Stay back!"

Goodluck heard more than one voice shouting the order. Hobbamock. Kuchamakin. Massasoit Ousamequin. No French were standing.

"Prisoners," he called out.

Hobbamock looked his way. "Why?"

Walter Goodluck blinked. "Battle's over. It wasn't their idea to attack us. Besides, some of us might get captured someday."

Hobbamock gave him a *very* dubious look.

"And you need to send some of them back with a message."

"We can send them a message." Hobbamock's voice was grim.

"No, we want these guys right here to go," Goodluck told him. "Their commanding officer may or may not believe them, but the rest of the French soldiers will."

Hobbamock considered that. "This bears thinking about." Then he turned and started bringing order out of the chaos of the battlefield.

Goodluck holstered his pistol, shouldered his rifle, and began doing what he could for the wounded. "Doctors. They're going to need doctors," he muttered.

"Walter Goodluck!" Hobbamock's voice broke into his thoughts. "Come!"

"Hobbamock, I can help..."

"Sawseunck and others will heal who they can. The English boats are approaching. We need you there."

Goodluck frowned and rose. He didn't want to, but Hobbamock was right. The risk of a misunderstanding when everyone was armed.... "Hobbamock, we need Sakaweston and Samoset."

"I have sent men to find them and the rest of the team. Uncas is assembling the men with shotguns."

Goodluck checked his weapons and slowly turned in place. The Algonquians controlled the eastern bank of the river and apparently five longboats. The three they'd swarmed from their canoes were gliding slowly toward the riverbank. They'd already taken possession of the two the French had grounded there.

He peered north. It looked like the English colonists had taken some prizes, too. Good. One of the larger English boats landed, and soldiers poured off. It was the Dutch squad from Fort Hope. Their sergeant quickly formed a rank near their boat, but out of everyone's way. The next boat was smaller and carried actual English colonists.

Edward Winslow was first out of the boat, with Lieutenant William Holmes right behind him. Winslow smiled and clasped arms as men greeted him, but he made his way straight to Massasoit Ousamequin.

"Edward! You have survived!"

One of the captured French boats reached shore. Sakaweston, Wequash Cook, and Eltweed Pomeroy splashed ashore.

"Walter!" Sakaweston thumped him heartily on the back.

"Good to see you, too, Sakaweston."

"I see you are victorious here. We were unable to stop two of the French boats. The fourth one waited until we all fought the first three, then skirted the shore. Later, another sailed close to the island after we had started this way."

Goodluck pointed. "These two landed rather than face you. The colonists have taken some, too. You need to be there when we talk."

"I understand."

Sakaweston turned to Wequash Cook. "Are you gathering the team?"

Wequash Cook was still for a moment, then suddenly shook his head. "I was thinking about what I just saw. The power of the People from the Sky."

"There are limits," Goodluck reminded him. "Ammunition."

"Oh, I know. Still..." Wequash Cook shook his head again. "The two girls who sent the writing about the team, they talked about the God of the English, too. You follow this same God, but differently, yes? I would hear more, Walter Goodluck." Then he moved off to gather the team.

Goodluck stared after the team's co-leader for a moment, then he and Sakaweston approached the spot where the English landed, a little upstream of where the French had. He was glad to see Massasoit Ousamequin and Edward Winslow approaching, too. They met up short of the river's edge.

"Who was in command?" Goodluck murmured.

"Colonel Fenwick," Winslow answered. "With Captain Endecott on one flank and Captain Mason on the other. Although Captain Endecott wears his subordination lightly."

Goodluck snorted. Then he noticed that the colonists were in formation.

George Fenwick turned to say something to John Endecott, and then the two of them came to meet them.

"Well fought," Fenwick told them. "Well fought, indeed."

"You carried out the feigned retreat perfectly," Goodluck returned. "I hope your casualties are not severe."

"A lot of good Englishmen are dead!" Endecott snapped. "Whereas the Indians..."

"Boarded three longboats and faced the crews of two others here." Sakaweston's voice carried but his tone was reasonable.

"Probably a massacre. Colonel, we need to get over there."

"A firefight at point-blank range," Goodluck told them. "Relatively little hand-to-hand combat."

Endecott snorted. "From these savages?"

"The new guns end the battle," Massasoit Ousamequin stated. He turned to Hobbamock and said something.

"We should plan what happens next," Hobbamock translated.

"We will give the French our terms," Endecott growled.

Hobbamock translated Massasoit Ousamequin's reply. "Massasoit Sassacus, Massasoit Canonicus, and I must speak. You—colonists, for you are English no longer—must speak. Let us speak together before any speak with the French."

"We don't have time for this. We must keep the pressure on the Fr—"

"This is not solely a military decision," Edward Winslow interrupted. "It is why Walter advocated so strongly for an executive branch." He smiled. "The Algonquians seem to have heard the same speech. That is the only way I can see Massasoit Ousamequin and Sassacus sharing command of the warriors while Canonicus took charge of the defense."

"That is... accurate," Massasoit Ousamequin allowed.

"Let us treat the wounded and bury the dead," Winslow suggested.

Massasoit Ousamequin held up his hand. "We carry our dead back. Bury them..." He turned to Hobbamock and explained in Wampanoag.

"Bury the warriors near the encampment where they can see the river. Yours, too. Let that be where we sign an alliance."

"Not yet!" Endecott insisted. "How many longboats got past you?"

"Three escaped," Sakaweston answered.

"About thirty soldiers, about twenty sailors," Endecott said. "Colonel, your men said that two hundred landed. That means there are eighty French soldiers at Sovereignty. One hundred ten is as almost as many as they had here."

"We cannot attack then," Colonel Fenwick pointed out. "Soldiers of any skill at all will fall back to the shore under the guns of their ships."

"You cannot leave them in control of the mouth of the Quinnehtukqut," Goodluck agreed. "The colonists and the Algonquian both need the river for supplies from Europe."

"There are too many French ships," Endecott stated. For a wonder, he wasn't arguing, just stating the obvious. "Unless you have ships...?"

Goodluck shook his head. "I have no idea how I am going to find the *Griffin*."

Hobbamock clapped him on the shoulder. "The ship sailed to New Amsterdam, yes? The team will take you there." He gestured toward the Dutch squad. "And a couple Dutch soldiers, to avoid misunderstandings. They will want to report to...whomever runs the Dutch colony."

"The Dutch have ships," Sakaweston pointed out. "How many, I do not know. Perhaps enough to cause the French to withdraw."

"We may be able to cause them to leave sooner than that." Goodluck turned and surveyed the...battlefield, he supposed was the right word. "There are wounded. Give them back to the French. They will have to care for them. Keep those who might be saved if they are not moved. Send those who will survive anyway."

"I do not know that many will survive." Hobbamock wasn't arguing with the idea, either, just pointing out the facts.

Goodluck gave them all a grim smile. "I am not suggesting this just because it is a good deed. The French have three longboats now. They've got one hundred ten men if Captain Endecott's estimate is correct—and I think it is. We add wounded to that, and all the French will be thinking is that it will take four trips to get everyone out to the ships.

"Meanwhile, we will surround the French troops at Sovereignty. Not to attack, but to make them think we greatly outnumber them." Goodluck spotted skepticism on several faces, Algonquian and English alike. "I got this from the great chief of the Shawnee tribe, Tecumseh. He and his tribe were allied to the English against the United States in the War of 1812. He and the British often made their numbers seem bigger than they were." He explained briefly.

"I like this," Massasoit Ousamequin declared. "What happened to Tecumseh?"

"He was killed in battle later in the war. His confederacy collapsed."

"They started too late, you said," Massasoit recalled. "We start early this time. Ally with colonies."

"Good, because I took the next part from George Washington...."

Outside Sovereignty
Saturday, August 29, 1637

The Pequot sachem Sassacus sighed. "I will say it, Walter Goodluck of the Diné. You are indeed a sachem to win such a battle without fighting. I still cannot tell if you force us to become like the People from the Sky to avoid what happened to us in your time."

"We up-timers and the down-time Germans are becoming a new people," Goodluck answered once Sassacus' words were translated.

"So are we, it seems." Sassacus did not sound entirely pleased by that. "Send some of these Germans. All of Canonicus' list. I understand the need. But we must remain Algonquian."

"I agree." That was already different than saying his people must remain Pequot. Goodluck figured the less he said right now, the better. He kept his eyes on the many campfires burning in a huge semicircle around the ruins of Sovereignty.

That afternoon, the longboats had disembarked French prisoners, both the few unwounded and walking wounded, about a quarter mile from Sovereignty, then hastily rowed back upstream. Tonight, the Algonquians and the colonists had lit the campfires.

The French had seen those campfires, and their remaining boats had begun ferrying men back to the ships offshore. By now the evacuation was nearly complete.

"We need warriors here." Massasoit Ousamequin's words were sour. "What is the word, Sakaweston?"

"A garrison."

"The team should lead it."

"No, Massasoit Ousamequin." Kuchamakin's disagreement was respectful. "The team is needed elsewhere. First, we must escort Sachem Walter to New Amsterdam so that he may return to Europe on the *Griffin*. Then we must go ranging for any other English who have fled from the French and bring them to the river towns."

The Algonquian and colonial leaders exchanged glances.

"Not me," John Endecott stated. "I do not want garrison duty."

"Uncas," Sassacus said. "And Captain Mason."

Uncas immediately frowned. "Do you send me away?"

"No. If all this is to work, I have to trust you out of my sight. You and Mason are able to work together. I have misgivings but it is necessary."

"Independent command," Sakaweston murmured. "Subject only to the councils. Not just Mohegans, of course."

Uncas gave him half a smile. "Well spoken. I cannot refuse— and it does need to be done. Captain Mason?"

Mason nodded. "We can do this."

"You must take the team back to the place of meeting in the morning," Massasoit Ousamequin told Kuchamakin.

Uncas was grinning now. "Massasoit Ousamequin. And Massasoit Sassacus. You must go with them and take the English leaders. Leave proven warriors to lead the others back. Ninigret of the Niantic. Miantonomo of the Narragansett." At their expressions, he shook his head. "Yes, it is strange. As recently as spring, I might have killed him. Now..." He shrugged. "From what Walter Goodluck and Sakaweston have said, we need every warrior."

Sunday, August 30, 1637

"Walter Goodluck, what do you think?" John Alden asked. "Should we fight, march, and sail on the Sabbath?"

He sounded genuinely curious. Walter smiled to himself. He might as well blow their minds.

"I had no problem marching and preparing to fight yesterday, John. The Sabbath is the seventh day, isn't it?"

He saw Alden blink.

"I am a Seventh-Day Adventist. I do not care what the rest of you do on Sunday."

Alden chuckled. "I will let the pastors deal with that."

The two of them, along with Hobbamock, Sakaweston, Wequash

Cook, and Kiswas, were on one of the three boats hurrying north on the Quinnehtukqut River. They'd all take a turn rowing soon, spelling the English who were currently manning the sweeps. There were two shifts of colonists, because they did not plan to stop for the night.

Dorchester
Monday, August 31, 1637

Sakaweston motioned toward where Ousamequin, Sassacus, and Canonicus stood with Edward Winslow, John Winthrop the Younger, Harry Stiles, and Roger Ludlow. He grinned. "*Massa-soitunk*. It is strange to need a plural."

Goodluck nodded. "The Algonquians have made a good start. Keihtánit watch over you."

"And you." Sakaweston was quiet for a moment. "Come back, if you can. Bring your family when it is safe."

Goodluck smiled. "I'm not sure what Helene will think of that idea." He grimaced. "It will be a quiet trip home."

Sakaweston nodded solemnly. "May we be friends with the no-longer-English for a long time."

"I will send what I can. And who I can."

The two men clasped forearms. Then Walter Goodluck approached the *massasoitunk*.

"May the Lord keep you safe on the journey," Winthrop said.

"Thank you. And may He watch over you here."

Massasoit Ousamequin handed Goodluck a yellow feather and a string of shells. "I hope to see you again. If it is many years, and I am gone, show these, and the Wampanoag—may it be all the Algonquian—will welcome you or your descendants."

Goodluck bowed and accepted the gifts.

One of the Dutch soldiers stepped forward. "I will get you into New Amsterdam, sir, if the . . . Algonquian can guide us through the forest."

Goodluck looked over to where the team was gathering. Individual men were saying goodbye to wives and children. "Just like in Europe," he murmured. "They will get us there, Corporal."

A few minutes later, the team set off. The Algonquians had repainted their faces with the quartered yellow, red, black, and white. Kuchamakin had a slight limp but insisted the walk would do him good.

Once the team was out of sight, and the children following them had returned, Massasoit Ousamequin turned to the others. "The French who burn villages are still a threat. Let us sit at the fire and smoke. We will talk land."

New Amsterdam
Monday, September 21, 1637

Two Dutch soldiers watched the *Griffin* depart. One of them shook his head. "I was on duty, Jan, when those Indians and Pieter and Andries appeared with that up-timer."

"He was not an up-timer," Jan objected. "He was an Indian."

"Up-timer Indian," Koenrad said. "They *walked* from Fort Hope. Strangest muskets I have ever seen. He was lucky enough to catch the *Griffin* still in port."

"Where did the rest of them go?" Jan asked.

"*West*, of all places. But they said they would be back in a few days."

Months later

A Munsee found his way to a village where he'd been a war captive years before. It was occupied, and an alert Shawnee quickly shouted at him.

The Munsee showed his open hands.

He was roughly shoved into the center of the village.

"Why are you here? Have you returned to spy?"

"My people have heard the story of the People from the Sky. They sent me because I can speak to you. They came to the land across the sea from a time yet to come. One of them is from a people far to sunsetting. Diné, that the white men call Navajo. I ask that I may tell the story as we heard it and then depart. Do with it as you will. Maybe you will tell the next people to sunsetting."

"Speak then, and we will hear."

~ Author's note ~

With the exception of the already established characters Fast as Lightning and Machk, all other Algonquian and English colonial characters are historical.

A Wide Latitude

Eric Flint

Hamburg, United States of Europe
September 3, 1637

Gordon Chehab had no idea what to expect from the mysterious meeting he was being escorted to by one of Estuban Miro's agents. But it was safe to say that nowhere near the top of any list he might have drawn up would *meet Rebecca Abrabanel* have appeared.

In part, his disorientation was due to the sharp and sudden change in lighting and atmosphere. He and the agent had come from a bright August day outside on the streets of Hamburg to the dim gloom of the cellar in the city's Rathaus. The cellar was the location of the Rathaus tavern, so had it been evening a number of lamps would have been lit and the place would have been...not bright, certainly, but at least boisterous.

Here, now, there were just three people sitting at a table in the dimmest of the cellar corners. Gordon recognized two of them, Rebecca and Estuban Miro, who served Prime Minister Ed Piazza in the same capacity that Francisco Nasi had served Mike Stearns, when he'd been the head of the USE's government. Spymaster, for lack of a better term.

The third man, he didn't know. He was young, a bit on the tall side—for a down-timer, anyway, which Gordon was sure he was—and had the vague air of a geek about him. From subtleties in his posture, Gordon thought he was another of Miro's people.

"Please, Gordon, have a seat," said Rebecca, gesturing to the chair across from her. She was flanked by Miro to her right and the young stranger to her left. The man who'd escorted Gordon here pulled up a chair from an adjoining table and sat a little ways back and to Miro's left. "I am afraid I cannot offer you any refreshments, since, as you can see"—she waved her hand about—"the cellar is empty."

"By design, I take it?" he asked.

She smiled, in the serene manner she had. He remembered, even though he hadn't seen her in... How long had it been?

More than a year and a half. Maybe two years. He and his brother Pete had set sail from Hamburg in April of the previous year. But he hadn't seen Rebecca for a number of months prior to that.

"Not entirely," she replied. "It is still early in the morning. The cellar would not normally be open at this time."

That was both true and not true. Certainly, the cellar wouldn't be open yet for business. But the tavern keeper and his employees would normally have been here already, setting up.

So. A black op. Well, medium gray, more likely. Neither Rebecca Abrabanel nor her boss Ed Piazza were the sort of people readily given to sliding stilettos between ribs—or ordering someone else to do it.

On the other hand, Gordon was pretty sure both of them fell quite a ways short of angelic status.

"I'm getting the feeling that you're offering me another job. Or would 'assignment' be a better description?"

Miro stuck out his hand and waggled it back and forth. "Either or both, depending on how you look at it."

Rebecca sniffed. "Why do spies enjoy ambivalence so much? I am offering you a job, Mr. Chehab. The official title—for you, not your brother—is 'envoy plenipotentiary.' That indicates that you are an official of the USE's government and are empowered to make a wide range of agreements with foreign nations or other bodies."

"How wide ranging?"

Rebecca smiled serenely. "As wide as you choose until such time as the USE decides you were an incompetent nincompoop and disavows your actions."

Gordon made a little snorting sound. "Why do politicians enjoy ambivalence so much? And what would Pete's title be?"

"Assistant to the envoy plenipotentiary." Rebecca cocked her head a bit. "Do you think he will resent the disparity in rank?"

"Pete? Hell, no. He'll make jokes about it." Gordon's hand made a little groping gesture atop the table, searching for a beer mug that wasn't there. Dammit, he could use a drink right about now.

"Let's put the titles aside. What would you want me to *do*?"

Rebecca studied him for a moment without speaking. A bit abruptly, she then said: "That largely depends upon you, actually. After reading the reports you've sent in, we have developed a great deal of confidence in your judgment."

Gordon was surprised to hear that. Pleased, too, of course, but . . .

"You don't think I'm too inclined to be a goody-two-shoes?"

When Rebecca made no immediate response, it occurred to Gordon that the idiomatic reference was pretty obscure. The woman was completely fluent in the English language, since she'd grown up on the island. In fact, she spoke it with a contemporary London accent which sounded closer to Appalachian dialect than it did to what twentieth-century Americans thought of as an "English accent."

"I have never been able to figure out the logic of that expression," she said. "The 'goody' part is clear enough, but what do two shoes—any number of shoes—have to do with anything?"

"Uh, I don't know myself. All I meant was—"

"I understood you. You wonder if we are not concerned that you are overly inclined to saving whales and hugging trees. Halting all progress for fear that an obscure bird or amphibian might be imperiled. Or perhaps more immediately to the point, wringing your hands over the plight of North America's indigenes instead of dealing with the issue in a practical manner that might produce some results."

He got a twisted smile on his face. "Yeah, that. My brother gives me a hard time about it pretty regularly."

"Which is one of the reasons you will be in charge of the mission and not him. This century is seventeenth enough as it is, all on its own."

She leaned back in her chair and regarded him for a moment. "There are times when your idealist impulses may prove to be a problem, true. Sometimes one has no choice but to be ruthless." She got something of a twisted smile on her own face.

"My husband has on occasion said the same thing to me that your brother says to you. But it is not a very big risk, we think. And we would far rather someone with your responsibilities err in that direction that in the all-too-easy direction of turning a blind eye to inconvenient realities."

She sat up straight again. "The essence of the USE's strategy in the New World has the following components, Mr. Chehab." She planted her forefinger on the table top. "First, we are already fighting wars on many fronts. The last thing we need is another—and insofar as we do need to engage in military action in the western hemisphere, the priority is naval, and the enemy is the Spanish empire. In particular, although we favor the legitimists over the usurper Gaston, we have no desire to get directly embroiled in the ongoing French civil war."

Now she planted her middle finger on the table. "Two. With regard to North America, our central goal is to do what we can to prevent any one power from becoming predominant on the continent. For a variety of reasons, the existence of many power centers, none of which is very strong, serves our interests—and, we think, will best serve the interests of the people living in North America as well. People of all races and origins, not just Europeans."

The ring finger joined the others. "Three. While we are willing to provide some weapons and some other military equipment to selected parties, the emphasis is on the words *some* and *selected*. We think technical guides and medicines will be a far more effective tool of diplomacy."

She laid her hand flat. "That is all there is, at least in broad outline." She nodded toward Estuban Miro and his two still unnamed agents. "They will want to spend some time debriefing you and discussing the particulars of the USE's strategy. And then, assuming you still wish to accept the position we have offered, you will be sailing back across the Atlantic. I just made a brief stop here on my way to the Netherlands in order to recruit you, so to speak. All that I have left to handle is a personal matter which...If you wish to discuss it privately, we can do so."

"Does it involve my brother and his wife?"

Rebecca nodded. Gordon shrugged. "There's no need for secrecy, that I can see. I assume she wants a divorce?"

"Yes."

"Don't blame her. Pete's been an ass about the whole thing."
He reached into his jacket pocket and drew out an envelope. "Pete
was expecting it too. This document—he's signed it, in front of
witnesses—turns over any pay he's owed for past services and
any he might be owed in the future from the USE to Penny.
That should be enough to support her and their little girl, even
if Penny isn't working."

Rebecca took the envelope from him, opened it, and quickly
read through the letter enclosed. "More than enough, I should
think. But how will your brother handle his own financial affairs?"

Gordon made another little snorting sound. "Pete? Don't worry
about him. He'll manage, one way or another—and before you ask,
no, I won't be using State Department money to keep him afloat."

Rebecca tucked the envelope away in a purse. "Actually, you
can if you so choose. In addition to your own salary, you will
have a rather large expense account, with no guidelines or restric-
tions on our part as to how you use those funds."

Her hand came out of the purse holding a larger envelope.
"You can draw the funds from Amsterdam's Wisselbank," she said,
as she handed it over. "They have a branch in New Amsterdam.
This contains all the information you need to do so."

"Can I use them to set up a whale sanctuary?"

Her smile, unusually for Rebecca, came very close to a grin.
"Legally, yes. I would recommend something more useful, however.
In the year 5397—you Christians call it the year 1637—whales
are not an endangered species."

Gordon thought his current status as a "Christian" was probably pretty shaky, but he wasn't going to argue the point. What
was most interesting to him was that Rebecca's statement about
funds reinforced her earlier explanation of the great leeway he
was being given.

Of course, looked at from one angle that leeway was inevi-
table. Even with radio communication—*some* communication,
at *some* times and in *some* places—diplomatic affairs were not
something that could be micromanaged across an ocean as huge
as the Atlantic.

"And now, I have to go," said Rebecca. She gestured toward
Estuban Miro. "He will handle everything from here."

And off she went.

✧   ✧   ✧

As it turned out, just as Gordon had presumed, both of the unnamed companions of Miro were his agents. And now, they had names.

The older one, who had escorted Gordon from the docks to the Rathaus, was Adam Neuschell. The tall younger one's name was Reitz Pauer. No further information was provided as to their place of origin or background.

Both of them would be accompanying Gordon back to North America. As far as their responsibilities were concerned, those of Pauer were simple and straightforward. One of the many refits, repairs and upgrades the *Challenger* was being provided with was a new and more powerful radio than the one which had been destroyed in the ship's first trip across the Atlantic. Reitz Pauer was the radio operator—and apparently could handle any other type of radio they might wind up using.

Neuschell's role in the expedition was a lot fuzzier. After listening to the man's circumlocutions and periphrases for a few minutes, Gordon decided to label his assignment as *spy* and leave it at that. He was perfectly happy to let Miro's agent handle the murkier aspects of the work they'd be doing. For one thing, he'd undoubtedly be better at it than Gordon himself. And for another, he was coming to have more appreciation for the phrase *plausible deniability*. Spies did sometimes get hung or shot, after all. Better Neuschell than him.

Most of the three hours that passed following Rebecca's departure were spent with Neuschell debriefing Gordon. The man's questions often brought out aspects of Gordon and his brother's activities in the New World over the past year and a half that Gordon himself hadn't thought much about. Call him agent, or spy, or whatever, he was clearly good at his job.

Once that was over, Gordon returned to the ship, only to find that Ingrid Skoglund was sitting on an upended suitcase—more like a small trunk—on the dock, reading a book. Ingrid was the mission's doctor and, for some time now, had been sharing the main cabin of the ship with Gordon.

He'd done his best to make her what up-timers sometimes called "an honest woman," but she'd refused his proposal of marriage. Twice, now. She'd given no explanation, but Gordon was pretty sure the reasons had little to do with himself. It was more a matter that the Swedish woman had become accustomed to running her own life as she saw fit, and feared that marriage—especially given some of the conventions of her time—might be chafing.

So be it. He just had to remind himself periodically that patience was a virtue. Reputed to be, anyway.

"What are you doing out here?" he asked.

"Maartens chased me off the ship. They're starting to work on our cabin now, and he tells me they won't be done for several days."

Claes Maartens was the ship's captain—at least, that was how Gordon viewed him. Maartens insisted that he was simply the *Challenger*'s "sailing master." Whatever title you chose, he was the one who actually ran the ship.

Ingrid pointed to her left, to an edifice that was set back from the docks and quite some distance away. "I obtained rooms for us at that lodging house. Sofia went ahead to get things ready for us."

She rose, reached down, and hefted the trunk. "I packed some of your things in here as well as my own."

"Here. I'll carry that."

Ingrid wrinkled her nose. "I handle patients who weigh far more than this. I can manage, thank you." She pointed to her side with her free hand. "Your job is to walk next to the street, so that you can be the one splattered by careless wagon drivers. And handle whatever drunks or ruffians might think to harass us."

The next few days passed pleasantly. Maartens made it clear that Gordon would just be making a nuisance of himself if he tried to assist in the refitting of the *Challenger*, so they spent their time instead being tourists. Both of them had been to Hamburg before, but they'd been too busy to spend much time just sightseeing.

Unfortunately, in the year 1637, there really wasn't enough to see in Hamburg to require several days of tourism. The somewhat gruesome truth was that, once you'd visited the Rathaus and the city's oldest church, St. Petri, the most interesting sight were the ruins of Hamburg's once-famous Wallanlagen, the fortifications that Admiral Simpson's ironclads had demolished when they passed through Hamburg on their way to the Baltic in April of 1634.

No one had proposed rebuilding those fortifications afterward. First, because Simpson's ten-inch guns had made clear that they'd be useless. Second, because Hamburg had been incorporated into the United States of Europe. The most powerful realm on the continent provided its own protection to its cities. And finally, because Hamburg was a boom town with a great need for building material—and the rubble that had once been the Wallanlagen was now the premier source of masonry in the area. Dismantling what was left of those once-great brick and stone walls had become a major industry in its own right.

So, they were left to their own devices, as the saying goes. Since those included plenty of leisure time and a sturdy and comfortable bed in their room, Gordon made no complaint. Neither did Ingrid.

September 20, 1637

Once they passed through the estuary of the Elbe and entered the Wadden Sea, Ingrid asked: "So where are we going now?"

His hands clasped and his forearms resting on the rail in the ship's bow, Gordon looked to the southwest. The Frisian Islands were down there, but they were too far away to be visible.

"The Gulf of St. Lawrence," he said, "and from there we'll go up the St. Lawrence River as far as we can. Hopefully, that'll be as far as Quebec. Champlain has been keeping his own counsel ever since the French civil war began. I'd be very surprised if he's a Gastonard, but he hasn't come out in favor of the legitimists, either. Not publicly, at any rate. I'd like to have a conversation with him, see where he stands—or is thinking of standing."

"As I recall your account of your conversation with Secretary of State Abrabanel, she was quite firm in stating that the USE has no desire—*particularly*, no desire—to get embroiled in the French civil war."

Gordon smiled. "*Directly* embroiled were her exact words. I'm not proposing we do so. I just want to have a chat with the leader of French Canada. Rebecca also stated that I had a wide latitude, remember?"

"Until they declare you a nincompoop." She shrugged. "At which point we are left to our own resources. Fortunately, I am a doctor. I can probably support both of us for a while. Until you get a new job as..."

She turned her head to look at him directly, cocking a skeptical eye. "By the way, what *are* you good at, Mr. Gordon? Besides meddling in the world's affairs."

Afterword

Rick Boatright
March 19, 1955–July 22, 2021

We dedicated this book to Rick Boatright, partly in the hope that he would live long enough to see it when it was published. Sadly, he didn't. He didn't even live long enough to see his own novel, *1637: Dr. Gribbleflotz and the Soul of Stoner*, when it came out in September. He died from complications due to pancreatic cancer, and of all cancers pancreatic is probably the most savage and relentless. Less than two months passed between the time Rick was diagnosed with the disease and the time it killed him.

I lost a very good friend on July 22, and I was by no means the only one who did. It is not an exaggeration to say that Rick Boatright was one of the nicest people I've ever met. If anyone disliked him, they kept it to themselves—which would have been a very wise move on their part. But I doubt any such person exists. Rick wasn't "nice" simply in the sense of being courteous and considerate. He was invariably helpful to people.

I won't say "helpful to me above all," but I'm in a select group of people whom Rick helped enormously for years—two decades, in my case. I met him not long after the publication of my novel *1632* in February of 2000. I hadn't originally intended the book to be the beginning of a series. I certainly had no inkling of the huge project it would turn into. (As of now, the Ring of Fire series comprises twenty-six novels of which I am either the author or co-author, thirty-seven novels written by other authors, seventeen anthologies of short fiction, and an electronic magazine that has been in continuous publication since May of 2007 and is now up to ninety-eight issues.)

One of the reasons I hesitated before deciding to create a series based on *1632* was that I knew just how daunting the task of researching the needed material was going to be. I was confident I could handle the historical material, but there was a tremendous amount of technical and scientific material I would also need to... Well, I won't say "master," because there was no chance of that. But I'd at least need to be knowledgeable enough that I could produce a work of fiction that didn't quickly become a source of derision and ridicule.

One of those technical fields that I was going to have to learn quickly because it would figure in the second novel of the series (*1633*, which I co-authored with David Weber) was radio. I'd been listening to radio since I was a toddler. But what did I actually *know* about it? How ham radio works, the impact of the Maunder Minimum on transmission in the seventeenth century, what sort of aerials my characters would need under conditions X, Y and Z (not to mention A, B and C)—oh, it went on and on and on.

Zip. That's what I knew. My ignorance was of that profound nature where the ignoramus has no idea where he or she can even start to learn about the subject.

Happily, I had noticed there was this fellow named Rick Boatright who'd been participating actively in the discussion conference on Baen Books' website that was devoted to the nascent Ring of Fire series. He seemed to know quite a bit about radio. So I got hold of his phone number and called him, asking for his help.

Rick told me later he thought at first that someone was playing a practical joke on him. Since when do authors call members of the hoi polloi on the telephone? (In fact, we do it all the time. One of the things a successful author learns very soon is that you're dead in the water unless you can build a network of people around you who can compensate for your own folly in presuming you could write a book involving a lot of stuff you don't have a clue about.)

Rick proved to be invaluable on the subject of radio—and you can find his knowledge and influence concerning radio in many of my books. But what I also realized quickly was that the man's knowledge was incredibly vast. I don't remember when I first ran across the term "polymath," but what I do remember is that I was skeptical of the concept—until I met Rick Boatright.

He liked to share his knowledge, too, and he was very adept at transmitting it in ways that non-polymaths like myself could grasp relatively quickly and easily. His first career had been that of a high school science teacher, and I think it may well have been his favorite one. (Alas, it doesn't pay well, especially in some states, so eventually he moved on and set up his own business.)

As the years went by, Rick became a major figure in the fluctuating group of people who are the center of what we often call "the 1632 community" for lack of a better term. And it *is* a collective enterprise. I occupy a central position in it, true, but it long ago became a literary project that expanded far beyond me.

Rick didn't write much fiction. A few short stories and vignettes, and he worked with Kerryn Offord in developing the two Doctor Gribbleflotz novels, *1636: The Chronicles of Dr. Gribbleflotz* and *1637: Dr. Gribbleflotz and the Soul of Stoner*. But his knowledge and many contributions to the series can be found everywhere.

I'm writing this essay of appreciation just one month after Rick passed away. Even in that short span of time, there must have been a dozen times—at least—when my hand started to reach for a telephone so I could call Rick and ask him a question. Nine times out of ten he'd have the answer, and the tenth time he'd know where to look for it. And the conversation itself would be a pleasure to have.

That was Rick Boatright.

Eric Flint
August 24, 2021